WILD ISLAND

JENNIFER LIVETT

First published in 2016

Allen & Unwin
83 Alexander Street
Crows Nest NSW 2065
Australia
Phone: (61 2) 8425 0100
Email: info@allenandunwin.com
Web: www.allenandunwin.com

Cataloguing-in-Publication details are available
from the National Library of Australia
www.trove.nla.gov.au

ISBN 978 1 76011 383 4

Set in 11.5/15.5 pt Dante MT Pro by Bookhouse, Sydney
Printed and bound in Australia by Griffin Press

10 9 8 7 6 5

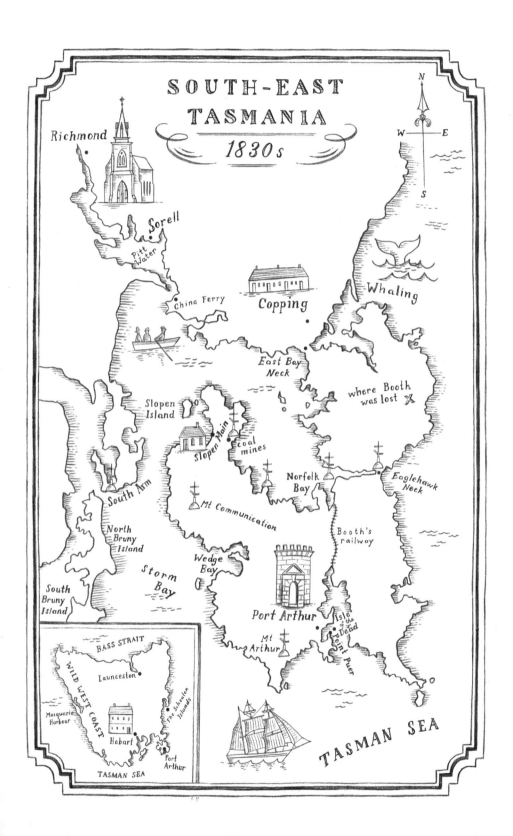

TZARA: It means, my dear Henry, that the causes we know everything about depend on causes we know very little about, which depend on causes we know absolutely nothing about. And it is the duty of the artist to jeer and howl and belch at the delusion that infinite generations of real effects can be inferred from the gross expression of apparent cause.

Tom Stoppard, *Travesties*

List of historical characters

Sir John Franklin Arctic explorer; Lieutenant Governor of Van Diemen's Land (VDL), 1837–44

Jane Franklin His wife

Eleanor Franklin Sir John's daughter by his first wife, Eleanor Porden

Miss Williamson Governess to Eleanor Franklin

Sophy Cracroft Jane Franklin's companion; niece to Sir John

Mary Franklin Jane Franklin's companion; niece to Sir John

Henry Elliot Sir John's young aide-de-camp

Charles O'Hara Booth Captain in the 21st Regiment; Commandant of Port Arthur Penal Station in VDL, 1833–44

Colonel George Arthur Lieutenant Governor of VDL for twelve years before Franklin was appointed

Eliza Arthur His wife

Archdeacon Hutchins Came to VDL with the Franklins

Alexander Maconochie Geographer, convict reformer and former naval officer; came to VDL with the Franklins as Sir John's private secretary

Mary Maconochie His wife

Dr Pilkington Surgeon to the 21st Regiment in VDL

Lizzie Eagle Dr Pilkington's stepdaughter

Thomas Lempriere Commissariat Officer at Port Arthur Penal Station

Charlotte Lempriere His wife

Dr Cornelius Gavin Casey Medico at Port Arthur

George Boyes Colonial Auditor in VDL, later Acting Colonial Secretary

'Bobby' Knopwood Chaplain in Hobart Town, VDL, since settlement

John Montagu Colonial Secretary in VDL

Matthew Forster Chief Police Magistrate in VDL

'Mad' Judge Montagu Judge in VDL; no relation to John Montagu

John Price Police Magistrate in VDL

Charles Swanston Director of the Derwent Bank in Hobart Town

Thomas Gregson Wealthy owner of 'Risdon', or 'Restdown', in VDL; later briefly Premier of Tasmania

Picton Beete, Wharton Young and John Peddie Charles Booth's friends in the 21st Regiment

John Gould The 'Bird Man': taxidermist, bird illustrator and collector

Eliza Gould Artist; wife to John Gould

Mathinna Aboriginal child taken in by Jane Franklin

Duterrau Artist

Miss Perigal Duterrau's sister-in-law

Thomas Boch Artist and former convict

Tom Cracroft Brother to Sophy Cracroft; a clerk in Sir John Franklin's office in VDL

Arthur Sweet Clerk; friend to Tom Cracroft

John Philip Gell Young clergyman sent from England by Dr Arnold of 'Rugby' to be Head of the new VDL College

Captain Ainsworth Later Major; aide to Sir John Franklin; courting Sophy Cracroft

Captain James Clark Ross Commander of the *Erebus*, Arctic explorer, leader of the 'Magnetic Expedition' of 1839–41

Captain Francis Crozier Commander of the *Terror*, Arctic explorer, Ross's close friend and second-in-command of the 'Magnetic Expedition'; courting Sophy Cracroft

Lieutenant Henry Porden Kay Cousin to Eleanor Franklin; came to VDL with the 'Magnetic Expedition'

'Mick' (Thomas) Walker Convict who, as leader of seven other convicts, escaped from Port Arthur in a whaleboat in 1839

Laplace Captain of the French exploratory ship *L'Artémise*
Mr Aislabie Clergyman at Richmond, VDL
'Tulip' Wright Constable in Hobart Town

List of fictional characters

Jane Eyre Orphan; governess at 'Thornfield Hall'

Edward Rochester Owner of 'Thornfield'

Adèle Pupil to Jane Eyre; Edward Rochester's ward

Rowland Rochester Older brother to Edward

Mrs Alice Fairfax Housekeeper at 'Thornfield Hall'; poor relation to the Rochesters

Bertha Mason Woman from the West Indies, possibly mad . . .

Grace Poole Bertha Mason's keeper

Harriet Adair Artist; a widow

Nina Harriet's stepmother

Gus Bergman Surveyor in VDL

St John Wallace Clergyman; cousin to Jane Eyre

Louisa Wallace His wife

George Quigley Captain of the *Adastra*

Mr and Mrs Chesney Property owners in VDL; passengers on the *Adastra*

Polly and Natty Their grandchildren

Lyddy Nurserymaid to Ned Chesney

James Seymour Doctor; passenger on the *Adastra*

Robert McLeod Newspaperman; passenger on the *Adastra*

Mrs T (Tench) Sailor-woman on the *Adastra*

Peg Groundwater Lodging-house keeper in VDL; an Orkney woman

Nellie Jack Peg's convict servant

Mrs Parry Property owner in VDL; friend to Knopwood

Augusta Drewitt Friend to Sophy Cracroft

Ada Sweet Shopkeeper; mother to Arthur Sweet

Seth Carmichael Former convict; landlord of the Eagle and Child Inn at New Norfolk; later a horse-breeder

Dinah Carmichael His wife

Catherine Tyndale Wife to a lieutenant in the 21st Regiment when it was in the West Indies

Prologue

READER, SHE DID NOT MARRY HIM. OR RATHER, WHEN AT LAST she did, it was not so straightforward as she implies in her memoirs. Jane Eyre is a truthful person and her story is fascinating, but some things she could not bring herself to say. Certain episodes in her past, she admits, 'form too distressing a recollection ever to be willingly dwelt upon'. When she announces in that jubilant sentence, 'Reader, I married him', and goes on to describe their quiet Church wedding, she is choosing to ignore the hasty ceremony that had taken place on the ship two months before.

They were married again when they returned to England—to make doubly certain all was legal, to sign their names in the parish records. Why mention that earlier wedding, so sombre, so desperate? In the heaving, creaking old *Adastra* on her way to the colony they never reached, with the fear of imminent death, and the odd little group of witnesses, of whom I was one.

My name is Harriet Adair, and forty years ago on that ship I was Jane Eyre's companion. That voyage also brought me friendship with another intrepid Jane: Lady Franklin. Her husband, Sir John, the Arctic Lion, was Lieutenant Governor of Van Diemen's Land during the six turbulent years when Jane Eyre and Edward Rochester had good reason to be closely interested in the island.

It is now, as I have said, four decades since that time, and those of us who know what really happened—about the Franklin debâcle, and

WILD ISLAND

the Rochester matter—become fewer each year. Mr Gregson therefore asked me to write my account of those days, which he intended to collate with his own and several others, but he died two years ago, and now all the papers have been passed to George Boyes's son. On the understanding, of course, that they shall not be used while any of those closely involved are still alive. I feel certain now that this will be necessary. Visiting London recently, I found my old friend, Sophy Cracroft, Sir John Franklin's niece and Jane Franklin's long-time companion, copying out Lady Franklin's letters for publication—but she is editing them ruthlessly, deleting whole paragraphs and pages. She destroys each original as she finishes it. Some she burns without copying. When she told me I cried out, 'How can you, Sophy? This is our history, our lives.'

She gave me one of her steely looks, half amused, half irritated. When she was young, she was slim, almost angular in a way that always seemed to me part of her character, but now in later life she is stout, with plump rosy cheeks that give her a benevolent look. This is misleading; her mind is as angular as ever.

'*Our* history?' she said. 'I was always taught, Harriet, that history is the record of great *men's* achievements. My uncle's discovery of the Northwest Passage is the true history of *my* life . . .'

Sophy loved her Aunt Jane dearly, but she comes from a devout Low-Church family and has severe ideas. She therefore intends to obscure Jane Franklin's part in those events in Van Diemen's Land that changed so many lives and led to Franklin's last fatal Arctic expedition. When Sir John vanished into the ice with the *Erebus* and *Terror* not much more than a year after the Franklins' return to London, Jane and Sophy were determined to save him. If physical rescue should prove impossible, then his fame at least must be preserved. For years they pleaded and flattered to raise money for search parties; they evaded the Admiralty's attempts to declare him dead, and fought the appalling claims of cannibalism. During the course of all this, Sophy came to believe that sometimes the end does justify the means. The destruction of her aunt's pages is nothing, now.

xiii

Any beginning must be somewhat arbitrary; we have agreed to start with the Franklins' arrival in Van Diemen's Land in January 1837. Someone else must tell it, since I did not arrive in the island until a year later—but those who were there have not forgotten.

PART ONE

1

BOOTH SHOULD HAVE BEEN IN HOBART TO ATTEND A HANGING that day. As Commandant of Port Arthur, the main penal station of Van Diemen's Land, he was required to witness certain judicial deaths; but on that January day in 1837, he was still in bed at seven in the morning. Most unusual for him, but it was not self-indulgence: rather, a soldier's habit of catching up on sleep when the opportunity arises. The weather had trapped him down at his station, on an isolated promontory eighty miles south-east of the town. Only two weeks until midsummer, and yet the wind had blown foully for three days: a strong sou'westerly with showers of rain, spitefully cold.

The day before, when the gales seemed to be dropping, he'd walked the five miles up the peninsula to the outstation at the coal mines, to see whether the *Vansittart*, the Government cutter, had managed to get down the estuary to pick him up. Even as he strode along he knew it would not be there. The wind was rising again, and on his way back he was caught in rain like the coming of the Flood. He reached his cottage again at half-past nine that evening, drenched and shivering, and immediately stripped and went to bed, giving Power orders not to call him until eight in the morning.

But the first muster bell brought him wide-awake at half-past five, and he lay listening to a shutter banging, the rushing wind, and thinking of his beloved semaphore stations. They would have to be kept closed again today. They were on hilltops, bore the brunt of the weather. Wind fretted and tangled the ropes, banged pulley-blocks against the masts, caused havoc if you let it. But if the duty men had frapped the arms down securely there should not be too much damage. If they'd taken care to keep the arm-lines separate from the haul-lines as he was always reminding them . . . The semaphores had brought him this appointment as Commandant, and not a day passed but he thanked God for it. Well, God and the former Lieutenant Governor, Colonel George Arthur. Two of a kind, really.

The job was a wonderful little plum: wholly unexpected at the time. Booth had arrived in Van Diemen's Land early in '33 with the Regiment, had waited on Governor Arthur and been frostily received. A cool word and out. Slightly alarming, since Booth's posting here—his life for the next six, eight, even twelve years—depended on Arthur. Did this mean His Excellency had heard of Booth's old court martial? The goat in the wardroom, the turtle in the bath? Stupid pranks which had seemed so amusingly necessary at that miserable time in the Indies more than a decade ago. It was all in the records; the Governor was sure to know.

He could not have heard of Booth's other sin? No, that was not in the records.

Booth had been left apparently forgotten in the barracks while his friends received placements, until at last there came an invitation to dine at Government House. His hopes rose, collapsed again as soon as he entered the reception room. He'd been warned that the Arthurs were strictly Evangelical, but this was so stark, comfortless, puritanical. What followed was more of the same. Conversation, stilted. One glass of bad Cape wine, a lengthy Grace and a dinner best forgotten. A meagre, dry occasion like the Governor himself. Although, Heavens Above, quiet little Eliza Arthur under her plain black gown was big with her thirteenth child. Arthur was fifty-one and she would be forty, surely. There must be juice in him somewhere.

The Arthurs' eldest son, Frederick, sat next to Booth. A pleasant lad, but too quiet. Seventeen: all knobbly wrists, Adam's apple, boots and blushing. He was really the second son, but his older brother, George, had died of consumption a few years before. Booth set himself to amuse young Fred. Uphill work. But just when the evening seemed interminable, a tumble of young children and half-grown daughters came in with the pudding.

Eliza Arthur grew motherly and the Governor unbent so far as to smile when a beautiful little girl recited her memory-work for the week, a psalm. *Deal bountifully with thy servant . . .* in a pure, piping little voice, then a breathy hesitation . . . *I am a stranger in the earth . . .* The little girl came across to Fred to be hoisted onto his lap. She told Booth, 'I am Fanny but I am called Mary. I am seven.' Booth's heart contorted and bled from the old wound because his own daughter would have been nine if he had not left her, his wife and son seven years ago in the West Indies, where they had died in penury probably.

But beautiful little Mary was continuing: George, Fred, Bella, Kate, Georgina, Eliza, Charlie, Edward, Sigi, John, Leonard. Her brothers and sisters. (Sigi?) Words had deserted Booth because the names of his own lost ones were filling his mind. Caralin, Rosa, Charlie. The irony being that he never had any trouble talking to children, nor indeed to anyone for that matter. Now Mary had given up waiting for him to say something sensible and was unfolding a drawing, a line of little stick men across the page.

'Soldiers,' he said, grasping. 'Making a signal, I think. A semaphore with flags? What are they saying, I wonder?'

'Why, so they are,' said Arthur, sternly mild. 'I believe they are saying Mary has done well and may have her jam pudding.'

Later, when the women and children were gone, Arthur said, 'Semaphores have been much in my mind.'

He wanted a network of signal towers to serve the south-east of Van Diemen's Land. To cover the distance between Hobart—here, the main harbour and centre of Government—and Port Arthur, his new penal settlement. Port Arthur had been a small timber-cutting camp, but would now become the main penal station of the island, replacing the old prisons at Sarah Island on the Wild West Coast, and Maria Island in the east. These had proved impractical because they were too far from Hobart Town, and communication could only be by sea, with its delays and dangers. But Port Arthur was only eighty miles away, and with semaphores . . . How many stations did Booth think would be needed over that distance? Could it be done—with convict labour and assistance from the Survey Department, of course? Booth was certain it could.

Within a few days, Captain Charles O'Hara Booth, latterly of blotted copybook and uncertain prospects, was Commandant of Port Arthur. Now, four years later, seven semaphores were in place, each with six moveable arms on its mast, allowing the signalling of numbers up to 999,999 with the addition of a jack staff and pennants. Each number represented a word or phrase in the codebook of Booth's devising. They were only using two hundred and twenty-seven numbers so far, but that would increase. At present a short signal and response could be returned in seven minutes. Booth thought they could get it down to four minutes if they built two more stations next year.

I mean this year, he amended his thoughts. Already January again, so soon. Nearly four years 'at the ends of the earth' as his sister Char said in her letters—but it was paradise to him. Everywhere in the landscape there was beauty barely explored, a new Eden. All he needed was a new Eve. Could he marry Lizzie this year? Should he? At Christmas there had been a rumour of the Regiment's recall; he discovered he was desperate to remain on the island. He had fallen by grace into a place he loved, and work he believed valuable, but how could he stay? Sell out of the Army? The sale of his commission would not keep him long, and some of it must be returned to Char, who had lent him money. And what civil position could he find here? Especially one that paid what he was earning now, and provided a free cottage. His salary was two hundred and seventy-three pounds fifteen shillings per annum, with a magistrate's allowance of ten shillings a day on top, but he always spent it all, and in fact, owed his agent twenty pounds at this moment.

The prison was something of a showpiece and visitors multiplied each year: Quaker observers from the Society of Friends, surveyors, auditors, engineers, missionaries and merely curious distinguished guests. Being naturally gregarious he enjoyed their varied company, but was often obliged to lodge and feed them at the Commandant's cottage, and found himself always supplying more in food and wine than his rations allowed. Could he afford to marry Lizzie?

Boyes, the Colonial Auditor, had told him every Governor of a British colony was in a similar position, having to supplement his salary from private income—with the exception of Governor Arthur. Boyes had looked at Booth and they had smiled. Arthur came to Van Diemen's Land with nothing—and left owning thousands of acres granted to him or bought cheaply, together with shares and investments yielding an annual income of five thousand pounds. Or so Robert Murray of the *Colonial Times* estimated, and Boyes believed he was not far wrong.

Booth's mind returned to his future. Surely the Regiment would not be recalled now, just when Arthur had left, and with the new Governor due in a month? And at this distance from Home, postings were often longer than usual. Governor Arthur had been twelve years in the island, recalled after twice the normal period. Booth had been one of the few chosen to accompany the Governor and his family as they boarded their ship for Home two months ago. Arthur unexpectedly weeping floods of tears, Mrs Arthur and the little Venuses, not.

Now the Governor was to be Sir John Franklin, the polar hero, Arctic Lion. Slow-witted, people said, and generally added, 'and Navy, of course', since that was the chief surprise. Army officers had been in power here since the day of settlement, which would change now, presumably. Franklin might want to appoint a new Commandant with a naval background. One of his own retinue, a younger man . . .

Booth had scarcely thought of his age until recently. He was almost the same age as the century: thirty-seven in August, although he looked younger because he was thin and agile and his hair was still thick and black, just beginning to recede in two arcs from a widow's peak. He was blessed, too, with an excellent constitution he'd come to take for granted. And then on Christmas Day—two weeks ago—he'd woken feeling seedy as hell for the first time in fourteen years. A return of yellow fever, caught when he was stationed in Saint Vincent. He must avoid a full bout. Couldn't afford to be ill.

Booth flung back the covers and sat on the side of the bed. As he did so, impatient footsteps approached along the hall. There was a rap on the door and it flew open to admit the protesting voice of his convict-assigned servant Power, and then his brindle terrier Fran, hurling herself in ecstasy onto the bed and then off again because she knew it was wrong. And the Irish accent of Casey, the station's young medico, peremptory as always: 'Get up, Charles! We have found you a body.'

A Dublin intonation like Lizzie's.

'Birch or Jones, I hope?'

'Birch,' said Casey. 'The flesh much nibbled by fishes to be sure, and all the whole of him swollen in an unlovely manner. Mutilated altogether. You will not like the look of him. But an arm remains *intacta* and it has Birch's tattoo at the wrist. A heart and two sets of initials. Now sit where you are and stop your talk.'

Casey produced a flexible tube about two feet long from his pocket and fastened one end in his right ear. A cold little white china cup at the other end was applied to Booth's lean ribs. The new snake ear trumpet, a Christmas gift from the old country.

Booth was thin by nature, but also because he spent his days tramping up and down his 'little kingdom' as he called it in letters home. Two peninsulas, each over twenty miles square, hanging one below the other by two narrow necks. The lower one, Tasman, was really the penal station, and the upper one, Forestier, was kept unpopulated as a barrier, except for a whaling station, and Captain

Spotswood's early land grant at the north end. In practice, both peninsulas fell to Booth's care. Some days he covered sixty miles on foot and by boat, hopping from promontory to promontory, sorting out problems at the boat-builders, outstations, jetties, coal mines—and his newest scheme, four miles of convict-powered railway from Port Arthur to Norfolk Bay, now half finished.

He walked about (like God in the Garden, he thought) because his position did not entitle him to a government-issue horse. Last winter he had bought one for himself, a biddable elderly nag named Jack, but his request for a forage allowance had been refused. Useful to ride quickly around the sprawling settlement, but the longer bush tracks were not as yet in a condition to allow riding.

For Booth, the long walks were the best part of his work. He tramped joyfully through dense, silent eucalypt forests where the sun fell in dazzling shafts through the canopy; and across sublime beaches and rocky headlands where gull rookeries pocked the tussocky ground and whitened the rocks with guano. In four years he'd come to love it all. Sometimes, hiking alone, he burst into song out of the fullness of his content. But occasionally now he felt his age. Lizzie was seventeen.

'Where was Birch found?'

'Floating in the shallows at Point Puer,' said Casey. 'Your chest is sound, but don't overdo things. Not that you'll take any notice.'

Birch and Jones, two young overseers from the boys' prison at Point Puer, had bolted on the eighteenth of December, an exquisite summer's day giving no warning of the sou'westerly that blew up in the night. Their curious escape engine washed up the following day—a raft with a clever outrigger and a well-equipped tool box lashed aboard. (How had they got away with that?) It was now down below the steps of Booth's cottage in the side-yard where he kept his collection of such things. Rafts, coracles, dugouts, leaky tubs: all inventive, eccentric. Made of pilfered scraps kept in dangerous secrecy and fashioned into the shapes of imagined freedom.

But why did they do it? Birch and Jones, for instance. They were overseers, well fed and housed, far better off than they would have been as apprentices with a hard master. Jones had been an excellent mechanical. Both were cheerful and content enough, it seemed. It irritated Booth, this waste of men, good brains. But some spirit seemed to seize them . . . He had felt it himself, of course. Had imagined living Crusoe-like on one of the little offshore islands, but with 'a good-tempered member of the fair sex to share my fate', as he'd written to his sister. Was Lizzie good-tempered? Not always. She was no Mrs Crusoe, certainly.

'I'll take breakfast with you,' said Casey, 'since Power is cossetting you and has made a kedgeree which it is your Christian duty to share. We'll do the inquest this morning as soon as I've had a closer look at the body. I shall want you there.'

Booth suppressed irritation. Casey behaved as though the MO outranked the Commandant. He was a civil appointment, twenty-seven, high-handed, from Dublin via Liverpool, where he had survived the cholera. Too brilliant for this place, that was the trouble. He had a hungry intelligence with nothing to feed on here. There were a thousand prospective patients—felons, military and civilian officers, wives and children—but the colony was mostly in rude health. Casey's daily lot was toothaches and common ailments, consumption and occasional accidents, with a score of lunatics at the asylum and an accouchement now and then. And floggings, of course.

After three years of this, dissatisfaction made Casey almost constantly irritable, although he'd cheered up no end last year when he had to cut Edward Howard's arm off. A difficult amputation just below the shoulder, done in only ten minutes from tourniquet to sewing up, with nothing but brandy and laudanum to quiet the patient. The main bone had been smashed when Howard, a convict bolter, was shot accidentally as he was retaken. The prisoner recovered remarkably quickly, but Casey's feat passed unnoticed. Six months later when the Colonial Surgeon, Dr James Scott, performed the same operation in

Hobart Town, all the senior medical men gathered to watch, loud with praise.

When Casey heard this he'd become morose and quarrelsome. He and Booth had nearly come to blows last November. Casey came raging in at midnight just as Booth returned from one of his scrambles up to Hobarton and back in the same day. Demanded to know where the hell Booth had been and why he, Casey, had not been told, etcetera, etcetera, insisting he was in charge when Booth was away.

Booth had been twenty hours on the go by then, having started for Hobart at four that morning. He wearily explained that this was a *military* establishment: the Commandant's second-in-command was the next ranking *military* officer, Lieutenant Stuart from the Coal Mines. Casey refused to believe it—in the coarsest, vilest language. Booth, exasperated, told him he was behaving like a jilted housemaid. Casey squared up belligerently and for a moment things looked ugly, but then he turned, slammed out and wrote to the Colonial Secretary in Hobarton, who confirmed what Booth had said—which only increased Casey's sullen resentment. The quarrel lasted until Booth's fever on Christmas Day, when Casey's attention was immediate, solicitous, and wonderfully effective. Yes, if ever Booth needed a medico, he'd want Casey—the proud, stubborn Irish bastard.

Power brought in hot water and Casey went out, no doubt to begin breakfast without waiting. Booth shivered as he washed and dressed. But it was never as cold here as at Home. Winter there now, January. Snowing in Basingstoke, probably. He wondered idly whether he would ever see it again. (He would not.) At the breakfast table he found Lempriere drinking coffee and talking to Casey about the weather. So that quarrel was mended, too. How could Casey quarrel with Lempriere, the Commissariat Officer, and the most affable creature in the world? About potatoes—how Irish!—in the allotment that Lempriere shared under regulations with the MO.

Lemp was describing now how one might construct a wind-measuring machine. The study of weather was one of his passionate hobbies, together with natural science, painting and drawing, and the study of the French horn.

'*Mon vieux*,' he greeted Booth. Lemp's forebears were from the Channel Islands, France and Portugal, but he'd been born in Hamburg, where his father was a merchant for a time. After fifteen years in Van Diemen's Land he spoke English daily, savouring its oddities; French for pleasure and to educate his children, and German in rare moments of melancholy and *Weltzschmerz*.

'I have been down at the office,' he said now. 'Killick is waiting to see you. He was on duty at Mount Arthur until last night and walked in at daybreak this morning. He says he saw a ship entering the Derwent as he started out, and later heard what he thinks was cannon-fire. He believes it's the new Governor arrived early. So I am come to ask if we can have our Metaphysicals tonight instead of tomorrow night? If it does prove to be the Governor you'll be called up to town and we shall miss again as we did last month.'

They had formed the Metaphysicals three years ago. A most select club, they joked: Lempriere, Booth and Casey, with the occasional guest. They debated any subject that took their fancy—from animal magnetism to *Zoonomia,* that strange work by Erasmus Darwin. Booth had borrowed the book from Casey and remembered it being mostly about composting, even of human corpses. But he was sometimes drowsy in the evenings after a vigorous day and several glasses of 'the blushful Hippocrene', and perhaps he'd got it wrong. Darwin's grandson had visited Hobart last year on the *Beagle*. Another 'Charles'. An amiable young man, people agreed, but not clever like his grandfather.

In the beginning, the Metaphysicals had met at each of their cottages in turn, but Lempriere's house, built for a family of four, now imperfectly contained Lempriere, his amiable wife Charlotte, their children Edward, Thomas, William, Francis and Mary, and the governess, Miss Wood. Their two servants slept in the kitchen, a brick box at the rear. The MO's cottage was even smaller.

'Can you find us a dinner, Power? Anything left of the Christmas ham?'

'Salt beef,' said Power gloomily. There being none fresh on account of the gale and the meat boat not come down. And the weather too bad for fishing and the ham-bone past using he would not be answerable, it must go for soup. Which meant it was gone already, finished up by Power and Mrs Power and their two older children, Billie and Lizzie. (Another pretty Lizzie.) Booth knew better than to argue. He was fond of the Powers, had stood godfather to young Billie and the new one, Harry.

He spent too much time having to think about food. But his kingdom of a thousand souls must be fed each day and nearly everything except vegetables brought in. No cattle or four-footed animals could be kept on the peninsula because they'd make an easy larder for escapees. Most of the meat was brought down by ship from New South Wales 'on the hoof' from Dr Imlay's brother's property. It came down the east coast, was landed near Imlay's whaling station at East Bay Neck, and driven across the narrow peninsula to Storm Bay, where it was slaughtered and shipped down to the lower peninsula on the more sheltered inner waters.

As it happened, the meat boat managed to get down as far as Wedge Bay that afternoon, having recently been fitted with a steam engine, one of the first in the island. With it came Gus Bergman, who walked the four miles to Port Arthur and came in soaked to the skin, bringing a new ham, a bottle of claret, and confirmation that Killick's thunder had indeed been for the Franklins' arrival. This sou'westerly had blown them here from Cape Town in only thirty-nine days.

Bergman was a surveyor. Clever, hardworking, amusing, he'd several times been a guest at the Metaphysicals. A Jewish, perhaps, with his finely curved beaky nose and mobile, intelligent face—but none the worse for that. He was here this time to set out the foundations for the new dormitory at Point Puer.

Over a stew with new potatoes, kale and turnips, they talked of the Governor's arrival. Hobarton had leapt into welcoming mood, Bergman reported. Like a fairground, in spite of the weather. Illuminations set up in every shop window and house. Bonfires tonight: fireworks, and the band of the 21st Regiment marching in the streets. The only sour note came from Mr Robert Murray, editor of the *Colonial Times,* who claimed this welcome had less to do with greeting Sir John than with yet another celebration of Governor Arthur's departure.

'The new broom,' said Lempriere. 'Changes, *n'est-ce pas?*'

'. . . and still nobody can tell me,' said Casey, 'why London would be after sending a naval man to lead a colony under military rule? Army and Navy together is a recipe for trouble . . .'

'All the senior posts are civil now,' objected Bergman.

'But they are all held by former Army men, Arthur's friends and relations,' said Casey. 'As Gilbert Robertson says in *The Courier,* England has put Sir John in the invidious position of a Whig King with a Tory ministry, and no power of changing it.'

'The King appointed Sir John. Being Navy himself, he wanted a naval man for it—so Frankland says.'

George Frankland, the Chief Surveyor, had high connections at Home and might be assumed to know.

'Lady Franklin is said to have had a hand in it too,' added Bergman. 'Sir John was offered the governing of Antigua but she thought it not enough. One of her friends who is lady-in-waiting to the Queen was asked to hint that something better was owed to the Arctic Lion.'

'But does he know anything of government? Managing a ship's crew is one thing. A colony of thirteen thousand scattered over a piece of land the size of Ireland—and three-quarters of it wilderness—is another matter entirely.'

'He has only to continue Arthur's work,' said Booth. 'People complain of Arthur, but he brought this island out of its first disorder into . . .'

'By employing his relatives and friends,' said Casey with a grimace, 'ruining his enemies, and hanging two hundred and seventy poor bastards in his time here.'

Booth shrugged. 'What else do you do with murderers and bushrangers? Especially when you've not enough prisons, overseers and constables. As for employing his friends, he had to have men he could trust . . .'

'So he makes his nephew Henry Arthur a magistrate—a known rogue, drunkard and fool? And Henry's brother Charles . . .'

'Charles is not like Henry, he's an excellent fellow.'

'I grant you, but . . .'

Power had made a 'boiled baby' to follow, a suet pudding filled with sweet dark-purple plums— an old variety, cropping heavily this year. The cabbages, too, looked set to be a bumper harvest again. Booth smiled wryly to himself. He would not repeat the mistake he had made two years ago when, with several tons' surplus, he had allotted a quarter of a cabbage a day as extra convict rations. A savage reprimand had arrived from the Governor—and yet Booth had come to admire Arthur by then, and to consider himself a friend of the family. But here was an abrupt lesson in the limits of Arthur's friendship. Booth was castigated for an inexcusable lack of judgement. Exceeding his authority. Wanton indulgence. All surplus crops must be dug in, sent to Hobarton, or used as animal fodder.

Booth had never spoken of this but it must have got about somehow, because James Scott, the Colonial Surgeon, meeting Booth in Hobarton soon after, had cornered him, murmuring, 'Expect nothing from that quarter, Booth, believe me. I do not mention names. I have treated the lady and her children. Seized her from the brink of death after one confinement—and was never offered so much as a glass of wine after a night of hard watching. Dismissed in the morning with a coolness that chilled my heart. And yet, do you know, I believe he loves her.'

And last year Booth's punishment records for Port Arthur had dropped, simply because the prison was running smoothly. Again came a savage letter from Arthur. Punishment was salutary, numbers must rise. And then, worse. A felon on trial in Hobart was sentenced to a chain gang and warned he'd be returned to Port Arthur if he erred again. Whereupon the man had shouted in court that he'd rather be there, where everything ran to rule. At least you were not at the whim of any devil of an overseer who flogged you at his pleasure and left you to rot afterwards. Arthur, in a white rage, had sent for Booth.

'We cannot have felons praising our prisons. Port Arthur must be a place of dread.'

Booth had seen too many strong, healthy backs turned to bloody pulp by the lash; too many able men screaming and weeping. He explained that if he kept his charges working long hours and well fed, they had neither the time nor the inclination for rebellion. The Government gained by labourers in good health. But he knew from these episodes that if Arthur ever heard about Caralin and the children, there would be no mercy. He'd be stripped of his command before you could say Jack Robinson. He had never told Lempriere or Casey about Caralin, although he'd come close some nights. The only people who knew were his three best friends who'd been in the Indies with him: John Peddie, Picton Beete, and Wharton Young, all now separated at posts around the island. They would never speak of it.

—⁂—

The weather cleared, and a signal came inviting Booth to the new Governor's first public levée for gentlemen, followed by a 'drawing-room' in the evening for wives, but naturally this could only include those who lived near Hobart Town. Booth could not attend. He was kept at the peninsula again, this time by a whaling infringement. He walked up to East Bay Neck, issued the fine and walked back, by which time the roof of the blacksmith's shop was collapsing. He was invited up to dine at Government House the following week, met Sir John at the Mess the following day, and scrambled back to the peninsula the day after.

'*Ensuite?*' demanded the Lemprieres when he settled by their fire on the night of his return. How did they appear, the new couple? What did they look like? What did she wear?

Booth smiled, shrugged. '*Bouleversement entier!* We're clearly in for a different regime absolutely. Chalk and cheese. Sir John is affable, gentlemanly . . . all you'd expect. A big man. He'd make four of me. Three of you, Thomas. Lady Franklin is a clever woman I should say—talks with great eagerness and attention. Not in an overbearing way . . . Her manner is friendly, no standing on ceremony.'

She had once been very pretty no doubt; was now old. Forty-five, she'd mentioned it herself. Her two companions were Sir John's nieces, Miss Sophy Cracroft and Miss Mary Franklin. Unassuming girls, evidently pleased with their daring adventure to the colonies. Miss Franklin was prettier and smiled more easily than Miss Cracroft, who might be fierce if roused. At any rate, Lempriere and Charlotte must judge for themselves, which they would have the opportunity of doing in six weeks' time, towards the end of March, when the Franklins would make their inaugural tour of the peninsula.

2

IT MAY SEEM ODD THAT I AGREED TO GO TO THE COLONY WHEN I knew almost nothing about it. A sea voyage of four or five months, Harriet, they said. Twelve thousand miles. And at once I began to think of how readily I could sell drawings of the strange flora and fauna of that place when we returned to England. I was worried about money—about the want of it, I mean.

I have always drawn, and for much of my life made a living by it, but four years before this time there had come a great change in my fortunes, and for a time I had no leisure to draw. After some months, however, I could resist no longer, and began sketching corners in the lonely mansion where I now found myself, and the room in which I was almost as much a prisoner as the patient I was nursing.

My troubles began with the death of my husband, Thomas Lawrence Adair, an artist more than twenty years older than I. Like many wives and daughters of artists, I was his assistant; I learned to grind his colours, prepare etching plates, and paint drapery and small commissions, generally portraits of women and children. When Tom died suddenly in the bleak January of 1831, many of his huge, laboured canvases of Biblical scenes were still unsold, stacked against the studio walls, and I discovered we owed debts everywhere. The bailiffs seized all our belongings, and I found myself at twenty-nine a widow nearly penniless, with the care also of Nina, my stepmother, who was ill and aging.

We moved into a tiny room and I tried to go on earning our living by the same means as before, but as a widow I could get no credit from the colourman or the oilshop, and was often in want of materials. Mr Linnell, the well-respected teacher, would advance me six and ninepence for a copy of certain Dutch paintings in the Pall Mall gallery, and I sold sketches of dogs or birds, and hand-coloured etchings.

In this manner we scraped along until Nina died two years later. She had been as true a mother and friend to me as anyone could have been, and with her loss I came to my lowest ebb. I understood now how impossible it would be to save against illness or old age. Friends said I would marry again, but I thought not. I therefore began to look for a situation as a drawing mistress in a school, or as a governess. This was easier said than done. I grew shabbier, thinner and more anxious by the day, and my appearance had no reassuring effect on prospective employers.

At last I obtained, by exchange of letters, a situation in a northern shire. There was to be a three-month trial, since no interview was possible at such a distance. The duties were described as 'nurse-companion to a patient sometimes difficult', which gave me the idea that it might be a child. The wages were suspiciously high, but this was explained as being on account of the isolated setting of the house, which did not attract servants. It was a wrench to leave my beloved London, but as the coach jolted north and the countryside opened around me, I began to believe the rural air might restore my health and spirits.

When I first saw 'Thornfield Hall' in the spring of '33 it seemed made for such a purpose. A Jacobean mansion of mellow rose-brick with clusters of barley-sugar chimneys, rooks in immemorial elms, ancient yews and pines. The great trees set the house rather gloomily in shadow, but the villages of Hay and Millcote at about two miles distant were sunny, the whole scene a perfect English pastoral—from a distance. Only later did I discover that the calm of 'Thornfield' was spurious, its peace a fiction.

The owner of the estate, Mr Edward Rochester, was away when I arrived. Mrs Alice Fairfax, the elderly housekeeper, was the person I must satisfy. My position in the house was ambiguous; I shall say more of it later. Mrs Fairfax explained that Mr Rochester was frequently out of England. She never knew when he'd be coming or going. She, too, was a widow escaped from genteel poverty, but in her case there were connections with the Rochester family. She had come to 'Thornfield' many years before as housekeeper-companion to the late Mrs Rochester, Edward Rochester's mother, who was her first cousin.

Mrs Fairfax was lonely. Indoor and out, there were sixteen servants, most of whom had been in the family's service for years, and they carried out their work each day with little need of direction. She could not be intimate with *them*, and there being no one else for company, she began to call me to her housekeeper's room several times a week for tea. Her innocent vices were soon apparent: a modest pride in the intricate white widow's caps she sewed for herself (long lace weepers hanging each side like the ears of an albino spaniel) and an old woman's eagerness to tell stories about the past.

Mrs Fairfax knew the present Mr Rochester disliked such talk and would call it gossip, but she carried on this minor rebellion almost indignantly. She would not *of course* speak of the family to anyone she could not trust, but I was a gentlewoman, and at any rate, this was not gossip in her view, but a way of honouring the dead. Telling how the Rochesters and Fairfaxes of earlier days had laughed and cried and quarrelled and married. How this one had a taste for mustard herrings and that one for gunpowder tea, until death gradually took them all and left her stranded among her furniture.

'The Rochesters and the Fairfaxes have always intermarried. George Fairfax, who . . . now there's my wool gone down . . . Thank you. When my cousin George—he was Lucy's cousin too, naturally . . .'

Like many of the elderly she was repetitive, her stories smooth as pebbles from the wash of time and handling. I could not always remember which George or Edward was which; whose pug it was that had bitten the Bishop—but Lucy was the late Mrs Rochester. She and Mrs Fairfax had been close as girls, but poor Lucy had not lived long into her second son's childhood. Perhaps it was just as well. She had not survived to know of the tragedy: her eldest son, the present Mr Edward Rochester's brother Rowland (her favourite—everyone's favourite, although one shouldn't say it) had been killed in the West Indies thirteen years ago in the slave rebellion.

If indeed he *was* killed . . . Sugar had been a shocking price those years, and cotton and coffee, too. Some people had refused to buy coffee in sympathy with the slaves. They had contrived substitutes from roasted corn and burned carrot powder, but these never tasted well to her. Rowland loved good coffee. How different the household would have been if he had lived!

'There is some doubt whether he really died?' I asked.

Well, she had heard Mr Edward say so, but Rowland must be dead—or why did he not return? No one would give up lightly such an inheritance as 'Thornfield'. There was more hesitation when she spoke of Rowland than in her other stories, as though she found herself near a boundary she knew she must not cross. I asked her if he had resembled Mr Edward.

No, she said. Rowland had been lighter in colouring and more cheerful in temperament: more a Fairfax, always merry, with a fondness for society, but a scholar, too. Excellent at the pianoforte, and with a fine singing voice. There had been eleven years between the two boys, so they had not been close. Lucy had borne three babes in between, but none survived. Rowland went away to college while Edward was still only a boy, and by the time he returned to 'Thornfield', Edward had gone to board with a tutor.

Mrs Fairfax hesitated again. 'Not to speak ill of the dead, but the tragedy was old Mr Rochester's fault. He fell ill one winter about fourteen years ago and began to think of making his will. He deplored the idea of dividing 'Thornfield' to leave half the estate to each brother, and so resolved to bequeath it wholly to Rowland. Edward's future would be secured by arranging his marriage to the stepdaughter of a certain wealthy Mr Mason, a friend of Mr Rochester's in his youth. Mason was a planter in the West Indies. Miss Cosway-Mason was to have a dowry of thirty thousand pounds! Hardly believable—but half of it was to be in property, a sugar plantation.

'To be sure, there had been unpleasant rumours about Mr Mason. His reputation was damaged somehow, but old Mr Rochester would insist on the marriage. This was in '23, eight years after the end of the war, and England was not so prosperous then as now. Money was tight, you remember, and business in a poor way from the long years of fighting Bonaparte.'

It was all leading up to that Yuletide of '25 when the banks suddenly closed and no one could get any money. The 'Black December' they called it afterwards.

'Mr Rochester was in trouble about money as early as '23. He had been forced to mortgage land. And there was also the question of carrying off Rowland's wedding to Lady Mary Faringdon in suitable style. Oh yes, the engagement had been a fact for several years. Only the sudden death of Lady Mary's brother, Rowland's close friend, had delayed an announcement of the betrothal. The match was such a source of pride to old Mr Rochester. Lady Mary would have had little in the way of dowry—the Faringdon estates are all entailed on the male line—but the family is old aristocracy and that's what counted with him.

'Edward Rochester had just finished Oxford and was travelling on the continent. Old Mr Rochester hated to travel and was not fully recovered from his illness, and so it was Rowland who went to Spanish Town to meet Mr Mason and his stepdaughter, to inspect the dowry property. But something went wrong. Old Mr Rochester received a letter and fell into a fury. Oh, he was in such a state! He set off at once to follow Rowland to the Indies (unheard of! Old Mr Rochester had such a cordial dislike to travel).

'And what happened next I do not fully understand to this day,' said Mrs Fairfax. She hesitated, pausing suddenly in her knitting, her lips pursed and her old face troubled. 'At any rate, when Mr Rochester came back he would say only that Rowland was dead, and Edward married and gone to the continent with his new wife, this heiress. And then a few months later, we heard she too was dead! A dreadful hole-in-the-corner business, all of it. No proper marriage, no funeral for Rowland or the deceased heiress.

'None of this is ever spoken of, of course,' she repeated. 'Perhaps I should not have mentioned it, but I know I can trust you to be discreet, my dear.'

Mrs Fairfax and I took tea together for two years and ten months. About six months into this time I met my employer at last, when Mr Edward Rochester arrived without warning one bleak evening. I was called to speak with him in the library, and saw a dark, restless man in his late thirties, sitting behind a desk. A craggy, unhappy face. After a first searching look at me, which would have shown him a tall, thin woman no longer young, of no interest but useful in her way, he turned his eyes back to the papers his agent was placing before him. He glanced up now and then as he spoke.

Mrs Fairfax was pleased with me, he said tersely. Did I find the work onerous, troublesome? No, sir, I said. Was my patient in good health? Did Dr Carter visit her regularly? I answered yes to both of these. He did not speak of visiting her, and a week or two later he left again just as suddenly. He came and went at intervals after that, and during another of his absences, the child Adèle arrived in the care of a French nurserymaid, with a trunk, four bandboxes, and a brief note from Rochester.

'Well, good gracious, she is Mr Edward's ward!' said Mrs Fairfax. 'Seven years old. A pretty little creature. Foreign ways of course, but a breath of young life in the house. As for whose child exactly, I cannot . . . It's not so long since we were at war with the French . . . She and her nurse will have the old nursery, and I am to employ a governess . . .'

The new governess came to 'Thornfield' in the early autumn of 1836. It was October and I was looking out of an upstairs window on the day she arrived, but it was weeks later before she first saw me. It was a radiant, glowing autumn, which you could only see in the kitchen garden, where the old apple trees, pears and plums were dropping leaves, or in the lanes beyond 'Thornfield' where the beeches were turning gold. The house itself was flanked by the two stands of tall pines always between us and the sun. On any but the clearest days of midsummer their violet shadows drowned the house.

When you first saw Miss Eyre, she looked small, thin, pale, plain. Grey bonnet, grey dress. The whole effect as colourless as a winter sky. As safely dull as porridge you'd have said, or like the hen-bird of some pair in which the male has all the colours. When I saw her face, however, I was not so sure. The constant drawing of faces gives you the habit of studying them, and there was something in Miss Eyre's expression that made you wonder about her history.

But I saw her very little, being now busier than before. Jane Eyre began to take my place as Mrs Fairfax's teatime companion, and it was not long before the servants' hall knew Miss Eyre had a quick, wild heart, a clever mind, a sharp tongue, and plenty of courage. The world has often found these qualities troublesome in women, and I wondered how she would fare when Mr Rochester returned.

By Christmas he was home, and within weeks she had fallen in love with him, and he with her, though neither seemed to recognise the other's feelings. The servants observed the two as they circled each other.

In the spring, Jane was called away to the deathbed of her aunt, a Mrs Reed, in a distant county. Jane, who had believed Mrs Reed was her only relative, now discovered the existence of her uncle, her father's brother, a bachelor living in Funchal, Madeira. Jane wrote to him and a correspondence began. All this came to me from letters Jane sent Mrs Fairfax. Rochester evidently heard it too, and perhaps he wondered whether Jane might go to Madeira—at any rate, as soon as she returned, he proposed to her.

This was nine months after she came to 'Thornfield', Midsummer's Eve of 1837. That magic night when the world pauses and turns. Earlier in the day, Leah, the housemaid, had brought the midsummer cushion into the kitchen—a square of meadow-turf set on a meat platter, with wildflowers stuck thickly into it. Unmarried women and girls would put a bloom from it under their pillow, in hope of seeing their future husband in a dream that night.

'No, thank you, Leah,' said Jane, passing through, 'If I ever come to want a husband, I'll trust in the Lord and look about for myself.'

Later, when Adèle was in bed, Jane went into the garden. It had been a day of heat and the air was balmy. Rochester joined her and they wandered in the scented twilight and on into the dark. There were accusations and tears, misunderstanding, explanations. As they embraced, the wind suddenly rose and the moon turned blood red. Rain began to pour down, and thunder and lightning rent the air, all heaven in a rage. As the lovers ran into the great hall the clock struck midnight and Rochester took Jane into his arms and pressed her wet face with kisses, murmuring, 'Jane, my Jane.'

'Let me go, sir,' she said smiling, struggling to escape. She had seen Mrs Fairfax holding her candle at the other end of the hall, astonished at the sight of the Master of 'Thornfield' dripping wet, clasping the orphan governess in his possessive embrace.

—◊—

On that same midsummer night in 1837, the King died at last in London: William the Fourth; the Sailor King; or Silly Billy, depending on your point of view. The Princess Victoria was eighteen, the same age as Jane Eyre, and just as intelligent, as uncompromising, as plain. And both were as eager for love—as I had been, at the same age. Many women are Jane Eyres at eighteen, ready to brave anything for the beloved, who is like no other; but we are sometimes forced to change as the years go by. The heart's hot beating continues invisibly, but we learn to disguise our feelings, to present a more cautious aspect to the world.

When I was seven, my father paid me a penny for a sketch of our dog, Rom. A whole penny for doing what I loved, what my deepest nature cried out to do. I was too young to think of it in such terms, but the tremendous satisfaction of the bargain was a lesson in itself, the dawning of a thought about how to live one's life. Father took the sketch of Rom away to sea with him. He was a Post Captain in Nelson's fleet, away at the war with Boney for most of my childhood. My poor mother had died soon after I was born. I was her fourth child, the only one to survive; and as she was without family, I grew up with my father's mother.

Grandmama was the daughter of a clergyman and the widow of one too, and pale watercolours had been among her own accomplishments as a girl, but even so, she found my continual sketching excessive (and paper was precious during the war). While not exactly immoral, it amounted to a passion, and therefore could not be entirely blameless. It was 'inordinate', a word she kept returning to; too much concerned with outward appearances, and it occupied hours better employed in other ways: sewing, good deeds, prayer. She encouraged my reading and playing the pianoforte in the hope that these would in time replace the drawing (both of these could at least be used in the service of the Lord) but they did not.

I was ten when Grandmama died and I was sent to my new stepmother, Nina, in London. This violent translation from a Hampshire village to the city was at first desperately unwelcome to me. My father was at sea; the sprawling paradise of garden and wooded lanes I was accustomed to had become dirty crowded streets; the windows in Nina's large, cluttered second-storey rooms revealed only dark roofs and chimneys. Later I thought them beautiful, but not at first. The only animals here seemed to be cats, mice, sooty pigeons and bony street horses. All these I liked well enough, especially the cats, but they could not compare with the village menagerie of dogs, hens, rabbits, cows, sheep, and more, now lost to me.

Nina had been the widow of an actor before she married my father, and an actress herself in her youth. Looking back I can only imagine they were one of those odd pairings war tends to bring about. My father was coolly rational, energetic, meticulously neat and self-disciplined.

Nina was sentimental, warm and famously untidy: her brown hair was always escaping from the bright turbans she wound carelessly about it. Her face reminded me of a gentle pony's. My father needed her gaiety as she needed his steadiness. Even so, their mutual happiness was no doubt aided by the war and his naval position, which kept them frequently apart. But they were happy, I believe.

Nowadays I think it could not have been easy for her to have a strange child thrust into her life. She managed by enlisting the help of her many friends—artists, actors, writers, musicians, both male and female: the demi-monde. At first I was shy of them, but soon became fascinated by their talk, their colourful ways. Under their good-natured, irregular care, I discovered a way of life entirely to my liking, which unfortunately lasted not much more than a year. Boney was captured and sent to Elba, and my father came home and noticed that the education I was deriving from this rackety company was rather too broad. He had earned a thousand pounds in prize money when his ship the *Resolute* captured the *Belle Isle*; it would pay for my schooling in Dublin.

'Dublin!' cried Nina. 'Are there no such establishments in London?'

She was a Londoner through and through, and by then she had taught me to love the city. She had once toured the provinces playing Lady Wishfort in *The Way of the World*, and shuddered at the memory. Yet she could not dissuade my father. The widow of his best friend, a fellow Post Captain, was struggling to keep body and soul together by running a ladies' academy in Dublin, and there I must go.

The long journeys that followed four times a year for me, across England and the Irish Sea, seem in memory to have taken place mostly at night and in winter. But all through the rattling cold, the boredom and fear, I always felt a current of humming excitement: the promise of new sights and places.

Waterloo came when I was twelve, and the following years were lean ones. My father, like so many naval men, was stranded ashore on half-pay because the fleet was in tatters after the decades of fighting. By the time I was fifteen he could no longer afford the school, and assuming I was sufficiently educated in any case, he called me back to London.

But I had fallen in love—like half the girls and teachers at the Academy—with Thomas Adair, our drawing master. An older girl nudged me and nodded at him in Church a few days before our lessons began. He was lean, wolfishly handsome, with Byronically hollowed cheeks, dark hair and a pointed chin. I believed at once the rumours she told me: he was half Irish, half Russian; he had escaped from the burning of Moscow by the skin of his teeth, and later fled a splendid career in London on account of a scandal involving the wife of some eminent person.

At our first lesson he loped into the room carrying a basket, set a white linen cloth in casual folds on a small table in the centre of the room while we watched and giggled, and laid out upon it lemons and grapes. It was January, in Dublin. They must have come from a hothouse. He half-peeled an orange so that the peel, still attached, curled out across white linen, dark wood. He carried the plaster cast of a beautiful veiled woman from a collection of such things on shelves in another corner, set this lady among the fruit, and bade us draw.

As he paced about the room, watching us begin, he intoned, "'She walks in beauty like the night of cloudless climes and starry skies." Do you know what that means, young ladies? It means she is dark and warm as the scented air of a summer evening in Italy. Put that into your drawing, *mesdemoiselles*—all the promise of summer, although we are in chilly Dublin, your young fingers are purple with chilblains, and she only a cold plaster bust.'

Later, when he came to look over my shoulder, he asked, 'A new girl?'

'Harriet Pym, sir.'

He used the pencil he was carrying to lift a long lock of my hair, and said, 'Harriet the Red.' An exaggeration: my hair was reddish brown. 'Are you fiery, Harriet? Aflame with the desire to draw?'

I looked at him. 'Yes, I am,' I said.

There are many opportunities to lean close together to study drawings, many times when the eyes of student and teacher meet, when the hot cheek of one feels the warm breath of the other. I was twelve at that first meeting; Tom was thirty-three, though he could have passed for ten years younger. He taught me chiaroscuro, perspective, and to measure faces—and many things besides. He kissed me behind a tree in St Stephen's Green on a sketching expedition when I was fifteen, and I knew I would die if I had to live without him. I wrote to him for a year after we were separated, letters of misery and burning passion. We eloped when I was seventeen.

There followed great troubles, but my father was brought to accept the marriage at last, and Tom and I went to the continent on a six-month wedding journey. It was 1820 and I was young and full of joy. Nothing could touch me: no crowded stifling carriages, no bleak wet days in flea-ridden inns, no greasy dinners of horse meat and black bread. Tom knew the poetry of each place, the paintings to see, the churches, palaces, the hill towns and fêtes. He was my teacher and sage, lover and friend, and I was blissfully happy. I discovered Paris, Florence and Geneva with lean wolfish Tom, all my very own, on days when the sky was blue as heaven and the nights were warm and full of promise. We were in Aix-en-Provence when he told me, greatly amused, that he had not a particle of Russian in him. He was the son of an Irish woman and a Liverpool Army man, both long dead. He had been brought up among cousins in a carpenter's yard in Putney. I did not care; I was happy.

Portraits were Tom's forte in those days, and the first shadow came when we returned to London and discovered the demand for these greatly diminished. With the war over, Captains and Admirals no longer needed to leave their likenesses at home for their loved ones—and money was short. Tom began then to paint grand Biblical scenes, gradually becoming possessed by them, spending less and less time on portraits.

During the next seven years I had three miscarriages and bore two infants. Both lived only a few weeks. I recovered easily in body, and yet the doctor said I could never, now, bear children. People remarked on how well I looked, and I strove to be cheerful for Tom's sake, but I felt always veiled in a kind of dark trance, half absent from myself and the world. Work was a solace, but it was a time of mourning; my father was drowned in the Mediterranean in the year '27. During all these years I struggled to be calm. Steady observation and detachment being habits drawing promotes in any case, I schooled myself to be like my father: measured, cool; since Tom, I now saw, was like Nina: hot-blooded, impatient, vigorous. These lessons of self-restraint and patience stood me in good stead in the later years of my marriage and during Nina's last illness.

But it was never easy to subdue my eagerness of spirit, and now, at 'Thornfield', in the days when Jane and Rochester's passion filled the house like a contagious summer fever, and England was preparing to celebrate a new young queen, the life in me that had been damped down and wintry for years, felt ready, suddenly, to burst out of containment.

I thought of my beloved London, of the parties there would be in the streets, illuminations along the river, music, dancing; of warm busy life going forward varied and glorious. Not standing still, frozen day after day, as it seemed to be in 'Thornfield's' attic. I could not help crying a little and thinking of the past. Then I reminded myself that if I had stayed in London I would probably be dead in a pauper's grave. I resolved to be thankful for 'Thornfield', and even for my cantankerous patient, and I fell to considering what changes might follow.

—◊—

Jane and Rochester were to marry four weeks after his midsummer proposal, allowing just enough time to call the banns and prepare for the wedding journey. When the morning came they walked together from 'Thornfield' to the Church across the park. By then they were so hungry for each other the air between them fairly crackled.

I was watching from my upstairs window as they set out. I did not go to the Church but I know what happened. At the moment when the vicar asked if anyone knew just cause why this man and woman should not be joined in holy matrimony, a man rose at the back of the Church. He said, 'Yes. Rochester cannot marry because he is married already. Fourteen years ago at Spanish Town in the West Indies, he was married to Bertha Antoinette Cosway-Mason who is at this moment a prisoner in the attic of "Thornfield Hall".'

The silence was instant, Jane told me later. She thought she had gone suddenly deaf, or that Time itself had come to a stop, like the cogs of a great clock between one second and the next. Then Rochester burst into accusations against the stranger, seized Jane by the hand, and strode out of the Church and back to 'Thornfield' with that dumbfounded little group stumbling behind. (There was the stranger, and Mr Gray, the lawyer, and Mr Wood, the clergyman, and the two elderly Miss Pattons from Hay village, who had been putting flowers on their mother's grave and were swept, wide-eyed, into the drama.) When they reached the Hall, Rochester pushed aside Mrs Fairfax, Adèle, and the huddle of servants waiting on the steps to give their good wishes, and strode on up to the attic and unlocked the door.

And there was I, Grace Poole, or so I was called sometimes, because it had been the name of Bertha's former keeper, a vicious old woman, by all accounts. I had been trying to keep Bertha quiet all morning, because she knew about the wedding, I'm sure. They seem to know things, mad people, without ever being told. They pick it up from the air around them as dogs do, I think. Or was she ever quite so mad as we all believed? Although Bertha never spoke properly and it was difficult to tell how much she understood, I am sure I could feel what she knew sometimes, as you can with an animal you know well.

Bertha herself had an animal's sensitivity to Rochester, as though she could smell him across long distances. When he was away she was docile. She would often sit quietly with her dark hair hanging down over the back of a chair while I sat behind her, brushing slowly until the hair shone like the feathers of a blackbird. But she seemed to sense her husband's return long before he arrived, and to become restless, prone to growling and fits of rebellion.

In the months while Jane Eyre and Rochester had been in the house together, Bertha had become agitated and unpredictable. I could not leave her for more than a few minutes. It was this that put an end to my teas with Mrs Fairfax. Bertha's imprisonment was mine too, you could say. I was drinking when I could, and praying a good deal. Praying and drinking. A more common combination than I knew then.

We had taken a drink or two the night before the wedding, Bertha and I. Or perhaps three or four. A drop or two of 'shrub' to start with—gin and lemon with a little hot water and sugar. Not ladylike, but then so much of my life has not been ladylike. And when the gin ran out, most of a bottle of claret. To keep out the cold, to warm the cockles. It was July but the nights were chilly. The fire in the grate wouldn't seem to draw properly and Bertha couldn't bear to be cold. She had been in the attic ten years by then, and I had been with her the last three.

She did not want to sleep, although commonly she slept a great deal, like the huge, drowsy, shabby bear I used to see on a chain in Glasshouse Yard. This night she was on the move all the time, up and down, in a way that made me uneasy. I brought the old red dress out of the chest for her to hold. She wound the fabric round her hand and put her thumb in her mouth the way little children hold a favourite piece of rag. The rest of the scarlet fabric trailed from her hands, and in the yellow candlelight it looked like flames, or blood. She dropped to the ground and crouched in the corner, holding the dress and crooning to it.

On that wedding morning when the noise came up the stairs and the door was thrown open, Bertha was crouched against the wall in the back corner. Rochester was raving and pointing, 'There you see her! Behold, gentlemen, my wife!' His face was twisted with rage hatred fury scorn. He looked more the maniac than Bertha.

Jane was white-faced, holding herself rigid; her elfish face a mask in which only the eyes moved. *His wife!* I had not known that. Mrs Fairfax and the servants believed Bertha was some mad bastard child or discarded mistress of old Mr Rochester. But, Edward Rochester's wife! I was so profoundly struck by this revelation that my attention was distracted from Bertha, who leapt from the wall and hurled herself at Rochester with a rising screech. Her hands snatched at his throat, tiger-violent. He seized her arms and battled with her as though glad of the excuse.

There was a cry from one of the men who had followed him up the stairs. It was Richard Mason, Bertha's stepbrother, the man who had come from the West Indies to stop the wedding, and now she had bitten him. In trying to get clear of the fray he knocked me aside, so I could not quiet her. Mason lurched into Rochester, who lost his balance and struck his head on the coal hod as he went down. Blood everywhere, suddenly. I pulled Bertha away to a chair. She sank down rocking, moaning, like a great lumpy old doll, and would not have made any more trouble; the fight had gone out of her but Rochester insisted on tying her arms with the straps I had never had to use.

Irrational, I know, but it's one of the things I find hardest to forgive him, and one of the reasons why I do not think I can ever be completely fair to his side of this story. I tell myself he had cause to be savage that day—his bride snatched away at the wedding hour, 'Thornfield's' secret torn open to the parish. But it was only ever a secret from the gentry, surely he knew that? And not all of them. Mr Woods, the clergyman, might cry out that he'd lived there twenty years and never heard of it, but servants and sharp-eyed children know everything that goes on in a great house.

You can't drag heavy buckets of coal, water, food and chamberpots up and down to the attics without servants talking. They did not know who the madwoman was, but you can be sure there had been plenty of guessing. About six months after I had arrived at 'Thornfield' I overheard Dawlish, the cook, and a young maidservant, Leah, talking about it. Leah had not been long in the house herself and was curious:

'That Grace Poole, or Mrs Adair, or whatever she calls herself, is no more nurse than I. She knows but one remedy—gin, or summat as strong, and as many doses a day as she can get.'

'Well, if it keeps t'other one quiet . . .' Dawlish said, kneading dough vigorously. 'There's noises in that attic come from no Christian soul. I'd not be shut up day and night with such a creetur—not fer all the hundert n' fifty guineas a year.'

'Hundert n' fifty! But that's ten times a wage!'

'And everything in food and keep with it.'

'But what can she do with all that?'

'Sits there countin' it in piles.' Dawlish was enjoying herself, warming to the sight in her imagination. 'Great heaps o' gold sov'rins,' she added. Then sharply, 'But it's nowt to me what she does with it, nor what she does to get it, neither. And you'd best make sure it's nowt to you, or you won't stop long in this house.'

I missed the rest: John the butler had come into the kitchen and he and Dawlish were both talking at once. They were husband and wife; had been at 'Thornfield' forty years. Like me, they knew almost everything about the madwoman except who she was. It was they who told me the story of old Grace Poole, a woman Rochester had hired to look after Bertha when he brought his wife back to 'Thornfield' ten years previously. Mrs Poole had been formerly a wardress at the Grimsby Retreat for the Insane, Dawlish said, a villainous old hag who fed Bertha gin and 'black drop', the strongest laudanum, for seven years. It kept the patient quiet most of the time, but there were terrible eruptions. The female servants whose bedrooms were near the attic often heard screams, which might have been Mrs Poole or Bertha or both. They had orders to keep away on pain of instant dismissal without a character. If the prisoner was cruelly used at times, what could they do?

No one was eager to interfere, therefore, when Dawlish noticed one winter's evening that Mrs Poole had not been in the kitchen all day. This was during one of Rochester's absences, and only he and Grace Poole had keys for the attic. John and Dawlish went up and listened outside the door. Nothing. Was Mrs Poole ill? Or had the madwoman murdered her? They agreed uneasily that she was probably sleeping off a prolonged bout of gin.

In the afternoon of the second day, John ordered Matthew, the groom, to fetch Dr Carter. When he arrived they broke in and found Grace Poole dead of an apoplexy behind the door. The madwoman was cowering in a back corner in a stench of her own excretions, apparently too terrified to come near the corpse.

Well, said Dawlish, if the poor creature had not been mad before, she would be now. Dawlish knew stories of people accidentally shut up with corpses, or even in a room where corpses had recently been, and none had come out with their full wits.

Rochester was still away when Grace Poole died and Dr Carter was desperate to find someone to care for Bertha. This was when I came to 'Thornfield' and discovered I was to be a madwoman's keeper, the second Mrs Poole. In the first days I regarded my charge with a mixture of disgust and wariness. Her hair was matted and filthy and she stank to a degree almost suffocating, but I was not afraid, being at that time too weary of my own life to care much whether I died or not. I did, however, take steps to make sure she should have no opportunity to attack me.

This was not difficult. The attic was divided into two parts; Bertha's cell was the cold, dark section at the back, divided by bars from my end of the room, which was large enough to contain a fireplace, a comfortable chair, a cot, and a small table under a skylight. I soon discovered a low door in the panelling behind my cot. It was fastened with rusted bolts, but I persisted until I could open it, and found a tiny outdoor space among the roof leads, where the steep angles of the gabled roof came down on three sides, and a high parapet closed off the fourth. When the sunshine from this doorway entered the attic, I heard the first nearly human sound from Bertha. A groan so filled with longing and anguish that tears came to my eyes, and I began to think of her as a woman rather than a wild beast, and wondered what misfortune had brought her to this.

My pity was greatly increased by finding a hideous garment in a chest in the corner, a thick white cotton jacket evidently made for pinioning the arms. The sight of it made Bertha scream and beat her head against the wall. She stopped when I threw it on the fire. I was about to add to the flames an old red dress also in the chest, but she gave a cry and put her arm through the bars. When I handed it to her she sank to the ground, pressing it against her face.

To show her I meant no harm, I began to tame her by means of food, as I had trained dogs and squirrels in my childhood. From the first I made sure that her meals each day were at regular times, and appetising. She was a greedy eater, which helped my cause, but it was like taming a lioness. I spoke to her frequently, though the only reply might be silence or growling. I spread a clean new dress on a chair outside her bars, and told her she might wear it if she would only wash herself. She hurled her tin jug and basin at the walls for days, but one day plunged her face into the water and tipped the rest over her head, which I took to be an attempt of sorts. I rewarded her with strawberries and cream and a hand mirror. She stared into this with apparent horror before she flung it, too, at the wall. Her next several meals were bread and water, and so it went. Any return to bad behaviour—this was frequent at first—was punished by bread and water (and greeted with howls and moans).

It was months before I could let her out into my part of the attic and properly clean her cell, and more than a year—the following summer—before we began to sit on the tiny square of roof-leads in the sun. This had to be given up when Rochester came home. Bertha escaped twice over the roof by crawling up the gable in an ape-like way, scarcely believable in so big a woman. She set fire to Rochester's room and later attacked a guest. It was her stepbrother, Richard Mason, although I did not know it at the time. I had no choice then but to return to a stricter regimen. After the failed wedding I discovered that Bertha and I were the same age: thirty-four that year. Our prospects for the future now seemed equally uncertain.

3

THE FRANKLINS' INAUGURAL VISIT TO THE PENINSULA BEGAN AT the coal mines, eight miles north-west of Port Arthur. The official party sailed down the estuary from Hobart at the end of March, and Booth rode up to meet them.

The outstation at the mines lies close to the shore, just behind a sandy beach, which runs out into the bay across two hundred yards of luminous shallows. Booth had designed a jetty seven hundred and sixty feet long and ten feet wide, to carry rails across the sands to where a sudden dark blue line indicates a fall into deep water. This tramway allowed convicts to push coal carts directly from the mines to transport ships anchored at the outer end, where the jetty was enlarged to form a wharf fifty feet wide. The *Eliza* anchored here, and Lady Franklin's first words on stepping ashore were an exclamation about the jetty.

'Beautiful,' she told Booth. In all her travels she had not seen anything quite like it, not even in Russia, where wood is used so exquisitely. She wanted to know if the timber was eucalyptus, or the remarkable native pine? The dense, slow-growing species, ideal for shipbuilding? Her interest was clearly unfeigned, but to Booth seemed odd for a woman, and yet he felt a similar pleasure in the jetty's lines. His greater astonishment came when she made it clear that she too would descend into the coal shaft. Sir John clearly enjoyed Booth's amazement.

'My wife is m-more than equal to it, Captain Booth,' he said.

Was he slow-witted, as rumour implied? What he said was cogent enough when you got to it, but his manner was ponderous, with an occasional stammer. Some big men are quick and agile; he was not. Lady Franklin smiled and said her boots were stout, her bonnet indestructible. But she would remove the bonnet if Captain Booth thought it advisable, if the coal galleries were low. Her clever face was eager. She stayed down the mine all the time of the inspection but later admitted she felt oppressed by the narrow passages and the surprising degree of heat underground. She made no complaint, however. Did not sigh, faint, or appear to think any special attention due to her, but was clearly relieved to reach the surface again.

The Colonial Secretary, Mr John Montagu, next in seniority to the Governor in the colony, had murmured, 'My dear lady!' when Lady Franklin spoke of going into the mine. Now, as they returned, he said to her, 'Did you find the Dark Pit illuminating, ma'am? Did the Nether Regions answer your expectations?'

Was it meant sarcastically? She gave him a long look before saying, 'Some experiences can only be got at first hand, do you not think? All their strange force expires in the retelling.'

It was difficult to imagine Montagu desiring any such experience, Booth thought, eyeing his immaculate black frock coat, tall black hat, urbane smile. Former Army, he had fought at Waterloo when he was seventeen and had been mentioned in despatches; yet that was hard to believe now. Paperwork—columns of figures, lists, private notes—rather than anything adventurous came to mind when you looked at him.

Montagu had come to the island in '23 as Governor Arthur's private secretary—through a family favour, people said. Montagu had recently married Arthur's niece, Jessie. 'Warming-Pan' Montagu, the newsapers called him. Not so much for his dislike of the cold, although that was well known, but because of his temporary stays in increasingly senior positions, keeping them warm for friends and relatives.

Un frisieux, said Lempriere. Cold-blooded? A cold fish? And was this merely descriptive, or was some moral judgement implied? At any rate, Montagu had made himself indispensable to Arthur in a number of barely legal dealings—or so the *Colonial Times* said. Arthur and Montagu had certainly planned the downfall of their friend Mr Burnett, the ill, inefficient, former Colonial Secretary, and as soon as he was ousted, Montagu had been given the position. He had expected to move up again when Arthur departed, some said: to be appointed Lieutenant Governor himself. If that was true, there was no disappointment on show now. He was paying court to the Franklins like any contented subordinate.

Mr Matthew Forster, Chief Police Magistrate, had also declined to go down the mine. In his case it was from complete lack of interest, Booth thought. Forster, another prominent 'Arthurite', was a 'sporting gentleman', which meant gambling—cards, horse racing, dog fighting, anything that offered itself. He had been a Brigade Major for years in Ireland, and retained a hearty, half-belligerent barracks manner, but looked now like a pugilist gone to seed. His black frock coat fitted too tightly across his wide shoulders and barrel chest; a great belly was pushed up above a low narrow waist—by a corset, surely—so that he resembled a pouter pigeon.

Even so, Forster was not unlikeable, to other men at least. Lizzie Eagle said he gave her the shudders. Certainly his head was overlarge, misshapen. His eyes bulged and his sight was poor, which explained the lorgnette always on a black silk ribbon around his neck. Forster was famously vain in spite of his disadvantages, or perhaps because of them. He wore a dandified cravat today, with a gold pin, and a double heavy gold watch chain. He was married to Jessie Montagu's sister, Helena, which made him brother-in-law to Montagu.

The party re-boarded the *Eliza* and sailed further up the bay into the inlet leading to Eaglehawk Neck. The waters on this inward, Hobarton side of the peninsula were sheltered, ending in a mile or so of beach with rocks at either end. They disembarked and Montagu and Forster walked over to the barracks, while the Franklins climbed the short, sandy path to the top of the dune that formed the spine of the Neck, to look out at the parallel beach on the eastern, ocean side. Here the sight was spectacular, a vast panorama of the open sea rolling in two thousand miles from New Zealand, crashing in great curling breakers onto a long crescent of pale sands.

The narrow neck on which they stood, Booth explained, formed the only land passage between Forestier Peninsula to the north and Tasman Peninsula to the south. This made the latter almost an island: a perfect natural prison, as Governor Arthur had recognised. Even so, in the first year or two after Port Arthur was established there had been escapes—until Ensign Peyton Jones of the 63rd Regiment conceived the idea of the dog-line. Booth pointed to the line of eleven lampposts spaced at intervals across the neck below them. Each post had a large, savage dog chained to it, with a barrel for a kennel. But the line had not worked at first.

'The first time I came up here there were nine dogs, and the corporal in charge regarded them rather as pets, I discovered. I walked straight between them to the hut, where he was asleep at the table with his head on his arms.'

Later that night, in the privacy of the officers' tent, the barracks having been given up to the visiting party, Booth came in for a ribbing over his evident bemusement at the Governor's wife. He shook his head, laughing at himself. Lady Franklin was so unlike her predecessor. Mrs Arthur had always been *enceinte* or too embroiled with children to venture far—even if she had wanted to, which she gave no indication of. Booth predicted he would not be the only one in Van Diemen's Land to be set aback by Lady Franklin. But you could not help liking her, admiring her. When you came across such quick understanding in a woman, such good humour . . . They mocked him all the more, of course.

Next day the weather changed. On the journey overland from Eaglehawk Neck down to Port Arthur it rained persistently. The visitors were caped, umbrella'd, and wrapped in shawls, cloaks, pelisses and surtouts. Pale faces peered out into the wet. The scarlet jackets and white cross-straps of the soldiers showed vividly against the shining grey-greens of the wet bush. Sir John rode Booth's horse (poor Jack!) and there were a variety of borrowed mounts for the other gentlemen. Convict bearers carried the makeshift sedan chairs for the ladies. Lowering skies pressed wreaths of mist down between the hills. Booth was disappointed. He had wanted the Franklins to have their first sight of the settlement cove with the sun on it, the whitewashed buildings looking sheltered and delightful as they so often did. Sir John dismounted and Lady Franklin too insisted on walking.

'Her Ladyship had us deployed in two minutes,' Booth mentally composed a letter to his sister Charlotte, dear Char: the family correspondent, who had seen Franklin's appointment to Van Diemen's Land in the *Gazette*, and demanded a full account of the Arctic Lion, The Man Who Ate His Boots, and his blue-stocking wife.

Booth must walk here beside her husband, said Lady Franklin, and Mr Montagu beside her, with Mr Forster on that side. Only afterwards did Booth understand that by this means she made certain he was talking to Sir John's 'good' ear during the first tour of the site. Sir John had been deaf on one side since the battle of Copenhagen, he told Booth later at dinner. The roar of the cannons beside him all day had damaged his hearing. Lady Franklin wanted him to let the doctors look at his ear, but he would not allow it.

'Only consider the great Duke's experience,' Franklin said, warming to his subject, no stammer now. Wellington had attended trials of the new howitzers during the War, and afterwards complained of a singing in the ears. England's greatest ear doctor poured a solution of lunar caustic—nitrate of silver, you know—into the Duke's ears, after which the Great Man was completely deaf on one side and suffered much with pain and headache.

'A barbaric treatment, to be sure,' said Casey that night. Booth was lodging with Casey; the Franklins were in the Commandant's cottage.

'But they had nothing else in those days. Perhaps the Governor's deafness accounts for the rumour of his slow wits?

'And no trouble yet from Montagu or Forster?' Casey added.

'No trouble,' said Booth, ignoring both the 'yet' and the one very small sign he had noticed. It had arisen on account of the continuing rain, which Lady Franklin hardly seemed to notice. At the boys' prison at Point Puer, stray drops evaded the brim of her bonnet and ran down her straight nose. She brushed them aside unheedingly, listening attentively to Sir John's questions and Booth's explanations. The boys were allowed to bathe in the sea in summer? Were taught trades as well as religion? She admired the boots made by the apprentice cobblers and the seating forms made by the carpenters. Where was the fresh water? Ah! A disadvantage, to have to haul it in. She tasted the soup and pronounced it 'palatable'.

Out in the rain again, Montagu walked beside her, trying to keep a large black umbrella over her head and his own, but in her bright eagerness Jane Franklin was always darting ahead of this protection. Just when he had the umbrella poised equally, she would move forward with an enquiry about sawpits, or to peer at some object of interest. Montagu's dilemma was amusingly clear. Must he stretch out his arm to make the umbrella cover her, thus baring his own beautiful tall black hat to the rain? Or put himself to an undignified trot to keep up with her? Montagu disliked rain as much as the cold, everyone knew. He believed himself more than commonly subject to the grippe. The little comedy appealed to Booth's strong sense of the ridiculous.

Montagu solved the problem by pausing abruptly as though recalling an urgent matter. He beckoned to Forster and they stood talking as Lady Franklin went on, her attention leaping ahead. Sir John's young aide moved in with his own umbrella, catching Booth's eye as he did so, and Booth saw that he too was amused. An indication that Montagu's loyalty would not stretch far? That his own wellbeing was paramount? Booth thought Lady Franklin had also noticed the little stratagem, although she gave no sign of it. The next day, as the rain continued, Montagu stayed indoors.

In a few words, Char, a more agreeable or pleasant visit could not have been, Booth continued the letter in his head. *Quite pleased at the satisfaction Her Ladyship, Sir John and all parties expressed with their trip.*

The single dissenting voice had been that of Mrs Evans, a sister-in-law of Sir John's, visiting the colony with her doctor husband. Several times she quietly lamented the hard lives of the convicts, clearly afraid to offend, but determined to show she was 'Anti-Transportation'. The prisoners were well fed and housed, she conceded, but nothing could make up for exile from England. Her protest became more visceral a fortnight after the Port Arthur visit, when the party reached Flinders Island. The Franklins had asked Booth to continue with them on this leg of the tour to see Wybalenna, where the remnants of the aboriginal tribes in Van Diemen's Land had been rounded up and transported to live, or conveniently die. When they came to the black people in the infirmary here, words failed Mrs Evans; she cried out in distress and hurried off to be sick.

Mind you, Booth had been shocked himself. None of the party was prepared for what they saw. Emaciated bodies lying in rooms filled with the stench of illness and death. The black people coughing, groaning, vomiting, or agonisingly silent, all effort on the next breath. Open sores unspeakable, cheap English clothes like a ghastly joke. Booth knew the stories of the last thirty years; barbarous cruelty on both sides, and far worse from whites than blacks, if you had to be truthful. The blacks had been hunted, driven over cliffs, shot, poisoned, burned, hacked . . . and the misery of it was horribly evident here, in the hopeless faces, the bright, haunted eyes.

As the party approached one dwelling, they saw an old woman sitting on the ground outside, staring out to sea, keening low and mournfully. A dirty petticoat hung round her shoulders. Her fingers fretted the neck of her ill-fitting dress. She stopped abruptly when Mr George Robinson, the Superintendent, approached her. He whisked away the petticoat, thrusting it at his assistant (his son) to be got out of sight.

Was Robinson a trumped-up, illiterate Cockney bricklayer—or a courageous half-saint? Booth had heard both. In Hobart he was known as 'the Conciliator' and praised for his efforts, but these people were dying with terrible speed under his regime.

Wybalenna meant 'black man's house', or so Robinson said. He knew some of the tribal languages, and with a show of ease translated the old woman's tremulous song.

'Over the water is her land, she smells it on the wind. The spirit of it calls to her night and day. She, the child of it, calls back in answer. She knew every bush and tree, every nest and burrow, the shape of each stone. If she cannot be buried there she does not know how she will find her ancestors when she dies. I tell her, Your Excellency, Your Ladyship, that Our Lord Jesus has strong powers. He will lead her to the ancestors.'

The Governor nodded sagely. His wife murmured something inaudible.

Mrs Evans only rejoined them when they started back to the ship. She seemed loath, now, to say anything about her recent experiences, preferring to tell Booth she believed she was acquainted with his sister. They had met while she was staying with relations in Mitcham. An unexpected connection—but then, not really unexpected, he thought. He had come to understand there are always more connections than we know about, across the widest spaces. So many links between the colony and England, most of them fluid. Water, ink, blood, each carrying its own cargo. Frail ships criss-crossing the seas, their holds packed with innocent-looking objects as dangerous as guns: china tea sets; bolts of flannel; packets of seeds and bank drafts. All bearing the message that there are certain ways in which life must be lived, and ways in which it most assuredly must not.

The message was scored all the deeper by ink on millions of pages carrying the stories we live by: the Bible, Shakespeare, Homer, the latest Romance or Newgate novel. Blood and more intimate fluids made their own connections, rarely spoken of in polite circles. Mrs

Evans, Char, himself; the Arthurites and the Franklins; all entwined in invisible currents across the surface of the globe.

What he could not write to Char, because it would sound like boasting of a too-readily assumed familiarity with the new Governor's wife, was that he had found Lady Franklin perilously easy to talk to. Wherever they stopped on the east coast she had spoken to settlers, had asked how they came there, sought their opinions of the colony, their views on the keeping of bees, fowl, sheep.

On one occasion, as they walked back to the ship afterwards, she and Booth were somewhat ahead of the rest of the party, and she said suddenly, 'You think I go too far in the questions I ask? Your face seemed to say it, Captain . . .' She smiled. 'It is my dear father's fault.'

She and her father were the best of companions, she said. Perhaps because her mother had died when she was six. Her father—he was a silk merchant—took her travelling with him from when she was very young. Her elder sister, Fanny, preferred to stay in London; Mary was a babe-in-arms. Her father had encouraged Jane's endless reading, writing and learning because he had no son. Her brother had died, full of promise, at fourteen. Her Uncle Guillemard, her mother's brother, had seen her eagerness for travel and study and had seemed to encourage it, but sometimes now, in retrospect, she could not help seeing in his methods a desire to show her she was not so clever as she thought.

In algebra, for instance, he would sometimes give her theorems far beyond her capacity, and was not displeased to see her cry with frustration at her own stupidity. One of his fond names for her was 'Poll-parrot'. Fond, but carrying the criticism that she repeated things she did not understand. She knew she irritated him, which made her awkward in his company. He had not meant to be unkind. She had much to thank him for and was grateful. It was just that he saw her father too proud of her, unwilling to curb, and wanted to warn her that women could not be like men, they were unfitted for it mentally and bodily.

Jane began to speak then of how one's actions could be misunderstood, and Booth found himself telling her how he had shot the albatross two days out of Tristan da Cunha because he wanted to test Coleridge's story of the Ancient Mariner. He would not be satisfied with superstition, even from a great poet whose works he loved and venerated. He wanted to know the truth of the world.

If she had not stopped dead in surprise at what he was saying, he would have gone on to tell her how much he had been affected by what he had done. He had learned that day how much an experiment may affect the experimenter. But her pause had given the main party a chance to catch up with them, and Sir John took her arm and asked her what they had been talking about so intently. 'Ancient Mariners,' she said, smiling fondly at him.

—⁂—

And after all this, on the last day and almost at the last minute, just as the official party was boarding the cutter to go back to Hobart, Montagu had handed Booth the letter. There had been a hundred opportunities to speak of it earlier, but this was planned, of course. Montagu had looked directly at him and said with a faint smile, 'A confidential matter, Booth.'

Booth handed it to his clerk with an order to take it up to his cottage, and had no time to think of it again until he returned there in the late afternoon. Two pages, one of them a letter, the other a covering note from Montagu. He read Montagu's first.

> . . . treat the enclosed as strictly confidential. You should not reply directly, but oblige by calling at the Colonial Office to discuss the matter when you are next visiting Hobarton in the course of your duties. You need not make occasion for a special journey up to town. Private enquiries must not be allowed to interrupt the business of His Majesty's Government.

Emphatic. And then the letter itself, from a firm of solicitors in England: Gray, Walsh and Tilney. Addressed to Mr John Montagu,

46

Colonial Secretary in Hobart Town, and dated seven months ago. Which probably meant that Montagu had kept it at least a month before handing it over.

> We present our compliments and take leave to beg the Colonial Secretary's assistance in furthering our enquiries concerning a Mr Rowland George Fairfax Rochester, Esquire. Would Mr Montagu kindly oblige by determining whether any official records are held by His Majesty's Government in the colony under Mr Rochester's name? To wit; grants of land issued, application for rescinding of quit rents, records of arrival, departure, marriage, or death?
>
> Mr Rochester's family was given to understand that he had been killed in 1823 in the Slave Rebellion in Demerara, however more recent advice suggests he may have recovered from his injuries and emigrated to Van Diemen's Land. We are further advised that Captain Charles O'Hara Booth, now stationed in Van Diemen's Land with the 21st Regiment, had dealings with Mr Rowland Rochester fourteen years ago in the West Indies when Booth was a Lieutenant there. Would the Colonial Secretary be so kind as to ascertain whether Captain Booth has any knowledge of Mr Rowland Rochester's subsequent or present whereabouts?

Booth sat for a few moments and then read the letter again, although the meaning was plain. He had been expecting something like this for a decade—not about Rowland Rochester, his conscience was clear there—but about Caralin and the children. If questions were asked about Rowland Rochester, then knowledge of Caralin was bound to come out—which would probably end any idea of marrying Lizzie. But why did Montagu ask him not to reply directly? Could the Colonial Secretary have some personal interest in the matter? In these small colonies the webs of kinship, loyalty and enmity could be as intricate and invisible as those in a country village. It had been the same in India.

Booth began a reply to Montagu and half an hour later had thrown two attempts in the fire. There was not even the distraction of mending his pen. Three days ago he had given up his quill and begun to use the new Government-issue steel nibs. The faint scratching of pen across paper made the dog Fran, asleep in front of the fire, open her eyes in hope of mice or rats. But she was growing accustomed to the noise and soon let them fall closed again. She was a brindle terrier, square and sturdy, Booth's favourite among his half a dozen gun-dogs. Better behaved than half the Regiment.

In the end he wrote four lines saying he was due in Hobarton in three weeks' time for the Hammond trial, and if the matter could wait until then, he would on that date give himself the pleasure of waiting on the Colonial Secretary. *Nil desperandum*, as Char would say. Perhaps it could all be mended. Except for Caralin and the children. Nothing could mend that.

4

THE DAY AFTER THE FAILED WEDDING AT 'THORNFIELD', I LEARNED from Dr Carter that my patient, Bertha, was in fact the sugar heiress Mrs Fairfax had spoken of, Miss Anna Cosway-Mason. She had married Edward Rochester in Spanish Town fourteen years before. Dr Carter's grey, tufted eyebrows twitched as he told me. He was one of those portly, elderly babies with a soft halo of white hair through which his pink scalp glowed.

'You did not know it?' I asked. I thought he might have been in the secret. He shook his head.

'I had formed the idea,' he said, 'as perhaps I was intended to do, that she was the unfortunate mistress of old Mr Rochester. Edward brought her here when his father was dying. I was called in to examine her and instructed that her presence was to be kept a perfect secret.'

'And Mrs Fairfax?'

'Much the same, I think. She knew you were the nurse, of course, but did not allow herself to know more. Did she never speak to you about your patient?'

'Never.'

Dr Carter had spent an hour attending to Rochester's head wound after the melee in the attic. He learned, then, that Edward Rochester's marriage had taken place in 1824 when Anna was said to be eighteen.

But the Mason family had lied about her age, Rochester claimed, and about her mental soundness. She had gone stark mad within a year of the marriage. Carter shook his head, whether in sympathy for Bertha or Rochester, or in perplexity at the whole condition of wedlock, I did not ask. As he spoke he examined Bertha. After the struggle she had seemed half-stupefied, had fallen into a heavy sleep and stayed so ever since. I was troubled because her condition did not seem natural to me, but Carter said he would reserve judgement until the following afternoon, when he would call to see her again.

Next day there came another blow to Rochester. Jane Eyre had left the house during the night, telling no one. He scoured the house and grounds, then rode off immediately in search of her—but could find no trace. I was more concerned with Bertha, who still did not wake. On the contrary, she seemed more deeply insensible than ever. Dr Carter's verdict was tentative and puzzled.

'I have seen nothing quite like it,' he said. 'There is no brain fever, but she is certainly in a most profound, unwakeable sleep.'

He bled her, taking a pint from each arm, but it brought no change. He said she must not lie always flat, for the damage it might do to her lungs and the sores that might form on her skin. He instructed me to roll her from one side onto the other, twice a day. Bertha could survive a long period without food, in his opinion, but water she must have, fortified with brandy and a cordial of his own devising. Matthew, the groom, would come morning and evening to help me. Dr Carter tied his bag and brushed the side of his tall hat with his coat sleeve as he spoke.

'Pray for her, Harriet. She is beyond my skill.' He rammed his hat on and departed.

After three weeks there was still no sign of Jane Eyre. Rochester continued to ride off each day and come back each evening with a face like a stone wall. At the end of the second week he shut himself in the library and took to sleeping on the sofa day and night. He rang the bell for a grilled chop at odd hours but ate little, Dawlish said. It was by then late August, sultry and hot. Mrs Fairfax seemed shocked and aged and kept her room. Dawlish cooked a meal once a day for the household, but fruit was coming off the laden trees, brought to the kitchen in the gardener's baskets, and I ate the late plums and early apples as I passed through. The kitchen was fragrant with the smell of boiling jam. The summer went on with no news of Jane Eyre—and Bertha slept. As she lay there on her back, her long black hair in two plaits down across her breast, she looked like some ancient queen lying in state. Like a sleeping princess in the old stories.

Rochester came up to see her. He stood for several minutes in silence and then said abruptly, 'Mrs Poole, Dr Carter tells me you are a woman of some education.' He corrected himself with a wry twist of the lips, 'Mrs Adair, I should say. Since there is little you can do at present for your patient, you would oblige me by giving lessons to Adèle for an hour or two each morning until I can arrange a school.'

Adèle came mournfully to show me a list of clothes to be taken to the Misses Bartons' Academy. Two plain black frocks, one plain black silk dress, four plain white pinafores, one plain merino . . . She was only just out of mourning for her mother and now the beloved colours must be laid aside or go into the dye bath and come out black again.

Dr Carter, who came regularly to see Bertha, one day stood panting in the doorway. 'Too much for me nowadays, three flights of stairs,' he said. 'And the weather so warm. I've asked Rochester to move you both to the ground floor. There's no need for secrecy now the whole shire knows the story.'

Adèle, staring at Bertha, asked him, 'When will she wake, *monsieur?*'

'I don't know, child,' he said. 'Perhaps tomorrow. Or it may take a hundred years as it does in fairy stories!'

Then Adèle wanted to hear the old stories about sleepers. She and I spent the long afternoons of that glorious St Martin's summer in the garden, walking, sitting on the swing, playing with a ball or hoop. I grew fond of Adèle. She corrected my French politely and chattered about her life in Paris with her mother and the other 'ladies'. She did not want to go to school. With a world-weary sigh she said, 'They will want me to be like an English girl, *et ça serait impossible, je crois.*'

The servants had instructions from Rochester that if Jane Eyre returned while he was out they were to keep her in the house at all costs. He told Mrs Fairfax it would be best to take Jane up to her old bedroom and lock her in until he returned. Mrs Fairfax was shocked. She fidgeted with her housekeeping keys until Rochester said, 'Leave them alone, madam, for God's sake.'

'It is all so wicked and wrong,' she stammered. 'I don't know what to do for the best. Miss Eyre—and that poor mad creature. I don't know what to say . . .'

Two weeks later she departed for Brighton to live with a distant cousin. Rochester had settled an allowance on her. He was always generous with money. An envelope also came to me that week. It contained a ten pound note and Rochester's scrawl on thick cream paper: 'Item: lessons for Adèle in addition to nursing duties.' It was far too much, and my first thought was to return it, but in the end I kept it. Bertha might die any day and my future must then be in doubt again.

—∞—

What came next was the fire, no doubt fed by the oak-panelled rooms full of furniture polished with years of beeswax, and the paintings along the gallery, dark portraits of former Rochesters which would burn fiercely. Afterwards it was blamed on Bertha, for no other reason except that she was there and mad, but it almost certainly began in the cluster of chimneys damaged by that lightning strike months before, on midsummer's eve. It had been a hot, dry summer, most of the fireplaces had been unused for months, but now it was late September and they were lit again. One must have caught on fire, sending sparks into the drifts of dry pine needles lodged in the roof.

Earlier that afternoon, we had moved Bertha down to Mrs Fairfax's rooms on the ground floor where she and I were now to live, so that when the cry of 'Fire!' arose, she was easily carried out onto the furthest part of the sunken lawn below the terrace. By that time a crowd of servants and tenant cottagers were milling there. Tongues

of red and orange flame licked into the sky. We called out names
through the smoke and din. Dawlish counted us over and over and
waited for her husband, who had gone back in to find Rochester.
In the end John came stumbling out, his head wrapped in soaked,
blackened cloths. Rochester was not with him.

At that moment a section of roof fell away and we saw two figures
up high, a man and a woman. The woman fell, her skirts lifting and
billowing before she disappeared into the hottest part of the fire.
The man hesitated. We saw now, with terrible certainty, that it was
Rochester. He retreated along a parapet, stumbled, slid down onto
a lower gable, and fell again into a patch of darkness. He was alive
when they picked him up. The water engines arrived from Millcot
and Hay but little could be done before morning. The dead woman
proved to be Leah, the housemaid, who must have been upstairs and
fled to the attic when the fire broke out.

—⚒—

A kind of silence came down on us after the fire: a dullness of
exhaustion and mourning. We were lodged at the George Inn at
Hay, where Rochester gradually began to recover. His injuries were
not so dreadful as had been feared, being chiefly damage to one eye,
one arm and a hand. He decided that 'Ferndean', a neglected house I
had always admired on a far corner of the estate, would become his
home as soon, as it could be made liveable. Bertha slept on.

I went walking each day to get out of the closeness of the inn, often
drawn in the direction of 'Thornfield'. The sight of the remains held
an eerie fascination even in daylight. Broken chimneystacks, blackened
ruins, and a rubble-strewn, unrecognisable space. Loose ends of
cloth and paper rippled in the wind, caught among the devastation
of brick and stone. On a blowy autumn day, rags of white cloud tearing
across a blue sky, I stood gazing at the scene until a movement on the
far side of the grounds caught my eye. A small woman in black. She
had been as still as I, staring at the ruin, but now she turned away
and set off walking. I could not see the face inside the bonnet, but

the figure was unmistakable: Jane Eyre. I set off in pursuit, unable to walk directly across the rubble, making my way round the perimeter and losing sight of her where ruined walls interrupted my view. By the time I reached the other side she had vanished.

That evening as I sat reading in the room I shared with Bertha at the George, there was a knock and it was her: Jane. We hesitated, embraced. I said I was pleased and relieved to see her well. She came smiling into the room, but the smile faded when she saw Bertha in the bed. She gazed for a minute and then asked me if I would go with her to Mr Rochester's room. There were matters they wished to discuss with me.

The George is one of those rabbit-warren inns, centuries old. The curved oak beams were once part of Tudor ships; now they supported crooked corridors, low doorways, unexpected steps. Not a straight wall in the place. Rochester's room was the largest, but even here there was only space for a curtained bed with a chest at the end, a night table, a chair each side of the fire, and a low stool. Rochester was seated in one of the chairs with a dark crimson counterpane tucked around him. His right forearm was bandaged and he had a patch over one eye. He looked like a domesticated pirate, slightly ridiculous, sadly tamed. Dawlish was nodding in the opposite chair, but at our coming she pulled herself awake, bobbed a curtsey and went out. Jane motioned me to the empty chair, and placed herself on the stool close to Rochester. He took her hand in his good one and they sat for a moment beaming at each other as though they'd lost a farthing and found a shilling, as my father used to say. In the conversation that followed it was clear they were a mutual pair, a joint self. There would be no more talk of her leaving, marriage or not.

'Mrs . . . Adair,' said Rochester. 'You see that Miss Eyre has appeared again, like the little witch she is. We have been making plans, deciding on a course of action in which we hope you will join us.'

I responded with a polite murmur but I was thinking about Jane, the subtle difference in her. She was as straight and determined as ever, but now with an easier, less defensive confidence.

'We intend to make a sea voyage,' Rochester was saying, 'taking my . . . Bertha Mason with us. We hope you will accompany us as the invalid's nurse and Miss Eyre's companion.'

The West Indies, I thought with a lifting heart, Spanish Town. It would be like Italy and the South of France: olive trees, white houses, sunshine and grateful warmth. Bertha would be placed in some kindly mission convent, we would make a leisurely tour back to England through the Mediterranean . . .

'I would be glad to,' I replied. 'I would be curious to see the West Indies.'

They looked at each other, smiling.

'We do not go to the West Indies. Van Diemen's Land is our destination.'

My astonishment amused them. Rochester explained that he had never been wholly satisfied with his father's account of Rowland's death and had set his lawyers to look into the matter. After much correspondence, they had discovered that when Rowland arrived in Spanish Town, he had fallen in love with Bertha and written to his father announcing his intention to give up his engagement to Lady Mary Faringdon and marry the heiress himself. It was this letter that made old Mr Rochester set off for the Indies so hurriedly. When he arrived, there had been a great quarrel and a scuffle between the two men, after which Bertha had been sent to a convent and Rowland had gone to Demerara. But it now seemed Rowland might have married Bertha before his father arrived.

'Can you imagine my feelings when I heard this?' said Rochester. 'If it was true, then my own tie to Bertha was bigamous and invalid! My years of suffering were at an end. I was free! I wanted to believe but dared not hope. Everything hinged on whether my brother had married Bertha, and whether he was still alive when my marriage to her took place, or whether he had died in Demerara beforehand. When I came to know Jane, I told her I was enquiring into the death of my brother, but I could not explain why it was of such vital importance to me!'

Through Army records, his solicitors had discovered references to a Lieutenant Charles O'Hara Booth of the 21st Regiment, who had found Rowland mortally ill at Demerara. They hoped Booth might know more of the matter—might even know whether Rowland was alive now, and where he could be found. But the 21st was now in Van Diemen's Land. Letters had been despatched months ago but no reply had come.

'When Miss Eyre disappeared,' Rochester glanced sideways to where she sat smiling at him, 'I became sunk again in Stygian gloom.'

Jane took up the story. When she ran away from 'Thornfield', she had intended to visit her uncle in Madeira, as he had been urging in his letters. She had therefore gone to her uncle's lawyer in London, only to discover that her uncle had died, leaving the largest part of his estate to her, and the residue to her cousins in England, whom she now heard of for the first time. She decided to visit them in the north, but could not forbear calling at Millcot on her way, to hear news of Rochester. In this way she had come to know of the fire.

Now Jane and Rochester had devised a new plan. 'Thornfield' was in ashes; there was no home for him until 'Ferndean' was refurbished, which would take many months. They would therefore travel to Van Diemen's Land and enquire personally about Rowland. This would be far better than the exchange of letters over months, years. There was nothing to prevent such a journey, everything to recommend it.

At first I thought they were mad, but gradually I understood. In England they could not live in the same house until they learned the truth about the marriage. After the *débâcle* of their wedding, convention would frown on it. But on a ship, or in a distant country, who could object? They would not be the first people to take refuge in the colonies from an awkward situation at home. I was wondering why they did not leave Bertha Mason in England, but Rochester answered my thought.

'I will not have it said that I abandoned my wife to die of neglect,' he scowled. 'For I must consider her to be my wife until the alternative is proved . . . And if she were to die while we were away, even of natural causes, there would be gossip. I will not have any vicious slur cast a shadow across my future with Miss Eyre.'

A transfigured smile from Jane.

'When we discover the truth and can marry at last,' Rochester continued (a leap of faith, I noted), 'it will be in all bright honesty with no doubtful stain. Dr Carter assures me the sea voyage will do the invalid no harm. It may even be beneficial.'

They glowed by the fire like a pair of children planning a great adventure, brimming with mutual tenderness and passionate hope. A quest for the truth: that was how they saw it. Jane would be Rochester's nurse, companion, faithful servant and protector. Sancho Panza to his Don Quixote, Sam Weller to his Pickwick, pageboy to Good King Wenceslas, gender notwithstanding. They would be together, that was the chief thing.

He was maimed, punished, repentant. She was rewarded for her suffering, burning with energy and joy. She would discover new worlds and give them to him. In the end there might be a husband for Bertha and a long-lost brother for Rochester, but if not, they could be together on land and sea for a year or two—and much might happen in that time. They had found each other again and England was too small to hold their need for each other. How could they keep still? The continent was tainted by Rochester's life there with former mistresses, the West Indies a place of bitter memories. Where better to go than towards the unknown regions?

Some sober reflection must have followed, because a few days later Rochester decided a nurse-companion was not sufficient to safeguard Jane's reputation on their travels, he must engage a lady's maid as well. Jane laughed and said she never had any difficulty in doing up her own buttons. If he must add another member to the party, a doctor would be of more use. For Bertha, she said; but I believe she was thinking of Rochester's own health.

The doctor they found, James Seymour, had served twice as Surgeon Superintendent on convict transports to New South Wales. Seymour was in England now, going back to stay permanently.

Shipping agents found Rochester a private cargo vessel, the *Adastra*, embarking at Deptford for New South Wales in a month. He was not of a temperament to linger once he had decided on action.

Just as this was settled, St John Wallace came to stay at the George. He was one of the three cousins Jane had discovered through her uncle. They were the children of her mother's stepsister, and all considerably older than Jane. St John was a clergyman recently home from missionary work in India. Both his sisters, Diana and Mary, were married and living in the north. When Jane wrote to tell them of her planned travel to the colony, St John replied saying he would come to Hay at once. Jane feared he would try to dissuade her, but it proved quite otherwise. He wanted to join them. The meeting took place in the private parlour at the George, a room taken over for Rochester's use now he was recovering. In my new role as Jane's *duenna*, I sat at one side.

The first astonishment was St John Wallace's appearance. He was so remarkably beautiful in face and figure that he might have been one of Nina's actor friends made up as a hero, if perhaps a somewhat effeminate one. Jane said afterwards that he had the face of a marble angel on a tomb, but to me there was something too sensuous for an angel in the curve of the lips, the arch of the brows, the impression that Mr Wallace knew exactly the effect he had on others. My grandmother's servant, old Sukie, would have called him 'neither flesh nor fowl nor good red herring', and I was surprised when he said his wife regretted she had been unable to accompany him.

He regarded Jane's letter as a Divine Direction. After three years in Delhi he had finished his report on missionary education in India and had been praying to be guided to his next service. Here it was. This journey to the colonies would allow him to make a similar study of the education afforded to convicts in Van Diemen's Land. He had written to the Church Missionary Society, the Women's League, Mrs Elizabeth Fry, the Anti-Transportation League, and the Wilberforce Committee. His salary would be paid by the Society for the Dissemination of the Bible in Foreign Parts.

'Oh Lord,' I heard Rochester mutter to Jane. 'Now I am truly punished for my sins.' She flashed him a warning smile but he only grumbled louder, 'Are we to take with us every Tom, Dick and St John?'

Jane's cousin heard it and looked startled. When he decided to laugh I began to like him. He turned his perfect profile downwards to a satchel and brought out a thick tract which he handed to Rochester: *An Account of English Efforts in the Progress of Christian Education at Kolcuttah and etc.* Among his friends at university, he said, were Mr William Broughton, now Bishop of Sydney, and Broughton's close friend Mr William Hutchins, who had sailed with Sir John Franklin a year ago to be Archdeacon of Van Diemen's Land.

Rochester groaned loudly and said, 'But your wife, sir? So recently home from India, and looking forward, no doubt, to a lengthy period in England? Will she like another voyage so soon? And one fraught with peril of every description? I am told ladies' hair does not grow well in the colony.'

St John smiled. 'My wife will not object,' he said. 'And while I understand that my cousin Jane already has an able companion (the smile was turned in my direction), I believe Mrs Adair will also be occupied with nursing duties? Who better than my wife, then, to be a second companion and chaperone?'

'A bulldog of a woman, no doubt,' Rochester remarked in another audible aside to Jane, as St John Wallace bent over his satchel again. Louder still, Rochester said, 'On your own head be it then, sir,' and rose and limped ostentatiously from the room, feigning a greater degree of disability than he really had, and adding grimly that Mr Wallace must of course stay at the George Inn at their expense as long as he wished. Cousin Jane must get to know Cousin St John (this was said with a mad wicked laugh in Jane's direction). But for himself, if Mr Wallace would excuse him, he had pressing business . . . elsewhere.

By late November our party was aboard the *Adastra* making our way down the Thames towards the Channel. England, with all its greatness and littleness, was falling behind in our widening wake. Ahead were strange islands.

5

MONTAGU ANSWERED BOOTH'S NOTE, ACCEPTING THE SUGGESTION that the Rochester matter could wait until Booth came up to Hobarton for the Hammond trial. But a week before that date, Hammond hanged himself in his cell and the trial was cancelled. A note from Montagu rearranged their meeting for the twenty-first of June. Booth would have liked it to be sooner. He was thinking about it too often. But on the sixteenth of June came a further postponement. This time no reason was given and no future date set. Did Montagu really think it of so little importance? Or was he, Booth, being left to stew in his own juice? Well, the answer was to try to forget it. There was plenty else to occupy him here.

Shelter had always been the most urgent task at Port Arthur. Timber had by necessity been used green, there being no time to let it season. As a consequence, all the wood in the buildings of the settlement was still half alive. It groaned and cracked like pistol shots in the night when the air cooled; it bent and sprang with every change of weather. On the second of July it began to rain and kept on for three days. Leaks announced themselves by 'plick, plick' in nearly every building. Swollen doors and windows stuck fast; the roof of the blacksmith's forge sagged again; the cabbage crop was a-swim in the field. Seven hundred prisoners were confined, cold, bored.

Booth plashed about directing repairs, mud sucking at his boots, his feet numb, water streaming from his tarpaulins, but not unhappy. The urgent practical work took his mind off other worries.

In Lempriere's crowded cottage, Charlotte and the children placed buckets, pans and chamberpots under the drips. They stared up at stains blooming on the ceiling. Like a dog! No, an elephant! Very like a whale. Lempriere brought out the Shakespeare and read *Hamlet* aloud. Mary, nearly seven, suddenly enacted her own mad scene: a fit of violent temper. In the hospital up the hill, Casey supervised the removal of supplies out of the path of a clay-coloured stream twisting across the storeroom floor.

On the morning of the seventh the rain stopped, the sky turned blue and the semaphore picked up a signal. *Captain Booth is required immediately at Hobarton.* Booth was irritated to find his mind turn immediately to the Rochester letter. Half an hour later came a second message: *Lieutenant Wharton Young drowned Little Swanport.*

Booth's throat and chest muscles seemed to constrict, bile rose into his mouth. He reached his cottage and shut himself in his room. Wharton. No, a mistake, surely. Wharton was such a strong swimmer. His father had been Governor of Trinidad in the 1820s and he'd swum every day. 'Beauty' Wharton, the serious one of their foursome, the youngest. Always Peddie, Picton Beate, Booth and Wharton Young. His elder brother Henry was also here in Van Diemen's Land with the 52nd Regiment. Less than a year ago, Wharton had married Amy Fenn Kemp, a daughter of Mr Anthony Fenn Kemp, the prominent settler. It was Wharton's horse Booth had ridden in the 'Gentlemen's Invitation' on that mad day at Kilkenny races. *A watery grave, a watery grave*; he could not stop his mind from repeating it.

When he emerged they told him a third signal had come: *Lieuts Stuart and MacKnight also required Hobarton.* The *Vansittart* was coming down to the coal mines to collect them. The oddity of this distracted him. All three chief officers on the peninsula called up to town together? Unprecedented. On account of a regimental funeral for Wharton? Possibly, but strange, even so. Some shuffling of duties became necessary. Lempriere would take charge here at the main station. Casey must do the four-hour walk north with Booth to the coal mines to relieve Stuart. MacKnight must walk in from Eaglehawk Neck to the coal mines to meet them.

Booth set off with Casey just as the short winter day folded into red-gold dusk. The rain had stopped, the cold stung their faces and made their eyes water. Booth wore forage gear with his shako, which was easier to wear than carry, and it kept his head warm. The haversack on his back held his regimentals and the Rochester letter. He decided he would see Montagu, by hook or by crook. Wet black forest closed around them and he breathed in deeply its smell of fresh leaf mould. Tall pale trunks of the eucalypts gleamed like church pillars in the light from their lanterns.

Silence fell between them the first hour. Not hostile; preoccupied with the dark track, the rhythm of tramping. After a time they began talking about the dead man and his brother, about Amy Kemp and her father, the Kilkenny Races . . . They reached the coal mines at nine and found MacKnight already there. They had stew and potatoes and turned in at midnight, and at four in the morning they were up again, waiting for the sloop coming down Storm Bay from Hobarton. Soon after midday they were in Hobart in cold sunshine, walking up the hill into the Barracks. As they crossed the parade ground, Dr Pilkington came out of the infirmary. He was staff surgeon of the 21st Regiment and Lizzie's stepfather.

'Booth, my dear. What a terrible, sad shame it is,' said the doctor. His tumbling black Irish curls were streaked with grey. 'I pity his father and his brother. Poor Wharton! And poor little Amy Kemp. A wife not hardly a minute and a widow now! And Private Tribute drowned too. Did you know that? Wharton's body comes down the coast today. Post-mortem tomorrow.'

Booth grimaced and felt sorrow overcoming him again, the weakness of tears. He looked back down the estuary, towards the way he had come. Blue hills and sea, pale beaches. 'Do you know what happened?'

'Sure and they say the boat swamped in the waves as it came near the strand.'

They stood a moment in silence before the doctor asked, 'Is it this has brought you to town, Charles? This terrible thing?'

'I suppose so. A summons, no explanation. The funeral perhaps . . . but it's odd that Stuart and MacKnight should be called as well. Unless there's something else? Have you heard anything?'

The doctor raised his eyebrows and beckoned Booth aside to a place where a short section of waist-high stone wall offered the opportunity to lean and look down at Government House and the cove.

'And that I have. It's as much of a secret as anything ever is in this place—which means only a dozen people know it. The Twenty-first is recalled. They'll give us a twelvemonth to pack up and settle our traps, I suppose.'

Booth said nothing. His mind had been so filled with Wharton's death that he'd forgotten this possibility. Now it felt like a blow to the gut, like hearing of another death.

'Five years,' Pilkington was saying. 'It was in my mind they would keep us longer here.'

'Where do we go this time?' Booth kept his voice deliberately even. Not, surely, back to the West Indies, not now. What a joke of the Almighty (or the devil) that would be.

'India is the word.' Pilkington shrugged.

'It may be no more than a rumour?'

'There's a Mess Meeting tomorrow night. I daresay that's why you're called. We'll know then for sure and certain. In the meantime, my dear fellow—will you tell me when we are to see you at home before you go back down to your felons? Lizzie and her mother will never let me hear the last of it if I've not brought you to dine. Name your day, my dear.'

—⁂—

In the high-ceilinged anteroom of the Colonial Office several groups of people waited: a shabby couple as silent and wide-eyed as their solemn child; two men in stained working clothes; a very neat young man sitting with a tall hat on his knees and a pair of yellow gloves thrown across it. Entry to the panelled doors of the inner sanctum was managed by a clerk at a desk in the corner: Willoughby, a rising young favourite. Booth greeted him and spoke. Willoughby disappeared and returned in a few minutes, holding up a sealed note like a conjuror showing a card. Mr Montagu regretted that he would have no opportunity of seeing Booth in the office today, but he and Mrs Montagu would be pleased if the Commandant could join them for dinner at 'Stowell' that evening.

—∾—

Hobartians joked that 'Stowell's' position revealed Montagu's ambitions. The Colonial Secretary had not built near the water as most officers did if they could afford to: his house was on the hill looking down on Government House. 'Stowell' had cost four thousand pounds, everybody knew; the money lent to Montagu by Arthur. Rumour added that some of the building materials had also been 'borrowed' from public works, but a threat of court action had silenced the newspapers on that matter. No one would be willing to give evidence against Montagu.

Booth had expected the evening to be gentlemen only, as it frequently was, but he found both Montagus and both Forsters in 'Stowell's' drawing room.

'Shocking,' said Mrs Forster. 'Such shocking news, Captain Booth? About Lieutenant Young?' She had a habit of framing her remarks as questions, as though seeking approval or expecting disagreement.

They spoke of the dangerous coasts of the island, the treacherous rocks, the violent power of the sea.

'We might have lost every man in the boat,' said Montagu comfortably as they settled on the elegant chairs, 'had it not been for the efforts of a convict by the name of Barnham—Lewis Barnham, a black man recently transported. He was among the group waiting on the beach, the only one who could swim. He took a rope out through the breakers, tied it to the painter and dragged the longboat ashore.'

'Poor Henry Young, to lose his brother?' said Mrs Forster. 'They made jokes of course, the younger Young and so forth? So terribly sad.'

Perhaps because they were sisters, Helena Forster and Jessie Montagu were inclined to address their remarks to each other, even in company, including others only obliquely, so that you were never quite sure whether you had been spoken to or not. When Booth first met them, they had been sitting side by side on a garden seat wearing similar fawn-coloured costumes with grey shawls. He had found himself thinking 'small marsupials', one of Lempriere's phrases. Utterly unfair. They were friendly, intelligent, capable women. And in their own way, influential no doubt. A word or two in a husbandly ear, in the privacy of the matrimonial bedroom. Hints about backsliding husbands; the unsuitability of certain wives.

Perhaps their similarity was more notable because of the great difference between their husbands. Did Mrs Montagu sigh with inward relief each time she saw her husband beside Forster? Montagu might be many things, but he looked every inch a gentleman. Forster, in elaborate evening dress tonight, had the appearance of a burly coxcomb, a brutish fop. The local press had recently castigated him again over his fondness for dog fighting and low company. One of his sayings was, 'Once I get my harpoon into a man I never let it out.' His laugh as he said it was not pleasant.

When the meal drew to an end and the ladies adjourned, the gentlemen did not stay at table for their port and cigars. Montagu rose when his wife did, inviting Forster and Booth to follow him to the study.

'I have a dislike to sitting over the ruins of a meal,' he said, smiling as though his own foibles amused him. 'Or even while the cloth is cleared. There is always a sense of disorder which does not suit my nature.'

He moved to a sideboard and poured brandies for Forster and Booth, and a digestive of ginger wine with a little water for himself.

'No doubt you have heard the news, Booth, although it is supposed to be a secret? That the Twenty-first is under orders for

India? Pilkington has told you, perhaps. I understand you are quite a favourite with that family.'

He smiled at Booth. He was said to hear everything, forget nothing.

'Rumours of recall are always about, sir,' Booth said. 'Especially when we have been several years at a station.'

'Oh, I think we can assure you that it's a fact, can't we, Matthew?' Montagu said to Forster, smiling still. 'The Twenty-first have orders for India. It will be announced tomorrow at the Mess Meeting, although it will be months before the first detachment sails.'

Montagu smoothed his coat tails carefully and sat down in the chair closest to the fire.

'Several questions now arise,' he continued. 'For instance, what is to be done about Government positions held by officers of the Regiment? We believe the Fifty-second will replace the Twenty-first, but it's not yet clear whether all posts presently held by the military will continue as such, or whether the Colonial Secretary at Home will convert some into civil appointments. There will also be news tomorrow of changes to London's convict arrangements. Transportation to New South Wales is likely to end soon. This Molesworth Committee at Home is full of radicals of every complexion. Anti-transportationists, abolitionists . . .'

Forster had remained standing sideways to the hearth, one elbow on the mantelpiece and one foot on the fender, drink in hand, the great curve of his belly outlined by his embroidered waistcoat.

'We may become the only destination for England's felons,' he said gruffly. 'Mixed blessing, I sh'ld say.'

'You will have seen the newspapers full of it,' Montagu said. 'The Government at Home demands cuts to expenditure in the colonies . . . Some addlepate has even suggested transporting convicts to Ireland. But for the time being it has been decided to continue sending them here. Which is fortunate for us. How else would we survive? There will be changes, however. Settlers are now to pay for the police department here, which may mean taxation—and of course, all the usual malcontents are instantly baying opposition to this. Gregson, Fenn

Kemp . . . They claim the police department is large and expensive only because the penal establishment makes it necessary. And if they are to pay tax, they cry, they must be allowed to vote their own representative onto the Legislative Council and Executive Councils.'

'Can't have that, says we,' growled Forster. 'Can't allow civil interference in a penal colony run by the Army. Old story.'

Montagu looked amused.

'You put it precisely, Matthew,' he said. 'If somewhat baldly. The interest lies in the detail. For instance, exactly this question of whether military or civil officers will best oversee the changes that are bound to come. Certain officers, in my view, should be induced to remain. Your own valuable work, Booth . . . you would not easily be replaced.'

Booth murmured, bowed, hoped he did not look as wary as he felt. It had happened before that Montagu made him feel complicit in some unspoken cabal. He spoke as though you were intimates, but just when you were on easy terms, he withdrew into cool formality, leaving in the air an implication that you had overstepped the mark, misunderstood his good manners or tried to presume on them.

'I wanted to let you know beforehand, Booth,' Montagu waved a hand to dismiss potential thanks, 'that at my instigation, Sir John will try to persuade you to seek permission to stay when the Regiment leaves. If you judge that would be in your best interests, then with his recommendation—and of course, my own,' he smiled, 'there should be no difficulty. You might decide to apply for your majority at the same time. I put it to you merely as a friend,' he paused, 'to give you time to think of it before tomorrow when Sir John wishes you to breakfast with him . . .'

'You are very kind, sir.'

'Not at all. Your staying would benefit us all.'

The room grew thickly warm from the generous, heaped-up fire; oil lamps; a great branch of candles with tall, steady flames. Heavy green velvet curtains shut out draughts, the dark, the difficult colony. One might have been in Basingstoke. Booth would have liked to go away and sleep. His head was fuzzy with weariness and he knew he had not the right kind of nature to keep up with Montagu. He liked to think he was clever enough in his own way; could design you a wharf, build you a bridge, a railway . . . but the sense of political deeps and shoals that overtook him in Montagu's company made him feel stupid. He preferred to walk miles in the clean rain—and he understood clearly what this meant: that he never had been, would never be, ambitious enough for his own good.

Forster crossed to the sideboard, refilled his brandy and brought his glass and the decanter back to the mantelpiece. Montagu's eyes made a memorandum of it.

'On another matter, sir,' Booth said. 'The letter concerning Mr Rowland Rochester. May I see you about it tomorrow?'

'Ah,' Montagu frowned, sipped his watered wine. 'No need after all, I think. Send it back to me. A mare's nest. I have looked into it. There are no records of a Mr Rochester in the colony. No reason why you need be involved.'

'But, sir,' said Booth. 'I believe Rochester might be here. Or at least, that he was in the colony at one time . . .'

Montagu frowned. Forster smiled at Montagu.

'I felt I should mention it . . .' Booth floundered on, 'I saw him two years ago.'

'The circumstances?'

'I had come up from the peninsula for Lieutenant Tunstall's wedding. I had leave to attend, you may remember, at Bothwell. I managed to get a lift upriver to the Black Snake Inn, and went into the stables there to hire a horse for the rest of the way. When I came riding out, the coach was there loading, and among the passengers just embarking was a man . . . My attention was drawn by his limp, I suppose. Rowland Rochester's leg was injured at Demerara and . . .'

'Did he see you? Did you speak to him?' Montagu interrupted, still frowning.

'I did not, but I believe he saw me and knew me. He looked at me as though he did not want to be . . .'

Montagu's frown relaxed. 'You are mistaken, Booth. You saw a man who gave you the impression of being someone you had known briefly many years before? No, no. There would be some record.'

'I wondered if he might be using another name,' said Booth.

Montagu smiled, raised his open hands in a triumphant gesture of, 'There, you see?' and said, 'Well, in that case how could we find him out to be Rochester? It is not for us to waste time looking into every possibility. What do you say, Matthew?'

Forster had his back to them, refilling his glass.

'*Makework* for lawyers,' he growled. 'Fees for this, that, and t'other. The man must be dead, I sh'd say,' he added, giving a leering, crooked smile at Montagu, who looked away at the fire.

A pause.

'Because, you know,' continued Montagu, smoothing his right hand gently over the back of his left, as though stroking a small pale animal, 'it's my feeling that we should be careful not to introduce irrelevant details. They will only protract the family's futile search. Raise false hopes. And it would be unfortunate for you, Booth, if old, almost forgotten matters were raised again—just as you apply for your Majority?'

Of course Montagu would know about the court martial. Booth's stomach turned as he waited for mention of Caralin, but after a moment the Colonial Secretary continued, 'In any case, once Molesworth brings in his report we shall all have enough to do.'

'At the time, sir, I felt certain it was Rowland Rochester,' said Booth, thinking, for some reason they're as reluctant as I am to open up this matter. Rochester is dead? Under awkward circumstances? There was a tap at the door. The maid said Mrs Montagu had made tea in the drawing room.

'Send the Rochester letter back to me. I'll deal with it,' Montagu murmured as they rose. 'And rest assured, Booth; Forster and I are well placed to defend your interests—if it should become necessary.'

The night air woke Booth as he walked back to the barracks, and later as he lay awake the conversation churned in his mind. He envied

Casey, who had the knack of falling asleep in an instant whatever the circumstances. He'd seen Casey deep asleep in the bottom of a whaleboat in heavy seas, with waves splashing over the gunwale onto his face.

—◊◊—

Sir John and his secretary, the eccentric Scotchman Captain Alexander Maconochie, were in the breakfast room when Booth reached Government House before eight next morning. Sir John was collecting a mounded plate of eggs, bacon, kidneys, cold meat and bread. Maconochie, whose opinions on diet were as curious as on every other subject, was eating porridge with salt. Over the next hour men flowed in and out.

"'*Monstrare*'", Maconochie said, with his rolling Scottish 'rrr's'. 'To demonstrate, to show. The tyrants and murrrderers of Shakespeare and Marrrlowe are mooral mornsters. Their evil rebounds upon their own pairrsons and upon the state itself.'

He was talking about Mrs Shelley's *Frankenstein* and the criminal mind, his thin body leaning forward to make the point, his wire spectacles slipping down his nose. Booth had heard Maconochie's opinions about the treatment of convicts before, and thought them half practical good sense and half idealistic madness. Maconochie had been in prison himself, probably the only officer in the colony who had been. During the war he had been a lieutenant on the *Grasshopper* when it was wrecked on the Dutch coast. The crew had been captured by the French; force marched from Holland to Verdun in midwinter and kept for two years in a French prison—which would no doubt colour one's views. But he had been a prisoner-of-war, not a convict. There was a difference.

Maconochie argued that the length of convict sentences should be less fixed, so that men might earn early release by a points system. Merit points would be awarded for good behaviour or special services. Well, that was sensible. Booth could think of at least thirty men at Port Arthur who could be released now, which would help the overcrowding and add labourers to the shortage in the colony. But he couldn't say so, of course: he'd be thought mad as Maconochie.

George Boyes, the Colonial Auditor, was listening with his customary sardonic smile. He was called 'Alphabetical' by his clerks on account of his large number of Christian names, George William Alfred Blamey Boyes, and because he liked everything precisely ordered. His long, thin arms were crossed, as usual, and he was leaning back as though distancing himself from Maconochie's fervour. Montagu came in. He had breakfasted at home with his wife and would take only coffee. He sat next to Boyes, choosing his seat with casual care, Booth thought. Dr Bedford looked in to tell Sir John he had seen Miss Eleanor Franklin. There was no measle in the case, simply a winter dose of the grippe, nothing to alarm.

Henry Elliot went out, came back to say that Dr Lillie, the new Presbyterian minister, was seeking an interview urgently. Forster came and sat beside Booth with a laden plate and asked him to dine at 'Wyvenhoe' the following evening. Forster's house was just below the barracks in Hampden Road. Amid all this Sir John looked beleaguered, Booth thought. He was trying to tell anyone who would listen about the *Griper* Arctic expedition in the year '24.

'She was a small ship but very comfortable, you know, very comfortable. Means for conveying hot air all around her. Harrumph. The Arctic clothing was made of two pieces of cloth glued together with liquid India rubber, making it air and watertight. And—um, aah—Captain Lyon's fur bag for sleeping was covered with this linen, too. His stockings were two glued together.'

Sir John chuckled. 'And the pillow. India rubber too. Ingenious. Kept flat, in general, for packing into the smallest space. But furnished with a cork at the corner. By blowing through this, the pillow was distended with air and formed a comfortable rest for the head. Only one disadvantage—the nauseous smell of the rubber. Very bad.'

Franklin would clearly have liked to continue talking. There were several more recent inventions of useful Arctic equipment . . . but at ten minutes to nine Montagu rose and Boyes followed. Henry Elliot ushered Sir John and Maconochie, still talking, into the office, where Booth's affairs were briskly considered, Sir John nodding benignly throughout. Booth would apply to stay as Military Commandant when his Regiment departed, and to be considered for his Majority. Letters from Sir John and Montagu would be sent in support.

—⁘—

At Forster's house that night there was no nonsense about moving away from the debris of a meal. The men sat, after the ladies had retired, over a soiled cloth and an ugly clutter of ravaged food, dishes, glasses, bottles, worthy of a Mess night. Broken bread, walnut shells, claret stains. Bloody meat congealing on a platter. A convict housemaid tried to remove this, but Forster stopped her. Although he had already eaten well, he kept picking at it with his fingers, wiping them on a napkin that had once been white linen but was acquiring a gruesome appearance.

Montagu would not have approved, Booth thought. Here were none of the niceties practised in his own house. But Montagu was not here—and this was gentlemen only: Booth and Forster, Captain Swanston, John Price. Price was a recent arrival in the colony. He had obtained land at the Huon River but was dissatisfied with it. He spoke little, looked arrogant and a trifle bored, a young man of aristocratic connections condescending to colonial society.

As Forster tore off another piece of meat and brought it dripping red juices to his mouth, Booth wondered what Montagu found to eat when he dined here. At 'Stowell' there had been a delicate soup followed by half crawfishes in pink sauce, and then, in the new Russian style, everything on the table together; ragoo of vegetables, a potato dish, roast fowl, savoury pie with a crust of melting perfection. Pears in marsala had followed, with *crème anglaise*. Mrs Montagu had corrected Booth pleasantly enough when he complimented the 'custard'.

At the Forster *ménage* there were no 'made' dishes. Brown Windsor soup, a plate piled with slabs of oily fish, the bloody beef, pot-greens. Cold mutton at the side, jugs of floury gravy, boiled potatoes and turnips. Honest barrack-room fare.

Charles Swanston was a man Booth found less easy to read than the others. He was older than most of the Arthur faction, nearly fifty now, and still called Captain by many—although as with Montagu and Forster, the title was now honorary. Like them, he had sold out of the Army years ago. Swanston was Director of the Derwent Bank and a prominent figure in Hobart. He had famously, in the year '14, ridden from Scutari to Baghdad carrying vital despatches. One thousand five hundred miles in forty-eight days. An average of thirty-one miles a day in unbearable heat. How could you survive that? Pity the poor horses. Those bad-tempered tough little Indian hill-ponies, probably.

Montagu would not have approved of the conversation here; the humour was broad, vulgar, especially from Forster. He told an obscene story about a local widow and an apple. Swanston did not comment, but Booth thought he saw disgust in those cool eyes. Forster was choking with hilarity. He had drunk a great deal, but was one of those men who appear almost unaltered until they keel over, except for a purpling of the face and a tendency to be tediously persistent and increasingly unintelligible on some topic. Forster's was horses. He was trying to persuade them to join him in buying a racehorse called Lady Dancer.

'I'm not interested, Forster,' said Swanston.

'Thirds, then,' said Forster. 'You, Booth. Fifty pounds shall buy you a leg of a Lady Dancer.' He winked, hung his tongue out, mock panting.

'Too rich for me,' Booth smiled.

'Gi' me y'r note of hand, tha'll do. Wha' say?'

Booth kept smiling, shook his head.

'Nonsense,' growled Forster. 'A bachelor may borrow, I s'pose? Swanston here'll lend it you. Apply Derwen' Bank first thing in mornin'. See good terms for Booth, eh Swanston? A li'l below goin' rate? Nag'll make y'r fortune.'

'I heard that too often in Ireland,' smiled Booth again. Forster had been in Limerick for fourteen years after the War. He should know how many men had been ruined by trusting in horses. But Forster continued to urge.

'Leave the man alone, Forster,' said Swanston lazily. 'You're being a bore. Booth knows his own business best. Perhaps you should take a leaf from his book.'

Forster muttered oaths, drank more, recovered his humour.

—◊—

At the Mess the following night, Booth lost money at cards. He went to see his agent the next morning, and by the end of their conversation had decided he definitely could not afford to get married—so he might as well buy the pretty little spy-glass, which was not expensive for the beautiful thing it was. It would be useful to have a second one.

Wharton's funeral was at three o'clock on the Wednesday. Afterwards Booth dined with the Pilkingtons, who for the first time left him alone with Lizzie after the meal. He understood; he was now to be treated as a suitor. The Pilkingtons would leave with the Regiment for India in a year. Decisions must be made, a little pressure applied. A year was barely long enough for an engagement. Young ladies and their mamas must have time to fuss. Lizzie's black curls were tied each side with little blue satin bows. She was little herself: small, white and soft, sweet and sharp. Everything was going swimmingly until he mentioned to her that he'd dined with the Forsters. And then, how did the mood change so quickly?

Lizzie said, 'Poor Mrs Forster, how she must suffer.' Booth did not like this but did not speak quickly enough to stop it. Lizzie rattled on about Forster's fondness for low company, villains and 'ladies of the pavement' as the newspapers called them. Booth said with a frown that it was not a fit subject—and yet he knew he had laughed over equally dangerous gossip with her before. Lizzie made a face at him and said (her accent so droll, so irresistible he'd let her talk at other times just to hear it) had he not seen the *Courier*?

Forster was known to visit the 'ladies' house in Harrington Street, which was under the protection of Constable Tulip Wright. Such comical things were written in the newspapers when the constable married the daughter of the licensee of the public house next door.

A 'he-Tulip and a she-Tulip' the paper called them, they were such dandies. You never saw such costumes. But Mrs Lowe, who ran the cat-house, claimed he had promised to marry her. She took 'Tulip' to court. Not for breach of promise, but on some trumped up charge—and Forster, a good friend to 'Tulip', had made sure the Constable was acquitted!

Lizzie laughed and her glossy black ringlets shook. She was playing with her small male lapdog, stroking its belly almost up to its prick, her hand delicate and smooth. Booth felt the stirring of arousal in his body even as his mind became deeply uneasy. He knew she was only doing what young girls do, showing off a pretended worldliness. But he said again, perhaps too severely, that these things were hardly fit to speak of, that newspapers and gossipers should mind their tongues. Lizzie was surprised and angry.

'But sure everyone knows it's the truth!' she cried. Booth was silent. Lizzie grew angrier still. 'Forster has given his wife a pox.'

Booth rose and left then, thinking perhaps Lizzie was too Irish for him. All the Irish are wild at heart, even the educated ones. It's the old lawless mad poet-warrior in them. He was glad to be going 'home' to the peace of the peninsula. A man needed eyes in the back of his head and the diplomacy of a Machiavelli for the intrigues of Hobarton. Well, at least the Rochester matter was buried, that was the chief thing. He did not like to think too much about how that desirable conclusion had been reached, but the relief remained. He could try to forget it again, and with it, all his past sins.

6

THE *ADASTRA* SAILED FROM DEPTFORD THAT NOVEMBER IN A grey drizzle of rain and we were all aboard, Jane and Rochester, Bertha and I—and unexpectedly, Adèle. Jane kept close to Rochester, her arm in his. He looked like a portrait of Napoleon, maimed hand thrust inside his jacket, a black patch over one eye. Surly, saturnine, damaged enough to wring the heart of any woman. Almost any woman.

Bertha lay motionless on the narrow bunk down in the cabin she was to share with me, still profoundly asleep—as indeed she had been through all the difficult journey from the George Inn. She had been brought aboard strapped to a litter carried by four crewmen; did not wake even when the pallet was tipped almost vertical to allow its descent below decks. The carriers showed a furtive curiosity. One crossed himself. They backed out of the cabin hurriedly as soon as she was in the bunk. She was travelling as Mrs Rowland Rochester, sister-in-law to Mr Edward Rochester. 'The unfortunate sleeping lady,' Captain Quigley said. It sounded to me like a freak show at a country fair.

Adèle was a late addition to our party. Two weeks before our departure, Jane and I travelled to her boarding school to say farewell, and found her despondent, runny-nosed and weepy, utterly unlike herself. The female headmistress soothed and simpered until Jane seemed persuaded that these were the predictable results of a spoilt child settling in. While they were speaking, Adèle fixed her eyes on mine for a long pleading moment and then hung her head. I was suddenly hot and desperate and began incautiously, 'Miss Eyre, I wonder . . .' without really knowing what to say, when the male superintendent, who was also present, made a foolish mistake. Raising his voice to speak over mine (I was clearly some sort of dependent, almost invisible, certainly inaudible), he said with a tolerant smile (patronising, unctuous, odious) that it was only natural for Miss Eyre to be worried. Miss Eyre was herself so young, so recently out of the schoolroom, that she could hardly be expected to understand the strict discipline necessary in the education of young girls. He thought this a compliment, even a joke. 'Spare the rod and we spoil the child, do we not, Miss Eyre?' he added, leering at her with terrible levity.

He could not know how badly Jane had suffered during her own school days, but he should have noticed the sombre stare she gave him. She looked away down the drab corridor as though seeing into her past. Her narrow form became even straighter. Her chin rose dangerously, her green eyes regarded him calmly with hidden thoughts like a cat. She asked to see the dormitory: a grim place, prison-grey, bare and bitingly cold. She asked to see the kitchen, which occasioned some flurry and vain attempts to dissuade her. The rank bouquet of odours in here began with the sickly reminder of many ancient meals in which grease had formed a large part. Boiled cabbage, something rancid, something acridly burned. Undernotes of mildewy dankness from the stone pantry, the sour reek of a sweating cook, a whiff of fear from the thin scullery maid.

Jane asked to see the library and discovered the miserable shelf of books did not include a copy of Bewick's *A History of British Birds,* nor a single volume by Sir Walter Scott or Lord Byron. Adèle was therefore with us on the *Adastra,* pale and slightly subdued but recovering swiftly. When she hugged me fiercely I said, 'Awful, was it?' She rolled her eyes and emitted a burst of indecipherable French.

We boarded the ship in elevated spirits, our nervous excitement enough to carry us through the early discomforts. I was to share a cabin with Bertha; Jane with Adèle. The ship had eight small cabins and two large ones, each of the latter taking half the wide stern window. One of these was the Captain's, the other was to be Rochester's. The small cabins were four each side, with a narrow row of storage lockers along the centre between them. An open space amidships served as general saloon and dining room.

Captain Quigley, a Yorkshireman of perhaps forty-five, weathered-looking, gentlemanly, was preoccupied with the ship's loading and departure, but he declared himself eager to arrange whatever might add to our comfort; and he was as good as his word in directly having the louvred panel in my cabin door repaired. The cabins were like wooden cells. The smell from the forward privvies, the 'heads', came and went with eddies of rain and wind. Everything felt damp and clammy. Most difficult to bear were the noises and the continual nauseous motion. At the Hall I had become accustomed to the quietness of wealth, but here on the ship was perpetual din: bells, shouts, hammerings, violent thumps. And always the rhythmic creaking and grating of timbers, the slop and drip of water.

The wife of the bosun, Mrs Farley, appeared with her sister Mrs Tench. There did not appear to be a Mr Tench, or if there was, he was never mentioned. The women wore canvas trousers under short skirts, with men's waistcoats and gold earrings. They lived a subterranean—or rather subaqueous—life in the lowest orlop, and would be our stewardesses for the voyage.

I left Jane and Adèle unpacking boxes to be 'struck below' when empty, and went next door to arrange Bertha's and my own belongings in the drawers under the bunks and on the hooks around the wooden walls. A knock came as I was finishing; it was Rochester with Dr Seymour. I had assumed the doctor would be an older man, but James Seymour was my own age, brown-haired, brisk and smiling. Rochester left us, saying the doctor would examine his patient. The cabin being dim, they had brought a lamp, which Seymour asked me to hold for him. He pulled the covers back from Bertha's large form, rolling them to the end of the bunk.

'You have been this lady's nurse for several years?' he asked. 'Were you formerly employed at a bedlam?'

'No, sir. I nursed my stepmother and husband before they died.'

He nodded, already examining Bertha's face and hair, turning her head gently in both his hands, lifting back her lips to look at her teeth. He peered into her eyes, pulling down each eyelid. Had she been used to taking laudanum, paregoric, chloral? Spirits, wine, ale? How much? Other medicaments? What did I give her now? Had she had monthly courses during my time with her? I told him she had not. He looked at me curiously.

'Mr Rochester tells me there are times when this woman is violent, dangerous to herself and others. Were you not afraid of her when you first came there?'

I said I had been pleased to have the situation, and Seymour frowned but made no reply. Between finger and thumb he took up a pinch of Bertha's skin, which was sagging where she had begun to lose flesh. Dispassionately, he examined her heavy brown body, her private parts. He tapped her chest, listened to the beating of her heart.

Straightening, he said, 'I would scarcely have believed it if I had not seen it. She has been well cared for. Is that your doing? Dr Carter speaks highly of you in his letter. Or else she has a remarkable constitution. Both, perhaps. What became of her child? Did it survive?'

'Child?' It took me a moment to understand. 'I did not know she had borne a child.'

He frowned again, more deeply this time, and said, 'Then you must forget again. Dr Carter assures me you have his full confidence, and therefore I assumed . . . It was foolish of me. Can I rely on your discretion?'

A child. Rochester's? Rowland's? Had it survived? I wondered whether Rochester knew.

—⁂—

On the third day the *Adastra* dropped down to the Nore, but we ran afoul of another ship's anchor lines and there was more delay. Three more days swinging slowly at anchor again, waiting for wind and tide. New passengers came aboard in a confusion of baggage, chatter, and introductions, and swept down to occupy the starboard cabins.

The first group was a family, a portly elderly couple, the Chesneys, with a plump two-year-old, Natty, his sister Polly, about the same age as Adèle, and a slightly older, pale, starved-looking girl. Mrs Chesney's round face beamed from within a black coalscuttle bonnet. The ribbons and shawl-ends of her mourning costume rippled in the damp wind. Her husband was a farmer in Van Diemen's Land. They had returned to the old country to settle up the affairs of a married son who had died in the cholera, and were now returning to the colony with their two orphaned grandchildren. The thin girl was Liddy, a new nursery maid.

'Workhouse,' mouthed Mrs Chesney, her head turned towards me and away from the girl, whose pinched face revealed nothing as she clutched the squirming Natty in her arms. When shouts and whistles heralded our moving at last, we gathered along the wet rails to watch everything familiar slide away behind us into the past. Rochester, Jane and I stood together, with Adèle holding my hand. Dr Seymour talked with a gentleman introduced as Mr Robert McLeod, a gingery Scotsman—brought up in Liverpool by an English mother, I heard him say, explaining his absence of brogue. No sign of St John Wallace and his wife. They had come aboard, the Captain said, but remained below.

Rochester said quietly to Jane, 'Now you will feel the pang of quitting England. It is only when leaving that one comprehends fully what it means to belong to the greatest nation on earth.'

'We take that England with us,' Jane replied, looking up at him.

'True,' Rochester agreed. 'And yet you will find that as we sail further away, it is hard to keep hold on the idea of England. Then one may be seized with the violent yearning to see it again; the castles and green fields, the old cobbled towns and village steeples.'

All we could see from the ship at that moment was the cluttered harbour receding. An English watercolour day: fine rain beading our capes and jackets; softening outlines into mist. A red muffler sang against shifting November greys. Certainly the cottages and castles were there, but so too were the new railway-cuttings being torn through the landscape, the smoke-billowing mills of new red-brick manufactories.

That evening, after Mrs Chesney and I had settled the children in their bunks, she confided that she knew McLeod, and his case was a sad one. He had lived in Van Diemen's Land for seven years with a wife and child. He had been by turns a schoolmaster and a newspaperman, a farmer-settler, and a senior clerk in the Colonial Office. But his wife had disliked the colony. She had been brought up in a town—Gloucester, from memory—and had found their property too lonely and strange. After a time she had refused to set foot outside her house. McLeod took her back to England, but she and her son had died of the scarlet fever last winter, leaving him free to return now to the island.

—⁂—

Dinner was soon the centre of every aimless day on the *Adastra*, for the passengers, at least. Captain Quigley frequently joined us for the meal, at one o'clock in the afternoon, according to naval habit. The Captains whom Quigley had served under during the War had always taken their dinner after the noon soundings. Newfangled post-war Captains might think it fashionable to take their dinner at four o'clock—or heaven forbid, at six! He saw no reason to change.

'You'll have to watch out, Quigley, steamships'll be overtaking you soon,' said Mr Chesney with loud good humour, talking and eating with equal force.

'It'll be a while before steamers make these long hauls, Mr Chesney, if ever they do,' said Quigley equably. 'They're useful in their way, but sail will hold its place.'

'Well, I don't know. I've a mind to put summat in steam. Ain't I right, doctor? You was a ship's surgeon?'

Seymour nodded. 'Even so, ships for me are pretty things seen from the shore, never comparable with *terra firma*.'

'Well then, sir, a question on your own ground.' Mr Chesney thumped his waistcoat under his ribs. 'There's times when I get the devil of a pain there . . .'

'Indigestion, sir?' asked the doctor. The Chesneys rolled with laughter.

Mr Chesney waved away the grey soups, vegetable in the first days, then pea or fish, which began each meal. He lived on boiled beef and dumplings with lavish helpings from his own jars of pickle, and slices off his own great yellow moon of cheese, which he brought to the table and offered generously about.

'Well, McLeod, you sold your property afore you left—and regret it now, I warrant? Wasn't you at the Pitt Water, neighbour with Robertson?'

Chesney gave an appreciative laugh, and added, 'Mr Gilbert Robertson, there's a rum 'un. Gen'leman farmer, newspaperman—and Lord knows what else. In the Black Wars, being a bit short of o' the ready at the time, he took Guv'ner Arthur's wages for leading out a Roving Party to bring in Chief Eumarrah—and then what does he do but get up in court and defend the prisoner! "Eumarrah and his people are rightful owners of this island," says Robertson, "and what they're doing now is defending it from the invader—which is us, see?" Well, Guv'ner Arthur didn't like that—so bang goes Robertson back in the jug again, where he'd been afore on account o' libel and slander agin the Guvment. And now he's bin an' bought another newspaper, I hear.'

'There are seven newspapers in the island,' said Mrs Chesney proudly, 'though the way news and gossip go around, you wonder why we need any.'

After the meal, Chesney took snuff and a number of tots of the Captain's rum and told us he and Mrs Chesney had gone out in the year '10. Hobart Town was still called 'the Camp' in those days.

'There was nothing but tents, a few huts, and the Gov'ment store. It had only been settled six years, o'course.'

'We would have starved but for kangaroo our first year,' Mrs Chesney said.

'Eighteen-oh-four they sent a party down from New South Wales to settle it. An' only because they thought the French was about ter grab it.'

Mrs Chesney explained how to make kangaroo soup in a Papin's Patent Digester, and Mr C's favourite, kangaroo 'steamer', a stew of salt pork and kangaroo.

'Aye,' he nodded. 'With a slice of pease pudding there's nowt to equal it.'

He speared another piece of cheese with his knife, and smiling widely, said Mrs Chesney would have it that cheese was considered common nowadays, servant's prog. But he'd been partial to it all his born days. It went with the pickle. Like him and Mrs Chesney, different as chalk and cheese, yet they'd got on right as a trivet for over forty years. Mrs Chesney smiled broadly and said she'd like to know which he thought she was, pickle or cheese or chalk?

'Ah,' he said, nodding, tapping the side of his nose. 'Pickle, my dear. Full of divers fruits and spices, ha, ha! The cheese is me, round and plain. Yeller I may be, but green I ain't! If you'd seen a halfer what we've seen . . .'

He shook his head at the impossibility of conveying his strange experiences and went on to describe the occasion on which a neighbour had had his arm shot away by a bushranger.

Mr Rochester and Jane listened to all this in reserved silence, until Chesney, when he finished his story, began to question Rochester about the 'sleeping lady'. Rochester replied curtly, barely civil. Yet Chesney persisted, and McLeod, too, appeared curious, until Rochester clearly made up his mind to be rid of the subject. With stony emphasis he gave the same careful account of Bertha's misfortunes that he had given to St John Wallace: her marriage to his brother Rowland when she was just out of a convent; Rowland's death, which had precipitated her into madness, followed by years in 'private seclusion'; and then a fit, a fall, leading to her present state of suspended animation. He made no mention of his own marriage to her.

He finished by saying he was travelling to the colony because his brother may not have died in the West Indies, as the family had believed, but in Van Diemen's Land. 'It is a painful story,' he added coldly, 'but no mystery. I have explained thus far in deference to an interest perhaps natural among fellow travellers—and to avoid impertinent speculation. Any further discussion would be offensive to me.'

Mr Chesney was silenced, for the time being at least.

—⁓—

After that conversation, Jane and Rochester spent most of their days in Rochester's private saloon, even taking their meals there. The weather, moderate while we were in the Thames, grew wilder as we headed for the Bay of Biscay. As the *Adastra* dipped into the black troughs of the sea, bucking and rolling her way up again to the foaming peaks, a terrible nausea arose in me. I crawled down to my bunk and there followed days and nights when I remember only the swirling wooden walls, ghastly retching and illness. Mrs Tench bathed my head with vinegar-water and gave me some vile dose.

When I finally woke one morning feeling I might live, the walls still creaked but the gale was over. I went on deck, righting myself against the plough and rise of the ship. The salt wind sucked away my breath, pulled at my clothes and filled me with sudden elation. Adèle and Polly Chesney chattered at my skirts, recounting all they had done while I was ill, and the ship heeled on towards a bare horizon. Later, lurching back down between decks, I came upon the Captain and Mr Chesney arguing. Robert McLeod stood listening, directly in my path.

'The cargo is right enough, Chesney,' the Captain was saying. 'There's been no great shift or we'd feel it in the lie of her.'

'It ain't that I question your judgement, Quigley, but I sh'd like to go down and see for meself. No need for you to come. Give me a feller with a light who knows his way. I need nowt else.'

'I've no man to spare just now. The gale's done its usual prying and loosening—nothing too bad, but extra work until all's set right again.'

'Ah, Mrs Adair,' said Chesney noticing me, half-joking. 'You're a stout-hearted woman? Not afraid of the dark places below? You'll fetch a lantern down to the hold wi' me while I look about? McLeod here won't disobey the Captain, and my wife would do it but she don't care for rats.'

'Mrs Adair,' said the Captain. 'I'm glad to see you well again.'

'It's too early for mutiny, Chesney,' said McLeod. 'Mrs Chesney won't like to see you hung from the yardarm. Not that I don't sympathise. I've been thinking of my books down there. Five hundred books, and reams of paper.'

'Five hundred volumes?' I repeated.

'Part of the Earl of Bylaugh's family library. My father was the Earl's land agent and I spent a good deal of time there when I was young. When I went back I found the books going to auction.'

'That's an immense cargo,' I said.

'It's nowt,' said Chesney. 'I've three thousand feet of building timber down there, mahogany windows and doors, two cottage pianofortes, twenty bolts of cloth, two harps. I sh'll make a penny or two in Hobarton. A'course, there might be damage, as what I'm saying to the Captin. The china, for instance. A dozen porcelain dinner services packed in straw and feather bolsters: who knows how they've fared?'

He looked gloomy, then brightened. 'The engine'll be none the worse. A steam engine for Hoskinson's flour mill. You'd be interested in that, McLeod.'

Conversation about the cargo dominated the meal that evening. Jane and Rochester were not present but the Wallaces came in at last. They had been as ill as I and both looked pale. Jane and I had briefly wondered together about St John's wife; had he chosen a homely-looking girl or someone as beautiful as himself? The latter, I saw now. Louisa Wallace's thick, heavy golden hair and dark brows and lashes made you remember the Viking blood in England. Her features were regular, her complexion of pearly English fairness, her eyes as blue as speedwells. She and St John were as well matched as a pair of china figurines. Or bookends rather, since they did not look at one another and there was a sense of constraint between them.

'They have quarrelled while they were ill, no doubt,' Mrs Chesney whispered.

'You have to furnish a whole country,' Mr Chesney continued between mouthfuls. 'If the colony has no history, bring the history with you. We've no castles in the island, no ruins, do y'see? No building older than thirty years.'

He seemed to be arguing that his cargo was a service to society. The colony must be made into a new England. He was bringing the furniture, windows, piannyforties and such, and soon Hobart Town would be just like Lunnon. He didn't claim to be book-learned—he was a sight too busy to be reading all day, but he liked a gurt big picture with plenty of action. A sea-battle, or Waterloo Field, or such. Looked well in the dining room and made summat to talk of when you was sat by some mule-ish dinner guest with nowt to say for hisself.

St John Wallace frowned and said he hoped Hobarton would never be *exactly* like London. 'Why transport the poverty, the divisions of wealth and rank? Why not learn from our mistakes and build a better city?'

I was about to defend London, but McLeod said, 'Then you are a follower of Edward Wakefield? He seems to think it possible to construct a perfect England in the colonies. I doubt it, myself.'

'I deplore Wakefield's ideas,' St John answered. 'He tries to persuade the British Government to let him buy land cheap from the native peoples and sell it to men of his own choosing—generally one of his brothers—who will form a governing rank. An oligarchy, no less. Most of his papers on the subject were written while Wakefield was in prison for abducting an heiress—running off with her before she came of age. Can you trust a man like that? Besides, he and his followers persecute the Church Missionary Society, of which I am a member, because we question both the legality and the humanity of what he proposes.'

McLeod shrugged. 'His settlement in South Australia does not progress quite as he wanted, apparently. His latest venture is the New Zealand Company. He's managed to persuade some influential men to join him. Sir William Molesworth is one—although for myself I don't understand how Molesworth can be allowed to chair a Committee on the colonies and at the same time enter into a commercial arrangement with Wakefield.'

Chesney stared at the men as if they were speaking Double Dutch, and then said, 'Brought anything besides books and paper, eh, McLeod? Summat to make a bit o' brass?'

McLeod smiled. Only a printing press. He hoped to begin another newspaper with his friend, Dr Ross. Hence the paper, too. There was a shortage of it in the island and in New South Wales.

'And you, sir?' Chesney asked St John.

'Nothing you would term cargo,' said St John Wallace, smiling, 'Only what I carry in my head. In my view we should revel in the fact that Van Diemen's Land has no famous battlefields steeped in ancient blood, no rotten or pocket boroughs held in the grip of some titled family. Here is the chance to create a new way of life. Not perfect—we shall never be that while we are on earth, but better than before.'

'Brought no cargo?' exclaimed Chesney. It sounded to him as though Wallace and McLeod had brought the heaviest cargo in the world—ideas, notions. And Radical ones, at that. 'It's a wonder we're not listing summat terrible. It's not the cargo we've to worry about, it's your brains a-turning on your pillow of a night!'

7

NOTHING CAME FROM LIZZIE ON BOOTH'S BIRTHDAY, LATE IN August. Last year she had sent him a booklet of flannel pen-wipers embroidered with a purple flower. Since that midwinter visit he'd been up to town twice, briefly, and both times had sent a note asking if he could call. No reply. The second time he'd looked for Pilkington at the Barracks, but the doctor was visiting the Orphan School at New Town that week. Booth told himself it was just as well: he could not afford to marry and that was that. But it was not, of course. He thought of her now more than ever, stirred by the recollection of her frail white neck, the secret darkness of her hair. He'd been too sharp about the Forster gossip, and in any case, he was dissatisfied with ending their flirtation in such a poor fashion.

The visits to town had also brought invitations to dine again at 'Stowell' with Montagu and 'Wyvenhoe' with Forster. He was pleased, but felt a sense of being drawn into the hands of a polite press gang. The other guests were always 'Arthurites': Swanston, almost invariably—and nearly as frequently now, John Price. Swanston did not like Price, it was clear. There would also be one or both of the Macdowell brothers: Edward, the Solicitor General, and Thomas, the newspaper editor. Edward was married to Swanston's daughter Jeannie. On one occasion the Treasurer was there: John Gregory, a thin, sallow man, almost a caricature of the desiccated miser. A man of Montagu's kind more than Forster's, he did not appear to be enjoying himself—but then he always looked like that. Certain glances between these men suggested complicity in matters from which Booth was excluded. Or did he imagine it?

Booth had received permission to stay as Military Commandant at Port Arthur when his Regiment moved on, and they had upped his salary a little in token recognition that there had been no increase in the four years since his arrival, but the promotion to Major was refused. Others had 'prior claim'.

To compound his dissatisfaction, misfortunes at the settlement seemed to multiply that spring. Two prisoners drowned at Hope Beach in September, and while he and Casey walked up to inspect the incident, two others, Cripps and Reid, bolted from Port Arthur.

Booth was furious. He liked both of them and had believed they liked, or at least respected, him. They were healthy young men, perfectly ready to be freed in a year or two and lead useful lives. Cripps was retaken a week later with a quantity of curious meat in his possession, and gave a confused account of Reid having drowned. The half-boiled, half-roasted flesh was sent to Hobarton and declared by the doctors to have human hairs in it. At a special Magistrate's sitting Booth committed Cripps for murder and sent him to Hobarton for trial. He was making yet another start on paperwork in arrears when a signal came that a whaler was moored too close to shore again, in breach of the Act. Walk up to the Neck again, serve papers imposing the fine, walk back. It was a ridiculous waste of his time. Why could it not be delegated to a clerk? No, not allowed.

Winter was persisting beyond its time. There were days when even Lempriere sounded merely stoical. His sons Thomas and William had scamped their lessons, gone fishing and lied about it, fought in the kitchen and broken Charlotte's best basin. He would have to give them a sound whipping. Was their bad behaviour caused by living at a penal settlement?

'And someone in the Store has allowed turpentine to drip into a sack of flour,' Lempriere added. 'A hundredweight ruined and tomorrow is Officer's Ration Day and we are so short of it. Always, everywhere, something to be irritable about if one allows oneself.'

Meanwhile, Corporals Annandale and Quinter were missing, not returned from the search party looking for Cripps and Reid. It seemed certain they must have perished, but the search for them went on in appalling weather until at last they were found, only half-dead.

And Lacey, convict supervisor at the mines, got drunk on his liquor ration and offered to fight the Master of the Swan River Packet, then swore long and inventively at Lieutenant Stuart in the presence of other convicts. Lacey, a pugnacious little gnome of a man, had helped to plan the coal galleries and was known to be a favourite of Booth's. How had he managed to get drunk on his tiny liquor ration? Smuggling? An illegal still? Impossible. Contact with whalers? Or planned mischief? Had the rest of them sacrificed their portions to Lacey and deliberately stirred him to fight because they were jealous of what they perceived as Booth's favouritism? Punishment must be seen to be done. But how, exactly, to carry it out?

A note came down from Edward Macdowell: Cripps not to be tried, insufficient evidence. Booth admitted to himself that he was pleased, but even this disturbed him. Was he peculiar in thinking that the eating of a companion was defensible if there was no murder involved? Would he himself, in extremis, eat Lempriere? Casey? Assuming they were already dead, of course. For example, if Casey had died that night two winters ago when they were lost together on the Tiers, and he, Booth, had been starving for days? He thought he might have.

He put the matter to Lemp. Would Thomas eat him? After all, when the spirit departs, the body is no more than a husk. Was it not tantamount to suicide to die when a supply of fresh meat was at hand? Lempriere snorted and said something guttural in German and then something smooth in French—something about difficult to swallow? In English he would only say Booth was working far too hard. He should acquire a hobby, like marriage or bee-keeping or learning the

French horn. In any case, there wasn't enough flesh on Booth to make a decent meal, nor would there ever be if he kept tramping up and down the peninsula at this rate.

In October Booth was called up to Hobart again to sit on the court martial of Private Ward. He was glad of the excuse, desperate to see Lizzie. But poor Ward. He'd been in hospital with disease of the brain a month ago, and had now been caught preparing to kill Captain MacKay for some imagined grievance. 'Discovered behind MacKay's quarters armed with a loaded musket and nine rounds of ball cartridge about him.' Fourteen years transportation if found guilty. Every day seemed to bring a new ugly knot of trouble on top of the regular grind, and no satisfaction in any of it except the recovery of young Annandale and Quinter. And perhaps if Lizzie . . .

Booth trekked up to Hobart and sat dutifully at Ward's court martial. A guilty verdict. He walked back to the Barracks and heard news just arrived: the King was dead, had died last June. Long live the Queen. Queen Victoria, how odd. He decided to walk to New Town without letting the Pilkingtons know he was coming. Bring them news of the King's death, a perfect excuse. And if they were not there he would lie in the grass of their garden and sleep. His spirits lifted as he walked. This evening spring had come at last—with blossom in the gardens, green fuzz on saplings, a ragged old woman, half drunk, selling flowers from a basket and singing. He bought two bunches of violets and an armful of drooping lilac that smelled of England. So the King had died in June and would never see another spring, and now there was a girl Lizzie's age on the throne.

The Pilkingtons were at home, and Mrs Pilkington went into Irish raptures over the flowers but Lizzie was cool. Said she had not received his notes last month in time to reply. She had been staying with her sister Nan and Nan's husband at Richmond. The King's death proved a useful topic until Pilkington came in and the atmosphere began to thaw. Taking a medical view of the royal demise, the doctor thought it interesting that poor old Billy Boy, who should have been dead anytime these three years, had managed to hang on to life until his niece reached her eighteenth birthday. The King had said he'd be damned if he'd die to suit the convenience of Victoria's mother and that bastard Conroy who wanted the regency in their hands. He'd keep going somehow until Victoria came of age.

'But sure there's little chance of the poor girl stopping long on the throne,' added Pilkington.

Many would frown on having a woman head of the kingdom. When she married, England would virtually pass into her husband's hands. Especially if she died in childbed and her child survived; her husband would have the Regency. Look at King George's daughter, the poor Princess Charlotte: she would have been queen this very moment if she'd survived her first lying-in. At any rate, the Queen would appoint a new Secretary of State for the Colonies, which would stir things up here.

Former comfortable relations were re-established during the evening. Lizzie's younger sister came in with two friends and conscripted them all to play 'Anagrams' at the dining-room table. When Lizzie won by swiftly changing Booth's 'L-E-O-P-A-R-D' into 'P-A-R-O-L-E-D ', smiling archly at him, he pleased her by saying, 'Bravo! I certainly know one young lady clever enough to rule the world.' Then she gave him a present, supposed to have been for his birthday in August: it was a china dog, a brown terrier which looked a little bit like Fran.

8

WE WERE TWO WEEKS PAST THE ISLAND, AS SAILORS CALL
Madeira, when Rochester began to be ill. The weather was warm
now, and the rest of us, even Mr Chesney, moulted our woollens and
emerged as thinner, summery creatures. Most of our time was spent
on deck under awnings, like some straggling, ill-assorted family at
a picnic.

Rochester generally stayed below in spite of the humid closeness
of the cabins and saloons. When he did emerge he wore a dark frock
coat and waistcoat, a black hat, which he was often forced to remove
on account of the wind, and gloves. It was as though, with a perverse
disregard for the present real conditions, he was dressing as if he
were still in an English autumn. At 'Thornfield' he had always been
scrupulously well attired, but with a degree of studied carelessness
which seemed like a show of patrician disdain for mere clothes. Now,
when there was excuse for laxity, he was too correct, making an
odd contrast with Jane, who looked like a child beside him in lilac
muslin—half-mourning for her uncle—and a calico sunbonnet. More
than once I saw her look at him anxiously, but she knew that any
fussing would irritate him.

Jane and I took turns in giving Adèle and Polly a lesson each day.
Apart from the lessons, Jane stayed below with Rochester in their

stifling seclusion. Liddy and Mrs Chesney were occupied with Natty, preventing him from tottering determinedly towards the side and trying to climb the rigging. The gentlemen occupied themselves with books and sports. They had the shark chains out and hauled in a great saw-toothed fish which was hacked into bloody portions for dinner, making surprisingly good eating. They practised target shooting at barrels tossed into the sea and read the sextant with Captain Quigley at the noon sightings. In the afternoons we played cards, at which Mrs Chesney excelled, or chess, at which Louisa and I were evenly matched. Seymour was better than either of us. We dozed, and lapsed in and out of straggling conversations as the hours passed. Rochester and Jane took no part in any of this. When they were on deck for brief airings, Rochester observed our activities sardonically; like a corpse at a feast, as my grandmother used to say.

On Sundays, Jane and Rochester made an exception to their usual withdrawal. They attended St John Wallace's morning service on the deck and afterwards dined with us. Our hymns rose thinly into sails, and on up into the vaporous blue. St John prayed for us all, for our safe arrival in the colony, and for the sick woman in our care, that she might be restored to health, as Our Lord Jesus had restored so many, even those lame, blind and afflicted for many years. Rochester seemed amused by this. He leaned towards Jane and murmured something that made her look at him reprovingly.

Louisa told me Lord Caldicott had so much admired St John's sermons as to offer him a living, but the congregation was small and wealthy, and St John considered his talents more needed among the less fortunate. A mixture of pride and resentment seemed to govern Louisa's attitude to this. Her sister was married to a clergyman who held a living in a pretty village near Bury St Edmunds.

We began our dinner that day with soup as usual, and by the time we had finished were hotter than ever in consequence. We were fanning ourselves, waiting for the next course in perspiring patience, when Rochester suddenly leapt to his feet without warning. While we looked on in astonishment he tore off his jacket, then his waistcoat and cravat, as though freeing himself from shackles. Using his one good hand and scrabbling with the maimed one, he flung each garment down, stood panting like someone escaped from a furious pursuit, and suddenly sat again without a word, his shirt open to the waist. In any man it would have been strange: in Rochester it was shocking.

Dr Seymour asked him if he was well. Was he overheated? Rochester did not appear to hear. The steward had served him beef, which he began to eat with a kind of weary persistence. Nothing further occurred, but later, when Rochester went below with Jane, the doctor followed. On his return a short time later, he was met with general enquiry.

'Mr Rochester is well,' Seymour said smiling, 'or at least well enough to consign me—and all medical men—to perdition. He declares himself sound as a bell and refuses to hear any other opinion.'

'That's reassuring, at least,' I said. 'It would be more alarming if he had *lost* the will to abuse you.'

Seymour smiled, nodded. 'Miss Eyre says much the same.'

Several days later, while Jane and Rochester were taking a turn around the deck, they paused near where Mrs Chesney and I were sitting. Jane murmured something to Rochester and moved to the companionway, evidently returning below to fetch something. He went to the side and stood motionless, a strange fixity in his attitude. After a moment he pointed out to sea and began muttering. Raising his chin, he snuffed the air like a dog finding a scent. A cold wave passed through me at the strangeness of it.

'Glittering, glittering,' he said loudly, pointing at the water, which sparkled with sharp tremulous points of light. 'Long grey hair and glittering eye. *"Wherefore stopp'st thou me?"* It is my father's eye. I'd know it anywhere. He was a devil in this life and left a devil's mischief behind him.'

Mrs Chesney gaped. I put down my book and went to his side.

'Mr Rochester, sir, will you come and sit in the shade?'

'There is no shade,' he said. 'I smell sun and rottenness. *Fee, fi, fo, fum.* D'you know that song, madam? *I smell the blood of an Englishman.*

Too bright, too hot, too red.' His tone began to falter. 'Pray excuse me, Mrs Poole . . . Ah! No, not Mrs Poole. Another woman who keeps changing! If they would only stay as they are! Pray excuse me, madam, I am not myself.'

He seemed to collect himself, seized my arm and pointed into the distance.

'Look!' he said. 'It comes again. The bird . . . red feathers. So steadily it approaches. Feathers. Help me, for God's sake, I am suffocating! Ugh! Ugh!'

He washed his hands vigorously across his face as though to clear an obstruction, staggering until he fell to the deck and lay in a glaze of sweat, muttering. At that moment Jane returned from below and Mrs Chesney arrived with the doctor and McLeod.

Between us we helped the stricken man down to his bunk. Jane went into the cabin with Rochester and the doctor, and I started to return to the deck, but as I passed the cabin I shared with Bertha, I heard the low sound of a woman singing. When I opened the door I saw it was Bertha, and again there passed through me that shudder engendered by the sight of something inexplicably strange. She was still asleep, lying flat with her eyes closed, her condition apparently unchanged—except that she was singing. Or not so much singing as humming; a wordless melody like that of a woman lulling a baby to sleep. Bertha, who for years had not spoken more than a few cracked words. Rochester's cabin door was wide open and the rise and fall of his delirious monologue made a counterpoint to Bertha's wandering tune, a weird duet. Rochester stopped first. She sang on, softer and softer until she ceased altogether.

Rochester's condition did not improve that night. The doctor administered paregoric, bled and cupped him, and at last he fell into a restless sleep.

I woke next morning to the sound of someone moving in the cabin. Bertha was sitting up in her bunk, shaking as though with palsy, breathing hard.

'Bertha!' I said foolishly.

'Bertha?' she said slowly. 'No, I am Anna. Anna Cosway-Mason.'

She paused, looking at me. 'I remember you . . . Not Grace Poole
. . .Who was Grace Poole?'

I was in such confusion that I could find no words to answer her.
She had pulled her hair out of its plaits and it hung in black abundance
around her face, which, ravaged though it was, still possessed a swarthy
beauty. At last I gathered enough presence of mind to say, 'Grace Poole
was your first nurse, and I . . . My name is Harriet.'

'Christophine is my nurse,' she said. 'But she would not come.
We are such a long time sailing to England. Are we near arriving?'

'We . . .' I began, but she did not wait.

'Christophine did not believe in England,' she went on slowly,
breathing heavily. '"No such place," she said. "Come," I begged her,
but she would not.'

Every movement was clearly exhausting to her. She tried to swing
round to sit on the side of the bed but fell back on the pillow, closing
her eyes.

'J'ai faim,' she said. 'Coffee. Chicken, bread, melon?'

I wanted to shout for someone, run in all directions. I hurried
in search of the doctor. I found him still in Rochester's cabin—in
his shirtsleeves, leaning over the sick man, who was waxy, deathly
pale. Jane was beside him. They had evidently been there all night.
She had a bowl of blood and rags on her lap and looked nearly as ill
as Rochester.

When James Seymour saw Bertha his astonishment was extreme—I
think he had not quite believed me—but it quickly turned to professional interest. Water she must have at once, he said, only sip by sip,
and later, weak beef tea. Her constitution must not be shocked by
too much sudden nourishment. Bertha made faces at the water and
accepted a spoonful of beef tea before her eyelids began to droop.
I thought she was relapsing into her former state, but Seymour pointed
out that this was a different kind of sleep. She lay curled on her side,
her brown face suffused by a flush. I could not help wondering how she
would manage the world this time when it had driven her mad before.

Our fellow passengers greeted the news with varying degrees of wonder, except St John, who said calmly, 'We pray for miracles and yet do not truly expect them. The proper response is not to wonder, but to rejoice and give thanks to the Lord.'

A few days later, after attending early to Bertha, I left her dozing and went along to Rochester's cabin, where the doctor was generally to be found at any hour these days. Jane was there too. I began to say that Bertha—Anna—seemed stronger this morning, but as I spoke I saw their eyes leave me and fasten on something behind. It was Bertha, dragging herself slowly along the short passageway like a wounded creature. She pushed me away when I went to help, and sagged against the door of Rochester's cabin, gripping the frame and staring inside.

'Jane Eyre,' she said.

Jane clasped the jar of leeches as though she might need to throw it at the madwoman, but Anna had turned to the doctor.

'I do not know you,' she said. And then, to the sick man, 'but I know you, Edward Rochester.' Tears rolled down her face. 'Where is Rowland?'

She began to shake in great palsied shudders and sank to the floor. I knelt beside her and said we were sailing to another country to find him. Mrs Tench came with hot water just then, and together we helped Anna back to our cabin.

I will not recount every small degree by which she came to the eating of broth and egg (she tightened her lips against gruel like a child) nor how the doctor insisted she build up her strength in short periods of exercise, but the result was that after ten days, Seymour declared she might dress and come in to dinner for an hour.

Clothes were a problem we had not considered when we brought her aboard. It had seemed so certain she would die. Although she had lost a good deal of flesh during the months of her strange state, she was still a large woman. Mrs Chesney, Polly, and Liddy went off to forage and returned with Louisa Wallace and arms full of clothing.

Anna sat on the side of the bed turning over the offerings, making little noises of astonishment and disapproval and muttering in French.

I began to understand that she expected to see the high-waisted fashions of fourteen years before: the style of her old red dress, too low-cut for these newly prudish days. In the year '37 the correct shape for a woman was that of an hourglass: a yard across the shoulders and hips, a handspan at the waist. Skirts were not yet as long as they later became, did not yet conceal the shoes. The expanse from neck to ankle was covered during the day. For evening, the shoulders and upper bosom might be bared if they were alabaster white and wreathed in silk flowers or lace. The *gigot*, or leg o' mutton, sleeve was still present, but waning.

At first it was just Anna we draped and pinned, while Adèle, Polly and Liddy knelt on the bunks dressing up Natty and each other, giggling, sorting through the clothes. Then Mrs Chesney tried on a dark green walking costume belonging to Louisa's mother, which Louisa meant to have remade. Bess Chesney believed she might squeeze into it if we laced her stays a little tighter, and what a surprise for Chesney if she went in to dinner like that!

Polly draped herself as a bride in Mrs Chesney's vast lace petticoat and was overtaken by hysteria. Liddy, wearing Mrs Chesney's striped poplin with a pillow underneath, showed an unexpected talent for comedy—and suddenly we were all helpless with laughter, gasping and wiping the tears from our eyes. Bertha alone did not laugh. She gazed from one to the other of us with an expression of mild puzzlement, but soon returned her attention to the clothing.

At the time I thought this wild mirth came from the monotony of the voyage, but looking back I think it was more. Seeing Anna lying still all those weeks, we had known in our hearts that any woman might come to this fate: madwoman, invalid, sleeping princess. Now it appeared that if Anna could escape the prison of Bertha, then anything was possible. We might each be more than we had imagined. We were seized with jubilant excitement.

No amount of thought could solve the problem of shoes. Her feet were a size larger than mine and three sizes larger than Mrs Chesney's.

She was forced to go barefoot until a crewman cobbled her a pair of leather sandals. Odd, but serviceable.

Accounts of Anna's progress had been relayed to the gentlemen, but only the doctor had seen her. For her *debut* Anna chose a red dress of Mrs Chesney's. It was too short—Anna was a tall woman—but would pass with a long black petticoat underneath. I looped her hair back into a coronet of braids. With a pair of Louisa's silver earrings and a dusting of pearl powder, she looked suddenly like a woman of consequence. Not English, something more dusky and exotic. We stared. She viewed herself piece by satisfactory piece in Mrs Chesney's hand-mirror, then brought it up and stared at her own face.

'*Madame, que vous êtes belle!*' cried Adèle, curtseying.

And now she did seem like a wonderful large doll: our creation. At the dinner hour when we arrived with her, each dressed in borrowed garments, our appearance produced as much astonishment among the gentlemen as we could have wished, and the occasion became a party, a rout. The gentlemen fell in with our mood, even St John. The Captain hoped Mrs Rochester felt more herself, and pressed her to take a little chicken (two non-layers from the hen coop sacrificed to the occasion) while she smiled cautiously, answered little, exclaimed in French from time to time. '*Vooly-voo?*' cried Mr Chesney, offering turnip. The meal passed in high good humour, subdued only by the knowledge that the doctor's place was empty because he and Jane were still with Rochester.

Wine was liberally served at dinner on the *Adastra*, and I suddenly wondered whether Anna might imbibe too freely, but she drank only two glasses. After the meal we went on deck to an afternoon of tropical warmth, with a blue sky, milky at the horizon, and a light wind. We were under full canvas, which rippled and snapped and sang. Anna clung to us, turned her face up to the air and closed her eyes, breathing deeply as though she smelt a divine perfume, although it was only the sour mixture we were accustomed to, of brine and tar and salt-pork boiling in the galley. She seemed to draw the warmth inside her, and for the rest of the voyage she was like a cat, always curled up in a warm spot, blinking gently, smiling. She preferred to doze randomly through all the twenty-four hours. When I became too tired to stay with her, Mrs Tench, Mrs Farley, or the Captain on his night watch, became her attendants. He treated her with courtly politeness as though she were some beautiful, large, damaged creature from a different order of being—which, in a sense, she was.

I came on deck a week later to find Jane and Anna standing at the rail with their backs towards me, two yards apart and not talking. They had met and murmured brief civilities, but showed no inclination to converse further. Jane, in any case, was generally with Rochester, whose condition had not changed.

As I approached them, I thought how profoundly different they were: Jane small, pale, slim as a child; Anna tall, brown and statuesque. Jane wore dove grey, the curved seams moulding her narrow body tightly from neck to waist, and yet a vital spirit animated that unremarkable exterior. Anna was in a flowing red sacque, bright and loose, but the embers of life burned very low within her, or as the Captain had said to me quietly, 'Hatches still battened down after great storm, signs of devastation apparent'. Jane wore her calico bonnet, while Anna's black hair was pulled back severely into a knot high at the back, with a green silk sash around it, the ends floating free. Jane looked utterly English, made of sugar and spice and all things nice, but also of prayer books and duties, tea and sombre warnings. What Anna was made of, we had yet to discover.

Jane turned as I approached. 'I came up to get a little air,' she said in a low voice, 'but I must go down again.'

'Mr Rochester is a little better, I hope?'

She looked at me and her mouth twisted out of control.

'No,' she said harshly. 'Dr Seymour believes he is dying. The fever has passed but he grows weaker. The cabin is dark but he complains of too much sun.'

She gazed bleakly into the distance. The doctor approached along the deck and was about to speak when Anna said unexpectedly in her slow way, 'You can save him if you want to.'

'Want to?' Jane was fierce, quick. 'Can you doubt it?'

Anna said calmly, 'Take him back to England. Now, quickly.'

For a moment I thought Jane might strike her.

'To England?' She did not raise her voice but it was bitter. 'We are in the middle of the ocean. And if I could, what then? Dr Seymour has done everything humanly possible.'

'England itself will cure him,' Anna said. 'He has had this sickness before—in Spanish Town and at Granbois. Breath not coming, pain in the chest. Christophine said, "When the fish comes out of water, at first it flaps, struggles, then it dies. Edward Rochester cannot breathe the air too far from England. He is not himself."'

Jane looked at me. 'He says this: "I am not myself."' But that is nonsense, superstition. If it were true, every Englishman who travelled to a foreign place would die.'

Anna shrugged. 'Englishmen are not all alike. Some carry enough Englishness in them to serve for a lifetime. Some become more English on a foreign shore. Many do die. Who is to say whether it is always a sickness of the body or sometimes of the mind? Is it possible to die of . . . *mal du pays*?'

'Homesickness,' I said.

Jane turned aside with a disbelieving shake of her head. Anna shrugged as though unwilling to attempt any further persuasion, but after a moment she said, 'When we were in the Islands, Edward always grew more ill as we journeyed south, better as we went north. Christophine noticed this. Soon we will cross the line of division the Captain says, the Equator.'

'Why should I believe you?' Jane cried, suddenly desperate. 'You hate him. You want him to die.' I knew she was recalling those nights at 'Thornfield' when Anna had escaped over the roof and attacked Rochester and Richard Mason while they were sleeping.

Anna's round brown face was expressionless, her manner unhurried.

'No,' she said. 'When Rowland vanished and they married me to Edward, yes, I hated him. Voices came in my head, saying, "Kill him." Then I hear other voices; the nuns, Christophine. "What I teach you, *bébé, dodo?* Have you learn nothing? Anyone can love a friend, what is hard is to love the enemy. But you must try. Hate is bad magic. Feed on your own self. Eat you up, make you sick."'

The impression of that Caribbean voice was so powerful I could almost see Christophine.

McLeod had now approached and was listening too.

'I could not forgive Edward Rochester and his father,' Anna continued, 'but Christophine sent help. Or perhaps it is God who sends it.' Anna put her arm around my shoulder. 'This one comes. Reads to me, gives me my red dress. Then I begin to think a little of other things, not just what they have done to me.'

Jane's face was white. She put her hand on Anna's arm, hesitant, vulnerable. 'I am sorry,' she said. 'But this is of such great importance to me . . . Were you married to Edward, or Rowland?'

Anna frowned. Not deliberately keeping Jane in suspense, I felt, but the question seemed to give rise to a crowded disorder in her thoughts. She began to speak hesitantly, as though setting it straight in her mind as she spoke.

'I married Rowland in the little chapel of Our Lady of Mercy. But then his father came and there were great quarrels and I was sent back to the nuns. They told me Rowland was dead. I was to have his child but it was born dead, they told me. A girl, born dead.'

Nobody spoke.

'Then my stepfather Mr Mason came. He brought Edward Rochester and his father to the convent,' she continued. 'They said, "Rowland is dead, you must marry his brother Edward now." I told them no, but always they came back. Sister Marie Augustine said, "You must do as they say." Later, after we were married, I had a letter.'

McLeod said, 'A letter from Rowland Rochester? After you were married to his brother Edward?'

'Yes.'

Sun poured onto the deck, a canvas above rippled and flapped, men were up there working and calling. Adèle and Polly continued some shrill game further along. The surface of the sea was inscrutable, showing nothing of the strange, teeming life beneath.

'I was frightened. Christophine brought the letter secretly and I did not know what to do. We had moved to 'Granbois' and it had taken long to find me, sent first to Spanish Town. Rowland was at Saint Vincent but he said he would come. I wrote to him. Come, I said, take me away. Christophine took the letter. I did not tell Edward because he hated me. He hated the islands, and Christophine most of all because the islands are strong in her.

'Many months went by and there came nothing. Edward and I sailed to Italy, France—many places—but we were always the same. We tried to find England but we never arrived. Antoinette Cosway was lost. She turned into Bertha Mason and I did not know her.'

Rochester was so weak he could barely move, but his eyes were alert and his hand clasped Jane's. Adèle and Polly had made a garland of white paper flowers threaded on cotton and Jane wore it resting on her neat head. This was the only sign of festivity. Captain Quigley asked Rochester if he understood the nature of the ceremony and with an effort he turned his eyes and answered yes, he desired to marry Jane Eyre for better or worse, ashes to ashes, dust to dust. The Captain paused, continued. When it was over Jane bent and kissed him lightly before us all. We gathered afterwards in the saloon for a glass of wine at the Captain's invitation. Jane stayed with Rochester. Mrs Chesney brought out a last plum cake, but we were subdued. The Captain cleared his throat and told us Dr Seymour had recommended to Miss Eyre—Mrs Rochester—that she follow Anna's advice and return to England with her husband as soon as possible. We exclaimed in surprise.

'Few ships return to England by this route,' the Captain added, 'but I have altered our course to put us in the way of one.'

'Do you believe it will save him?' Louisa Wallace asked the doctor.

He looked wearily at our puzzled faces. 'Stranger things are known. The mind and spirit have profound effects on the body. If Rochester is suffering from some kind of tropical fever it may ease his mind to know he's on his way home. If he remains on the *Adastra* . . .' He made a helpless gesture.

And so, I thought, I shall never see Van Diemen's Land. The Captain warned Jane it might be days before we spoke a ship able to take us back to England, but the following afternoon there came a cry from the mast top and a barque grew slowly larger to our view as though summoned from behind the horizon. The *Constantia*, heading to Liverpool from Sierra Leone, could take only two passengers. Jane did not want to leave Adèle.

After hasty negotiation it was agreed that room could be made for the child, but no one else. Anna's views and mine were sought. Anna shrugged and said calmly, 'They must go, of course,' but I could not be sure she understood what this meant; that she and I must go on alone, and manage as best we could. I said they had my blessing. The doctor, Wallace, Quigley and the Chesneys assured me they would help us once we reached the island, and I felt a rising interest, a flutter of pleasurable excitement and fear.

While the pinnace was being launched to carry our passengers across to the *Constantia*, Jane and I packed a small trunk and a holdall. She gave me a banker's draft for five hundred pounds, and letters of introduction. Sailors arrived to take Rochester to the deck and we followed as he was carried up on the same pallet Bertha had once occupied. Jane kept close at his side.

'I will write care of the Derwent Bank,' she said to me as they readied the bosun's sling for her.

The wind had risen and the light was fading. The short tropical dusk had begun. Shouts and orders flung through the wind, men clambered up the ratlines to alter the sails, and the ship swung slowly about. We embraced awkwardly and she was strapped into the sling and lowered over the side. I was left with the feeling of her thin body, wiry with energy and determination. The doctor brought Adèle forward but she suddenly wailed, 'No, no. I will stay with Polly, and Harriet, and Anna.'

My eyes were streaming. The *Constantia* was gradually being borne away from the *Adastra*. McLeod lifted Adèle briskly, hauled himself into the bosun's cradle and was dropped with her down into the boat, where she fell weeping into Jane's arms. McLeod was winched back up and we watched as the pinnace set off towards the other ship. Even as Jane, Rochester and Adèle were hauled aboard the *Constantia*, her stern lanterns were lit, more sail bellied out and she began to veer away. We stood and watched until she disappeared. I could not stop weeping, praying silently for Adèle, and for Jane, who might be a widow before she reached England. And for Anna and me on our way to the colonies, and for poor Edward Rochester, three-quarters dead.

9

'HEADS WILL ROLL,' PREDICTED LEMPRIERE, BEAMING, PASSING the claret to Boyes. It was the phrase that appealed to him, not the thought of bloodshed.

'One head should go, at least,' said Boyes. 'But I'm not sure it will. And there you have the problem in a nutshell.' He gazed at the ruby lights in his glass, lips compressed.

Even when Boyes was at his most informal, Booth thought, he still looked like a Colonial Auditor. It was something to do with his dry smile, his long thin narrow figure, as neat as a column of figures.

Lempriere shook his head and seized a folded newspaper lying on a side table. 'Franklin must do something. Montagu has gone too far this time. Robert Murray defends him in the *Times*, of course, and Thomas Macdowell ignores the whole matter in the *Chronicle*—because they are both Arthurites—but Gilbert Robertson in the *Colonist* has attacked. You see?' He pointed to the page. 'Robertson calls it "the climax to the presumption of the Arthur faction".'

He read aloud: 'John Montagu has declared himself Governor of this colony. This attempt to defeat the ends of justice is conduct disqualifying all persons implicated, from holding office ... and those persons are Captain Forster and Mr Montagu, brothers-in-law, fellow Councillors and conspirators in this plot.'

'What plot?' asked Booth. He was too tired to talk or to think; could follow the conversation only by a constant effort of will. It was a month to Christmas. They were in his cottage, sitting round the fire after a dinner that had not been one of Power's best, thought Booth, although it might simply be that he had no appetite himself. The others had eaten briskly enough. They were four this evening, an unusual foursome. They met in town, but it was rare for them to be on the peninsula all together. Boyes was here to oversee an extraordinary audit for the accession of the new queen. Amounts produced, whether boots, bricks, cabbages or coal, must tally exactly with quantities used, sold or stored. Boyes would inspect the records himself this time, rather than delegating it, as with the quarterly audit.

Bergman was here for another round of surveying at Point Puer. His amused brown face conveyed a lively temperament wholly different from Boyes's cool detachment, and yet the two men had much in common and were close friends. Booth had been looking forward to the evening, but had woken this morning feeling bilious and ill, lethargic and restless at once. A touch of the yellow fever again. He'd fought it off for nearly a year, and now Casey wasn't here to give him the usual dose. Transferred at his own request, posted to New Norfolk. A blow, but probably for the best. His replacement, Dr Benson, had agreed with Booth's self-diagnosis, bled him, and administered some filthy draught. Tonight he felt better but weak, labouring under the weight of an enormous lassitude.

'At any rate,' said Boyes. 'You're looking at last week's *Colonist*. Matters have moved on. The plot thickens.'

'What plot?' Booth repeated.

'The newspapers call it "The Clapperton Affair",' said Boyes with a twist of the lips. The intrigues of Hobarton were a perpetual source of sardonic amusement to him, and not a little irritation. 'When Alfred Stephen lost his wife last year, he was left with several small children and a heavy load of work as Solicitor General. He found an emancipist called Clapperton to employ as house steward, general factotum, and for eight months everything went like clockwork.

Then Stephen discovered Clapperton had stolen all the monies given to him to pay household accounts, and was adding insult to injury by telling the tradesmen Stephen refused to pay.

'Stephen brought charges against Clapperton, who was sentenced to transportation. As you know, for those already here, that means hard labour on a road gang, or a spell at Port Arthur. But some weeks later the Stephen children went to play with the Montagu children—and found Clapperton cooking in the kitchen at "Stowell"! They told their father, of course, and it turns out that Matthew Forster, who was magistrate at Clapperton's hearing, had assigned the man to Montagu's household at Montagu's request. Completely improper—against every rule. But Clapperton is an excellent cook, apparently.

'You may laugh, gentlemen,' Boyes continued, looking down his thin nose at Bergman and Lempriere, 'but the matter is profoundly serious. Not only for Montagu and Franklin, but for all of us. It's the first major hurdle of Franklin's term here. If the matter becomes known to Whitehall, Franklin's manner of dealing with it will be carefully scrutinised. And it might well affect the outcome of the Molesworth Enquiry, which is in full hunting cry. It's exactly the kind of abuse of the assignment system our masters are on the *qui vive* for. Especially those who would like to abandon assignment—and transportation altogether.'

'Molesworth?' said Lempriere, delighted. 'What a picture the name conjures! An elderly judge—long face, grand wig, *pince-nez*.'

'So you might imagine,' said Boyes nodding, 'but William Molesworth is twenty-seven, ambitious, arrogant, and not long sent down from university after a blazing row with his tutor. A thousand times more dangerous to Montagu than a woolsack of elderly judges. Molesworth is desperate to make his political mark, and his overbearing, well-connected mother supports him. If Molesworth gets wind of the Clapperton case—and he will if Franklin dismisses Montagu—then Montagu loses everything. His career will be finished at the age of forty-five, just when he's managed to scheme and haul himself to within reach of his goal, which is to secure a Lieutenant

Governorship for himself. And if Franklin *doesn't* dismiss Montagu, then he'd better have a watertight excuse for not doing so, or it will look as though he is ready to ignore this kind of illegality.'

Gus Bergman laughed again. 'If Arthur were still here, Gilbert Robertson would be behind bars by now for splashing the case all over the newspapers.'

'If Arthur were here the problem wouldn't have arisen,' said Boyes. 'Montagu would not have dared to have Clapperton assigned to him. Arthur kept Montagu and Forster in check, and now he's gone they'll test the water to see exactly how much they can get away with. Arthur used the law to his own advantage, but he was careful never to overstep in any way he could be held accountable for.'

Lempriere shrugged. 'Then surely Sir John has no choice. He must dismiss Montagu, reprimand Forster, and let them take the consequences.'

'That's exactly what Maconochie, Franklin's secretary, is advising. But Franklin doesn't seem to find it so straightforward,' said Boyes. 'For two reasons, I think. Sir John is deeply religious, and genuinely hesitates to ruin a man's career. Doesn't believe in casting the first stone. And he likes Montagu—as he tends to like everyone. He also believes he needs Montagu's help; Franklin's been here less than a year, and he wants to keep the administration in the hands of a man who knows it well. Montagu is an excellent Colonial Secretary.'

'*Et alors?*'

'Well, Franklin may yet listen to Maconochie. I hope he does. In the meantime, he's ordered Clapperton to a road gang. But the worst is, Montagu has evidently taken fright and decided the best form of defence is attack. He's leapt to accuse Franklin of bias, of taking Alfred Stephen's part, of being weak, failing to support his senior officers, etcetera, etcetera. In short, he'll say anything to put himself back where he sweats to be, in the right.'

'The Arthurites are used to having their own way,' grumbled Lempriere. 'Now they cannot believe it when they are opposed. They should remember they set the precedent for dismissing a Colonial Secretary when they got rid of poor Burnett.'

Booth had liked Burnett, who had been dismissed for selling part of his land grant, a minor breach of regulations, commonly ignored. Not nearly as serious as this Clapperton business, and yet Arthur had abandoned Burnett and given the position of Colonial Secretary to Montagu. The four men sat considering.

'Arthur and Montagu had clearly been planning Burnett's fall for some time,' said Bergman. 'Burnett was inefficient and ill, and they couldn't stand it. Arthur held a mortgage on a property of Burnett's and asked for repayment just when Burnett was in greatest difficulties.'

'I'm sure Montagu remembers,' said Boyes. 'And no doubt it fuels his fears. Burnett has returned to England practically a pauper, looking desperately for another appointment. Most of our generation depends on the King's shilling to keep us from the Workhouse. Montagu came out of the war with nothing, like so many of us. Dismissal means not only the loss of salary, but of reputation—which makes it difficult to secure another position. If he's disgraced, Montagu will have to take any post he can find: clerk, tutor, private secretary—which is precisely why his present outbursts against Sir John are so violent. His aim is clearly to turn the story about until he appears to be the injured party.' He shrugged his thin shoulders. 'Otherwise his hopes are gone.'

'The Arthur faction will save him,' said Lempriere. 'They'll stick together.'

'Will they though?' asked Bergman. 'I'm not so sure. Arthur held them together, as I said before, and now he's gone they are less united. It may be a matter of *sauve qui peut*. They must fear what else may come to light if their affairs begin to be examined by the Colonial Office in London. Henry Melville's new book is full of allegations against Arthur and his friends. If only a quarter is true, they'd have embarrassing questions to answer. *The History of the Island of Van Diemen's Land*. Have you seen it? Melville sent it to England last year to be published; he was afraid Arthur might somehow stop it if he went ahead with it here.'

'Ah, well,' said Lempriere. 'Perhaps Franklin will find the strength to dismiss Montagu. He had Gregson released from prison, which was a blow against the Arthurites.'

'But did he know that?' said Bergman. 'I don't think so. Franklin had only just arrived. He was shown a petition and set Gregson free as a piece of inaugural grace. He had no idea of the strength of the Arthur faction then. Does he even now?'

No one answered.

'It's an interesting study in human nature.' Boyes was pensive. 'Franklin, who believes a man must be forgiven to seventy times seven as the Bible says—and Montagu, who can't comprehend how one could have the advantage and not use it. Franklin, who feels a duty to love his fellow men, and Montagu, who takes violent, irrational hatreds against certain individuals. He loathes Maconochie, and Alfred Stephen, and Cheyne, the new Superintendent of Public Works . . .'

Another short, comfortable silence.

'All this talk of factions, opposing sides,' said Booth irritably. 'I don't like it. The newspapers start it. Why can't a man be a friend to both Franklin and Montagu?'

The other three considered him.

'You look as though you could do with a week in bed,' said Bergman.

'A touch of the old fever, that's all.'

'You're fortunate down here. A safe distance from these slings and arrows.'

'Tempests in teacups,' said Booth wearily.

'Sometimes. This may be more.'

'It must be especially galling to Montagu that it's Alfred Stephen who's brought this Clapperton business down on them,' said Lempriere. 'Wasn't Stephen a friend to the Arthur faction at one time?'

'They fell out a year ago over that row at the inn at New Norfolk.'

'A quarrel over a late-night card game? That doesn't sound like Montagu.'

'No, nobody's suggesting Montagu was actually involved, but he was there. It was the Governor's nephew, Henry Arthur, at the centre of it. "Shots were fired," the *Courier* said, when someone accused Henry Arthur of cheating.'

'That's hardly new . . .'

Bergman smiled. 'You can't help wondering what England would think if they could hear us: the Bennett affair, the Clapperton case, the Greenwood business—and half a dozen others.'

'When Arthur was here these things could be kept quiet,' said Boyes, shrugging. 'But it's curious. Something about that night at New Norfolk made his followers very nervous. They certainly closed ranks to keep it from him. He was waiting to hear of his next appointment at the time, and a scandal at that moment was the last thing he wanted. And then Henry Arthur resigned and went to Port Phillip; Alfred Stephen quarrelled with the others, and is off to Sydney.'

'Henry Arthur and Thomas Mason are a pair of rogues. And as for John Price, a more unpleasant . . .'

'He's to marry Franklin's niece.'

Another silence.

'Can no one persuade her against it? Invent a delay while her parents' approval is sought?

'She is an orphan. Sir John is her guardian. She needs only his permission . . .'

Boyes shrugged, sighed. 'The Franklins have known Price less than six months—and he certainly appears eligible at first sight. Third son of a baronet—who is said, however, to be both eccentric and impoverished. John Price has sold his worthless land at the Huon to Lady Franklin.'

'It's not worthless,' Bergman protested. 'It's heavily wooded, and needs more effort and outlay to develop than John Price expected. Lady Franklin's plan for it seems excellent to me, although the press is quick to mock her. Gilbert Robertson is the only one who understands.'

Booth had heard Jane Franklin speak of her idea of forming a new settlement at the Huon River, and had thought it excellent as well, but too difficult to put into practice. During the inaugural tour, Jane had learned that many settlers could not buy land in the island because it was sold only in large parcels, generally more than two hundred acres, often more than five hundred, which put it beyond the reach of those with modest capital. They wanted smallholdings of five, ten or twenty acres, which at present they were forced to rent from the owners of big properties.

Small tenant farmers were thus at the mercy of wealthy landlords, many of whom were absentees living in England. The rents left the island, but worse still, tenants could not afford to make improvements because these became the property of the landowner. Even clearing was often done at the tenant's expense, to the benefit of the owner. There had been cases where smallholders had built huts, barns or fencing, and were afterwards given notice to quit, so the improved property could be rented at a higher rate to a newcomer.

England's policy could not be changed, so Lady Franklin had begun a private scheme. As Bergman now explained, her six hundred acres on the Huon River was gradually being surveyed and carved into allotments of five or ten acres. (In a few cases the measure was as little as one or two.) She was selling these to poorer settlers who could prove their *bona fides*—had even sold one to a former convict. Repayment was set at ridiculously low interest, and even this was deferred for the first few years, allowing the new owners to put what little money they had into developing the land. The scheme was in its infancy, and yet, Bergman said, he had already seen one grateful farmer trying to press two grimy ten-shilling notes into Lady Franklin's hand with gruff thanks.

'It's a pity she didn't buy land nearer the town for it.'

'You know there is none, except what would cost a fortune. Most of the desirable land was granted or sold in the early days, and Arthur took the rest.'

'If John Price has sold his land, where will he live with his bride?'

'He's leased a small farm on the eastern shore near the Mad Judge's property.'

Boyes was evidently still thinking of Mary Franklin, because he said suddenly, 'A young woman dances with a presentable young man once or twice and fancies herself in love. If you tell her he's a vicious specimen, she'll probably cling to him all the more loyally and think the worse of you. Pray for your daughters, gentlemen.'

'If Franklin doesn't dismiss Montagu, he'll have more to worry about than his unfortunate niece,' said Lempriere.

'True. But I'm inclined to agree with Booth; why let oneself be forced into partisanship? I shall be a "trimmer", as people used to say bitterly in my father's time,' said Boyes. 'One who trims his sails to the prevailing wind. A kinder name is "diplomat".'

'But suppose you have to defend a principle, or a friend?' asked Bergman.

'How often does it come to that?'

'I prefer to keep out of it,' said Booth.

'Perhaps you can, down here. But as our friend Maconochie might put it,' said Bergman, '"He who wad sup wi' the devil maun keep a lang spune."'

He smiled, rose, and thanked Booth for the evening.

10

ON THE *ADASTRA* MEALS CAME AND WENT; WE SAILED ON AND ON.

Nights seemed even longer as we reached the middle of the voyage, in spite of the increasing hours of daylight. The cabins were too hot for sleep and the dark hours stretched and warped like a vast slow arc from dusk to dawn. I would often return to the deck and lean on the rail gazing at the heavens lit with stars, the inky roiling sea. Quigley might pause to talk if he was on watch; St John, McLeod and Seymour were also regulars. Bess Chesney and Louisa either slept soundly or endured their wakefulness below. With the ship aslant, rushing steadily on through the warm dark, it seemed natural to be silent, or to speak of things too private for the sunlight. One night I asked Seymour whether he believed Anna's recovery would be permanent.

'I have been thinking about it,' he replied, 'and the truth is, I do not know. It is clearly an affliction in which the body and mind—or spirit, if you like—are connected, and this kind of ailment we know little about. Some physicians think the mind is like a great house: a Gothic castle with secret chambers, dark corners, winding stairways. As I say, we simply don't know.'

His expression was unreadable, his face half in shadow. 'Shall I tell you why I concluded Jane Eyre and Rochester should turn back?' I was eager to hear his reasons. We had all, I think, wondered at the decision. 'It was because although Rochester's case is curious, I have seen another, very similar, on my first voyage out. I was assistant surgeon on a transport carrying two hundred and thirty felons and twelve passengers. One of these was a Mr Thomas McClelland—young, handsome, well bred—going out to the colony to be Attorney General. This is not confidential, I should say; unfortunately it is now well known in Hobarton.

'For the first few weeks you'd have thought McClelland the sanest man alive, but three weeks into the voyage he began to complain that he did not really wish to leave England; the position had been obtained for him by influential friends. He begged the Captain to turn back. The Captain treated this with kindly amusement at first, but McClelland became increasingly agitated and would not eat.

'He tried to throw himself overboard, and at last showed such strong signs of derangement that we were forced to lock him in his cabin, and later, to restrain him. I began to think he could not reach Van Diemen's Land alive. More strangely still, when we did arrive he recovered his sanity with astonishing swiftness. He said Hobarton was more like England than he had expected. Unfortunately, after a year he relapsed into madness again. In McClelland's case, as in Rochester's, the affliction seemed to bear some relation to the fact of leaving England, a fear that in a strange colony he might change, lose hold of the self he had always known . . .'

St John Wallace had joined us, his face like that of a stern angel in the light of the translucent moon, now far over in its arc. He gave a soft laugh and said, 'And yet rightly considered, it hardly matters where we are in this world, since our true task is to prepare for the next. We are all colonists after a fashion. Pilgrims, exiles, on the way back to our true home.'

He must have been pleased with this conceit because he used it in his sermon the following Sunday, speaking of homesickness for God as the essential condition of mankind. He quoted Wordsworth, saying we are all born into the world 'trailing clouds of glory'—faint memories of the spiritual home from which we come. Each newborn infant suffers a Fall out of Eden into the World, as Adam and Eve did. And although these 'intimations of immortality' fade as we grow, what remains of them is our natural attraction to Beauty and Virtue. We are homesick for God. By cleaving to the Good and the True we find our way home. If we turn aside to sin, we wander lost through many lifetimes. He concluded by saying the felons in Van Diemen's Land were in this state and must be helped to set their feet on the Way again.

'"Many lifetimes", Wallace?' Seymour said half-teasingly as we went in to dinner afterwards. 'Hardly an orthodox position? Does your time in India incline you to believe in reincarnation?'

'Orthodox or not,' interrupted McLeod, 'you are dangerously mistaken, Wallace. Poverty and ignorance are the major cause of vice. No *poetry*,' he infused the word with contempt, 'should obscure the fact that the strongest impulses of humanity are the same as those in animals—hunger, fear, and the will to live and multiply. Poetry cannot be consulted on matters of social justice.'

McLeod seemed intensely irritated by Wallace's views and from that day seemed constantly looking for ways of stirring him to anger, one of his favourite subjects being the age of the earth. McLeod insisted that Lyell's geology and the discovery of the speed of light had proved the universe ancient beyond calculation. How could anyone now believe the world was only four thousand years old, as theologians claimed? And created in seven days? St John maintained a saintly calm under these attacks, which—intentionally or not—had the effect of infuriating McLeod still further.

But he was hurling himself uselessly against the implacable wall of St John's certainties. These were mysteries we were not meant to understand, was the constant mild reply. And what's more, according to the men of science McLeod put so much faith in, the substance we were pleased to call matter was made up of atoms like dust, which could be changed at God's Will. Take the stars: Orion's Belt, for example, the only constellation visible from both northern and southern hemispheres. (It must have been night again, on deck again.)

'That reddish star at the base? That is Bait-al-Jeux, or Betelgeuse, part of the Winter Triangle. I have been reading Edmund Chilmead's translation of *Riti Ebraici*, a history of the Jewish peoples, where he mentions that the curious name comes from a mistranslation of the Arabic into Latin—by which we know that Betelgeuse must have been visible to Jesus. But the most interesting thing is this: Sir John Herschel, our Astronomer Royal, tells us Betelgeuse has begun—two years ago—to suddenly grow in brightness, until now it surpasses Rigel. The universe is changing, we are born into vital times and called to action.'

'My action would not be yours,' said McLeod.

'No, indeed. Each must find his appointed way.'

—ɷ—

With the departure of Jane and Rochester, the talk also turned again to speculation about Rowland Rochester.

'But if he is alive and heir to an estate in England,' McLeod asked, 'why did he go to Van Diemen's Land?'

'Perhaps he had some friend there?' asked Mrs Chesney.

'He knew Lieutenant Booth and others in the twenty-first,' I said. 'But that Regiment was not sent to Van Diemen's Land until eight years after Rowland left the West Indies.'

'Booth is a Captain now. Has been for some years,' said McLeod.

'You are acquainted with him?'

'I have met him through my friend Dr James Ross. Ross's wife, Susan, has a sister, Charlotte, who is married to Thomas Lempriere, Booth's Commissariat Officer at Port Arthur. Ross is not a medico but a scholar, a former editor of the *Hobart Town Gazette*.'

Natty climbed onto Mrs Chesney's lap and began to grizzle and pull at her sewing.

'Chesney?' she said, trying to sew at arm's length. 'Parson Knopwood might know something of Mr Rowland Rochester?'

I scooped Natty off her lap. He squirmed and squealed.

'Aye, it's possible,' said Chesney.

'By Parson Knopwood I mean Mr Robert Knopwood,' Mrs Chesney explained, 'chaplain in the colony since Hobarton was settled. He knows everyone's connections and keeps his memory wonderfully. He must be seventy now. I don't mean he gives such things out gossiping. Only what can properly be told.'

'Aye, and you'd be surprised what *can't* be told,' added Chesney with a grunt of laughter. 'A good many families in the island have secrets. '

'Van Diemen's Land is full of stories,' said his wife. 'On account of we've most of us come there full-grown, with our stories ready-made.'

'But you'd best not believe everything you hear!' Chesney grinned. 'I've heard tales that fanciful you'd swear they come out o' books, but I know for a fact they're true as I sit here. Others sound that real you'd stake your life on 'em, and they're nowt but a pack of lies!'

'Mr Jorgen Jorgensen,' said Mrs Chesney, nodding. 'A convict, and now a constable . . . but is he King of Iceland? Him and his fat wife, poor Norah. Now there's a madwoman for you. Trying to take her own life, and him at his wit's end trying to prevent it. Half the things he says are true as bread and butter, but as for the rest . . .'

'Gus Bergman might know of Rochester,' said Chesney. 'He goes tramping all about the island with his surveys.'

'Mr Bergman is a Jewish,' Mrs Chesney said to me, 'but a lovely man.'

Such meandering conversations drifted on with the slowly passing days.

—ᴍ—

Anna thrived in the hot weather, although she slept long hours. She spoke little, often sitting silent for half an hour gazing unseeingly into the distance. I made many sketches of her like this. Quigley asked me privately if I could spare one, and bore it away in triumph. Anna did not care for reading but would pore over the illustrations in Mrs Chesney's old copies of *The Ladies Cabinet of Fashions*. Through these she became reconciled to current modes and began to make herself one of the wide linen collars then in fashion. Her stitching was clumsy at first, but she soon began to recover what had clearly been a great skill.

When Mrs Chesney exclaimed over the fine work, Anna said slowly, 'Two gifts the nuns gave me: sewing and music. Also we learned deportment, cleanliness, good manners and kindness to God's poor. And what to say to yourself when you think a sin. You say, *Save me Lord, I perish.*'

I was puzzled. 'A convent school? Are you of the Roman Church, Anna?'

Her mother was, she said. Her stepfather, Mr Mason, had no religion. When he sent her to the convent he'd shrugged and said, 'She's the daughter of a mad Creole whore. She'll go to the devil one way as quick as another.'

Mrs Chesney looked at me, looked away.

—⁂—

Neptune, or Badger Bag, as sailors call him, came aboard as we crossed the Line, and two of the crew who had not 'crossed' before were baptised with buckets of rancid slops and ritual humiliations.

'It has to be done,' Quigley said. 'We sailors are a superstitious lot. It's no light matter to cross from the top of the world to the bottom.'

Even before this, evenings of gaiety had begun. Lanterns were hung at dusk and there was a seraphine for music. It was a new instrument, like a small pianoforte. Its tone was too bright and jangling for me, but it served to accompany the dancing. Wallace danced well, but he would often retire to his cabin rather than join in. The doctor and McLeod danced with Louisa, although McLeod did not know the steps and had to be pushed and pulled through a set of 'Strip the Willow' with laughter and breathless cries of instruction.

'Oh, Mr McLeod,' gasped Mrs Chesney, weeping with mirth. 'You'll be the death of me. I always did love to dance.'

'Hah!' he cried, 'I have the way of it now. Come, give me your arm, madam, we'll go about once more.'

'Oh, no, no,' she moaned, mopping her red face. 'Here is Harriet playing for us all this time. Louisa will take the instrument a while, won't you, my dear? Do you go round with Harriet, Mr McLeod.'

When she had recovered, Mrs Chesney said it was as good as a 'rout', a 'levvy' or a 'swarry', all of which were plentiful in Hobarton, she reassured us.

On another night the Captain brought a guitar into the saloon, saying to Anna, 'This is the instrument I spoke of.' She plucked the strings slowly, twisted the pegs, and after a time played songs so melancholy they made you want to weep. Later, the rhythms became more troubling, lopsided beats like an overtaxed heart.

—⁓—

Another long, hot afternoon. After a silence, James Seymour said idly: 'I have been told—that Mr Algy Montagu, the Mad Judge in Hobarton, was brought up by the poet Wordsworth and his sister Dorothy. Can it be true?'

I listened more closely now when there was talk of Van Diemen's Land, which began to seem to me peopled only with convicts, eccentrics and misfits.

'Why yes,' said Bess Chesney, 'Judge Montagu's history is a tragical one; his grandmama was murdered on the steps of the Opera House in Covent Garding by a clergyman mad for love.'

Seymour laughed and looked at McLeod, who nodded and said, 'Judge Montagu's grandmother was Mrs Martha Ray, the opera singer, mistress of the Earl of Sandwich, by whom she had—illegitimately, of course—the Judge's father, Basil Montagu. Mrs Ray came out of the theatre one night after watching a comedy, and just as she reached her carriage a clergyman in love with her came up and shot her in the head with a pistol. He then tried to shoot himself, but missed. He was hanged afterwards in a celebrated case.

'Then Algy Montagu's mother died when he was four, and his father, Basil, a friend of Wordsworth's, thought it better the child be brought up in the country with the poet and his sister rather than in the smoke of London, where Basil was in legal practice.'

'The Judge is related to John Montagu, the Colonial Secretary, I suppose?'

'You might suppose it,' said Mr Chesney, 'but you would be wrong.'

'Different families altogether,' supplied his wife, 'and the Judge is not truly mad at all.'

He was only called so, she explained, on account of his bad temper in the court.

When he first came out to Van Diemen's Land eight or nine years ago, Mr Chesney interrupted, the Judge was only twenty-six, and had in his care a family friend, the wife of Mr Henry Savery, a gentleman convict in the colony, a writer and newspaperman transported for forgery. Savery's wife Eliza had started out from England earlier that year in the *Jessie Lawson*, but the ship was wrecked.

('Yes, it was, poor woman,' murmured Mrs Chesney.)

Mrs Savery and her son being rescued, Chesney went on, they transferred to the *Henry Wellesley* and continued their journey. And no doubt she was in need of comfort after the shipwreck—but Mr Algy Montagu comforted her somewhat *more* than required, apparently . . .

'Whereupon, when they reached Hobarton and Henry Savery heard of it, what does he do but cut his own throat from ear to ear,' interjected Bess triumphantly. 'He was only saved by Doctor Crowther, who sewed his head back on.'

'And after all that, Savery's wife did not stop in Hobarton,' added Chesney. 'Savery being soon arrested for debt, she took the next ship home. You wouldn't do that, Bess, if I was took for debt?'

'Best not try me,' said his wife, pursing her lips at her knitting. 'There's no knowing.'

'At any rate,' said McLeod, 'Savery recovered himself enough to write the colony's first novel, *Quintus Servinton*.'

'Any good?' asked Seymour.

'No,' said McLeod.

—⚌—

Three weeks later the weather began to cool again, and towards the end of February 1838 we resumed our winter clothes. Squalls appeared like bruises on the horizon, sped towards us, passed over the ship in rods of icy rain, and vanished into the distance. The ship heeled on at speed, floor and table at an incline. When it was necessary to move about, which we did less and less, we lurched and staggered.

Rochester's saloon became a nest for Anna. Pillows and blankets were tumbled on the bunks, with clothing, scraps of sewing. I looked for her there to measure a half-sewn bodice, and found Louisa instead, curled up on pillows in the corner of the bunk under the stern window. Her thick golden hair was loose in heavy locks almost to her waist. She looked ten years younger. She had been asleep and she was still rosy with it. There was a half-empty bottle beside her, a jug of water, a glass, and the perfumed scent of gin.

'Harriet. Come in. Shut the door. Talk to me.'

But it was she who talked, her tongue loosened by gin and sleep. Mrs Tench had given her the gin for her terrible monthly pains. I said my stepmother had given it to me for the same reason. The doctor had assured Louisa the spasms would cease when she married, but St John had proved not demanding in That Way and the cramps continued. St John believed that side of marriage was only for the procreation of children, and for three years he had thought it too soon for that—and then they had gone to India, where he judged the climate unhealthy for infants—and now this voyage was a time of abstinence and prayer to prepare him for the work ahead.

'I should like to have a child,' she added. 'It would be a way of passing the time. Did you never want a child, Harriet?'

I told my tale briefly, but the thought of my poor babes overwhelmed me and I had to stop.

'Oh, I'm sorry, Harriet,' she said. 'I don't know why girls are so eager to marry. We imagine only being loved and know nothing of what may be really in store.'

St John was not ordained when she met him. When he decided to take Holy Orders everyone believed he would soon be a Bishop, he was such a scholar. She had imagined living in a pretty cathedral close, like Salisbury or Winchester: never dreamed of India or Van Diemen's Land. In India there had been plenty of servants at least: *dhobi wallahs* and *punkah wallahs*, *ayahs* and *amahs*. In Van Diemen's Land they would all be convicts, which was not a pleasant thought.

—⁂—

I do not remember exactly when I knew Anna and Quigley were lovers, but in the latter part of the voyage she no longer used our cabin or Rochester's. She and the Captain made no secret of their happiness. What I found curious was that in spite of this she seemed unshaken in her determination to find Rowland. Several times I tried to hint that this might be awkward if she remained attached to the Captain, but this was met only with a blank stare of incomprehension, and at last I gave up and determined to wait and see what time would bring.

—⁂—

The ship called at the Cape for re-victualling but we stayed only a few hours in the end, and did not take on supplies, because there had been an outbreak of fever. We had enough salt beef and biscuit for another month, Quigley said, and what we lost in fresh vegetables we would gain in reaching our destination the sooner. We had not long left the port when strong winds drove us south, and a maelstrom of noise and water lashed the ship for a week. Meals became monotonous. 'Fishy' soup—so-called, Seymour said, because it was a matter of doubt whether it contained any fish, though it certainly smelt of it—followed by lobscouse or salmagundi of salt beef. A plague of fleas had erupted. There was much surreptitious scratching. The children were grizzly and the adults irritable. A quarrel arose at dinner one day.

'Governor Arthur was not well liked, I know,' said St John, 'but men who act on principle are frequently maligned. Arthur is a model Christian and family man.'

'That's as may be,' growled Chesney. 'But it's my belief religion is in the heart and not in the knees, as the saying goes. There's Christians of the spirit and Christians of the letter.'

'Colonel Arthur is a devoted Churchman,' Wallace insisted, his beautiful face severe.

Mr Chesney had not attended St John's last two Sunday services.

'Ah well, if it's pious-faced pew-fillers you want, then Arthur is your man,' said Chesney. 'But his greed for money and property is not what the Good Book recommends. I don't call it Christian to wait until a man's in money troubles and then buy up his property at half value. That's what Arthur did to Knopwood.'

He looked around the table to emphasise the point. 'Parson Knopwood loved his little house and garden. Everyone admired "Cottage Green", and the truth is, it lies on prime land above the cove at Hobarton, and Arthur decided he would have it by fair means or foul.'

Seymour said, 'Knopwood was in debt.'

'Mr Knopwood is reputed to be a spendthrift,' agreed St John. 'How else, with a generous stipend and neither wife nor child, could he get in debt? He'd wasted a fortune in England before he went to the colony.'

'You don't know your facts, sir,' replied Chesney immediately. 'It was his father wasted the family money. And I won't deny Knopwood likes his port wine, his giblet pie and roast fowl with a good bread sauce . . . ' (Mrs Chesney groaned), but he'll share them with anyone. As to family, he adopted little Betsey Mack, a foundling, and doted on her twenty years until she were grown and married. When she died of a fever his heart near broke. It's true he's an old-fashioned hunting-and-shooting parson and no saint—but there's one o' them in every second parish in England. Or was, 'til a few years since. Nowadays,' he added, looking hard at Wallace, 'there's a new breed o' hoity-toity dry-as-dusts who fancy they ain't flesh and blood like the rest of us.'

'I understood the foundling girl was Knopwood's own daughter by a convict "housekeeper" . . .'

'Ladies present,' said Quigley mechanically. He was talking to Anna, only half listening to the conversation.

'That's a wicked lie put about by his enemies,' said Chesney with disgust.

'Colonel Arthur is a family man,' repeated Wallace. 'His wife is dutiful . . .'

'Aye, Arthur's a family man!' said Chesney with a wry look. 'If that means handing out public offices to all your kinsfolk! Montagu, Forster, Henry Arthur and the rest.'

'It's a convict settlement. Arthur had to have men he could trust.'

'What do you know of it, sir? You wasn't there! He had to have toadying, fawning, canting, grasping *creatures*!' said Chesney.

'Gentlemen, please!' said the Captain. 'Ladies, let us have some general topic.'

'You had best both save your breath to cool your porridge,' said McLeod. 'Colonel Arthur and his faction have been abused and praised in equal measure, at Home and in the island, but his enemies have never managed to prove anything against him.'

'And why?' cried Chesney. 'Because he has the courts in his pocket, that's why! He is a pence-counting, paper-thumbing, self-serving jack-in-office.'

'The truth is less simple than you admit, Chesney.'

Chesney reddened and swelled, and cracked a walnut so hard it was crushed to fragments. Inclining his head towards Wallace, chin thrust forward, he said, 'If that's your opinion, defend it. The ship is not an ideal field, but I've no objection to stepping on deck to settle the matter. Or ain't you man enough?'

Wallace said, 'A duel? That would be unwise for both of us.'

This was a taunt in itself. Wallace had been surprisingly accurate at the pistol shooting on deck. Chesney had not managed to hit anything. I looked at Louisa. She was speaking to McLeod and seemed unperturbed by the mounting row.

Chesney crumpled his napkin and threw it on the table, 'Why you . . .'

Mrs Chesney clutched her husband's sleeve. 'Chesney! Consider! What are you doing?'

'Wasn't it just last year, Chesney,' asked Quigley conversationally, 'that your friend Gregson fought a duel in Hobarton with Mr Jellicoe over the same matter? Gregson got off scot-free,' he added to Anna, 'but still Jellicoe limps . . .'

Mr Chesney bellowed, 'Scot-free! Gregson is persecuted! I've a letter from my son telling me that Arthur's nephew Henry—a dyed-in-the-wool villain—has insulted Gregson in the public press. Gregson gave the rogue a horsewhipping for it, and was called to court and found guilty, of course! Fined two hundred pounds for thrashing a known rogue! *And* sent to prison for three months! Well, if I had a horsewhip . . . but pistols will do. We'll soon see, Wallace, whether your pair of pretty toys make a decent hole.'

He filled his mouth with more beef and chewed pugnaciously. Mrs Chesney rose to her feet with a fork in one hand, making stabbing motions in the air to punctuate her words.

'That's the last straw on the camel's hat! Shame on you all. How can you sit there, Captain? The Lord knows it would be hard for a widow to survive in Hobarton—which, though I love it, I don't deny is a hard place. Every second finger a fish hook to swindle and cheat a poor body. Chesney, how can you?'

Mr Chesney opened his mouth to reply but made a choking, retching sound, turned blue in the face and collapsed in his chair, clutching at his heart. The doctor was out of his seat and with him in an instant. For a time it seemed we might have two more patients aboard, since Wallace looked more ill than Chesney until the latter recovered. The whole affair was ridiculous, as Seymour said, but it could have ended badly.

—⚉—

On the morning of the thirtieth March the *Adastra* sighted Van Diemen's Land, a smudge on the horizon which appeared almost unchanging hour after hour, but next morning we woke to see high cliffs and a narrow, fluted pillar of rock standing offshore. Seals basked on the rocks at the base and slid easily into the sea at our approach.

We waited for the tide, and towards noon entered the estuary leading up to Hobarton and began beating slowly up-river against a northerly wind. We leaned on the rail to watch the sun shining on wooded hills and pale beaches on both sides of the wide estuary. Smoke rose from a ridge in a lavender-grey haze and we smelt it clearly. Clearings became more frequent, with cabins or huts, and the pilot came aboard and said it had been an uncommonly hot day. A northerly was unusual here, except on rare days in late summer, as now.

Hobart in the distance was a picturesque cove with a great blue mountain behind. Called the Table Mountain at first, Mrs Chesney said, but Mount Wellington now. By the time the sun began to descend behind it, silhouetting its huge purple profile against a salmon-coloured sky, we were close enough to make out Government House, a long whitewashed wooden building among trees. The harbour directly in front of it was busy with two large ships and many small craft and dories. The smell of smoke grew more prominent than ever. Watermen from the shore had surrounded us in small boats, resting on their oars, and suddenly there came a vigorous yell from one of them, followed by a rapid chorus of shouting. This is the last coherent thing I remember before everything became confusion, pandemonium, then a frenzy of action. The fire was aboard our vessel. Piles of corded luggage on deck were in the way, and so were we. Men swung up and down the ratlines shouting. The doctor herded women and children into a group. McLeod and Chesney disappeared. Smoke billowed around us, clouds of choking grey-black, making our eyes water and bringing moments of near-darkness. Natty began to whimper and the girls clung to our skirts and hands.

It was the hideous blaze of 'Thornfield' all over again, more terrifying here because we were trapped. Mrs Tench appeared from the smoke and led us blindly along, every familiar thing obscured. I clung tightly to Polly's hand, my holdall slung across me like a satchel, my other hand gripping the back of Liddy's skirt. My throat filled with suffocating smoke, my heart pounded and leapt. Mrs Chesney and Anna, Liddy and Natty were pushed and pulled into the longboat, which was then dropped down into the smoke. A splash as it reached the water. Polly, Louisa and I waited, then scrambled down by rope ladder into a dory. Mrs Tench and Mrs Farley clambered in after us and the *Adastra* disappeared in engulfing smoke. The rower, a gnarled waterman with a pipe between his teeth, stared grimly as we pulled away.

When we reached the wharf a sailor helped us to where Mrs Chesney, Anna and Louisa had sunk onto the wooden steps of a warehouse. Liddy and Polly clung to us. Natty's little face was swollen from crying. I stood on the top step and tried to see across the water above the crowd, but dizziness and weakness overcame me and I almost fainted down onto the step again. It was twilight now, growing darker every minute, eels of lamplight wriggling on the dark waves, and the sounds of crackling and crashing coming to us with sinister clarity.

Mr Chesney, torn and dirty, came pushing through with another gentleman: their neighbour from Richmond, Mr William Parry. He was in town on a visit after the harvest. Mr Parry's mother lived in town and had offered to take the Chesneys in for the night. I urged him to go. A cold evening breeze had banished the heat and the children should be indoors. Chesney was persuaded at last; he believed Wallace and McLeod were on their way to find us.

After a time, Wallace appeared and tried to comfort Louisa, who began to weep uncontrollably when she saw him. He said the *Adastra* must be towed away from the other shipping and scuttled, and we saw, indeed, that the dark cloud with the orange blaze at its centre was growing smaller as the ship moved back out into the wide river. There were shouts, 'She is going . . .' A general groan and gasp from the watchers. 'Gone . . .'

Down goes the Earl of Bylaugh's library, I thought, the seeds and fabrics and windows and china. I imagined the boxes of books and paper bursting open as they tumbled over and over in the currents and fell to the bottom. Bales of bright fabric unwinding in great slow ribbony folds through the dark water. Seeds and teacups and saucers scattering into the tide; writing slopes and chairs, windows and oaken doors sinking down, down to the seabed. The printing press, the harp and the steam engine emitting last watery sounds as they plunged in an uprush of bubbles, far beyond reach, fathoms deep.

PART TWO

11

EARLY IN THE MORNING OF THE DAY WHEN THE *ADASTRA* SANK, George Boyes was upstairs in Hobart Town's new Treasury building, standing at the window of his office. At about the time the ship entered the estuary fifty miles downriver, he was looking out towards Government House next door. The Vice-Regal residence was still 'the old place' at this time, a whitewashed wooden building set on ten acres along the shore in the centre of the town's cove. Ten acres had seemed enough when Hobart was only a clearing above the beach, dotted with tents and huts. The Governor's cottage had been begun in those early days as a *bungalow* in the Indian style, but by the time the Franklins arrived thirty-four years later, haphazard additions and 'improvements' had turned it into a long barn-like structure two storeys high.

Hasty construction and poor foundations were now causing trouble. A chunk of ceiling had come down during Governor Arthur's final months, narrowly missing him and his secretary and bending an iron poker. Every year the place seemed a little less dignified, more crowded by the busy harbour and burgeoning town. Which might well be a metaphor for the Governor's own situation, thought Boyes wryly.

To some, Hobarton's Government House was irredeemably ugly. Boyes allowed it a certain ramshackle charm, pale among the trees with its red brick chimneys—if seen from the east in a boat offshore, say—and far enough away. The northern aspect was not so bad either; the carriage drive came in there. The shabbiest sides were those adjacent to the town, west and south, where a clutter of kitchens, sculleries, laundries, drying yards, stores, outhouses, stables and offices straggled out to the boundaries.

All this would be demolished when the long-planned new Government House was built, but at present it was a warren of constant activity which never failed to interest Boyes—there was always something in it that made him wonder at the human condition.

He now saw Snachall, Jane Franklin's maid, emerge from between the carriage-house and stables. She walked up to the sentry box, spoke to the guard, and came through in Boyes's direction. Minutes later his clerk came in with a note from Lady Franklin.

It was a printed card, but the words *Lady Franklin requests the pleasure* had been crossed out with a stroke, and the charming message written on the back—yes, it was charming, it always was—conveyed urgency. Jane Franklin 'depended upon him' to bring his wife Mary to dinner that evening. She had 'a particular wish' to see them. No apology for the late summons—she did not say 'summons', but clearly it was. 'An impromptu gathering . . .' The *Neptune* was in. Captain Hasluck and his first lieutenant would dine at Government House with them *en famille*. All of which meant that Boyes must leave early, ride home and warn Mary, order the carriage out and miss his favourite part of the day, a golden late-summer evening in the garden with his family. This northerly would drop by midday. They could have walked down to the bay and taken the dory out for an hour's fishing.

In spite of these regrets, as soon as he and Mary arrived at Government House that night, Boyes admitted to himself that Jane Franklin had been right to send for him. The Montagus were there—and inexplicably, the Maconochies also. Disaster. Montagu had taken a violent dislike to Alexander Maconochie, Sir John Franklin's private secretary, from the day they met. For no clear reason at first, but during the recent Clapperton Affair, Montagu had come to know that Maconochie was advising the Governor to dismiss him, and he now regarded Maconochie with vindictive loathing.

Sir John had not followed his secretary's advice, but Montagu, saved by the skin of his teeth, had sworn he would never meet Maconochie again in public or private. He was known to be a good hater. Throughout the row Maconochie, the mad Scotchman, had displayed the absent-minded good temper of one preoccupied with ideas, yet he must know Montagu had wrecked several careers before now. Whitehall would not tolerate quarrels among its colonial officers. Even Franklin's tenure and reputation might suffer if there was an eruption.

As Boyes led Mary in among the other guests to greet the Franklins, he considered the situation. How had it come about that the two couples were here together? Had the Maconochies come to dinner without warning? It was possible. They lived with their children in a tiny cottage in the grounds of Government House, and were eccentric. But no, Jane's call for help had come this morning. Boyes believed that after a year he could judge her well enough to know this was not an error. It seemed to him far more likely that she had issued the invitations deliberately, believing she could act as a peacemaker.

She was cursed with a regrettable urge to do good, a tendency to *embroil* herself in matters better left alone, a passionate eagerness for life which she expected everyone to share. An elderly gentleman had once told her admiringly that the Greeks have a word for it: *kefi*. Boyes did not like this story. The Greeks who sprang to his mind were Helen of Troy, Antigone, Electra, Clytemnestra: women who caused a great deal of trouble to their friends and relations.

They were dining *en famille*, as Lady Franklin had said in her note: not in the dining room but on a long section of broad enclosed verandah looking out across an informal garden to the harbour. This verandah had been open and almost unused while Colonel Arthur was governor. Neither he nor his wife Eliza had time for the picturesque. He kept an unsleeping eye on his wicked kingdom, she was busy with her hive of children. But when Jane Franklin first saw it, in spite of the weather that day, which was frightful, she was seized, she told Boyes, by the memory of delightful terraces in the Mediterranean looking down on sunny little ports. The verandah would be perfect for summer gatherings. Her husband would like to drink his tea—or something stronger—in contemplation of the shipping.

It was one of her first mistakes about Hobarton. She soon discovered the afternoon sea breeze, which whirled up tablecloths, needlework, papers and hair and drove the ladies indoors. Not easily beaten, she had the verandah enclosed with three-quarter-length windows, and plants in tubs brought in to give the air of a conservatory.

'Family' was always a generous term with the Franklins, and there were rarely less than a dozen sitting down to dine. Tonight, Eleanor Franklin, Sir John's daughter by his first wife, sat beside her governess Miss Williamson, an elderly, somewhat crotchety, spinster. Ella was fourteen and 'difficult'. Miss Williamson was close enough to say a quiet word or put out a restraining hand. It was sometimes enough. The child's face was almost laughably like her father's, round and plump-cheeked, but it was inclined to carry a scowl quite foreign to John Franklin.

Sophy Cracroft was there, but not her cousin Mary, who was staying at New Town with Mrs Price, her fiancée's mother. Sophy was flirting as usual with Sir John's aide, the Honourable Henry Elliot. He and Sophy played at mutual interest, but each knew perfectly well that when Henry chose a bride it would be in England under the watchful eye of his father, Lord Minto—and it would be someone a good deal more eligible than Sophy, who possessed neither fortune nor rank. This might have been painful for the girl, but Boyes and his wife had watched Miss Cracroft and decided privately that for all her flirting she did not want a husband, and regarded the young men who passed through with spinsterish detachment. 'Not the marrying kind?' Mary suggested. And yet Sophy had something, they agreed. Not beauty but intelligence, and a kind of inward smouldering which a man might easily misinterpret as readiness for physical passion. Henry

Elliot, a family friend, was young, witty, handsome and amiable, and thus a safe and useful partner, Mary argued.

'Family', for Lady Franklin, also meant anyone who had come out on the *Fairlie* with them; thus the Maconochies, Archdeacon Hutchins, and another strange Scotchman, the cowherd from Leith, Mr John Hepburn, one of Sir John's crewmen in the Arctic on his early, near fatal journey. Visiting naval officers or scientists, too, were 'family', no matter what their nationality. Tonight there was no language barrier; Captain Hasluck and his first lieutenant were English. Jane Franklin's French was fluent, but during her travels she had made herself clearly understood to Italians, Turks, Egyptians, Arabs, Greeks, Russians, Armenians and Americans.

As soon as they sat at table, Sophy, on Boyes's left, gave him a histrionic look and began to brief him in a series of desperate asides. He was right. Aunt had convinced herself that a Franklin family dinner would dispel Montagu's enmity against Maconochie, but she had been seized by terrible doubts as the evening approached. A lost cause, Boyes thought. It only remained to see what form the explosion would take and how the damage might be contained.

The pea and ham soup was tense but calm. Montagu and Maconochie had been placed as far from each other as possible. Sophy began to talk about the new young Queen and Lord Melbourne, and Lord Melbourne's wicked mad wife, and their sad mad son, while all the time watching the table nervously. By the second remove Boyes had begun to think he was mistaken. The evening might pass quietly after all. Montagu seemed content to be visibly contemptuous. Mary Boyes was on his left and Lady Franklin on his right; he was responding to their attempts at conversation with cold monosyllables. With any luck he might hesitate to let factional politics show in front of the visiting naval officers. You could never tell who might come to hear of it in London.

On Boyes's right was Mary Maconochie, silent, darting hostile glances at Montagu across the table. Her husband was eating his fish with untroubled enjoyment and lecturing Miss Williamson, using the prongs of a fork to draw on the tablecloth. Lady Franklin spoke across a pause in which Maconochie's accent and the clink of cutlery were the loudest sounds in the world.

'Captain Hasluck has been admiring our harbour,' she told her husband.

Sir John nodded, smiling. 'A great asset,' he said in his calm, slow way. 'A deep-water harbour at the end of the main street. Indeed, a valuable asset.'

'Is the interior of the island accessible, sir?' asked Hasluck. 'Does agriculture extend far?'

'North and east, yes. Handsome properties. You would be astonished,' Sir John rumbled on. 'But to west and south, no. Impossible. Which is to say, r-rugged . . .'

'Mountainous, from the charts, sir?' said Hasluck. He sensed a growing uneasiness in the air but laboured on.

'M-m-m, yes,' said Sir John, nodding. 'But of great b-beauty. Or so we hear. We hope to make a tour in that region next spring, don't we, m'dear?'

'There is a road then, sir?'

'No, no road,' Sir John laughed. 'The surveyors are carving a track, and if necessary we shall make our own. Explorers, eh?'

'A carriage road runs up through the centre of the island,' said Lady Franklin. 'From Hobarton here, to Launceston at Port Dalrymple in the north. Some enterprising gentlemen from there have recently begun to make a settlement across the Bass Strait at Port Phillip on the mainland of New Holland. The town is to be named for Lord Melbourne.'

'And if you're minded, Hasluck,' added Sir John, 'to take a landsman's view while you're here (ha! ha!), Mr Cox's coach makes the journey up twice a week. Pretty countryside. Said to resemble the L-lake District at Home.'

'You will understand, Captain Hasluck,' Lady Franklin leant forward, spoke urgently, 'how much we wish to advance commerce between south and north here. The chief impediment at present lies in fording the Derwent River. Hobarton is on the southern shore, as you see. The river near the town here is far too wide to bridge, and therefore the coach must travel twenty miles upriver to Black Snake to cross where it is narrower. At present this is accomplished by ferry, but there have been tragic accidents. A causeway and bridge are in building, and the completion will be a great thing. It is one of Colonel Arthur's valuable schemes—and Mr Montagu, of course,' she added hastily, 'has pursued it since the Colonel's departure.'

Montagu looked at her and inclined his head a contemptuous inch. Lady Franklin flushed. Mrs Maconochie gave Montagu a basilisk stare and said loudly, 'Of course, Captain Hasluck, when the crossing is finished, the land beyond the river will increase greatly in value. Do you not own a very vast piece of land there, Mr Montagu?'

Boyes said quickly, 'Further up beyond the causeway there's another pleasant hamlet. Its official name is Elizabeth Town but the inhabitants call it New Norfolk, many having come from Norfolk Island when that was resumed for a penal settlement. Our Government cottage and farm is at New Norfolk. We call it His Excellency's "country seat".'

'We *laughingly* call it that,' explained Jane Franklin, following his lead. 'But do not imagine a Petit Trianon or anything of that sort, Captain. The place is neglected and a little too thoroughly *en plein air*. The wind whistles through it.'

'But it sits so picturesquely by the river, my lady?' said Henry Elliot. 'A little paradise in my view.'

'Oh, I grant you, Henry, the sweetest spot imaginable. A perfect refuge from civilisation.'

Maconochie, hearing this last remark, called cheerfully across the table some Latin tag about civilisation and rustication, which he then translated into impenetrable Scottish-English, blank to the growing hostility. Boyes and Elliot both began to speak but paused to give way to each other. Mrs Maconochie's voice drove harshly through.

'As to that, my dear, a new scene of civilisation would be well enough. But at present Van Diemen's Land is nothing but a little stage where the tragedy of misused power is played out every day.'

'Have you seen our new theatre, Hasluck?' asked Henry Elliot. 'We have Mrs Robinson in *The Bandit of the Rhine* this season, disguised as a . . .'

'Disguised!' cried Mrs Maconochie in quivering tones. 'There are venomous reptiles in this island disguised as gentlemen. There are wolves in sheep's clothing. There are TOADS of loathsome complexion!'

Montagu threw down his napkin, pushed back his chair and made to rise, saying distinctly, 'Lamentable, hardly unexpected . . . madwoman . . . want of breeding . . .' but Captain Hasluck was now also on his feet and speaking urgently. The alarm of his words made itself felt on the whole company, and as he spoke Eleanor Franklin also rose, with a sharp cry of, 'Oh, look!'

'Your Excellency, Lady Franklin, pray excuse me,' said Hasluck. 'I believe there is a brig afire in the harbour. If I am not mistaken she lies directly between the *Neptune* and the *Calcutta*. The *Calcutta* has her masts unstepped and cannot move. May I beg your permission, sir, to go to my ship? My lady, will you excuse us?'

Eleanor Franklin called, 'Oh do look, Papa! Such fountains! They have set the pumps. What ship is she?'

Elaborate consternation, a pantomime babble of relief. Lady Franklin rose and led a clustering at the windows so that Sir John and their guests could watch the burning vessel. Eleanor Franklin prattled on and for once was not reproved. Jane Franklin rang the bell for a telescope. Hasluck and his lieutenant left with Henry Elliot, who was asked to return to explain what was happening. Mutton would be kept for him, said Lady Franklin. And rhubarb tart.

As Mrs Maconochie rose trembling from the table, Boyes upset a glass of wine into her lap. Her anger was already passing into furious wild sobs. She gave a gasp and wail, holding out her skirts. Boyes, apologising, led her from the room. Her husband would have stayed, but Mary Boyes took him firmly by the arm and followed them. The party gradually settled. Boyes and Mary returned but the Maconochies did not. Nobody mentioned them. It grew dark. The burning ship could be seen heading out into the river, towed by the new steam tug. The ladies left the gentlemen to their port.

Henry Elliot returned soon after the gentlemen had rejoined the ladies in the drawing room. Sophy was at the pianoforte playing a tricky scherzo. She knew everyone expected her to stop, and indeed, would have been glad to. She knew she did not play particularly well, and was struggling with four sharps, which for some reason she always found more difficult than four flats, but a sense of duty made her persist through the repeat. When at last she finished, Henry told them the ship was the *Adastra*, Master Captain Quigley, and her voyage a curious one altogether, apparently. There had been a deathbed marriage and the strange return to health of a beautiful Creole madwoman.

It was just the kind of story to catch Lady Franklin's attention, to penetrate the violent throbbing of the headache beginning to grip her. She was subject to these attacks, usually after high emotion. She felt now the familiar tightness in her brain, the slow onset of nausea, the flickering rim of lights beginning to close off her vision from the edges, the first deep pain. She longed for her visitors to be gone so that she might fall into silence and darkness with fifteen perhaps thirty-five perhaps sixty ruby drops of laudanum in a glass of water. With an odd fixed smile she endured farewells and thanks.

When at last she could begin to make her way upstairs, half-blindly now, she stopped and turned. She asked Henry Elliot to see that the Captain of the *Adastra* and his passengers received invitations to the formal reception for the *Neptune* a few days hence. Sir John would like to hear more about the voyage of the lost ship.

12

OUR FIRST NIGHT IN THE COLONY—OR WHAT REMAINED OF THE
night—was spent at the Hope and Anchor Inn, merely because it was
barely two hundred yards from the wharf, the nearest respectable
hostelry, said McLeod. Although all the inn's conveyances had long
since been retired for the night, he persuaded them to rouse a groom
and send a wagonette to fetch Anna, Louisa and me. The gentlemen
would walk. McLeod and Quigley had found us as the entertaining
spectacle came to an end and the crowd began to disperse. James
Seymour was at the hospital with an injured crewman.

I was worried about Anna. She was still not strong, and even
Louisa and I were near collapsing with shock and weariness. But
Anna revived at the sight of Quigley, though his face and clothes were
disfigured with soot. When the wagonette arrived we summoned our
last desperate energies and rose to mount into it, but as Louisa began
to follow Anna, a pony trap approached from the other direction and
drew up alongside us. During the evening St John had managed to
send a note to Archdeacon Hutchins, and here was a servant with
orders to take the Wallaces to the clergyman's house.

It was thus only Anna and I, Quigley and McLeod who entered
the inn—just as a single bell began tolling. A death knell for the
Adastra, I thought, but McLeod said it was the curfew. Convict-assigned

servants must not be in the streets after this time, eleven o'clock. So early! I felt whole days and nights had passed since we had scrambled from the ship. The innkeeper's wife showed a lively interest in the evening's drama. I responded as well as I could, tired to the bone and stifling an impulse towards manic laughter as I looked about me. Twelve thousand perilous miles we had come—to this. It might have been any down-at-heel English coaching-inn from Land's End to John O'Groats.

The smell of stale beer and roast meat filled the entry, and as we went to climb the stairs we passed the door of a loud smoky taproom. Sporting prints hung on the staircase; brown oil-cloth and drugget covered the floors; there was a long-case clock on the landing. Stopped, of course. The cheap ewer and basin in our room came from an English pottery, the dented pewter might have belonged to the George Inn at Hay. What else had I expected? I don't know. The familiarity should have been comforting, but I felt obscurely deceived, caught in an illusion as deep as life. As if all these months we had been going nowhere.

I lay awake, my mind running uselessly like a mouse on a tread-mill. The room was strangely motionless after the ship; the taproom downstairs continued noisy. There were other sounds too, familiar yet strange, for it was months since we'd heard them; a town clock somewhere rang the hours and quarters, dogs barked and a rooster crowed although it was far from dawn. I prayed, dropped in and out of turbulent dreams. A bell began ringing and the stables of the inn came alive with footsteps and whistling. The jangle and whicker of horses came next, and then bells and more bells. From the prison up in Campbell Street near the Scotch Church, the maidservant said when she came with hot water.

Anna was slow to wake and I was reluctant to urge her, but we managed to meet Quigley, Seymour and McLeod for a late breakfast in a private back parlour where everything except the greasy fried eggs was brown. Quigley had been out early. The fire had arisen from the combustion of McLeod's paper, he said, which had probably become damp during the voyage, heating as it began to rot. The insurance would pay, but there was no Lloyd's agent in Hobart. He must go to New South Wales to file the insurance and meet his co-owner of the *Adastra*, who was also there. He was worried for his crew, stranded here without pay or work. He would take most of them with him on the *Marian Watson*, leaving Hobarton for New South Wales in four days. He wanted us to go too: to abandon the search for Rowland.

'What can Captain Booth tell you that will be to anyone's advantage?' he argued, speaking to Anna, glancing at me. 'Rowland Rochester is dead by all accounts. And if not, how long are you to look for him? Winter is coming. Sydney is warmer in winter, Anna. You will prefer it. And if you do find Rochester he may not thank you. Let sleeping dogs lie, eh? What do you say, m'dear?'

Similar thoughts had occupied me during the night. The search for Rowland, which had seemed so reasonable in the presence of Jane and Rochester, those two inspired romantics, now began to look like mere folly. The Captain's argument was tempting, except that I would have to explain our decision to Jane and Rochester at some future time. In any event, Anna would have none of it. Oblivious to complications, or apparently so, she smiled and said we would find Rowland first—and then go to Sydney. I found it hard to understand why she should still wish to find Rowland when she seemed so attached to Quigley, but we could not change her mind. In the end it was agreed that she and I would wait in Hobart Town until he returned.

'Four weeks,' he said. The *Marian Watson* was the only ship regularly making the run to Sydney and back, generally in that time. 'Six at most. Do what you can in four weeks,' he said to me. If he could bring back another ship, we would leave for England. Otherwise, well, it would depend . . .

Mr Chesney came in cock-a-hoop, brushing aside the loss of his cargo. Unfortunate, yes, but it was insured, and nothing compared to the good news he'd just learned. The summer harvest across the island had fetched unheard-of prices, most of it sold to the new settlement at Port Phillip, or Melbourne, where everything was wanted. Potatoes had fetched twenty pounds the ton! Chesney could not wait to discover what profit his son had made. The Chesneys' neighbours, whose mother had taken them in last night, were returning to Richmond today with an empty cart. With no cargo to wait for now, Chesney was eager to go with them.

'Port Phillip is barren as a desert,' he said with satisfaction. 'Lieutenant Collins tried to settle there thirty years a'gone and gave it up. If Fawlkner and his lads are to stay there, they'll need our crops forever and a day. A ready-made market on our doorstep!'

And Chesney's friend Mr Thomas Gregson was released from prison. The new Governor had accepted a petition against the sentence. Ha! A blow to the Arthur faction! If this was Sir John Franklin showing his colours, they suited old Chesney. Arthur gone, a benevolent new Governor in place, and ready markets for the crops. Lord! A new golden age at hand. Nowt to do but fill your pockets.

Our sea legs buckling, we walked slowly down to the Wharf again with Chesney to say our farewells, only to find there was an hour to wait while the ferry was loaded. Mrs Chesney had taken Liddy and the children along to the warehouses, or godowns, or *ghauts* as Louisa would say, at the other end of the cove, but Anna could not walk so far. We sat waiting on two kitchen chairs, which providentially formed part of the freight surrounding us: laden hand-carts, chicken coops, crates and boxes, garden tools, a goat. Chesney talked to anyone who came within range. The weather was more summer than autumn, warm and sunny. Dazzling water, layers of blue hills along the opposite shore fading downriver, where a white lighthouse shone on a rocky outcrop.

To me the whole scene resembled a stage set, like the inn. 'An English Wharf', with colours falsely bright because the sun was so strong. Not really England, nobody fooled for a minute, everyone accepting the counterfeit as they do in the theatre. Behind us, at the back of the town, Mount Wellington loomed like painted scenery from a different play altogether, some Gothic drama.

Mrs Chesney's returning party became visible while still some way off. She had acquired a new basket and several brown-paper parcels; a mop; a bucket; and two gentlemen. One of these, a portly figure pacing beside her in clerical black, proved to be Mr Aislabie, the vicar at Richmond, also waiting for the ferry. The other, a shabbier, laughing man, carried Natty on his shoulders, bending to talk to shy Liddy. He was forty perhaps, sturdy and muscular-looking in a brown jacket, the pockets sagging because they evidently carried many odds and ends. His black hair was too long, hanging in loose waves and curls that lifted in the breeze because Natty had seized his hat. He wore several days' growth of beard.

'This is Mr Bergman,' said Bess Chesney, 'the surveyor we spoke of on the ship. I have been asking him whether he has heard of Mr Rowland Rochester but he thinks not.'

'I am not in a fit state for introductions,' said Bergman with a brown grin. He swung Natty to the ground, retrieved his hat and passed his hand across the dark stubble on his chin. 'I come from two weeks of camping at the Huon River, surveying Lady Franklin's new settlement. I have hardly been an hour off the cutter.'

'He has come out of his way to help,' Bess Chesney explained. 'I'm much obliged, Mr Bergman.'

He said a few sympathetic words about the loss of the *Adastra* before bowing and striding away. His pleasant face might be Jewish, I thought—or not, but it was gypsyish, clever-looking.

Anna and I parted from the Chesneys with embraces and tears, promising to visit them at 'Kenton' before we quitted the island, as they demanded a hundred times.

—⟡—

The Derwent Bank was as English as the inn; mahogany and brass, the smell of beeswax polish and money. While I waited with St John Wallace in the reverent hush—Anna chose to stay at the inn, Louisa was still recovering at the Archdeacon's—I became aware of just how shabby I was. An elderly clerk took our draft away to some *sanctum sanctorum* and returned to say the Bank would cash it at a discount of fifty percent. Faced with my astonishment, he acknowledged kindly that it was a high rate, but the signatory, Mr Edward Rochester, was in failing health. (This was my first example of the swift rumour mill of Van Diemen's Land.) If Mr Rochester should not reach England alive—which Heaven forbid, of course—the bank might incur 'prolonged expense in securing its equity'.

'Is fifty percent legal?' I protested. 'In England the rate is set at four percent to prevent usury. This colony follows the laws of England, does it not?'

The clerk was happy to explain, with a broad condescending smile. 'The Usury Laws are one of the few exceptions here to the law of England. In a new colony it is important to encourage investors by affording them the opportunity of making higher gains.' I retrieved the draft, not quite snatching. I would spend my own money and ask for reimbursement from Jane and Rochester when we reached England again. It did cross my mind that Rochester might be dead and Jane in straitened circumstances, but being angry at the bank's rapacity, I brushed the thought aside.

St John looked at me questioningly but did not interfere. When we emerged from the bank he asked how we would manage and seemed satisfied when I explained. I returned to the inn, and when Anna was ready we walked slowly to a dressmaker's in Elizabeth Street—again chosen only because it was close. Luck was with us. The pretty young assistant was tiny, neat, dark, French, and aghast at our sad sartorial state. She fetched the proprietress, Madame Delage, a Scotchwoman married to a Frenchman who had escaped to Edinburgh in the Terror. We heard the story during the next several hours of choosing and fitting. Monsieur Delage owned the draper's and haberdasher's shop adjoining his wife's premises; the young assistant was his niece; 'a wee marvel,' said Madame. While Anna was being fitted I crossed the road to a stationer's for the other necessities of life: pen and ink, pencils, writing paper and sketchbook.

It makes me smile to recall the gowns we chose that day, ridiculous now, but at the time I thought Anna looked like Spanish royalty in her ruby satinette. A lavender-and-yellow Madras wanted letting out; two more walking-costumes would be made up from pattern books. Anna refused to wear white because her mother had always worn it, and black because Christophine thought it unlucky. I chose three skirts for myself: dove-grey, blue-grey and black, with four matching bodices. And so to stays, petticoats, small linen, nightgowns, gloves, stockings, combs, hairbrushes, handkerchiefs, silk flowers, ribbons, fans . . .

With an eye on the mounting cost I tried gently to curb Anna's childlike desire for everything she saw, but still the total came to one hundred and eighty-six pounds eight shillings and threepence halfpenny. Shoes and boots we bought afterwards at a nearby cobbler's; another forty-three guineas. I kept reminding myself that our return passages would be paid by the insurance, and that we would spend nothing once we were aboard ship, bound for Home again. In the meantime we must look our parts: a well-to-do invalid widow and her meek dove-grey companion.

I was puzzled by Madame's pleasure when I paid with sterling, but later discovered it was commonplace in the colony to settle only a fraction of any bill, putting the rest on account. Or to pay with a mixture of the curious local currency: Spanish dollars, Indian rupees, specie from New South Wales, or the four-pound notes issued by the Van Diemen's Land Bank and engraved by a convict artist.

—✺—

My views of Montagu are coloured by what happened later, of course, and I don't claim to be unprejudiced, but I detected no whiff of sulphur about him that day. I'd expected a bluff military man, all ruddy nose and side-whiskers, but Montagu was as sleek as an otter, urbane and charming. As he murmured about the loss of the *Adastra*, I felt our value being weighed in his private balance, reckoned down to the last jot and tittle. He made me think of a plover, or peewit, one of those neat grey, black and white birds that look like gentlemen pacing gravely forward with their hands behind their backs. Much later I remembered how fierce plovers can be, how they protect their territory by swooping to attack the heads of their enemies.

'Unfortunately,' Montagu's smile was regretful, 'my clerks find no record of a Mr Rowland Rochester in the colony. The Doctor and Mr McLeod will have told you, Mrs Rochester, that we keep very precise records, but there is nothing.'

Anna and I had come to the Colonial Office with St John Wallace, Doctor Seymour and McLeod. St John thought it would be useful to have Seymour and McLeod with us, since they knew Montagu and the colony, and would have a better grasp of any names and places the Colonial Secretary might mention.

Now Montagu gave the shadow of a shrug. 'Not a few who come to the colonies are—how shall I put it—seeking to begin afresh? Many continue to New South Wales, of course.'

'We are advised Captain Booth may know something of the matter?' said McLeod.

'The events you refer to took place many years ago. Which of us can trust our recollections over such a time?' Montagu smiled broadly, secure, I supposed, in his own reputation for an infallible memory.

'Certainly you could go down to see Captain Booth,' he added, 'if you consider it worthwhile. A permit could be arranged.' He turned to Anna again. 'There can be no unauthorised visits to the peninsula, Mrs Rochester, as you will readily understand. Only felons of the worst description and most desperate character are sent to Port Arthur. They are the smallest proportion of convicts arriving—and reoffenders, of course. Nine-tenths of transportees are assigned as domestic servants, or to work on roads and buildings, or in Government offices.'

'I believe Mrs Rochester is eager to learn whatever Captain Booth can tell us,' said McLeod. 'We would be obliged to you, sir, for a permit.'

'Very well. I believe your time will be wasted, frankly, but you must be the judge, of course. It should not take more than a few weeks. How long are you in the island?'

'A few *weeks?*' McLeod was clearly surprised. He looked at Seymour and was about to speak again when the door was flung open without a knock and two gentlemen came in. The first was what I had expected Montagu to be: big, florid, heavy-breathing. He was startlingly ugly yet dressed like a fashion plate. A toad in a frock coat. His eyes protruded, oyster-like, from a grey pouchy face. His nose was a 'colonial strawberry', bulbous and purplish.

'John, I must speak with you,' he said abruptly to Montagu.

'May I present Mr Matthew Forster, our Chief Police Magistrate,' said Montagu, rising. His tone suggested he disliked the unceremonious intrusion, but Forster took no notice. 'And Mr John Price, our Assistant Chief Police Magistrate.'

Price was not much beyond thirty, taller and more pleasant in appearance than Forster, but with the same arrogance. He wore a monocle and Forster a lorgnette. The sight of two men staring thus through eyeglasses might have been humorous, but something about these two stifled any impulse to laugh. They quizzed Anna and me with careless insolence. Montagu said he believed he would have the pleasure of seeing us again at Lady Franklin's reception for the *Neptune*. He must have rung a bell, for an aide appeared and we were smiled out before we knew it.

—⚬—

The invitation to the reception was unexpected. I had not imagined joining the social life of the colony. Left to myself I would have sent apologies, but Anna gazed at the pasteboard like a castaway seeing a ship, and Seymour said that to have any chance of finding Rowland we must enter the proper circles.

McLeod left for Richmond to see his friend Dr Ross, intending to return for the reception. James Seymour had affairs of his own, and Quigley, waiting to leave for Sydney, came and went, busy with arrangements for his crew. Anna and I moved from the Hope and Anchor to lodgings in a large stone cottage on Battery Point. Mrs Groundwater, the landlady, was an Orkney woman, her lilting voice carrying the attractive Scotch-Welsh modulations of her birthplace, with many odd words and phrases. Her husband and son were whalers, away at sea two years at a time. She let by the quarter only, which meant we would lose money if we left early, but we were the sole guests, the house was clean and quiet, and I was content. We had a bedroom each with a small sitting room between us: three guineas a week with breakfast and dinner, washing and coals extra.

Anna had never dealt with money and refused to begin. At 'Coulibri', when she was a child, everything was simply there: clothes, food, servants—that was how she preferred it. There had been no need for money at the convent, nor while she was with the Rochesters. Even so, I insisted on showing her where I had put the unused bank draft and what remained of my funds. If anything should happen to me she must know where to find it. She was more interested in unpacking the altered costume just delivered. With it came a note from McLeod. His friend Dr Ross being gravely ill, he could not return for the reception.

—⚅—

On the given night we joined a queue of men and women most variously arrayed, in every style from last-century court dress to the latest fashions and the barely formal. As our names were announced we curtsied past the official party, propelled swiftly onward by the queue behind us. Sir John looked like an amiable bear in naval evening dress, the crown of his head bald, a crescent of dark little curls at ear level. Lady Franklin, small and neat beside him, made me think of Jane Eyre as she might be in another twenty-five years; there was the same cool intelligent appraisal, the feeling of energy suppressed.

Anna had hoped for dancing, but although an ensemble was playing, the object seemed to be merely to form groups and talk. St John Wallace and Louisa appeared with Mr Hutchins, the Archdeacon, who was younger than I had expected, about my own age, with a broad smiling face and square jaw. He introduced Mr Phillip Palmer, the Rural Dean, one of those clergymen whose stomach precedes them, and Palmer's wife, another Harriet, and her sister Rachel Owen, recently arrived from Wales. They were very Welsh, the Owen ladies, with lilting soft accents. The accents on all sides struck me forcibly: Scots, Welsh, Irish, and so many regional English intonations.

'. . . only two servants at the Archdeacon's house, both convicts,' Louisa was saying in an undertone, when a stir came in the crowd near us and the official party came through the gathering, shaking hands and pausing to speak briefly. Sir John, with his wife and a young male aide, stopped abruptly when he came to us.

'Ah, Quigley. Some time since we've met. And now this loss. Terrible. I am sorry for it,' Sir John rumbled.

'Thank you, sir.'

'Deeply affecting sight, ship ablaze. Saw it many times in the war, of course. Never fails to strike me to the heart.'

'Thank you, sir.'

'She was with Lloyd's? A1?'

'Yes, sir, she was.'

'I believe you must go to New South Wales. We have no Lloyd's agent here, have we, Henry?' he said to the young aide.

'No, sir.'

'But your greatest difficulty, you know, Quigley, will be in finding another command. Mm, yes. Shipbuilding grows apace here, but is still in its infancy. And most vessels arriving have a full complement of officers. Too many of us about since the war.' He laughed his comfortable laugh. 'We are items at a discount, we old salts.'

Lady Franklin turned to us. She was not dressed in high fashion except for her light brown hair, pulled up into a knot in the French way, with a loose curl each side.

'You have felt no ill effects, I hope, Mrs Rochester, from your evening in the cold?'

Her voice, unexpectedly low and husky yet precise and clear, was part of her charm. Anna smiled her broad smile, curtsied, did not speak.

'I believe you are come in search of your husband's grave?' Jane Franklin persisted. 'I know I would feel as you do. Most women could not rest until they learned the circumstances of their husband's death.'

'He is not dead.' This flat utterance from Anna was a stone cast into the calm waters of social exchange. 'If he was dead I would feel it. I would know.'

Jane Franklin was visibly affected. Two decades later she would repeat almost the same words when the Admiralty told her Franklin was to be declared lost. If she had heard a prophecy of it she could not have looked more shaken.

'But, I understood . . .' she said.

James Seymour interposed, 'It is not easy for Mrs Rochester to believe, Lady Franklin. Although her husband's death occurred more than a decade ago, it is hardly six weeks since . . . Mrs Rochester's health allowed her to be told of it.'

Anna smiled. 'He is not dead,' she repeated almost gaily.

Now it had become merely an awkward moment and Jane Franklin was composed.

'You are going down to the peninsula to see Captain Booth?' she smiled at me. 'Please give him my kind regards. We are so fond of him. And the Lemprieres—delightful.'

'It seems there may be some delay, Lady Franklin,' I said. 'The permit may take several weeks, we understand.'

'Not generally,' she said, frowning. 'I don't see why. Miss Cracroft goes down on Tuesday in the *Vansittart* with Miss Drewitt. Why do you not go with them? Would you arrange it, Henry?' She spoke to the young aide again, ignoring our thanks and adding, 'Leave your cards when you return, bring me news of our friends.'

She took her husband's arm, beginning to steer him towards the next group. He parted reluctantly from Quigley and the officers of the *Neptune*, by now deep in talk of euphroes, knees, and guttered shrattnels.

'You are like me, Quigley,' Sir John said. 'We are sailors. Nothing else will do for us. "The sea has soaked our hearts through." Do you know that line? It is said of Ulysses in "Chapman's Homer", you know. "The sea had soaked his heart through." My wife read it to me and it struck me so deeply I have never forgot it.'

Later that night Quigley made his adieux with Anna, and at dawn sailed for New South Wales. The following day she asked me where Edward was and when he would return.

I had been startled by Lady Franklin's offer of help. Why take any trouble for perfect strangers? Later I understood her as one of those to whom any knot or problem is irresistible, finding solutions a matter of satisfaction.

13

WE STARTED FOR PORT ARTHUR AT DAWN; THE AIR SHARP COLD, the wide river a shining mirror of dark hills and streaked, salmon-pink sky. By the time the waterman had rowed us out to the *Vansittart*, a light breeze was ploughing the image into furrows. I would have liked to stay on deck, but we were ushered down into the cabin. Plain Miss Cracroft and her pretty friend Miss Drewitt sat facing Anna and me.

Sophy Cracroft said she believed it would be calm, but whether or not, she always chewed a square of seaweed against *mal de mer*. It was effective on account of the affinity of elements, she added. She offered the little box to her friend and to Anna, who both declined. I accepted and then struggled to get my hand out of my new tight glove while Miss Cracroft waited not quite patiently: a young lady of strong opinions who would not suffer fools gladly. The pastille was dark and salty like liquorice. Miss Drewitt stifled yawns behind her gloved hand.

The *Vansittart* shook out more sail and picked up the wind. Miss Cracroft explained that her visit to the peninsula was to condole with Mrs Cart, the wife of the Superintendent of Point Puer, the boys' prison at Port Arthur. The Carts' baby, Edward, a beautiful child, had accidentally been given four grains of opium last week instead of a quarter of a grain. He had fallen into convulsions and died. Miss

Drewitt was to stay a month with her sister, whose husband was an officer at the Wedge Bay outstation. Through the porthole I watched the morning unfold into one of those translucent autumn days I came to know as so frequent in the island. Anna's face showed its usual unreadable repose. I wondered whether, like me, she had misgivings. I was feeling slightly sick and hoping Captain Booth would tell us Rowland Rochester was dead.

Quigley had said the *Vansittart* would probably take us only as far as Norfolk Bay, where Booth's new convict railway would carry us the further four miles overland down the peninsula into Port Arthur. But Sophy said no, not this time. She had travelled on the railway before and had not enjoyed the experience.

'A wooden box on wheels with *no* hood or covering, propelled by convicts *panting* alongside and *leaping* up to rest on a side-peg each time we *hurtled* down some *precipitious* slope. Like the most *violent switchback ride*. I was certain we should be *hurled* out on our heads, or *dashed* to pieces against a *tree* . . .'

To spare her a repetition of this, the weather being fine, the *Vansittart* would take us all the way round the southern cape and into the bay at Port Arthur.

On reaching this anchorage we could see no settlement, only heavily wooded arms of land and a small island, cleared of vegetation but for a few trees at the margins of the water. The Isle of the Dead, Sophy explained, lying in the bay between us and Port Arthur. As its name suggested, it was now a graveyard. Military and civilian officers and their families were buried with headstones; convicts were laid anonymously in the soil.

A whale boat approached, with six men at the oars and a military officer in the stern. As it made fast alongside, the officer rose and climbed nimbly up to the *Vansittart*'s deck to introduce himself: Commandant Booth. The military title had not suggested this—a thin, youngish man, joking with Sophy about her dislike of his railway. The convicts looked like any wharfingers except for their yellow and grey woollen clothing. I would have liked to study their faces, but after one glance kept my eyes on the view or on their tattooed brown hands pulling the oars.

Port Arthur was a miniature version of Hobart in a far smaller cove. Only a handful of these whitewashed buildings were cottages, the others being wooden workshops and huts, barracks, a stockade and a hospital. Only two buildings were of stone: a powder magazine like a squat little crenellated tower, and, under scaffolding, a Church up the slope at the back of the clearing.

We set off walking towards a hillside cottage set slightly apart from the rest of the settlement. Anna could make only slow progress, leaning on Booth's arm, and we stopped when she cried suddenly, 'Ajoupa!' and pointed at the little house. It had green wooden shutters, or *jalousies*, and an enclosed verandah on three sides. A kitchen garden lay on one side in a state of late summer decline. Behind and above, on the crest of the hill, was the signal tower, a mast with a yardarm and flags.

Booth seemed taken aback.

'I haven't heard that word since I left the Indies,' he said. 'This is the Commandant's Cottage, Mrs Rochester, my humble abode. But it does resemble an *ajoupa*. Nobody has remarked on it before. Perhaps the idea was in my mind when I had the verandah and shutters added.'

His parlour was a bachelor's room, four comfortable chairs on an India rug by the fire, a round table and a desk piled with papers, ledgers, drawing instruments, rocks and a gunpowder flask. The Lemprieres were there to greet us. Charlotte Lempriere, a smiling, friendly woman, showed us the offices, and when we returned to the parlour she presided over making the tea. Her husband thanked us for the provisions we'd brought and invited us to dine with them that night. Booth and Sophy Cracroft departed again for the Carts' cottage at Point Puer in the next bay, while Charlotte took us down the hill to our quarters at the 'Museum'. Miss Drewitt would stay with us for the night and travel on to Wedge Bay next day.

The Museum was a small wooden hut. Its central door led into a cluttered room which had clearly once been a place for storage and display and was now overwhelmed. Stuffed animals and birds filled the shelves among books, jars, snakeskins, rocks, nests, eggs, seashells and the orange carapace of a giant crab. Boxes were stacked on two tables, on a schoolroom desk, on the floor. Fishing rods and butterfly nets leaned against a wall; an old school cupboard held bulging sacks. A path had been left through this conglomeration to a door in the centre of the back wall, which brought us into a second chamber, sparsely furnished by comparison.

There were three narrow metal cot-beds in a row, separated by small side-cupboards—or in one case a three-legged stool. The dormitory impression was confirmed by a mirror hung on the wall, a kitchen chair, and a row of wooden pegs for clothes. A tiny round table held a ewer and basin and three candlesticks. This had been a storeroom, Charlotte apologised, but the shortage of accommodation meant it must presently be used for guests. Booth's servant, Power, came with hot water, and Charlotte and he left us. An hour later he returned and led us back to the Commandant's cottage.

Booth was amiable and talkative, but could not seem to begin the discussion we were so eager for. This is not hindsight. I remember finding his unease almost palpable at the time, and thinking it came from having bad news to deliver. He, too, apologised for our quarters, explaining that Mr Bergman, the surveyor, was occupying the spare room at the Commandant's cottage. It was hardly more than a cupboard, in any case, utterly unsuitable for three ladies, or even two. He sympathised about the *Adastra*, showed us fossils and shells, threw coals on the fire and riddled it up violently with the poker, and at last said to Anna that he doubted he could help her. His acquaintance with Mr Rowland Rochester had been brief. She waited in her silent, unnerving way, her eyes fixed on him.

'I know you have suffered a great deal,' he said, 'but, forgive me, do you think it wise to go on searching after so many years?'

For a moment she said nothing, and then replied slowly, 'You think I should not ask, not care what happened to my husband?'

Booth looked uncomfortable. 'No, indeed. I meant only . . . Have you considered what the consequences may be? I hesitate to alarm you, but it would be wrong not to warn . . . Supposing, for instance, Mrs Rochester, that your husband has believed you were dead? He may have . . . formed another attachment?'

There was a longish silence. Anna kept her great dark eyes on him and at last said in her unhurried way, 'When I was a child we were told Saint Paul had a thorn in his flesh. I supposed it to be a real thorn, but Sister Marie Augustine said no, *c'est un façon de parler*. A way to speak of something that pricks and torments so one cannot forget. Rowland Rochester is the same for me.'

From Booth's face you'd have thought she had picked up the poker and struck him.

'If he is alive I want to know why he did not come back to help me,' she continued. 'And if he is dead I want to know that too.'

'I see,' Booth said. And then, more gently, 'Well, I will tell you what I can. Some of it I believe you already know.'

He sat in the chair behind his desk and at last began.

'I was one of several officers of the Twenty-first Regiment sent to Demerara in August 'twenty-three at the time of the slave rebellion. We took small detachments from the Georgetown Rifle Corps and marched out to the plantations where there was unrest. To show the flag, mop up generally. One group went to Mahaica to relieve the station there, my party went to Nabaclis.

'At a small plantation called Belleur we discovered a man half-dead in a shanty. The slaves claimed they had found him. He had a bullet wound in the leg—the bone was broken—and a high fever. His head was on a rolled-up, mildewed jacket, and inside this was a parcel of waxed cloth containing four thousand pounds in Bank of England drafts, paper money and specie. Two of the bank drafts were directed to a Mr Rowland Rochester, but we could not be sure that was the name of the sick man, of course. We did our best for him, but we also had other urgent concerns. The fighting seemed set to break out again.'

Somehow the patient clung to life, and against all expectations began to recover. As soon as he could speak, he told them he was Rowland Rochester, but that he was estranged from his family and did not wish to have his plight made known to them. The money came from his having recently sold a small estate to the owner of an adjoining property. He would say nothing, at first, of how he had come to the condition in which they found him.

When the time came for the 21st to leave Demerara they took him back with them to Saint Vincent. During his convalescence Rowland wrote letters, and at one time received a reply that agitated him considerably, but he did not volunteer any explanation. As soon as he was strong enough, he moved out of the infirmary to a house in the hills where it was cooler, cared for by a quadroon family he employed as servants. Booth saw him less frequently after that. Four or five months later, Rochester, walking with a stick, came to say he was leaving for Spanish Town. Later, perhaps a year later, Booth heard that Rowland had died of a fever there.

Anna's face dropped. Booth turned away, picked up a fossil from his desk and turned it in his hands.

'How did you learn of his death?' I asked.

'One of the sergeants who had been in Demerara with me, a man called Elton, was in Spanish Town for some reason, and on his return he mentioned having heard it.'

'Is Sergeant Elton in Van Diemen's Land now?'

'No, he died when we were in Ireland.'

'Rowland Rochester was well when he left Saint Vincent? Why should he suddenly die?'

Booth shrugged, smiled faintly. 'No mystery there. The mystery is how anyone survives. Yellow fever, or a dozen other kinds of fever, a man already weak . . .'

'Were there other soldiers in your Regiment who knew Rowland Rochester? Did he have a particular friend?'

'Our surgeon, Dr Beckett, had a good deal to do with him of course; they played chess together. But Beckett died of fever before we

162

left the posting. And as I said, after Rowland moved into the hills we saw him less. A couple of times he spoke of the Reverend Smith in Demerara as a friend, but Smith was accused of helping the slaves during the rebellion. He stood trial and was sentenced to hang, but he'd been consumptive for years and died before the sentence could be carried out.'

I searched my mind for questions. 'Rowland's injuries—do you think the slaves were to blame, that he was caught up in the rebellion?'

'No. He told me his wounds came from a duel.'

'A *duel*?'

Booth shrugged again. 'Common enough in those days.'

'Did he never mention Van Diemen's Land?'

'No,' he smiled again, 'and if he had, I would not have known where it was, then. After we left the Indies we had a stint back at home and four years in Ireland before we came here—and when we were told our next posting was Van Diemen's Land, we thought it was near New Zealand. What brought Rowland Rochester here?'

'We don't know.'

He said gently, addressing Anna again. 'Rowland never spoke of his family. Have you considered, Mrs Rochester, that if he is alive, and has not communicated with any of his people for fourteen years, it may be that he prefers not to?'

She did not reply. Again he turned away from the look on her face.

'Rowland had quarrelled with his father,' I said. 'We know that. But old Mr Rochester is dead now and Rowland's brother, Edward, is the only one left except for Anna. If he knew this it might make a difference.'

Booth shook his head. 'I'm sorry to have no better news.'

We sat in silence. I know now, of course, that he was not telling all he knew. Even then I suspected there might be something else, but I assumed his reticence came from a desire not to give Anna more pain. In any case, you can hardly accuse your amiable host of deceit. And wasn't this the answer I wanted? Booth put down the fossil and stood.

'I am sorry, Mrs Rochester,' he repeated. He clearly wished to end the interview but could hardly urge us out: a much-tried woman who had come halfway around the world for bad news. I went to Anna's side and said we must leave the Commandant to his affairs. She did not move.

'Anna, it is not the end,' I urged. 'We can go to Spanish Town, to Saint Vincent. Find Rowland's agent, speak to other people.'

Anna sat as though deaf and dumb, her staring eyes, brimming with tears, fixed on Booth. After a time he could clearly stand it no longer. He said he could make no promises but would enquire further if that was what she wanted. There were two other officers of the 21st who had known Rochester briefly. They were stationed in outlying parts of Van Diemen's Land. He did not believe they knew any more than he, but—he shrugged—he would try. It would take several weeks to receive replies.

Anna looked at him as though he were a beatific vision. He looked away.

—※—

The Lemprieres' door was opened that evening by a small boy wearing a shako made of cardboard, tied under his chin with a bootlace. He carried a wooden rifle over his shoulder.

'Sentry duty tonight, Thomas?' said Booth.

The boy nodded, shy and stern. He led us along the central hall of the cottage towards laughter and voices, pushed open a door and marched away. The room was astonishing. Leafy eucalyptus branches covered the walls in bosky profusion. Ferns, garlands of paper flowers and festoons of greenery were looped with paper-chains and bows of pleated paper. Squeezed into the centre of the room was a long table spread with several overlapping white cloths and places for eight people. Charlotte Lempriere stood with Mr Bergman, looking up at her husband, who was standing on a chair, plump, joyful, excited, holding a sizeable branch in both hands and using the leafy end to brush the ceiling vigorously.

'*Et voila!*' he cried, pausing as he caught sight of us. 'Welcome, *chers amis*. Now you will be in at the kill!'

As he spoke, a brown spider the size of a saucer ran rapidly from under the leaves, across the ceiling and down the wall. Charlotte lunged at it with a table napkin but only knocked a paper bow fluttering to the floor. More leaves and decorations were lifted and inspected, amid little shrieks from Miss Drewitt, but the creature had vanished. The search was abandoned and the seating arranged so that Bergman, who declared that he did not fear the insect, was positioned with his back to where it was last seen. We sat. There was a sighing and settling and the last guest arrived: Lieutenant Stuart from the Coal Mines. I was seated between him and Bergman, who had Miss Drewitt on his other side. Anna was between Booth and Lempriere, smiling, comfortably beginning a half-French, half-English conversation with the latter.

When Miss Drewitt leaned across to introduce me to Bergman, I said, 'We have met, in Hobart.'

'I was rather hoping you'd forgotten,' he said, smiling. 'I was not at my best that day. Now you see me to better advantage I hope. A new man.'

His loose black curls were cut short now, and he was close-shaven. The gypsyish smile remained. He was not handsome, but his brown eyes were full of amusement and energy, and his long brown face gave the impression of kindness and cleverness. In his black cut-away coat he looked thinner than in the loose brown forage gear.

'I have been warned that many in this island are not what they appear to be at first sight,' I said. 'Perhaps you have other aspects also?'

'Oh, half a dozen. But I won't tell you what they are, I'll let you discover them as we become better acquainted. This colony tends to make new men out of the old Adam—remakes us, whether we know it or not. And you, Mrs Adair? You're an artist, I believe—and therefore perhaps have just the one settled character—a rather singular one?'

'Singular and plural,' I said, trying to match his jocular tone, but before I could continue there was a cry from Lempriere. *Non, non! C'est impossible*! He had noticed that, concealed by the tablecloth, makeshift additions to the table had brought together too many table legs and props at the point where Bergman was sitting, forcing him to arrange his legs somewhat unnaturally around the obstacle.

'It's nothing,' said Bergman. 'My legs have grown immensely flexible from climbing up and down Booth's confounded signal towers. Let me lecture Mrs Adair in peace.'

Charlotte Lempriere soothed her husband and the servant deposited a tureen of soup with an unpolished thump. Lempriere said Grace and we passed the bowls about.

'This claret is excellent, Booth,' said Stuart. 'I hope it's not the same shipment the boys plundered.' He turned to me and added, 'Two dozen cases of what Booth calls his "vinous fluid" were broken into and sampled by boys on one of the transports. They clearly found it to their taste. They were discovered in a state of inebriation . . .'

'. . . not unlike our own regimental indulgences,' finished Bergman.

'Steady, Gus,' said Stuart, 'You'll give Mrs Adair the wrong impression. Besides, it's ungrateful; the Army taught you everything you know. Make him talk to you about surveying, ma'am, or music. He can be quite sensible on those subjects.'

Bergman asked me whether I played or sang, and we talked about London, where he had been born, until Augusta Drewitt claimed his attention from the other side, and Stuart began to explain to me the difference between the artificial horizon on a ship, and the one presumed in perspective drawing.

'The vanishing point in drawing is *more* imaginary . . . the artificial horizon is real in *itself*, but it is not actually on the horizon. It is in the dish of mercury held between the gimbals . . .'

'Can one thing be *more* imaginary than another?'

Conversation around the table had divided into groups. Charlotte Lempriere was talking to Booth and Anna. Fragments drifted free:

'. . . entire gross of candles chewed by mice. Soap, also, they seem to . . .'

'. . . laughing-jackass bird, which the children say . . .'

'Decent sort of hack for thirty pounds . . .'

Soup and fish were followed by a goose, rather tough, a round of beef, and a baked ham studded with cloves: Bergman's contribution, said Stuart.

'Charlotte, what a stunning feed!' Booth called.

Lempriere rose to his feet, tapping his wine glass with a fork.

'Ladies and gentlemen, is anyone still troubled by the pangs of hunger?'

Groans.

'Then please be upstanding for the loyal toast! To our young Queen. God bless her and long may she reign!'

'To the Queen!'

'The Queen, the Queen.'

When the gentlemen were seated again, Booth remained standing.

'Ladies and gentlemen, I should like to propose another toast. We are gathered here in genial concord to celebrate, belatedly, the birthday of our esteemed friend and colleague, Mr Thomas Lempriere. As you know, our usual revelries were postponed this year on account of the arrival of little Lucy two months ago. You should understand, ladies,' he turned to us, 'that every February the Lemprieres put on a great scald to celebrate the day when Thomas Lempriere entered the world, in a place and time very far from here.'

'Steady, mon ami. Not so very far in time,' said Lempriere.

'I won't press the point,' Booth smiled. 'Although it may seem to those of us still in the first flush of youth (cheers from Stuart) that forty-one years (cries of astonishment, more cheers) is an attainment of great venerableness and wisdom. You have gathered to yourself a lady of shining worth (hear! hear!) . . . a family of great . . . exuberance (laughter) . . . a position of honour in our little community and strong affection in our hearts. A man of science and the arts, equally excellent in learning and sensibility, whose multiple exertions on behalf of this colony are a matter of wonder: ladies and gentlemen, I give you Thomas Lempriere and his delightful spouse, the fair Charlotte.'

The toast was drunk amid table-thumping from Stuart until Charlotte begged him to desist in case the extensions should collapse under the dishes. Lempriere rose and thanked Booth for mentioning how much of his happiness lay in his family, his friends, his most welcome guests.

'We should thank the Lord every day that "the lines have been laid to us in pleasant places" on this beautiful island . . .' he said. He spoke of the exciting duty of pursuing the study of natural history in this curious place. He referred to his youth, and asked for blessings on those dear to him in Hobarton and other parts of the world. He blew his nose and sat down. I glanced at Booth, expecting to see a smile for this display of sentiment, and was surprised to catch on the Commandant's face a wave of similar feeling.

A distribution of plum pies and crumb tarts revived the conversation until Charlotte Lempriere gave the signal for the ladies to retire. Having shown us the offices and the tiny parlour, she excused herself to attend to the baby. I had wondered if Anna would be tired by the evening, but although she was quiet she seemed happy. Augusta Drewitt, pursing her lips at herself in a wall mirror, began to put drops from a tiny vial into her eyes. 'Belladonna. For sparkle, you know. Do you never use it?'

Anna and I watched as she dropped the poison into her eyes.

'Rouge is quite *passé* in London, worse luck,' she went on. 'I always think I need a little colour, but one looks a superannuated fright if one wears it now. Do you think Captain Booth the more handsome, or Lieutenant Stuart, or Mr Bergman?'

She went on without pausing, 'Bergman has had a convict mistress five years. He has a son by her and is much attached to them, apparently. He is wealthy but a Jewish, of course. I wonder why Captain Booth has never married? He is thirty-seven, you know, and must have means. I should hardly wish to marry out here, in any case.'

She moved to the cottage piano, plinked a few chords and began turning sheets of music.

'Will you play, Mrs Adair? Mrs Rochester? Or shall I?'

She launched into an *écossaise*. Anna sat by the fire slowly turning the pages of an album of engravings: *Picturesque Scenes of England and Wales*. Exactly the kind of prints I had hand-coloured for a few pence each, in that winter after Tom died. Nina and I were so poor I might have stolen a loaf or a piece of blanket if I'd not had that work. I went to the window, held the curtain aside and stood looking down the dark slope to the sentry box with its soft lamplight, wondering whether the prisoners could hear the piano. Miss Drewitt lost her place and came to an abrupt halt. In the sudden silence it seemed to my imagination that the frail music had been vanquished by the strangeness of the thickly treed hills and the water lapping its own song into that cove since the beginning of time. Miss Drewitt recovered and plinked on. I wondered what Mr Bergman's mistress was like, and what she had done to deserve transportation.

When the gentlemen came in, the parlour grew crowded. Lempriere was saying to Stuart, 'But the pursuit of the sciences cuts across every boundary of country and race. Napoleon's armies had orders to let Sir Humphry Davy and the young Faraday pass through the battle lines . . .'

A high young voice called in triumph from the doorway, 'Papa knows, don't you, Papa? Papa was a spy!'

A small girl appeared. She wore a white nightgown and clasped a thick red counterpane around her shoulders that trailed behind her.

'Mary!' said Lempriere. '*Qu'est-ce que tu fais?* Where is Miss Wood?'

'She is sitting in a chair making noises, Papa. I think she is ill.'

Mary came up to Bergman and said, 'The others are asleep but I cannot sleep.' She turned to Booth. 'I have made some paintings with the colour-box you gave me. Could I ride Jack tomorrow?'

Booth smoothed her hair. 'We'll have to see what your mama says,' he answered smiling. He chose a custard tart from a dish on the table. 'One of these and then you must go back to bed.'

'You spoil her, Booth,' said Lempriere.

There was a knock on the door and a thick shout of 'Mary?' A woman came in. She was at the petticoat-and-stays part of undress and had thrown over the top a voluminous brown shawl. A white cotton cap, strings hanging loose, was crammed over hair partly in curl papers. She had been drinking.

'Oh, I do beg your pardon,' she said in tones of slurred politeness. 'Come, Miss Mary!' And descending into a whimper, 'Now come along, do!'

The governess subsided into tears, and followed Charlotte Lempriere out with Mary, snuffling into a large handkerchief. An odd intrusion, a reminder of what I might have been, might still have to be. The conversation resumed slowly.

'Settlers like Gregson and Fenn Kemp won't stop until they get a voice in Government,' said Stuart.

'Well, I don't know how they'll do it,' said Booth. He yawned. 'Oh, excuse me! Life is too short. I'd rather spend time building jetties and dining with friends.'

'"The summer of a dormouse,"' said Bergman smiling. 'Do you remember what Byron says? "When one subtracts from life infancy, which is vegetation—and sleep, eating and swilling, buttoning and unbuttoning—how much remains of downright existence? The summer of a dormouse."'

Lempriere brought out a violin. We must try a Mendelssohn song for two voices he had sent for. Bergman sang the low part, playing it on the violin at the same time, Augusta was soprano and I accompanied on the piano, managing the lovely little piece with some false notes and laughter. Lempriere, deeply affected by the music, seized his trumpet when we finished, vowing to play a dirge for those in peril on the sea. It was after midnight now, and Charlotte reminded him of the children already abed.

'Only softly, *ma chère*,' he said, taking up her hand and kissing it. But he put the trumpet aside and the evening came to an end.

—⟶—

We stayed five more days waiting for the *Vansittart*'s return. The next day I accompanied the party that conveyed Augusta Drewitt along the four-mile track to Wedge Bay. Anna was content to sit in Charlotte Lempriere's kitchen playing with the family's collection of curious pets, among them a wombat which slept in her lap like a fat little bear, and a tame orphan kangaroo or joey, whose pouch was a canvas bag hanging from the doorknob. It dived in head first, leaving its long back legs poking out like a bundle of sticks.

Charlotte kindly supplied me with a pair of thick cotton duck trousers and a short canvas skirt, and we set off on the narrow road through the dense forest. Augusta rode Jack. I was pleased to stretch my legs. Two convicts pulled a small cart carrying Augusta's luggage, Bergman's box of surveying chain—the 'Gunter's' chain—and sacks of flour and sugar rations. The track was black sand netted with root fibres, boggy in places. My new boots were soon unrecognisable. The weather was perfect for walking: a brilliant autumn day.

Bergman and Booth explained as we went the difficulties of the 'chain and compass' method of surveying. By stretching the 'Gunter's' chain along the land to determine length; and using a circumferentor, or tripod-mounted compass, for direction; and a theodolyte, the world could be divided up with imaginary lines. But in practice, when the land was not flat and clear, the readings were part guesswork, and errors were common in the surveying done during the early years of the colony. 'Triangulation' was a better method, but it used sextant readings, and therefore needed cairns on hilltops for the sightings. These were expensive and laborious to build, and Whitehall had stopped the money for them, forcing Sir John Franklin to order a return to the old method.

Wedge Bay proved to be an exquisite curve of long white beach with rocky outcrops each end. A whale-shaped island lay in the distance offshore, humped at one end, tapering away to the sea at the other. Two tiny huts formed the outstation, with neat garden beds around them, and a track behind leading to the signal on top of the ridge. Augusta's sister, Evie, and Evie's husband, Sergeant William Wade, were a pleasant couple, plainly happy with each other and their resourceful life. They made tea in a billycan over the fire outside, the baby being asleep indoors, and we shared the 'scran' Power had given us: bread, cold meat and cake. When the men climbed to the signal, I left Augusta and her sister unpacking and walked down to the shore to sketch.

After a time, Bergman joined me and looked at my drawing.

'Your line is skilful and accurate,' he said, 'but you also manage to convey the scale of the scene, the sense of this landscape extending beyond . . .'

I told him that in France, when I was young, I had seen two works by Madame Vallayer-Coster which perfectly captured this effect for me and made me strive to achieve it.

'Curiously, these were not landscapes but still lives,' I added. '"Still Life with Parrot and the Fruits of Summer", and "Still Life with Bird in a Gilded Cage". Quiet interior scenes—and yet the painter had imbued her work with a mysterious light which made you imagine a window just outside the edge of the canvas, and beyond it the orchards and vineyards where this fruit grew—and even beyond that, the distant lands where parrots live.'

Each grape seemed a little green world you were inspired to wonder at, to see how astonishing it is that such things should exist at all, even though we take them for granted every day. A half-peeled lemon suggested some invisible human hand—and there were roses, in bud and full-blown, others already dropping petals.

'An allegory of our brief lives?'

'Yes, but more than that, too. I felt the painter wanted us to think of the glorious breadth of the world and our little knowledge of it,' I said. 'I thought she herself might be a prisoner, like the birds she painted; in exile like them and yearning to go home, and yet acknowledging the beauty of her enforced surroundings.'

I had desperately wanted to buy one of those paintings. My father had given me a generous amount of wedding money, but Tom had taken charge of it and he did not care for them. A pang of unwanted knowledge had come to me at that moment. I suddenly knew I was less free as a wife than I had been as a daughter. Even gifts to me, even my earnings, belonged by law to my husband.

I did not tell Bergman this. It seemed a too-intimate and distorted glimpse of my life with Tom. For a time we had been happy together.

Bergman and I walked along the sands as we talked, picking up little orange crab-shells so perfect they looked alive, but they were empty, hollow and light. There were myriad shells: whorled, bone-white skeletons, and whole, perfect ones, barred and patterned; tiny fluted scallop shells on which a miniature Venus might have risen from the sea—and feathers, and brown sea-wrack with dark pods to pop between the fingers. Everything smelled of brine; the water had the hard sparkling blue of autumn.

When Charlotte asked me later what I thought of the place, I said I found it beautiful, which was true: the tall straight gums in their subtle colours, the glorious hills and sea. But I did not like to say that it seemed to me a strange, cruel kind of beauty, charged with a quality I could not name, but which felt profoundly alien to me. Some little nuts and seed-pods Bergman collected for me seemed emblems of this, each one an exquisite, sharp, dry little puzzle, the geometry of a different world—only understandable, perhaps, to the people so savagely exiled from it. I found myself thinking how wrong a word like 'meadow' sounded in this colony.

—⁂—

Two days of rain followed, spent in Booth's or the Lemprieres' cottage, talking, playing cards, at the piano, or copying out music. Bergman proved to have a pleasant baritone, and we sang—everybody sang. I visited the little school house, made jam tarts with Charlotte, read to the children. Lempriere showed me his portrait of Booth, just finished. He was dissatisfied with its air of stiffness—all Booth's fault. The Commandant could so seldom be got to sit still, Lempriere had been forced to sketch the face while Booth was sitting as a magistrate. And from the neck down it was not Booth at all! It was Lempriere's eldest son Edward, wearing Booth's dress-jacket and epaulettes. Booth judged it a capital likeness. He was pleased to look suitably severe.

On the third day it turned fine again. Sophy returned from the Carts and there was a general expedition to a fishing spot nearby. She was more friendly now, grasping my arm almost possessively to tell me *sotto voce* that she was relieved to be away from the Carts' deep mourning, which was 'frightful'. She flirted with Booth but ignored Bergman, who grilled fish over a fire on the rocks. Booth pointed to a promontory where he and his number one whaleboat crew had nearly captured a whale a few months earlier. It had escaped in the end, but gave them an hour or two of capital sport. Bergman showed me a scrimshaw medallion with a similar landscape etched into it: a cliff, a ship leaning into the wind, a whale breaching. Sophy took it out of my hands and played with it carelessly until the fine leather cord snapped and the medallion disappeared into the water.

Edward and Thomas leapt in with joyful shouts, reckless of their clothes and the icy sea, and floundered about waist-deep, retrieving shells and weed until they were shuddering with cold. Poor Sophy's apologies faded at last as Bergman insisted that he liked the thought of it lying there in the depths, waiting. Perhaps in a hundred years it might be brought to the surface in a net, or as in a fairytale, someone might find it in the belly of a great fish. Or the tides might wash it up on the sands.

'Someone, a complete stranger to us, will wear it again in the future.'

Sophy took me aside later and told me that although Mr Bergman appeared pleasant, he was immoral. He was known to have a child by his convict housekeeper. A boy. I said Augusta had mentioned it.

14

FOUR WEEKS, QUIGLEY HAD SAID, SIX AT MOST. BY THE END OF
May it was seven, and there was no news from him and nothing
from Booth. The *Marian Watson* returned, but he was not aboard. We
settled in our lodgings to wait, but Anna was bored from the first and
showed signs of increasing melancholy as the days passed. *'Je m'ennuie,'*
was her lethargic refrain. She was always a late riser, and would have
stayed in bed all day if I had not coaxed and bullied her out.

The weather was partly to blame. Autumns in Van Diemen's
Land are frequently times of late radiance, warm golden after-ends
of summer. I know this now—but it was not so that year. Two days
after we returned from the peninsula the rains came, bringing an early
winter. When it was not wet it was bitingly cold. In our landlady's
Orcadian dialect the weather was masculine, with a wealth of terms
denoting fine distinctions of foulness, and I soon became accustomed
to Peg Groundwater's morning greetings: 'He maks a feer skuther',
with a shake of the head. Or a 'feer gushel', or a 'sweevle' when
it was windy. And 'Snae on t'moon'en!' when it snowed on Mount
Wellington, the weather gauge for the town.

If the weather had been fine I might have been able to persuade
Anna to walk a little and explore the town, but after one attempt
she would not even attend Church on Sundays. She complained of

being cold even in front of the blazing fire, and I ordered extra coal in quantities that made thrifty Mrs Groundwater stare, and gave me wakeful nights over our dwindling funds.

Many afternoons we spent playing simple card games, the stakes being buttons from Peg's button jar. Anna was childishly gleeful when she won, sulky when she lost. The lamp was lit at four in the afternoon and the evenings were long. Most of the time she sat by the fire in a huddle of shawls. She liked oysters and toast, roast fowl and hot chocolate, not tea. She asked for mulled wine, or Negus, and James Seymour, who came to see her once a week, agreed it might serve as a tonic. Peg Groundwater did not like to have wine in the house, but as a medicine it was permissible.

Apart from the doctor and Peg, we saw no one. Louisa and St John had left Hobarton for Richmond, where they were to stay with Mr Aislabie, the vicar. St John would begin his report with the small Richmond gaol, to provide a comparison with the main prison at Port Arthur when he went there later. McLeod was also at Richmond, still with Dr Ross and his family. Ross continued unwell.

I wrote to Jane Eyre and Mrs Fairfax, and on three occasions was able to explore the town for an hour in the morning while Anna slept, but Peg said she became agitated if I was not there when she woke. I was now almost Anna's prisoner, as she had once been mine. No invitation came from Government House—which was partly my own fault. We did not leave visiting cards when we returned from the peninsula, for we had none. It had not seemed worth the expense of having them printed when we knew nobody and were soon to leave. But as time went by and I grew desperate to keep Anna in spirits, I regretted this and was thinking of ordering them when an invitation arrived. Lady Franklin had found us somehow, or perhaps it was Sophy. The Governor's wife would be 'at home' on this day, at this hour.

—∿—

Sophy made introductions. Mrs George Frankland of 'Secheron', wife of the Chief Surveyor; Mrs Josiah Spode of 'Boa Vista', wife of the

Superintendent of Convicts; Mrs John Montagu of 'Stowell', wife of the Colonial Secretary; Mrs Matthew Forster of 'Wyvenhoe', wife of the Chief Police Magistrate; Mrs John Gregory, the wife of the Treasurer. These ladies smiled in a small way, but did not trouble to feign any interest in us. They conversed about children and domestic matters, favouring us with the same faint smiles now and again to show we were included.

There were few gentlemen present; the Reverend Knopwood turned out to be one of them. With snow-white hair in elfin locks and a benign smile, he was thin and straight as an old schoolmaster. His hands, trembling slightly, rattled his teacup and saucer. He sat by the fire with Mrs Parry, a widow. His friend for years, he said. She too was in black, and as thin as he, but she carried herself more firmly, sat fiercely upright in her chair. She held a speaking tube in one hand, the ring-laden knuckles of the other clasped over the head of a black and ivory cane. Her little King Charles spaniel snored in her lap. In spite of the ear trumpet she seemed to hear perfectly well. Knopwood asked me what I thought of the town and I said I was surprised to see it so flourishing. I had imagined bark huts and bushrangers.

'Hush, my dear,' he said softly. 'You won't mind . . . I beg you not to speak of bushrangers before Mrs Parry. She lost a son by the violence of such poor wretched souls some years since.'

When I raised the subject of Rowland Rochester, Knopwood said he thought he knew the name but could not quite recall . . . If God preserved him he would be seventy-five next month and had seen more curious things than he could tell. Twelve men hanged in a row on a public gibbet in Hobarton. Families of aborigines coming into the kitchen of his dear old house above the shore, 'Cottage Green', twenty years ago, to cook potatoes in the fire. The black people had been handsome in those early days, but now—such a terrible shame . . .

He had seen so much—a lost husband was nothing! People were here one moment and gone the next. Life is an odd journey and we might as well face it smiling and singing. Who said that? Virgil? Rowland Rochester . . . He felt sure he would remember. The other day a line had come to him; 'a slumber did my spirit seal', and he'd been delighted because he thought it was his own invention. Then he remembered it was Wordsworth!

'I met him, you know, William Wordsworth,' Knopwood nodded. 'He was up at Cambridge in my time. Younger than me, of course. He was at St John's, I was Caius. It was just before the revolution in France and he was going for Holy Orders too. Ha! He might have come to Van Diemen's Land instead of me. But it could never have been the other way round. You'd never wring a jot of poetry out of me. No indeed, not with a laundry mangle!'

He had met Lord Nelson too, in the year 1793. 'Good Lord, what a time ago that is. Forty-five years.'

He turned his head to assess me with his best eye, the other being of slightly milky appearance. He had been a young curate in the Reverend Edward Nelson's parish of Burnham Thorpe. Captain Nelson, as he was in those days, was the Reverend's son, and came into the congregation some Sundays. And now he was Lord Nelson, famous and dead these thirty-three years and the world a different place. As for Hobarton, Knopwood believed you might meet anyone here. More than one family was rumoured to be secretly related to the crowned heads of Europe.

'Your friend Mrs Rochester is from the Indies?' he said, his bright as a boot-button good eye following Anna, across the room with Sophy. 'I was at Port Royal, Jamaica, in the year '03. We sailed home by the Windward Passage in the shortest time ever known then: twenty-three days, five hours and a half, from Cape Tiberoon to Chatham Dockyard! I daresay they've done it quicker since. Everything is quicker now. Well, I'll soon be on my last voyage out. The great leap into the dark, as Thomas Hobbes said. Ain't that so, madam?' he turned to Mrs Parry. 'We are both ready for the great leap.'

Hmph, she said. He might leap if he chose, but she'd thank the Almighty to spare her until her little dog died, then she'd go in peace. As for Nelson, he'd fought off the French and died a hero—and what had been the use of it, that long war? Everyone was as Frenchified nowadays as if the little Corsican had won! And would it have been such a bad thing? All the world French, even this colony? There are worse things.

Knopwood asked her about Rowland Rochester. Yes, Mrs Parry thought she'd heard him mention the name. Well, it would surely come to him, and he would send me a note to Mrs Groundwater's, if he lived. The doctors had said he must die twenty years ago.

'Mrs Adair doesn't want to hear that,' said Mrs Parry.

'Yes, she does, madam. She ought to hear it. It is a lesson in what one may survive with the Lord's help.'

He had had a stone and should have been cut for it but there was no surgeon in Hobarton to do it in those days. He had suffered agonies when the doctors passed a bougie up into his bladder and poured caustic in to dissolve it. Three times in a week they'd treated it, until he thought he'd go mad with pain, but the remedy had worked. The Lord had granted him another twenty years. He was certain he would remember where he'd heard of Rowland Rochester—as soon as we parted, probably.

—◊◊◊—

A note came from Booth. He would be in Hobarton for the Government Ball in two weeks on the thirtieth of May, and if convenient, would call on us the following day to give us further news. When I read this to Anna a smile slowly appeared on her placid face. 'He has discovered Rowland,' she said.

'I don't think it can be that,' I said gently, 'or he would surely have said so. It may be some small clue.' I was annoyed with Booth for not giving any hint of whether the news would be welcome or not, and I prepared myself to distract Anna from dwelling too much on it, but this proved unnecessary. We, too, had received an invitation to the ball, and her mind became fixed on the need for a dark red velvet cloak, with a lining of merino and a fur collar against the cold.

—◊◊◊—

Quigley arrived on the *Lady Phillipa* two days before the ball, to Anna's joy and my considerable relief. He had found a temporary command as Master of this brig on a trading run between Hobart, Port Phillip, Sydney, Moreton Bay, and back to Sydney again. A stopgap for a few months until the summer, when the ship would make an England voyage. We must stay in Van Diemen's Land until he returned to take us to Sydney and Home. He had not yet received the insurance monies. They would come, but with these landlubbers everything took so long; 'They would none of them survive at sea.'

The ball was not only to celebrate the Queen's Birthday: the Franklins were entertaining the officers of the *Conway*, about to leave Hobarton after two months of repairs and revictualling. Killing two birds with one set of *expensive* wax candles, said Sophy Cracroft. She was moving about the ballroom speaking to different groups before the dancing commenced. What did we think of the illuminations? A hundred pounds! Just for a crown in lamps over the entrance and candles for the ballroom. Of course the local merchants made sure the price of every article was double to Government House. The hire of the set of huge silver sconces was extra. These had originally been sent out for the Presbyterian Church, but when they arrived they were judged too popishly ornate to use, and were now hired out to every public gathering in the colony.

'Not above four hundred people, I think?' she said, over the music. 'Aunt and I sent out a thousand invitations. But we have had such bad weather, and the bushrangers are out.'

Captain Hasluck of the *Conway* wrote his name on my card for two dances. Bergman arrived late, but proved to be a capable dancer. He took me in to supper, where we found Robert McLeod eating chicken and ham. He was in town only briefly, he said, attending to some business for James Ross.

'He is still not well. He was about to open a school at his house, 'Carrington' in Richmond, but that must be delayed. Susan Ross has enough to do with an ailing husband and thirteen children.'

He asked me what we had learned from Booth and, including Bergman in the explanation, I told them, adding that we might hear more tomorrow.

'But I don't see Booth here?' said McLeod.

I had been looking for him too, with no success. I wanted some forewarning of whether his news next day was likely to cheer Anna or dismay her.

'He has probably been delayed,' said Bergman. 'At any rate, Anna appears happy enough,' he added, watching her with Quigley.

Shortly after midnight, Lady Franklin was obliged to retire, seized with one of her headaches. Mr Robert Murray of the *Colonial Times* had recently noted with his usual asperity that these appeared to attack her ladyship after a few hours in company with the respectable classes of the town. He implied that she found the worthy burghers dull. He did not say quarrelsome, narrow-minded, stubborn and money-grubbing. As he had written on other occasions, many of them were all those things and proud of it.

Bergman suggested a breath of air, and he and I left the din and went into a windowed corridor overlooking the garden and entry. Several coaches were waiting in darkness although the ball would not end for hours yet. You could hear the occasional harrumph of a horse and the jangle of harness. The rain had stopped and the sky was frostily clear. An upper window was open and the air coming in smelt of smoke and damp earth. Through the dripping trees the black lines of ships' rigging rose and fell, and the river wrinkled silver and black under the moon's path. A cluster of candles near us had burned down until they were guttering low, drowning amid stalactites of wax. A man appeared at the end of the corridor and came towards us.

'Lord! It's hot as the devil in there. Chatter and noise fit to burst your brains. No wonder Lady Franklin has the headache. I can't bear it myself.'

It was Dr Pilkington, easing his high collar, stretching his chin up out of it. 'Mrs Adair, Bergman. Booth not here tonight? I thought he was going to escape for a few days? He works too hard, that he does.'

'Things are brisk down there at the moment. So many new transportees this year—and more expected,' said Bergman.

'I don't know where he'll put them. The Government at Whitehall wants reports, but it's sure and certain no one reads them, for they understand nothing of how matters are here.' Pilkington shook his head. 'Do they think penitentiary buildings spring up from the ground by nature in this part of the world?' He shrugged. 'Well, my girls are missing Booth. He has a little flirtation with Lizzie, d'y' know.'

I said I had been looking for Booth myself but had not seen him. 'But Miss Lizzie Eagle does not seem to lack partners, even without Captain Booth,' I added. Elfin small, with raven-black Irish hair and a fine pale complexion, she would have graced a ballroom anywhere.

'Hm,' said Pilkington. 'Well, the young ladies will soon have to choose among their beaux. The Twenty-first Regiment sails for India before the end of the year. The Governor would like to be on his way too, by all accounts. Will you look at him there now? Hands behind his back, legs braced apart as though he's on the deck of a ship. And it's my belief that's where he'd rather be.'

'Have you heard Henry Elliot's story?' asked Bergman, 'Sir John looked up at a great mass of fleecy clouds and said, "Look at that, Henry, ice-continents in the sky. A great Arctic in the heavens. What would it be to sail a barky into that, eh?"'

Pilkington was silent for a moment before he answered, 'When a man's lived in those out-of-the-way places for months, years . . . he's never the same, I suppose. Or perhaps it takes an uncommon kind of a man to venture there in the first place?'

Music from the dancing was a bright thread in the corridor. Pilkington shivered, sneezed and blew his nose on a great silk handkerchief. 'It's turning colder again,' he said. 'And my dear Mrs Adair you have no wrap at all. Let us go in before we catch our deaths.'

As we turned back there was a commotion. A soldier plunged into the corridor on a surge of freezing air, pulling off riding gloves and putting his shako under his arm. We followed him into the ballroom and stood inside the doorway as he made his way through to the

Governor. The news was clearly unwelcome. Henry Elliot went to the musicians and halted them, and the room fell quiet.

Sir John's round face was solemn as he announced that he had just received a message he knew would be as painful to all as it was to him. 'Commandant Captain Charles O'Hara Booth is lost on the Forestier Peninsula. He has been missing since last Thursday, south of East Bay Neck.' He frowned and consulted the paper in his hand. 'Near Dr Imlay's whaling station. Mr Thomas Lempriere is leading a search party from Port Arthur, and another party will leave immediately from Hobarton.' He scanned the gathering. 'Volunteers are to assemble in the small reception room opposite us here.' He asked us to pray for Booth.

For a moment I felt faint. Bergman had turned away to say something to Pilkington. By the time he turned back to me I had recovered myself.

'Will you excuse me, Mrs Adair? Are you ill? Are you sure? Of course I shall join the search, but I will stay until I see you well.'

'You must go,' I said. I could easily find my way to Anna and the Captain, or Dr Pilkington would take me.

'Indeed, indeed. Go, Bergman,' said Pilkington, his face grave. I will see to Mrs Adair. And I must find my wife and Lizzie.'

We repeated our assurances until Bergman gave a bow and hurried away. The Doctor and I attempted to move back to the ballroom, but the hall was filling with people. We began a slow progress through the milling throng, who seemed caught in a slow turbulence, like leaves in a river's eddies. As we passed we caught snatches of talk. Three nights out, freezing conditions, people shook their heads. And most of the officers from Port Arthur would be out with the search party: what a moment for a mass escape if the felons knew of it!

Rumours crossed the ballroom faster than we did. People kept stopping Pilkington to ask or tell, and I was forced to wait because he'd taken my arm firmly under his elbow, and each time I tried to escape, it tightened involuntarily. One man claimed Sir John was not revealing all he knew. Booth had been walking with a convict, a man called Tanner. The convict had returned to the settlement—supposedly to report the Commandant missing, but it was more likely that he wished to rouse others to revolt. Tanner was a vicious felon who had been sentenced to twenty-five lashes by Booth a few weeks earlier. The convict had now taken his revenge, probably.

Augusta Drewitt caught my arm on the other side and whispered that I must not be alarmed, but a convict called Tucker, goaded by an unmerciful flogging from Booth, had murdered the Commandant and called the convicts to revolt. She therefore intended to continue dancing all night, Government House being the safest place in the colony. Why go home to be murdered in her bed? But it was apparent that few shared her feelings. Servants were sent for wraps and carriages, and a scurry outwards began. Mr Littlejohn's band played on but the dancers dwindled. The crowd at last began to thin, but hours seemed to pass and still I could see neither Anna nor Quigley. When only eight couples were left, they were not among them. I went to look in the ladies' dressing room while the doctor attended to his wife and stepdaughter. Anna was not there, and her cloak and boots were gone. She had taken them a long while ago, the maids thought.

I changed my slippers for boots, collected my wrap, and returned to where Pilkington was trying to cheer his distraught wife and Lizzie. They clung together, white and tearful, looking as if they might collapse at any moment. The doctor hastened away to call their carriage, promising they would convey me home on their way. I said we had come in sedan chairs which were ordered to return for us, but the doctor believed they would take some other fare in the present confusion. He thought Quigley must have gone to join the search party, asking some other family to take Anna. I considered this unlikely but did not know what else to believe.

Lady Franklin came downstairs on Sophy Cracroft's arm. She looked ill, but spoke sympathetically to Lizzie and her mother and suggested the remainder of the supper should be wrapped to send with the search party. Sophy went to give this order and Lady Franklin turned to me and asked if she might take my arm for a moment.

Her face was ghastly pale. We walked a few steps to another group, and she spoke disjointedly of Booth's fine qualities and the sudden treacherous changes in the island weather.

This must have been the moment when Dr Pilkington sent a servant to fetch Mrs Pilkington and Lizzie to the carriage. He had been called to attend a woman having a fit in the morning room. Mrs Pilkington and Lizzie went home, not understanding that I was to have accompanied them. By the time Lady Franklin and Sophy disappeared upstairs again, as they soon did, the ballroom was almost empty and I could see no one I recognised. I made my way through the hall and out into the entry. It was after four o'clock. I was weary but the cold revived me. I looked about for the sedan chairs, but there were none. I now felt an urgent desire to be home, to know Anna had reached there safely.

The Franklins' Scottish steward, Mr Hepburn, saw me standing irresolute, and in the ensuing conversation I spoke about sedan chairs, and perhaps he did too; his strong accent made it hard to tell. We were floundering by the time Bergman came by on his way out, and Hepburn insisted on explaining my plight. Bergman seemed to grasp the import, and went to see whether one of the two carriages preparing to leave could take me, but one was going in the wrong direction, the other overladen already. They were the last.

'It's no matter. I shall wait here until it grows light. Or I can easily walk,' I said. Bergman looked at me dubiously.

'We can walk together if you'll allow me?' he said. 'Or would you prefer to wait here until daylight? It will be another hour or more. I'm on my way home to change. My house is in the Battery. You are at Mrs Groundwater's? They are not far apart. It is generally frowned upon in Hobarton for a lady to walk alone with a gentleman to whom she is not related, but in these circumstances . . .'

'You'll miss the search party.'

'No, the first one went half an hour ago, the military contingent. Another leaves at dawn with civilian volunteers. It gives us time to assemble more lanterns, ropes, blankets.'

I explained I was anxious to get back to the lodgings to make certain of Anna. He nodded briefly, said, 'May I?', tucked my arm under his without fuss, and we set off into the cold dark. His breathing warmth was pleasant, comforting, his greatcoat rough, smelling faintly of tar and smoke. We fell into step. The cold came up through the soles of my boots and my feet began to grow numb.

'Do you think Booth has a chance?' I asked.

'He's been lost before and survived. He and Casey were out for two nights on the Tiers a couple of years ago.'

'In weather as cold as this?'

'No.'

'Have you ever been lost?'

'When I first arrived. A colleague and I stumbled about in the bush at Jerusalem Corners for two days. Our donkey, Nelly, led us out when she was hungry, and tired of going in circles. And you?'

'Only in London.'

He gave a huff of laughter. Walking briskly on, we passed the garden gate of a large house, where three people stood under the light of a lantern on a pole. One was a maidservant, shivering, grasping a shawl round her and holding a large tin jug. Beside her was a youngish man too thinly clad, carrying a little girl of about four. The child was bundled warmly in a coat, mittens and a little woollen cap, with a cup in one hand and an apple in the other. The man had looped a muffler loosely about his own neck and hers. As we went by he and Bergman raised their hats to each other.

'The Mad Judge,' he told me when we were some yards distant. 'His little girl likes to give the dairyman's carthorse an apple, and collect her own cup of milk.'

'I'll never understand this place,' I said. 'Where else would you see such a thing?'

As we reached Peg Groundwater's gate and started up the front path, the door opened as though she had been watching for us. Without speaking she handed me two pieces of paper, a page of my sketchbook torn in half. She held up her candle while I read the pencilled notes. The first was in a childish, straggling copperplate:

Chère *Harriet,*
Poor Cpn Booth dead with Pierre Maman Papa Edwd Rchstr. Too much time wasted my life and yours. I pray for you and Christophine, adieux, Anna.

The second was in a neater, smaller hand:

Dear Harriet,
Forgive this haste we leave on the instant or lose the tide. We carry the search party on our way. Poor Booth. No finding Rowland now. Return VDL for you in spring. Anna's happiness will ever be my first object. Yr srvnt, Ned Quigley

Thrusting the notes at Bergman, I flew down the hall to Anna's room. Discarded clothes were strewn about. One of the rough sandals she had worn on the *Adastra* lay in a tangle on the floor. All my hard-won calm was gone, turned into doubts and fears. There was a knock and Bergman came in. He looked at my face and said, 'Quigley's a good man. They'll be back in the spring. Are you all right? Mrs Groundwater is bringing a hot drink.'

He came and took my cold hands between his, saying, 'What can I do? If I can help, you know you have only to ask.'

We stood like that a moment and I felt, as before, his warm energy passing into me. Peg Groundwater came in as a clock chimed the quarter and he said he must go. Peg and I went to my room, where she had made up the fire, and when she saw I was not ill to collapsing, she left me to rest, as I asked. I opened the curtains and sat by the window, waiting for the day. The first pale grey light showed roofs and grass white with frost. Booth would need our prayers.

In those first hours my thoughts were all of Booth, Anna and Quigley. The agitation I felt was for their safety—abundant fears and dire imaginings. Yet after another day and night when there had been no news of Booth, I found a change entering my thoughts.

Booth was dead, surely, and therefore at peace. I was profoundly sorry for it, and for the dreadful manner of it, but it was over now, and Quigley was right: the search for Rowland was therefore at an end. As for Anna, I had had four months on the *Adastra* to study Quigley, and I believed he would take care of her. All of which meant that for two or three months, until spring—September, say—I was free. For so many years my life had been constrained by the needs of others, my grandmother, Nina, Tom, Anna—that the idea brought a curious flattened excitement.

I counted up the money Anna had left in the cache: nine pounds and some shillings. Together with the ten pounds I had hidden in the spine of a book and the money in my purse, I had twenty-four pounds. My lodgings for the quarter were paid, my return fare to England not in doubt, and my clothes were new. If I wished to, I might buy books and drawing materials, take a ferry across the river, walk all day, buy a currant bun.

In the weeks before the ball I must admit I had sometimes felt impatient with Anna, but after she was gone I missed her. I had strange dreams. In one I was caring for a babe-in-arms, which I knew, somehow, was Anna. I was forced to set it down on the ground because of its struggles, whereupon it turned into a wonderful vase as tall as myself, painted with fruit and flowers, but I was angry because it would not speak to me. In another I was unwrapping an infant from swaddling clothes to bathe it. I undressed it as one would peel an onion, and with horror at last, found nothing there at all.

15

ABOUT THE TIME WHEN NEWS OF HIS BEING LOST ARRIVED AT the ball, Booth lay huddled in marshy scrub south of Lagoon Bay. Rain had saturated his clothing, which was now stiffening with ice. His tinderbox was soaked, his musket jammed. The dogs were with him, sleeping curled against his chest and back, but a fiery numbness burned in his swollen hands and feet. He could no longer move. From time to time a palsied shuddering ran through him. This was his third night out.

The wind had been coming from the south-west on the previous Thursday morning when he started out from King George Sound with Turner, heading for the whaling stations. Lempriere had worried about him taking Turner, the convict coxswain of the Woody Island Boat, but Turner was safe enough. Surly, but not malicious; a strong walker and useful companion. They had tramped north-east across the Tiers, climbing steadily, but lost the track when the dogs, Fran, Sandy and young Spring, put up a kangaroo. Turner took the game-bag ahead to retrieve the kill, and at that moment a bolt of pain started up in Booth's chest. It stretched across his heart and pressed hard down like a bar of steel. He gasped and stopped. This must be death. Fran stopped too, turned and looked at him expectantly, stood waiting.

He slid into a sitting position against a tree as the pain gave a last violent squeeze and began to recede. The dense undergrowth sheltered him, but as he gazed up at the sky he saw the weather was breaking. Pewter-coloured clouds massing and rolling, wind thrashing the tops of the gum trees. There was an interval of darkness and silence. He must have dozed. When he was able to stand again the pain was gone and there was no sign of Turner. He shouted. No reply but the wind.

As he moved on he thought he glimpsed the convict out of the corner of his eye, but it was a pale grey strip of hanging bark flinging itself against a tree. The rain came, daylight faded, the first bitter night was endless. He prayed, found one part of his mind reciting the Lord's Prayer while another tried to reckon his position. During the night he could feel the frost entering him, turning his body to stone. When at last a slow, overcast dawn lightened the world, he found it hard to move. He dragged himself into a sitting position, hauled himself gradually to his feet and stumbled on. Every gully, ravine, boulder outcrop looked the same. When he stopped there was a buzzing in his ears. Rain and wind ceased briefly and a perfect silence fell. A lone bird called in the dripping canopy. He found a patch of weak winter sun, fell into it and slept.

When he woke the cold stars were out again and once more he thought he saw someone slide between the trees. A green dress. Caralin. *Spare Thou them O God which confess their faults. Restore Thou them that are penitent.* Was it Sunday? *Forgive us our trespasses . . . manifold sins and wickedness . . .* Perhaps God was punishing him for deserting Caralin and his children? No, he did not believe that. Too many evil bastards flourishing like green bay trees. And God would understand: at the time it had simply been the way of the world, men had their mistresses and bastards. How many of his Regiment had taken native women to their beds in India and deserted them when they moved on? But he could not forget his children's birthdays. The ninth of October and the twenty-sixth of April had become terrible dates to him.

Then the posting to Van Diemen's Land and shooting the albatross on the way. As the broken suffering thing crashed to the deck it fixed him with a bright beady dying eye, full of question. From that moment life had seemed different, not to be used up as easily as possible in pleasure or lazy ambition, but having some new meaning he must learn. For one thing, his memory of the last few years of his life had twisted traitorously in his mind and he knew suddenly what damage he had done, what suffering he had caused. It was like one of those black and white trick pictures—a candlestick one moment, two old witches in profile the next. The pains in his chest began from that time, randomly, as though the dead bird were hanging round his neck, weighing on his heart. For some reason it was also associated in his mind with an earlier sea voyage, when his ship had called at Saint Helena. He had visited the estate where Napoleon died in exile. Peered through the great iron gates and wondered what thoughts Boney had on his deathbed. All those dead and dying men.

At the first convict muster after Arthur appointed him Commandant, Booth looked along the lines of prisoners and saw boys as young as seven. There was nowhere to put them in those days except in the main prison among the old lags. He knew what awaited them, however vigilant the guards. What had become of his own children? Lempriere's much-loved children, Power's children, were a continual reproach.

He had suggested to Arthur the establishment of a separate prison for boys up to fourteen, and Arthur was pleased with the idea. He obtained permission to let them swim in the cove in summer, and their thin white bodies seared his heart again. They bore the scars of old beatings. Limbs were bent with rickets or broken bones ill-healed. He wanted desperately to like them, wanted them to like him—but most were brutal, vicious, foul-mouthed and wild; untameable, disgusting, resentful and sly.

He wrote endlessly to the authorities. A lack of sewing thread and needles, not sent with the bolts of cloth, left the boys half naked one summer. Late in the season he gave up waiting and sent for the necessary items from a mercer in Hobarton—and then spent months answering reprimands from Arthur. At least they were regularly fed. He gave prizes out of his own pocket for diligence: books, small toys.

The boys fought over them or with them, tore them apart. There were small successes, unspeakable failures.

Three years ago he had decided to forget Caralin and marry gentle, doe-eyed, wealthy Phoebe. The week they were to announce the engagement she was taken ill. A summer fever, the doctor said; nothing to alarm. She died three weeks later. Booth told himself he was a scientific man of the new age, and yet he found it hard to rid himself of the thought that she was the victim of a curse set on him. He had not married Caralin, now he would not be allowed to marry. Was that why he hesitated about Lizzie? Ridiculous. He did not believe such things.

Now, lost in the night, he had a vision of himself from far up in the darkness looking down. A scrap of flesh and bone on a tiny dark island in a glimmering sea. Yet everyone was so convinced of their own strutting importance. *The summer of a dormouse.* If he could have stretched his sore, dead mouth he would have laughed and laughed.

And then the stars began to sing, one at a time, joining together until they formed a chord of unbearable beauty. *Lord, oh lord, our light shining in darkness; lucerna pedibus meis; a lantern unto my feet.* Time and space collapsed in pain. The darkness began to be pierced by irregular scuffling, screams and the clamour of voices: a woman weeping, a baby crying, a bugle's deep mellow fart. Years later it was daylight again. The dogs were on their feet, restless, alert. Daphne gave a sharp yelp. He heard the call of a bugle. Lempriere. More bugle notes surrounded him faintly, disappeared. The dogs whined. Spring went bounding off, came back. Bugle calls passed into silence and imagination. He kept dropping into an abyss.

They found him in mid-afternoon on Monday, when one of Frances Spotswood's party caught sight of Sandy and raised a shout. Lempriere's group arrived later, the Hobart contingent close behind. Shocked by Booth's emaciation, the filth that caked him, the stubbled, wrecked face like yellow parchment stretched over a skull, they milled around, desperate to help. They built a fire, cut the boots from his swollen feet and put him too close to the blaze. It caused him agonies when his frostbitten toes began to thaw too quickly. They gave him food and drink and he vomited. They wrapped him in blankets that allowed leeches to continue bleeding him inside the woollen cocoon. In spite of their kindness he survived.

All of June he lay in bed looking out at the winter sky. He knew his collection of escape engines lay below the steps, although he could not see them. He had always admired the machines. Now he thought of the men who had made and used them, imagined their nights at sea or in the bush.

—⁓—

In the second week of July I received a note from Booth saying he was sorry to put me to the inconvenience of travelling down to Port Arthur again, but it would be some time before he could make the journey to Hobart, and he believed I would be as anxious as he to resume our discussion. I was not anxious to resume it at all. I wanted Rowland Rochester to be dead, a swift passage Home in Spring, and a simple, unvarnished story to tell Jane and Rochester.

The day after this came a note from Mrs Chesney urging me to visit them at 'Kenton'. There was a PS:

> Please my dear ask our agent Mr Mather to send the following to be added to our acount there being none bought since I was away.
>
> 2 silver thimble one paper mixed needles
>
> 3 pr small tortusseshell sidecombs—you will no what kind
>
> 3 capcauls—white ribbon for trimming
>
> 2 Ridding Combs—head lice at a plaugue!
>
> 15 yds strong canvas for mens trowsers
>
> 2 lbs arsenic—mice and rats bad
>
> 4 lbs epsom salts and ribbon for shoes
>
> Mr Chesney wishes one pound erly turnip seed and a hat of his normal kind Beaver Felt his being Blown away into the sea when he was riding and Sugar Plumbs for the children.

I made arrangements to return from Port Arthur by way of the Chesneys.

—⚉—

When I saw Booth again it was a bright winter morning, pleasant in the sun, icy out of it. He had insisted on dressing, said Power disapprovingly. I found him in a wicker chair on the verandah, padded with cushions, his possum-fur rug across his knees. St John Wallace and Gus Bergman were with him. Six weeks had passed since Booth's rescue, but I have never seen a man so thin. His jacket hung on his narrow chest. He looked weak but cheerful, calm in a way he had not been during our earlier visit.

'So Mrs Rochester has gone with Quigley,' Booth said, taking my hand in his bony grip for a second. It was like holding a bunch of keys. 'You see I have asked Mr Wallace to join us, and Gus Bergman, too. I believe you will understand why when you hear what I have to say.'

He spoke falteringly of the kindness he had received during his illness. Power fussed around him. Lempriere played chess with him and neglected his trumpet practice. Charlotte Lempriere made broths and custards. He had received notes from the Governor and Lady Franklin, Montagu and Forster. Port wine came from Casey, letters and books from Dr and Mrs Pilkington, and Lizzie. There had been no convict rebellion. The prisoners had expressed concern for his welfare. Booth's eyes filled with the unstoppable tears of illness and he turned to look out at the water.

He spoke of Caralin, his common-law-wife in the West Indies: he believed she must be dead; he could get no news of his children.

'Why did you not take her back to England with you?' asked St John.

'I wanted to break the news to my father first. I would need his help, and to borrow money. Do you know what he said? "Do you want to kill your mother? Ruin Charlotte's engagement? Put an end to your own chances in the Army? You'll turn yourself—and this mulatto woman and her piccaninnies—into paupers." And I understood suddenly that Caralin would be humiliated at every turn. She would hate it.'

There was silence.

Because of Caralin, Booth continued, he had understood Anna's quest from the start, the painful longing to know about a lost loved one. But he also knew that if Caralin was not dead, if she had deliberately severed contact with him because she had found a new way of life, enquiries from him might imperil or destroy it.

During his time in the bush, he added matter-of-factly, he had heard the stars singing and had come to believe that if he were rescued, it would be a sign God had forgiven him. Nevertheless, it was hard to forgive himself. He had come to the terrible knowledge that some wrongs cannot be righted. The reparation owed must be paid to strangers. He would tell everything he knew about Rowland Rochester.

Power came in with coffee and bread and urged Booth to eat. Booth smiled and his thin hands obediently took the bread. Power waited until the Commandant had taken a mouthful and then, with a satisfied grunt, left the room. Booth laid the food aside and said, 'Rowland Rochester is in Van Diemen's Land, or has been. I saw him here two years ago.'

Bergman made an exclamation. I said, 'You *saw* him?'

Booth coloured faintly at our astonishment and looked for a second like his old self. 'I salved my conscience by arguing that it did not affect the outcome. When I spoke to you I still believed Rowland was dead. Now I am not so sure.'

Booth explained that when Rowland left Saint Vincent he did not go alone. He took with him a young Englishwoman, the wife of a Lieutenant in the 21st. She was a girl of seventeen or eighteen, with a baby boy always sickly. Her husband was only a year or two older, still wanting a barrack-room life of drinking and gaming with his friends, while she lived neglected in the hills.

'She and Rowland had formed an attachment?' This was Bergman, who must surely, I thought, be thinking of his own situation. Why did he not marry his convict woman if he was so fond of her and the child?

'No. I don't think so. It was generally thought she simply used him as an escort home to England. And yet on the day when I saw Rowland at the Black Snake Inn, two years ago last February, this woman was with him.'

He shook his head. 'It happened by mere chance. I had leave to go to Oatlands for the wedding of a friend. I hired a horse at New Town but it cast a shoe after Austins Ferry and I had to stop at the Black Snake to have it re-shod. The coach for Port Dalrymple came in as I was waiting. There were passengers getting out and in, and something about one man—his limp, I suppose—caught my eye. And then the woman turned and I recognised her. It came into my mind that they might have married bigamously under another name—in which case they certainly would not want their earlier connections known.'

Booth smiled wryly. 'I was in a mood to oblige them. I had my own secret and was in no hurry to expose others in a similar fix. If it had been only Rowland I would have approached him, or asked openly later in barracks whether anyone else had seen him, but the woman gave it all a different complexion. I was curious though, as you can imagine, and made a few careful enquiries later, but no one seemed to have heard of Rowland since Saint Vincent. I came back down here and almost forgot it until nearly a year later.

'To explain this I have to go back four years. Soon after I arrived here I began to notice a convict named Thomas Walker, or "Mick" Walker. He was a head taller than most of his fellow prisoners, uncommonly good-looking, and uncommon in other ways, too. He could read and write, and although his record was bad—continual attempts at escape—he was well behaved, courteous, articulate. I would have used him as a clerk, but he told me he was a good oarsman and I needed a man for the number one whaleboat, the Commandant's boat. In fact he proved so useful I was sorry to lose him when he came up for his ticket-of-leave in '35. On my recommendation he was appointed constable at New Norfolk.'

'Former convicts are often made constables,' said Bergman, seeing my surprise. 'Especially if they have any education and have been of good conduct.'

Booth nodded. 'There are backsliders, of course, but I did not expect Mick Walker to be one of them. To my great surprise, he was returned to Port Arthur a year or so later, convicted of housebreaking. I ordered him back on the number one whaleboat, telling him he'd been a fool to reoffend. Then he said the charge against him was false, trumped up by the 'Arthur faction' to disguise the death of a man called George Fairfax.'

'George Fairfax!'

Booth nodded at me.

'You recognise the name, of course, and so did I. I ordered him to be silent at once because we were in a muster group, but his coming out with that name shocked me, because I associated it with Rowland Rochester.'

Booth's voice was growing hoarse. He had a fit of coughing, drank some water and coughed again.

'When we found Rowland in Demerara fifteen years before,' he continued, 'the name on the documents in his jacket was Rowland George Fairfax Rochester, which struck me as unusual. Every schoolboy knows "Black Tom" Fairfax, one of Cromwell's heroes in the Civil War, but the Earls of Rochester were Royalists, and I remember saying something to Rowland about it being odd to have Roundheads and Cavaliers in the same family. As soon as Walker said "George Fairfax", my mind leapt to the idea that if Rowland had taken a false name, it might well be that. Therefore, I concluded that Rowland Rochester, alias George Fairfax, was dead.

'I had Walker called in to hear privately what else he might say. But he'd changed his mind and wouldn't speak of it again. He'd decided it might be the worse for him if he was thought to have "blabbed".'

Booth shrugged. He raised his hands, still discoloured from frostbite, let them fall in a gesture of defeat.

'What could I do? If I wrote to Arthur, my letter must go through the Colonial Secretary, Montagu. It would never have reached the Governor; it would have been returned with some scalding comment on my lack of judgement in listening to a convict. My name would be black-marked for the future—without doing Walker any good. I asked him about the names, Rowland Rochester, George Fairfax, but they meant nothing to him.'

Booth coughed again and turned to Bergman, indicating that he should continue.

'It is rare that several senior members of the Arthur faction would be in New Norfolk together,' said Bergman, 'but they were there in February that year for a meeting with the Bridge Association, and there was some kind of quarrel afterwards.'

'The Government had talked of building a bridge at New Norfolk for at least five years,' he added, 'but nothing was done, and at last the New Norfolk settlers determined to build it themselves, by subscription. By February '36 they'd made representations to the Executive Council, and it became necessary to have a general meeting. Whatever happened took place after the meeting, late that night, at the Eagle and Child—and it must have been serious, because the Arthurites quarrelled over it. Henry Arthur resigned and went to the new settlement at Port Phillip. Alfred Stephen moved to New South Wales.'

Power came in again and Bergman fell silent. It was past midday. We moved into the dining room, Booth slow but determined, speaking about general matters while Power served an excellent thick soup and bread. Afterwards, Booth told us that in the end he had done nothing about Walker's story, even after the arrival of the letter from Rochester's lawyer, which had been like a prod to his conscience. He recounted his evening with Montagu and Forster and his feeling that they did not want the matter discussed. At this point he had another paroxysm of coughing and was clearly reaching the end of his strength.

'I want to add,' he insisted when he recovered himself, 'that I am now far less certain that George Fairfax and Rowland Rochester are the same man. The quarrel at New Norfolk was on the eighth or ninth of February, and I travelled up to the wedding on the tenth, the day I saw Rowland Rochester. Once I knew this, I asked Bergman to visit the graveyard for me, to discover whether there is a Fairfax buried there.'

Bergman nodded. 'A headstone with only the name George Fairfax, and the dates: seventeen sixty-eight to eighteen thirty-six.'

'I assume that makes him too old to be Rowland Rochester?' said Booth.

'Yes,' I said. 'Rowland was born in seventeen eighty-nine.' My mind had gone back to Mrs Fairfax's stories. 'There was a scapegrace older cousin called George, the black sheep of the family. Could that be why Rowland came to the colony? Because George Fairfax was here?'

There was a silence before Booth said, 'You see why you may stir up a hornet's nest if you continue to ask questions about Rochester and Fairfax?'

St John Wallace had not spoken so far, but his silence and the severity of his face had emitted cold disapproval. Now he spread his hands and said, frowning, 'If we were certain that George Fairfax was, in fact Rowland Rochester, then my duty as proxy to my cousin Jane would be clear. But as that now appears impossible, I don't understand why I am here, Captain?'

'I assume that Mr and Mrs Rochester will want to know more of Walker's story—if he can be brought to tell it—in case it does cast light on Rowland's whereabouts. And I thought that might be your province, Mr Wallace. After all, you are here to speak with the convicts, to examine them as to their education and their prospects. Walker might say more to you than to me.'

St John Wallace's reluctance was clear, but at Booth's urging he agreed to speak to Walker, although he held little hope of finding out anything.

I asked Booth the name of the woman who was Rowland's companion.

'Catherine Tyndale.'

'Is her husband still with the Twenty-first? Perhaps he . . .'

'Tyndale shot himself soon after his wife left with Rowland. The official verdict was "an accident while cleaning his gun". It was not investigated out of respect to the family, but also because the provocation probably came from our commanding officer, Major Champion, who loathed Tyndale, and singled him out for continual minor punishments. Champion made all our lives a misery. He was afterwards murdered by another of his victims, Private Ballasty, who shot Champion dead as he rode into barracks—and was hanged for it.'

Exhausted, Booth told us, as we gathered to leave, that he'd written to Dr Pilkington and Lizzy Eagle. Smiling through his fatigue, he said she had agreed to marry him.

—⁂—

My plan to return to Hobarton via the Chesneys had to be given up. It rained heavily for two days, and a signal warned that the floods were out at Sorell and Richmond. I returned to Hobart on the *Vansittart* on the fourth of August. Three letters were waiting for me at the post office. The first was from Jane Eyre, written on the sixth of February.

My dear Harriet,

I confess I feel the oddity of writing this to send halfway around the world, trusting to its arrival in a country we failed to reach ourselves. It is little more than two months since we left you, but how much longer it seems! As you may imagine, thoughts of you are never far from my mind. I wonder each day how you are faring, what you may discover, and when we will see you again.

As to our own circumstances, I begin with what is nearest my heart, and what you will doubtless first wish to know: Mr Rochester is recovered! Whatever the cause of his illness, his health began to improve from the moment we turned back towards England. By the time we disembarked at Liverpool

200

he was weak but vastly improved. He is now in good health and spirits and insists my affection caused me to exaggerate the severity of his condition. I am not persuaded. I can never forget those days when we feared he would not live.

Adèle too, is flourishing.

There was a paragraph here about the plans for Adèle's schooling nearby, and two enclosed notes from her, one for me and one for Polly.

Edward and I have now been at 'Ferndean' for two weeks in great mutual contentment. This will be our home. Even now in winter it is beautiful. Snow is falling into the woods as I look out from where I write. I cannot recall whether you ever saw 'Ferndean', but you will understand, I am sure, when I say I have few regrets about the loss of 'Thornfield' with its burden of sad memories. In spring we begin our schemes of improvement. By the time you receive this it will be summer here, and the work long commenced. Edward plans to have the trees cleared some further distance around the house to allow of more light entering the rooms . . .

A page here about refurbishments to 'Ferndean' and the garden, and news of Dawlish and John, who had resumed their former capacities as cook and butler.

We trust you will arrive—I mean, of course, have by now arrived—in the colony without further alarms. Mr Rochester asks me to say he desires Bertha Mason to have everything due to a gentlewoman, without extravagance, of course. We depend on you to judge what is fitting, and beg you will use the enclosed towards her comfort and your own.

Five ten-pound notes were folded in.

You must know how eagerly we look for a word from you. To think of you in those distant regions at our bidding inspires anxious thoughts, even without the mystery of Mr

Rochester's brother, which renders your journey a matter of such profound interest to us. It is impossible to convey our thanks, dear Harriet. We must remain in your debt and endeavour to show you on your return how we value your help. Believe me when I say you are always in our thoughts. I will write no more, being in haste to send this. We pray for you daily, knowing you are in God's care, which has brought us out of dire troubles and into a happiness greater than any I have ever known.

Jane Rochester

The second was a note from Lady Franklin, saying she would be obliged if I would make it convenient to call at Government House at three in the afternoon on the following Wednesday or Thursday.

The third was from Robert McLeod in Richmond. Dr James Ross had died on the first of August. His wife Susan was left in difficult circumstances with thirteen children.

I spent some time considering how best to answer Jane, and at last wrote that Anna had gone away with Quigley, but Captain Booth was kindly assisting me with enquiries about Rowland in the island.

16

LADY FRANKLIN WAS UPSTAIRS IN HER 'OFFICE', THE MAID TOLD me. Later, when I used the word, Jane Franklin explained gently that she preferred to say 'writing room' or 'anteroom', but the servants were apt to forget. The 'office' was a *gentleman's* place of business. She shuddered at the idea of being thought one of those 'bold, masculine, independent women who ape men'.

I understood. Mr Robert Murray, editor of the *Colonial Times*, had recently accused the Governor's wife of being secretly at work on a novel, which he claimed was a satirical attack on Hobart society designed to allow her London friends to mock the raw colonials. A woman with an 'office' might be that kind of woman. *The Advertiser* had followed Murray's lead, but said the book was not fiction but a lampooning history of the island—cribbed from Mr Henry Melville's *The History of Van Diemen's Land*, since Lady Franklin could know nothing of the matter herself. It would annoy the Arthurites, which was no doubt the lady's intention.

Various explanations were offered in Hobart as to why Robert Murray had decided to loathe the Franklins. Some said it was because he had been left off the guest-list for their first levee, either by accident or because Murray was a gentleman convict, transported for the 'gentleman's crime' of bigamy. Others said Sir John had refused to shake his hand when they were introduced. Gus Bergman believed Murray and Montagu considered themselves to be the only aristocrats in the island, and hated having to defer to a couple of nobodies. Murray claimed to be the bastard son of one of the royal princes; Montagu was kin to the Duke of Manchester. For them the Franklins represented a despised new order arisen since the war.

Lady Franklin's father was 'in trade', a cloth merchant; Franklin's was even more deplorable, a shopkeeper! Nobodies. Murray was a dour Scot, a John Knox of our times—and former Army, with nothing but contempt for the Navy. His writing was clever and full of barbed wit, but humourless. To him, Jane Franklin was the pretentious wife of a naval fool, famous not for *finding* the Northwest Passage, but for disastrously *failing* to find it. You could imagine him deciding to take the new couple down a peg or two before he'd ever seen them.

Others, like Boyes, added cynically that battles sold newspapers. Jane Franklin believed the word 'blue-stocking' had done the damage. It was used to describe her in an English newspaper sent out to announce their appointment, and was not accurate, she insisted. But it seemed to have made the pressmen in the colony bristle like hedgehogs. How little they understood her. A paid female scribbler? Horrors! She shrank from any kind of public notice.

Not 'office', therefore. 'Writing room', 'anteroom'; they had a more courtly ring. They brought to mind Miss Hester Stanhope, say, writing invitations for her uncle the Prime Minister; or Wordsworth's sister Dorothy, copying the immortal lines. Women writing in the service of men: no one could object to that.

Jane Franklin thanked me for coming and apologised; I was prompt to the hour and now she must ask me to excuse her for three minutes while she finished a letter to her father. Half-a-dozen lines, no more. The *Thomasina's* sailing had been brought forward to catch this evening's tide and the mail must be aboard by four. She hoped I might find something of interest among the books on the table.

She resumed her writing and I turned the books over. An album of pressed seaweeds, two volumes of sermons, Charles Pasley's *Essay on the Military Policy and Institutions of the British Empire,* Lyell's *Principles of Geology,* Bentham's *Panopticon Versus New South Wales.* There were London newspapers several months old, and the local *Colonial Times,* folded open at a page where one passage had a faint exclamation mark in pencil at the side:

> Mr District Constable 'Tulip' Wright appeared with Mrs Cooper a well-known 'Nymph of the Pave' who was to answer Mrs East for assaulting her together with John Younghusband a 'man about town' with cakes for sale. The witness showing evidence of exchange of pugilistic compliments said she was bathing her black eye when Mrs Thompson came out with a log of she-oak and threw it—called him a varmint—a wretch—a stinking cakeman and said she'd larn him . . .

Whose pencil mark was it? Would Lady Franklin read such things? I discreetly considered the room. More books, in two tall bookcases and on small tables. Chairs in green velvet, a tapestry firescreen. A vase of leaves giving off a faintly bitter, musty smell—or perhaps that came from the 'cabinet of curiosities' bulging with specimens. Fossils, shells and bones, birds' eggs, seedpods, butterflies pinned in rows, brown unidentifiable lumps. It resembled the assortment in Booth's rooms. I later found such collections to be ubiquitous in the houses of the colony. This room's general effect was warm and peaceful, however, a place of private studious pleasure. It was genuinely an 'anteroom'; at the further end a door led into the bedchamber.

It did not escape Lady Franklin that I was taking notice. She paused in her writing and said, 'These furnishings are old favourites. I have carried them to many countries. With my chair, my Turkey rug, flowers and a few books, I have felt at home from the Nile to Saint Petersburg. My "campaign furniture", I call it.'

She smiled, blotted and sealed her pages, scrawled a direction, wiped her pen, pulled the bell to summon a servant. Later, when she was so vilified in the newspapers, people said she had no sense of humour, but in fact she frequently made wry little jokes. Like that one, they were often so subtle they passed without notice. I once heard her say among a mixed group that her husband and Mr Thomas Archer, two huge men, 'were the *bulk* of the Legislative Council'. It was received in heavy silence.

'Captain Booth says in his note he is quite recovered, but of course he would say that. I hope you really found him well?'

She came over and sat in the shabby velvet chair and spoke of Booth's ordeal. She asked about the families on the peninsula with friendly interest and wanted to know what I thought of the Port Arthur Church. She shouldn't have told Booth she thought the gable ends 'clumsy', but he had taken it in good part, dear man. Architecture was one of her interests. She was about to have plans drawn up for a new Government House to be built on the Domain. This place was falling about their ears. There were two or three convict architects here—or she might persuade Mr William Porden Kay, her stepdaughter's cousin, to come out from home. He, too, was studying to be an architect. Noticing that I'd picked up Pasley's essay, she asked if I'd read it. I told her it had been one of my father's favourites. He'd read parts of it aloud to me when I was a child. She said her own father had done the same.

'So Booth is to marry Miss Lizzie Eagle? And Mrs Rochester is gone to New Holland? Where did you discover Mr Rochester's grave?'

'We were not able to, my lady. He may have lived here under another name. It may be impossible to . . .'

'Another name?' She was interested, a bird poised above a worm-hole, a game dog stilled to point. 'Ah well, I won't pry. After all, the impulse to escape is easy to understand. Who has not at some time imagined changing their too-familiar self for some other? Not that I mean to condone deception. I need not fear you will misunderstand me, Mrs Adair?'

'No, my lady,' I said.

'This colony is small, the walls have ears, there are few educated women and too many gossips. In short, a good deal of mischief may be done by a word in the wrong company.'

When I came to know her better I understood that she tried to practise the reserve she was advising, but her impulse was always towards candour, discussion, an exchange of ideas about the difficult, fascinating world.

'When I think of what this place could be . . .' she said, 'Athens, Dublin, Edinburgh . . . They are all small, out-of-the-way cities, and yet each has been a distinguished centre of learning. Distance is nothing these days. Traffic to this part of the world will increase as England comes to know more of our island's beauty and rare interest.'

She peered at me keenly. These penetrating stares were greatly disliked by some people. They were misleading. She was short-sighted even then, but would seldom use spectacles. Her eyes would trouble her greatly in the years to come.

She paused, changed the subject. A parcel of gifts had come to her from the peninsula: a seaweed collection, a bushranger's skull—Mr Lempriere had kindly boiled it for several hours to enlarge the sutures, the phrenology was curious—and a number of drawings, including three of mine. She had been astonished to find them so accomplished. (Tact was never her most reliable quality. She could be a model of diplomacy or blunt as a bargee.) Giving me no pause to reply, she said she was pleased to have the sketches. She was making a collection of views in the colony. On seeing their quality she and Miss Cracroft had formed a plan (plans flew from her brain like the sparks from Port Arthur coal). Perhaps I had heard that Mr John Gould, who had published *A Century of Birds from the Himalaya Mountains*, was shortly to arrive in the colony with his wife?

'Oh, good heavens! No, I did not know it, but I am so very glad! I am acquainted with the Goulds, my lady,' I said. 'I knew Eliza Gould in London when she was Miss Coxen. We were close friends. I would love to see her again.'

Lady Franklin sat expressionless for a moment and then said, 'Twenty years ago I would have thought that an extraordinary coincidence, but I have come to know the smallness of the human portion of the world. It does not surprise me now.'

She said Sir John was anxious to give the Goulds every assistance. Mr Gould would be away from Hobarton on collecting excursions, gathering material for a book on the birds of New Holland. This would leave Mrs Gould much alone, making drawings from the specimens as they were obtained. It was therefore Lady Franklin's scheme that rather than working solitary in lodgings, Eliza Gould must stay at Government House and draw in a room here. Eleanor Franklin and Miss Cracroft would attend once a week with Eleanor's governess, Miss Williamson, as a lesson. Lady Franklin would join the circle herself when at liberty. If I was agreeable we would decide on a fee to cover my labours and such drawings as could be useful to the Goulds, and she might wish to purchase some of my sketches herself.

Unfortunately, she added, her stepdaughter showed no gift for drawing, but she must persevere. The child was not yet fifteen; much might yet be done with her education. I heard the doubt in Lady Franklin's tone and only understood it when I came to know Eleanor, whose intelligence was acute in many directions, but whose stubborn lack of interest in certain subjects was often a refusal to like what her stepmother liked.

'Sophy, on the other hand,' continued Lady Franklin, 'has quite a talent.'

Drawing had been one of their regular pastimes on the *Fairlie* during the voyage out, but Eleanor had showed a little spirit of resistance to learning. Some degree of resentment was to be expected, of course.

'I lost my own mother when I was a child, and I know I would not have taken kindly to a stepmother,' she admitted.

Eleanor's mother had died of consumption not long after the child's birth. Sophy was ten years old when baby Eleanor was taken in by the Cracrofts, so the girls were more like sisters than cousins.

'And the bond between sisters may be close and yet occasionally troubled, I know. I have always been closer to my sister Mary—Mrs Simpkinson—than to my older sister Fanny, who is Mrs Majendie now. Do you have sisters, Mrs Adair?'

But at that moment the clock struck four and she rose, looked out of the window, and briskly led the way downstairs.

'That was the carriage returning with Sophy and Eleanor. They were to call for Mr Knopwood. He is in town a few days to see his doctor and lawyer. Not in good health, poor man. We'll take tea with them. Sophy needs proper companionship. Since her cousin Mary married Mr Price last month, she has only Miss Williamson—apart from the Maconochies, of course . . .'

She hesitated, did not finish the sentence, began again.

'I had hopes of Mr St John Wallace's wife as a friend for Sophy, but now Mrs Wallace is expecting a child, it is unlikely . . .'

Half my mind continued to listen while the other half took in the idea of Louisa expecting a child. I was pleased for her, but immensely surprised. Their marriage must be in a healthier state than had seemed at all likely from her revelations on the *Adastra*.

Sophy had charge of the tea things. Eleanor was talking ponies and dogs to Knopwood, who was warming his hands at the fire. His white hair seemed sparser, a more ethereal cloud; he was thinner and frailer, but smiling still. He clasped my hand and said, 'Ah, Mrs Adair! I wish I had known we were to meet! Mr Rowland Rochester! You see I have not forgot. I knew I had seen the name! I have set them aside for you but they are at my house. I meant to send them but I have been ill, you know.'

I thanked him and tried to discover what he had found.

'Why, the books I promised you!'

He seemed to imagine we'd spoken of it before. Sophy supplied him with tea and a buttery muffin that engrossed his attention. After a pause I tried again, but he had forgotten Rowland and wanted to talk about the villainous lawyer in England who could not be brought to send him the two thousand pounds left to him in his sister's will.

There was another sign of age in the way he began to repeat himself. He thanked Jane Franklin, as I had heard him do twice before, for her kindness in asking him to dine last Christmas. He followed this by saying calmly that he doubted he would last another summer. By the coming Yuletide he hoped to be with Betsey, his dear dead girl.

'Tush!' said Jane Franklin kindly. 'You have many more Christmasses yet to spend with us—or you will have to answer to me, sir.'

He laughed weakly and said, 'If I am not with you then I will be answering to God, ma'am, and so it seems I am answerable every way!'

They chuckled gently but her face was sad.

—⁂—

Elizabeth Coxen at nineteen had been a quiet, sweet-natured girl, painfully shy in company, yet humorous and quick in private. We first encountered each other in a bookshop called Benson's, just off the Strand, in the year '21. Benson's in those days had a room set aside for the sale of hand-coloured prints, painted fans and drawings. There was a fashion for animal subjects, and Elizabeth and I were both selling these, one or two a week. It was one of those friendships that blossom immediately out of mutual liking, mutual interests, and we began meeting to draw and talk at the new zoological gardens in Regent's Park, and this continued after Eliza married John Gould. He was always pleasant to me in a rather lofty way. I'm afraid I thought him a pompous little man—and Tom couldn't bear him. Gould opened a taxidermist's shop in Broad Street, Soho, and being largely self-taught, went briefly to Scotland to learn more from Mr John Edmonstone, a freed black slave from Guyana, who was demonstrating taxidermy to medical students at the University of Edinburgh.

Now, meeting again, Eliza and I talked of those days, and of her children. She had been forced to leave her two little daughters and her son Charles, her lovely Charley, with her mother in London. Her eldest son Henry had come with them—he was seven—and so had her nephew, who was fourteen and also named Henry, but known as 'Scrammy' because his right hand was deformed. It had been accidentally shot by a relative when he was younger. In a month Scrammy would sail to Sydney alone and set off to the back country of New South Wales to find his uncles, Eliza's brothers, who had taken up land there. She looked forward to spending several months with them on the way home, when her husband's collecting in Van Diemen's Land was finished.

'It is so good,' Eliza whispered, pressing my hand, 'to see a familiar face among strangers.' Such very kindly people, she added hastily. Nothing could be kinder than the attentions she and her husband had received since their arrival. They had also brought a maid-companion, Mary Watson, a cheerful, practical young woman, more friend than servant, who took care of little Henry, and her husband's manservant James Benstead, and Mr John Gilbert, a colleague of Gould's, a fellow naturalist.

John Gould's assurance of manner had increased with his fame. He was already called 'the Bird Man' and clearly relished the title. Sophy and Henry Elliot were amused by his swaggering, and agreed Gould had the habit of thinking well of himself on all possible occasions. Jane Franklin, overhearing this, said that in her view he was entitled to do so. Undoubtedly he did have a rare talent for locating birds, even those shy or seldom seen, and no one could quarrel with his skills at recording and preserving them. He had also mastered the curious art of 'pishing'—making soft twitterings and calls fatally enticing to birds. It was like her to know such a word. She seemed to have an endless degree of tolerance for Gould. What might have irritated her in someone else was forgivable in him, perhaps because he shared her passionate eagerness for knowledge, and seemed to take it for granted that a woman might feel the same.

She also thought it admirable that while he had started life as a gardener like his father, Gould had mastered Latin and rudimentary French so that he could use the Linnaeus system of classification. She often looked through the books he had brought with him, his Forsfield and Vigors, his Sparmann, Cuvier's *The Animal Kingdom*, and Temminck's *Manuel d'ornithologie, ou Tableau Systématique des Oiseaux qui se trouvent en Europe.* These were kept in the workroom assigned to the Goulds, which soon became known as the Bird Room.

In reality it was two rooms, a disused brick kitchen dating from the earliest years of the colony, and a low-ceilinged chamber connected to it, once a small servants' hall, probably. This had plenty of south light from old-fashioned windows looking out onto the laundry yard. It contained a long scrubbed table at which Eliza and I worked, and shelving for birds, cages, and other necessaries. Stray cats attracted by the birds used to prowl the area at night, leaving the smell of toms rank against the doorway in the morning—which may be the reason why I have never since been able to like the scent of lavender. It retains for me an association with cat urine and bird slaughter, lavender oil being used to protect the bird-skins against infestation by insects. Thyme and rosemary were employed for the same purpose, the dried herbs packed between the feathered skins as they were layered into boxes.

Like any alchemist, Gould closely guarded the recipes he used in his taxidermy, but I know they included alum, boracic powder and carbolic acid, with naptha, strychnine, and many forms of arsenic. On the shelves he kept jars of Fowler's solution, one percent of arsenic, and *liquor arsenii* and *hydrargyri rodidi*, white arsenic; and there was 'Paris green', and 'King's yellow', or orpiment, which I had used for making Tom's colours. The skinning had to be carried out in the most precise fashion, and John Gould went at this delicate work in the old kitchen with the care of a surgeon and the avidity of a butcher.

He prepared only a handful of stuffed, mounted birds while he was in Hobart, most of them gifts for the Franklins. Among them was a little goshawk everyone declared wonderfully lifelike—and it was, but I had become fond of it while it was alive, caged, and privately thought it perverse to kill any creature to give it a spurious semblance of life. What had disappeared with its life was its character, as I explained to Bergman, who called in one day when I was alone there. It had been an intelligent bird, quick to recognise certain voices and people. Bergman's brown face tilted slightly to one side, considering.

'That's hard for you,' he said. 'But we're back to the old subject, time. Taxidermy, embalming—they're some of the ways in which humans try to defy death. Art is the same, isn't it? Sculpture, your drawings, portraiture—all ways of countering mortality.'

He was at Government House to attend a meeting in preparation for the voyage to the South Cape and Port Davey. Surveyors and hydrographers would carry out further coastal mapping, John Gould would capture birds, Lady Franklin would observe. Bergman had called to say he had suddenly wondered whether George Fairfax's presence at the Bridge Meeting meant he owned land in the area. On searching the records he had discovered this was so.

'A property across the river from the town at New Norfolk was owned in the name of George Fairfax from the year 'twenty-seven, but resumed to the Crown in mid-'thirty-five, six months before the quarrel at the Eagle.'

'Why would it be resumed to the Government?'

'Several reasons: neglect is the most common. Failure to improve the land in some stipulated way over a period of years, or non-payment of rates or dues—or because the Government wants the land back for its own purposes—something like the bridge.'

'I wonder if there's any record of Fairfax objecting to the process? We might discover an address through those papers.'

'I thought of that. There's nothing—which is interesting in itself. It suggests that he certainly wasn't living in the area. Perhaps not in Hobart, or even in the island.'

We talked for a time about what this might mean, but came to no conclusions, and soon drifted back to the more interesting topic of art and mortality. We were still talking half an hour later when Eliza came in.

—⁂—

Louisa and St John returned from Port Arthur in September and were among many who came to the Bird Room to meet the Goulds and exclaim over the doomed creatures in the cages, the skins, eggs and nests; to see the delicate skeletons soaking in spirits of salts or laid out to dry, to admire drawings in progress. Louisa's condition was now very apparent.

'December,' she replied tonelessly in answer to my question, and looking directly at me, grimaced. I was puzzled. She had said she wanted a child. St John had news, he said, and we walked down through the shrubbery to a seat near the water. It was early spring, still cool but pleasant in the sunshine.

St John had had several conversations with 'Mick' Walker, but the convict refused to say anything about New Norfolk. Walker was an extraordinary man, added St John; of uncommon personal attractiveness. His face had what one could only call nobility, a pure, classical form of beauty rare in men, like the head on a Greek or Roman coin—miraculously unmarred by the bad life he had lived. The man's physique was no less striking. He was strong and well formed, a natural athlete—like the Adam of some new and better race, fresh from the hand of God.

St John seemed unaware of the extraordinary emphasis into which his enthusiasm had led him, but Louisa was looking at me with a peculiar little smile.

The convict could read and write, but little else, St John continued—unless he was concealing it. The man was willing to learn, but hesitant in case he should be made to look foolish in front of the other convicts, for whom he was a natural leader. One of these was an unfortunate named John Thomas, known as 'Dido'. He had a club foot and a partially cleft palate which made him unable to speak clearly. In spite of his afflictions, Dido was immensely strong in the arms and shoulders, an able rower like Walker, one of the Commandant's number two crew. Walker seemed to be Dido's protector and spokesman. His dealings with these men, St John said, had convinced him that many prisoners could be made into useful Christian citizens. With the right teaching they could then train others, as recommended in Lancaster's monitorial system.

Louisa continued to stare at me during this with the same small sour smile, raising her eyebrows from time to time. She pulled some eucalytpus leaves from a tree and twisted them in her gloved hands, sniffing their pungent scent.

'You see how it is,' she said when her husband stopped. 'My husband has found a lost sheep—a whole flock—and makes it his business to bring them back into the fold. In two days' time he goes down to Port Arthur again for another month. I am to go to the Chesneys.'

They were again staying with Archdeacon Hutchins but must hastily find other quarters now. The Archdeacon had been obliged to offer refuge to Mr Palmer, the Rural Dean, and Palmer's wife Harriet, and Harriet's sister Miss Rachel Owen. The Church house they had been occupying in Argyle Street had burned down the night before.

—m—

Eleanor Franklin made no great progress at drawing but toiled breathily, more patient when her stepmother was not present, which was most of the time, since Jane Franklin frequently joined John Gould's party on his excursions. Eleanor had the same plump, round face and light-brown hair as her father. She was also like him in being immensely devout. When she was nine she had decided to marry a clergyman, she told me, and was now waiting for a suitable one to appear. She did not care for landscapes, only pictures of animals and scenes of moral or religious sentiment.

'What shall I do with this part?' she would cry. 'Oh, do fill it for me, Mrs Gould, Mrs Adair.'

Pleased by the smallest encouragement but confident without it, she announced with satisfaction at the end of each morning, 'I am vastly improved, am I not? Is this not very lifelike?'

'If it is, it's because Eliza or Harriet has made it so,' said Sophy.

'I shall show Papa. He will like it.'

Sophy's drawings were not conventional but they were lively and frequently captured the subject in a few naive lines. This did not satisfy her, she was determined to do 'proper' watercolours. Mary

Maconochie, the wife of Sir John's secretary, and her eldest daughter, Mary-Ann, also came to draw at first, but music was their real passion, Mrs Maconochie said. Their attendance soon lapsed. Sophy was indulgent. The Maconochies were in straitened circumstances; they employed only one servant and had little leisure.

On the first morning, when I prepared to leave at noon, Sophy objected. I must take luncheon with them as Eliza did. It had been understood. And Eliza wished to spend the afternoon with her son— but perhaps Sophy and I might walk? This soon became the pattern of the days I spent at the Bird Room, our afternoons being frequently a scramble up the hill to the Government Gardens on the 'Domain' about two miles away.

The gardens were on the hillside facing away from the town, looking down to the Derwent River, their entrance being through an arch in a handsome high brick wall of considerable length, which faced north. Governor Arthur had had this built for the growing of grapes, espaliered apricots and peaches. Fireplaces had been made at regular intervals so the wall could be warmed in cold seasons. Almonds and apricots did particularly well there. The blossom was out that September and this was a sight Sophy craved, a reminder of Home. Occasionally we had the use of a carriage and Eliza and little Henry came too, especially if we were gathering herbs for the Bird Room or flowers for Government House. When there were horses to spare we rode with Eleanor and two grooms. I had not ridden since I was at school in Ireland, but the distance was not great, and I soon began to enjoy it again. Miss Williamson was too old to ride.

Sophy was a little bored, a little lonely. After eighteen months in the island she could not wait to return to England. Jane Franklin had offered to pay her passage to travel home with some suitable family, but Sophy would not go without Aunt and Nuncle. In the meantime she wanted company other than Eleanor and Miss Williamson. The local ladies? Sophy clicked her tongue with annoyance. If she or Aunt appeared to favour the womenfolk of one official over another there were cries of 'faction', and in any case the military wives were dull,

dull, dull. A respectable chaperone increased her freedom. I was a temporary visitor, not part of any quarrelsome little clique, with no aristocratic relations or pretentions to *ton* to make me dangerous. (Sophy could be as blunt as her aunt.)

As for Mary Maconochie and her daughter, they were delightful, said Sophy carefully. She and Aunt were *very* fond of them, but . . . In close quarters on the *Fairlie* they had revealed an alarming tendency to question *everything*, even religion, and they were encouraged in this by Captain Maconochie, who was half genius—and one had to admit—half mad. Sophy's mother and father would not like her to be too intimate with such radicals.

Plunged into all this new activity, I deliberately pushed Rowland Rochester to the back of my mind. I could not forget him, but my congenial work with Eliza was now the vital, pleasurable centre of my life. Until I could discover what Knopwood had found, I would simply enjoy each day, I decided.

At the end of September, however, a crisis erupted which had the Maconochies at its centre—and on the heels of this came news of Knopwood's death.

—⁂—

During the 'Maconochie Affair', as it became known, signs of a household in distress were everywhere at Government House, as they had been at 'Thornfield' in those days which now seemed so distant. Lady Franklin shut herself in her room, and Marie the French maid went up and down with vinegar-water, gruel and camomile tea. The housekeeper, Mrs Childs, was aggrieved because she could elicit no instructions about meals or any other household matter. Sophy was flustered, indignant, and refused to take it upon herself to give orders. Dead flowers lingered for days in the great hall vase as a sign of Mrs Childs' dissatisfaction. They were taken out at last, but not replaced.

Mary Maconochie had demanded entry to Jane's room, reported Eleanor, and when refused, hammered on the door with her fists and then rushed away, weeping, down the stairs. Eleanor and Miss

Williamson were sent to stay at the Government Farm at New Norfolk. Urgent male voices rose behind closed doors. For a few days the commotion was a mystery, and then John Gould explained the trouble to Eliza and me. I remember that day because of the swallows, which had just returned for spring. Gould had been out before dawn to hunt them. Eliza and I were already working when he came in carrying two small, feathered corpses and set about measuring them with calipers. Eliza was in the middle of an intricate drawing so I took notes for him while she continued.

'This is *Hirundo javanica* . . . total length six inches. Bill, half an inch. Wing, four and five-eighths. Tail, three inches. Tarsi, half an inch. Bye the bye, I have discovered the cause of the commotion is Captain Maconochie. Wait, this is odd. This bird *is javanica*, I suppose? But look at this, Eliza! The tail . . . Here in Sparmann, *javanica* is pictured with the square tail, do you see? Now look again at this one I have got today; the tail is *rounded*. The question is, has Sparmann's been correctly drawn? You see why I insist on accuracy? Let me compare it with Temminck's description. Where is *Planches Coloriées*?'

I went into the next room to fetch the book while he continued, 'What? Oh, Maconochie . . . Well, it seems that Lady Franklin, reading a London newspaper just arrived, came across an article about the Assignment System in Van Diemen's Land. It carries Sir John's name as author, but was not writ by him at all—voices opinions quite contrary to his. Maconochie is the culprit. He has written the thing and sent it to England—but he claims the papers were clearly marked as his own and must therefore have been deliberately misrepresented by those in Whitehall with an axe to grind. Which is probably true. Anti-transportation and anti-slavery sentiment is used by Whigs and Tories alike these days, most of them wholly ignorant of the real circumstances here. Ah, thank you, Hetty.

'Well, Temminck calls it *Hirondelle orientale,* but it is identical to Sparmann's *javanicus;* the same square tail. The one I have here appears to be distinct from both.'

There was triumph in his voice, but he was cautious, and never permitted himself to assume a success until his insights were confirmed, as this one later was. He did show his excitement by shutting the large book with a whump of satisfaction. This was the bird he later called *neoxena*, one of thirty new species he exhibited in England four years later.

—⁂—

Sophy came to the Bird Room to vent her outrage. Sir John had received a reprimand from London. Maconochie had sent his report in the Government bag, and therefore it was assumed to contain Sir John's opinions. It had been tabled in Parliament in London without due process through the Colonial Office. Nuncle was deeply angry with Maconochie, but his Christian principles required forgiveness, and his nature inclined the same way. He had been hesitant about bringing Maconochie to the colony, but Sir John Barrow, Nuncle's old friend in the Admiralty, had recommended the Scotchman, and Aunt Jane had urged it too. She thought it would be valuable to have with them a man who had studied penal systems, as Maconochie had.

But even on the *Fairlie* it was not only Sophy who began to have doubts. Maconochie had explained to Lady Franklin his idea that all human beings were once black-skinned. Increased civilisation wrought internal changes, which gradually lightened the skin. He allowed his children to read anything except the Bible. One of his lectures on the ship, on human physical types, had been so indelicate it scattered the ladies into blushing flight.

Jane Franklin was now conscience-stricken at her part in employing Maconochie. She agreed he was culpable and must be dismissed . . . but he had no private income, and Mary and the children must not be allowed to suffer. Four months of intimacy on the *Fairlie* could not be set aside. How could they be left penniless? The Home Government must be persuaded to give Maconochie some other post here. It might take a year, but . . .

219

In Bergman's opinion the Maconochie Affair had only hastened changes already on the way. The Assignment System had been under attack in England for some time. His was by no means a lone voice, but newspaper editors, settlers, and above all John Montagu, were determined to vilify Maconochie as a traitor and a fool.

'Montagu hates Maconochie,' explained Bergman, 'and will add fuel to the flames if he can. And it's true that Maconochie's report will give the Molesworth Committee in London exactly the excuse they've been looking for to abolish assignment—perhaps even transportation altogether. If they do, the island will suffer. How can properties and businesses be worked without convict labour? There are no free labourers to speak of. Settlers come here to work for themselves, not labour for others.'

He told us that there were not nearly enough ticket-of-leave-men and free labourers to fill the need here. And even if there were, they'd have to be paid, which would bring profits down to nothing.

'What will happen to the convicts if they are not to be assigned?'

'That is the great question. England seems to favour keeping them in prison for the whole length of their sentences. That would be very bad policy. At present about nine-tenths of convict arrivals are immediately assigned to households, and thus are fed, clothed and sheltered by their masters. If the decision is made to introduce the kind of "probation prisons" the reformers want, all the prisoners' keep becomes an expense on the public purse. Settlers will have to be taxed to provide the revenue, and will have their servants withdrawn at the same time! A double blow. Worse still—we are refused any representation on the Government councils because it's a penal settlement. Gregson, Fenn Kemp and others have been complaining about that for years.

'And where will the prisoners be housed? There are not enough buildings now. The irony is that Maconochie is not in favour of probation prisons himself. He argues that keeping hundreds of offenders penned together is the worst answer, and any man who's been in the Army would say he's right.'

He shrugged. 'And if taxes don't bring in enough revenue, the Governor is supposed to sell land to make up the difference—but the only land left these days is isolated, or unsuitable for crops or animals, certainly not worth twelve shillings an acre, which is the price they're insisting Sir John ask for it.

'Montagu is as bitter against Sir John as he is against Maconochie. He blames Franklin for bringing the mad Scotchman here, and makes no secret of having written to England to try to prevent Maconochie ever having another Government appointment. He was furious to discover Sir John has written recommending Maconochie for other posts in Hobarton.'

—⁂—

At this moment of crisis the Franklins could not attend Knopwood's funeral, nor could they easily send an empty carriage as a mark of respect as they would do at Home, since the funeral was to be at Knopwood's tiny Church at Clarence Plains—on the eastern side of the river, miles down the estuary. In these circumstances Henry Elliot was sent to represent them. I went down on the steam-packet hired by a group of Knopwood's old friends to convey members of the public who wished to attend. I went because I'd liked the old gentleman, but also, I admit, because I half-hoped he might have left 'the books' for me, whatever they were.

As the crowd of mourners filed off the ferry onto the jetty near the Clarence windmill, the spring wind fluttered an orchard of blossom near the path. Wattle shone in golden bursts among the darker green of the hills. New wheat showed in a faint wash of green across the fields. The congregation was too great for the tiny wooden Church and many stood outside in the sun. Men, women and children, black-garbed and silent, stood in the field with heads bowed. Sheep nibbled across the paddocks behind the graveyard, shadows of the clouds raced over the ground in dark fleeing patches. On such a day it would be hard to leave the world and lie in the earth. Reverend Naylor read aloud Knopwood's words:

Friends die, and years expire, and we ourselves shall do the same . . .

Sophy gave a shudder when I described the scene next day.

'How I should hate to be buried here! I pray nightly that I may survive until we reach England again,' she said.

Father Philip Connolly, the Catholic priest, was at the funeral, loud with drink and weeping for his dear old friend, although many in Hobart had thought it a scandal to see the Church of England minister on familiar terms with the Papist. It was Father Connolly who gave Henry Elliot a parcel, which Henry brought to me in the Bird Room next day. Rectangular, the hard shape of wrapped books, it was addressed in an old man's shaky hand: 'Mrs Adair in care of Lady Franklin, Government House, Hobarton'. Three books, two bound beautifully in leather: *Gulliver's Travels* and *Robinson Crusoe,* and an unbound copy of *The Tempest,* sewn coarsely along the spine. The Swift carried a bookplate, a leafy border framing an empty shield on which was written in faded ink: '*Ex Libris* Rowland George Fairfax Rochester'. There was also a loose fragment of paper carrying a note in Knopwood's writing: 'Purchased Hobarton 1837'.

17

BEFORE THE ARRIVAL OF THESE BOOKS, ROWLAND HAD BEEN merely an irritating puzzle to me, an enigma compounded of fragments. Eleven years older than his brother Edward, if he were alive he would be fifty-one now. Personable, by all accounts: a fair-haired, cheerful man. Musical, but 'a scholar too', Mrs Fairfax had said. Certainly Anna had loved him, and Lady Mary Faringdon too, presumably. And Catherine Tyndale? Women are capable of loving even the most blighted failure of a man, of course, but I doubted he was that. And now, in the books, certain marginal annotations in spidery writing made me feel a startling, breathing presence; a man who read attentively, whose questions were as important to him as mine to me. *What latitude is this?* he asked himself at one point in the Defoe. *Shall I ever see it?* And almost hidden in an inner margin close to the spine: *If Friday had been a woman? Would Crusoe have kept his religion then, or brought up a tribe of little brown Crusoes? What story would Friday tell of their meeting?*

The two largest bookshops in the town, Fullers and Solomons, assured me the books had never graced their shelves. Oldham's, Beddome's and Meredith's, 'OBM's', was equally certain. I went next to Davis's Seed and Stationery Warehouse, where I had purchased my writing and drawing materials on the day after our arrival. I could not recall seeing any books, but Davis's advertisement in the *Courier* claimed 'upwards of 5,000 volumes on well-assorted subjects': a sizeable number for a seller of seeds.

A door at the back of the shop led to a narrow corridor, and thence to a warren of book-crammed alcoves smelling of glue, paper and dust. A labyrinth; at its heart no Minotaur, but two affable, bespectacled gentlemen pottering gently in an alcove equipped for repairing and binding books. Mr and Mr Davis, father and son. Seeds were their bread-and-butter, stationery a sideline, books their abiding pleasure, they said happily. They were not so much sellers as *collectors*, although they reluctantly admitted they *might* sell a book, if pressed. Both men were walking catalogues of their stock, which was at least as extensive as they claimed.

They had not sold these items to Mr Knopwood, poor old gentleman, but they knew where he had obtained them. They recognised this copy of *Gulliver's Travels* (a *very* fine binding), as having been for sale for many months on a stall at the weekly market down by the Rivulet. They had considered buying it but already carried three copies. The seller was Mr Harry Bentley, a notorious rag-and bone man who set up most Thursdays between the Dog Woman and the cage-birds.

When I left the Davises I was carrying four books I had not intended to buy and they had not intended to sell. The following Thursday I went early to the market before I was expected at the Bird Room, and found it to be like any such event in England: the same bellowing dusty beasts, the hawkers and pedlars, stalls and tents. The bird-seller was a fat young man seated on a yellow chair with a pair of parrots on his shoulders. On the fence behind him hung cages of canaries, pigeons and finches. The Dog Woman next to him sat on the ground with her back against the fence, legs stretched out in front, feet lolling outwards like those of a rag doll. Six puppies in a box wrestled sleepily beside her. Four other dogs were tethered to the fence: one pair old and resigned, the other young and hopeful.

Next was Mr Harry Bentley, a man of unfathomable age in a long green coat and brown wool cap, one side of his face disfigured by a livid scar, which dragged it into a permanent leer. On the fence behind him hung old clothes. Coats hunched with the burden of hard times, boots suspended by their laces. Bits of china and a few tattered almanacs lay on a cloth beside him. He glanced at the books I showed him, and said, 'Ain't no call, see? Munce they was sat there afore Parson took 'em.'

The Dog Woman nodded and cackled.

''e 'ad a li'l white dorg,' she said. 'Li'l dorg fer you, missus?'

I shook my head. 'Mr Knopwood bought them from you?'

Harry Bentley drank from a bottle and passed it to her. After a moment's thought I indicated a glass jar with the tiny skeleton of a mermaid in it and handed him four shillings, though it was not worth sixpence, and he told me he'd had the books from a woman at a farm. Where was the farm, and who was the woman? He shrugged, spat to one side. With a few more coins I learned it was out Copping way, near Bream Creek or thereabouts. The woman was 'the wife of him as kep' the Eagle 'n' Chile at New Norfolk'.

'Carmichael,' said the Dog Woman, 'Seth Carmichael.'

They could not or would not say more, but this was enough. The Inn at New Norfolk again. I walked back to the Bird Room, recalling that Copping lay beyond Richmond and Sorell and wondering if I could reach it from the Chesneys'. But how had the woman come by the books? Stolen them from a dead man?

I was about to recount all this to Eliza, but when I reached the Bird Room, saw she was being sick into a basin. When the spasm was over she confessed she was now certain she was carrying another child, which she had been trying to avoid. Poor John was vexed. Their plans for the summer must be altered. They had intended to travel to the new Wakefield Colony in South Australia in January, and then to 'Yarrundi', her brother's property in New South Wales. Now she would have to remain here while John went alone, returning before the baby came. To make matters worse, the strong odours of the Bird Room seemed to increase her nausea each morning, just as many new specimens had come in. Would I come every day until she recovered, instead of only three days as at present?

During early November, therefore, Eliza joined me at around noon, and in the mornings I worked alone, apart from visitors. Sophy was the most frequent of these, agitated by 'appalling' news—the Montagus and their children were moving into Government House—at Aunt Jane's invitation!

'After the trouble that man has caused! Now the vile creature and his wife and children must stay with us as though they were *friends*,' she cried. 'November, December . . . Their ship sails in *March*. The whole *summer*.'

The Colonial Secretary was taking his family home on eighteen months leave. In the meantime they could not live in 'Stowell' because the entire contents had been sold at auction, bringing four thousand pounds. The house itself had been up for sale for months, but there were no buyers and it was now let unfurnished.

'Why can't they stay with the Forsters?' Sophy demanded.

Jane Franklin said it was only right to take them in. Montagu, after all, was the most senior official next to Sir John. Gus Bergman laughed and said he thought there was a good deal of method, as usual, in what others were pleased to call Lady Franklin's madness, 'a characteristic mixture of impulsive generosity and acute intelligence'. For one thing, this was a shrewd way of securing the definite departure of the Maconochies, whose disorganised leave-taking might otherwise take months. And perhaps Lady Franklin, like many others, believed the Montagus were not really intending to return to the island. Even *The True Colonist* had asked why the Colonial Secretary had sold every last teaspoon if he was to return in eighteen months.

'Montagu probably hopes to obtain a better post somewhere closer to Home,' Bergman said. 'But in any event, whether it turns out to be a last friendly gesture or a useful insurance for the future, this seems to me good strategy on Jane Franklin's part.'

Finding spare rooms was the difficulty. Eliza must stay on of course, now that her interesting condition was known. And charming

Captain Laplace from *L'Artemise*, the visiting French corvette, was staying for a month with his two senior officers while his ship was in dry dock. Three bedrooms were uninhabitable, and another must be kept for Sophy's younger brother, Tom, expected from England any day. Miss Williamson, Eleanor's governess, could not be asked to move. So it must be Sophy who decamped for a few months to make way for the Montagus.

—∞—

Booth married Lizzie Eagle at St David's Church that month. He was well, but far from robust. The Franklins lent them Government Cottage at New Norfolk for the wedding journey. The week after they returned, Dr Pilkington and Lizzie's mother and younger sisters left with the Regiment for India. Her elder sister Nan remained at Richmond with her husband and small children.

The summer began early. There were hot days in November, and on one of them Eliza, Sophy, Miss Williamson and I were walking under the trees near the shore when Miss Williamson discovered she had left her peppermint drops behind. I went back to fetch them and witnessed an amusing incident. As I explained to Bergman, it seemed so very typical of each character involved.

Returning down a narrow servants' back staircase, I was surprised to find Sir John, Henry Elliot, Montagu and Boyes coming up towards me in single file. They must have come through the stables from the Treasury rather than walk round the outside of the building in the heat. Sir John, as wide as the staircase, heaved to a standstill on the tiny landing, puffing like a grampus. Without seeing me he mopped his face with a handkerchief and drew out a pocket watch. A small window behind him threw light over his shoulder and onto the glass face of the instrument, which reflected a quivering luminous oval onto the ceiling. The watery patch of light danced and trembled as Sir John moved the watch. He gave a grunt of pleasure and began to twist it deliberately to skim the light about. In looking up he noticed me and said, 'Ah, Mrs Adair.

Caught playing like a schoolboy. Do you see my Ariel? It resembles a sprite, eh?'

He made the light perform a rapid circle on the walls and ceiling, rumbled a laugh, shook his head.

'Light!' he said. 'What an astonishing thing it is. We take it for granted every minute, but what a mystery! By the grace of God we live in it as fish in the sea, and yet we know so little about it except the vast speed of its rays. And now Dr Richardson sends me an article on a new wonder. Can you believe this, Mrs Adair? A sheet of glass is coated with a preparation of seaweed and silver—seaweed! Silver! I do not wholly understand it—but by means of an apparatus—a light-box of sorts—there appears on the glass a perfect image of a landscape or person, which may be subjected to chemicals and so fixed in place like a painting!

'Ask Lady Franklin,' he advised me, nodding, 'she has read it more thoroughly than I. Will such a contrivance rival you artists, do you suppose? Or could it be used as an aid in some manner?'

He went on to talk about the light of the Arctic, the 'ice blink' and the mysterious auroras which glimmer and flash across the sky in huge wild winter patterns, pink and green, like a mirage of some vast country among the stars . . . Montagu waited two steps below with an air of boredom. He did not look at the light on the ceiling but down at the dust on his polished boots. He stooped, had discovered a coin in a dark corner of the stair, a farthing, some servant's loss. He glanced about as though he might find another.

'Sir . . .' said Henry Elliot. 'Mr Lillie will be waiting.'

Lillie was the new Presbyterian minister, zealous for the rights of his small congregation.

'Ah, yes. Mr Lillie's problems are intractable, I fear . . .' Sir John sighed and turned to Montagu. 'Ready, John?'

'Excellency . . .' drawled Montagu, in a tone that made Henry Elliot look at him sharply. Boyes noticed too, Sir John did not. They filed past me, smiling, Sir John talking again about light, Montagu turning the farthing in his fingers behind his back.

—*m*—

Much of the hectic coming and going at this time was in preparation for the Sailing Regatta. Regattas had been held randomly under previous governors, but Sir John had decided to institute an annual event for the first of December, to mark the day when Abel Tasman discovered Van Diemen's Land. Lady Franklin suggested an emblem of wattle sprigs and oak leaves, tied together with royal blue ribbon, signifying England and the colony united. The newspapers sneered at Her Helpful Ladyship: the wattle had finished blooming, and even for clever Lady Franklin would not come again out of season. They criticised the waste of time and the expense, the encouragement of wanton pleasure-seeking. Government House seethed with bustle and heat.

Against all predictions the Regatta was a triumph in the end. Heavenly sunshine, brilliant but mild; the Derwent glittering like splintered sapphires as the rowing crews flashed to and fro. The gubernatorial box fluttered with blue ribbons, ships' pennants and an abundance of flowers. Sir John carried a bunch of dark red roses, Lady Franklin smiled. Arm in arm they came forth and wandered among the cheering crowds who, mellowed by free cheese and beer, waved indulgently at their foolish superiors.

Eliza and I watched for a time and then sat in the shade on a blanket with young Henry, Miss Williamson, and Eliza's servant, Mary Watson. After a time Bergman joined us, and removing his hat, sat down beside me with a smile, which gave me the opportunity to tell him what I had learned about Rowland Rochester's books.

'I am to go to the Chesneys' at Christmas,' I said. 'Is it a difficult journey to Copping from there?'

He was about to reply when St John Wallace also arrived and seated himself. Louisa could not be there, her confinement was near. St John had taken her to visit the cottage this morning and she was now resting . . . Oh, had he not mentioned? He had rented a furnished cottage.

'Louisa will wish you to see it as soon as we are settled. It is a short walk from St David's, and in the other direction only a mile or two from the Cascades Female Factory. Lady Franklin plans to begin a Ladies Committee to visit the prisoners in the New Year, and Louisa will wish to take part, of course.'

I doubted it. John Gould arrived to urge us towards the Governor's tent for luncheon. He and Eliza set off and Mary followed with little Henry; Bergman and I rambled behind as usual. He carried the folded picnic blanket.

'Copping is about twenty miles from the Chesneys at Richmond,' he said, resuming our earlier talk. 'If the weather is good it can be done easily enough with a little planning.' He said he was going down to the Huon over Christmas—he had bought ten acres from Lady Franklin—but he would come to the Chesneys when he returned, and see what could be arranged.

'If Anna and the Captain return soon, I may not be able to go to the Chesneys at all,' I said. 'Quigley may wish to start again for England without delay. Unless they've forgotten me,' I added jokingly, 'left me marooned here.'

'Would that be so terrible?' he asked, smiling. He took his hat off because the light breeze kept threatening to blow it away. His black hair lifted; his brown face was full of life, the lines at the corners of his eyes vivid in the sunlight. 'You could stay, we could marry.'

This came so abruptly I did not take it in for a moment. When I did, I said, 'Oh, but I must go back!'

'Why?' he objected. 'Quigley will take Anna to England—if she still wishes to go. Any news about Rowland Rochester can be conveyed by letter.'

'I don't . . . I hardly know what to say. You've taken me by surprise.'

'How can I believe that? You must surely have thought of it. We've hardly stopped talking since the day we met, we gravitate together at every gathering, play music together, and are both unattached.'

I had of course. But because I knew of his convict mistress, and because we both knew my stay in the island would be brief, I had considered our flirtation simply a kind of manner that develops in society between a man and woman whose real lives are elsewhere, but who are thrown together and feel they might as well make the best of the situation. We had talked, yes, but only superficially of personal matters. Our conversation was light banter, agreement and disagreement about books and music or the island's politics, or occasionally about Rowland Rochester. I could see now, though, that he thought I was only pretending surprise; that I had solicited this proposal always intending to refuse. Speaking curtly and low, I said, 'I believed you were not unattached.'

'Ah,' he said, with a trace of bitterness. 'I should have guessed. "The island is full of noises"—but not always harmless here. Alice left me a year ago. Her common-law husband was serving a sentence at Port Arthur. When he was released on a ticket-of-leave and posted at Jericho as a constable, she went to him. I did not foresee it—but I should have. They grew up together in London as barrow children, costermongers. Looked after each other in back alleys from the time they were twelve or thirteen. Intensely loyal.'

'I'm sorry.' I was damp and clammy from the heat and agitation.

He shrugged slightly, frowned. 'We had nothing in common except her son, Tom. He was five when they came to live with me, ten when they left. I'd begun to think of him as my own. He has a great talent for figures which I had hoped . . .'

He made a helpless, dismissive gesture. We were still making our way across the dry grass towards the Governor's marquee, but the public refreshment tents were in the same direction, and it being past noon, many were heading that way. We were becoming part of a crowd.

'I'm sorry,' I repeated.

'Or is it the other story that deters you?' he continued coolly. 'It's half-true, but I would not be ashamed if it were wholly so. My father was Jewish, though he never practised his religion. I regret it now—that he so rarely spoke of it—and that I never asked him. I was embarrassed about it in those days. My mother was half-Irish—which some people consider as bad or worse,' he added, with a smile.

'No, not that! I've never thought of staying; living here forever . . .' As I said this I was seized by a breathless panic, a feeling of being suddenly trapped.

'And yet you've said you find it beautiful?'

'Oh, beautiful,' I said. 'Hills, brilliant water, fair skies . . . and apart from that? Nothing. Only prisons. A place of prisons.'

'"Then is the world one", as Rosencrantz says. Or is it Guildenstern? The world is full of prisons, Hetta, we make our own. It takes courage for a woman to live here, I understand that. But look at Charlotte Lempriere, Bess Chesney, Mary Boyes?'

'I don't think I lack courage . . .' I knew I sounded too defensive; I did lack the courage for it. I intended to explain that the Goulds had asked me to work with them in London on the new book, but instead found myself saying, 'You miss the child, and might reasonably still expect to have children of your own. But I cannot . . . I . . .'

My voice sounded angry with the effort of keeping back tears because what rose to my mind was the poor little bluish face of my last baby when she was four weeks old and dying. They put her in the crib beside my bed and in my delirium I imagined that if only I could reach her she might live, but I was too weak from loss of blood, too near death myself, and when they gave her to me she was warm for such a short time and then so cold. I had learned to avoid the floods of useless weeping by swallowing hard and concentrating hard on some nearby object, but Gus Bergman undid me by taking my hand and saying, 'Oh, Hetta, I'm so sorry.' He added after a minute that he was sorry on my account, for my grief, but for himself it made no difference. It had never been an urgent matter for him, children.

'Tom was an unexpected gift,' he added, 'Not replaceable.'

I could not answer, in utter confusion now, because I had taken off my gloves, and as he held my hand a treacherous flow of leaping warm energy entered my skin and ran up my arm to my heart and head, and suddenly I was stirred to the depths as not for years, uncertain of everything.

We were awkwardly, farcically, paused in the middle of a moving crowd, jostled together with the picnic blanket and his hat between us, and now his hat blew away and a black man brought it back. A lion of a black man, with a fierce, smiling face. Broad and strong in the shoulders and narrow in the hips, he was elegantly dressed in light summer trousers and a dark-blue jacket, and with him were two young ladies, one on each arm. He threw back his head and laughed, greeting Bergman like a long-lost friend in a strong Scottish accent—at which I could hardly refrain from laughing although I was still on the quivering edge of tears. Bergman introduced us: Mr Gilbert Robertson, editor of *The Advertiser*, and his daughters.

I knew of him. Everyone in the colony knew of him. The son of a wealthy Scotch sugar-plantation owner and his Creole mistress, he was one of the great characters of the town. Outspoken in defence of the aboriginal people, he showed a keen interest in new methods of agriculture, which he promoted in his editorials. He had been a neighbour of the Chesneys at Richmond for a time, and was later imprisoned by Arthur for his trenchant criticisms. Now he was sharpening his pen on the Franklins. While he and Bergman spoke I gathered my wits, hauled together the pieces of myself threatening to fly apart, like a vessel exploding from amidships.

We walked on with Mr Robertson and his daughters, who only parted from us when we reached the marquee. Bergman and I stopped and looked at each other. We would both have said more, but the opportunity was gone; we were obstructing the entry. A couple closed in behind us. Bergman said quietly and quickly that of course he would not attempt to persuade me if I was intent on going home. He had seen too many marriages made unhappy because one wished to leave and one to stay. He gave a slight bow and walked away.

For the next several hours I drank tea, watched the boat races again, spoke rationally—I suppose I did—desperate to be alone. By the time I reached my room I was furious with myself for having been so weakly tearful, and cross with Bergman for bringing me to that point. Why had I said all that? All the wrong things? Why had he chosen such an impossible place to choose to speak? And he had not asked me to take time to consider further. He had not said he loved me. He had expected me to be pleased by his proposal, to accept gratefully. Did he think I was the kind of woman to spend all her life in an out-of-the-way colony? I had been right to refuse. Of course I had.

I suddenly, desperately, wanted London. Filthy, noisy, crowded, unpredictable: a proper, ancient city. I wanted the solid weight of history in brick and stone all around me and beneath my feet, holding me steady. And above me, too, in the canopies of ancient oaks, domes and spires, the proper stars. The colony had no depth by comparison, nothing to keep you from spinning off into the wilderness. How could I promise never to see London again? And yet many had no choice. How did they feel, those who could never go back?

Next morning I began a note explaining to Bergman, but was not sure what I wanted to say. He might write to me, I thought, or come to the Bird Room to renew the conversation. For a week I lived in expectation of this, but when a note did arrive from him at the end of that time, it was a formal goodbye. He was setting off for the Huon, and doubted whether we would meet again before I left the island. He would be in touch with the Chesneys about my visit to Copping. He wished me all good things for the future. This note inspired another fit of tears, another round of self-questioning, yet it brought the same conclusion: why marry again? Why stay in the colony when I might live in London?

The following day I had a note from Louisa. She and St John had not yet removed from the Archdeacon's. Would I call there on Sunday morning when the rest of the household would be at Church? Come alone.

—∞—

She answered the door herself, huge in a shapeless sacque of an unbecoming yellowy green. Her hair was dragged back, bundled into a knot. She began talking before I was wholly inside, furious about St John's renting the cottage. Another year here! He was infatuated with Mick Walker and Dido Thomas and his other black sheep, and planned to spend months at the peninsula again, while she was stuck in town with the baby, entertaining Ladies Committees.

'But the cottage is lovely, I've walked past it,' I said. 'You'll be freer there. You can do as you like . . .'

'I want to go home,' she said. 'But St John has new reasons every day why we cannot. The reports must be finished. Jane Franklin must have her chapel at the Huon—and her College, her Museum. All these *whims* she has . . . like the snakes. Have you heard that absurdity? She decided when they were first here to pay a bounty of sixpence a head to get rid of the snakes—and caused havoc! Convicts left their jobs to hunt the creatures, sackfuls poured in, and it cost the Government six or seven hundred pounds.'

'The Government paid nothing,' I said. 'The newspapers repeat the error, but Jane Franklin paid it all.'

'*Schemes*,' said Louisa, ignoring this, 'which bring men gathering around her to *discuss*. I could almost feel sorry for her,' she continued angrily. 'She does it because she's bored with her great slow Governor-husband, bored with her *marriage blanc*, like me.'

'The Franklins a *marriage blanc*? I don't think . . .'

'Of course they keep up appearances, as we all do. But his parts were frozen off in the Arctic twelve years ago. Didn't you know?'

'Where did you . . . ?'

'The Dorcas Society. All the wives. Jessie Montagu, Helena Forster. Mrs Gregory, the Treasurer's wife—the woman who looks as though she chews lemons. I sit with Jeannie Macdowell, the wife of the Solicitor General, Edward Macdowell. She's Swanston's daughter. We sew ugly little shifts for the infants at the female factory, but really it's an excuse to gossip. They say that's why Jane Franklin has no children, because Franklin is not capable now.'

'But there can be more than one reason . . .'

'Helena Forster says it's true.'

'How would she know? At any rate,' I smiled, nodding at the mound she was carrying, 'yours is hardly a white marriage.'

A pause.

'I used to think you so clever, Harriet,' she said, 'I thought you'd guessed. You can't have forgotten what I said on the ship?'

'No, but . . . then . . . ?'

'McLeod.'

I tried not to gape. 'Does St John know?'

'He must know it's not his own, of course!' she said contemptuously. 'He's not a fool. But he's watched me increasing like a whale, like a great fat sow—and never said a word! Can you believe it, Harriet? Not a word. Perhaps he thinks it's parthenogenesis. He probably prays for me, an unchaste woman. Perhaps he's forgiven me. Or this silence is his way of punishing me. I don't know what he thinks.'

'Perhaps he *doesn't* know,' I said. 'If you resumed your normal married life after we landed in early April there's not much time to account for. Only two or three weeks. Men don't think so much about these things, the dates. If it's born now, December . . . he may think it's simply before time, an eight-month child?'

She gave me a look. 'We have not "resumed", as you put it. Nothing—since we left England. How could it be his?'

Another pause.

'Why don't you talk to him about it?'

She grimaced. 'I'm frightened of what he might do. If he asks me whose it is, what shall I say? Or he might insist that it is his own—pretend I'm mad or lying when I say it's not. Or write to my father, send me back with no money, nothing. Harriet,' she seized my arm, 'promise me if I die you'll take the child home. I've sent a letter to my sister telling her that if the worst happens you'll bring it to her.'

Her voice trembled. She released my arm, paced away, fell heavily into a chair.

'Does McLeod know it's his child?' I asked.

She shrugged. 'I haven't told him. When we were at Richmond I saw him sometimes, but he's so taken up with the Ross family . . . He might not believe me. Or again, he might deny everything. If it's a boy he might want it, but a girl . . .' She shrugged. 'An amusing situation, *n'est-ce pas?*'

She looked the picture of misery.

'That is why, if I die,' she went on, '—and I know I will die, it will be my punishment—you must promise me to take the child back to England, Harriet, to my mother or sister. St John will probably put it in the Orphan School, or employ some convict hag to feed it on sugar-water and gin.'

'You're not going to die.'

'It's upside down, a true antipodean. A "gumsucker", a "currency lass". Ugh!' She pulled her face into such grimaces I had to laugh.

'A breech delivery isn't so uncommon,' I said. 'They often turn at the last minute . . .'

'Don't try to comfort me, Harriet. I know what it means. It makes it far more likely that I will die, or the child will, or both of us.'

'No, it doesn't. Charlotte Lempriere has six children and one was . . .'

'I'm much beyond the age at which most women have their first child, and what about Lucy Granger? Do you know where her baby is? In the Orphanage, where *Ewing* is supervisor . . .' She shuddered.

Lieutenant Granger had drowned the week before his wife's confinement and she had died in labour. As for the Orphanage, it was widely rumoured that Reverend Ewing had 'favourites' among the little girls, whom he would fondle and caress, but nothing had been proved. Louisa got up with a grunt and moved restlessly about.

'I should have taken some ghastly dose. Mrs Tench would have known. Like a scullery maid. And now I shall be forced to stay in this loathsome place until St John makes up his mind to leave. Or until I die. Look, I've written out my mother's address.'

'Perhaps St John would let you go home with the child, while he stays?'

She shook her head. But I saw that what I'd suspected on the ship was true; she loved St John and would not leave him.

'At least I'm better off than Mary Price, whose husband is a brute. He wants her to do filthy things in the bedroom and when she objects he strikes her.'

'Louisa! Good Lord! Who says these things?'

She shrugged. 'Mary told Sophy Cracroft and Sophy has told Jane Franklin, so they say. But the servants hear things too.'

Later, as I was leaving she added, 'And since you're so thick with the Franklins, you'd better hint they'd be wise to attend the Dorcas Society. Jane Franklin is supposed to be patroness but she never goes and the other women don't like it.'

'But Eliza Arthur never attended, Sophy Cracroft says.'

'She had the excuse of a dozen children. Jane Franklin has none— nothing to do. Saint Jane. But she's not such a paragon of virtue. When she was in Egypt five years ago she behaved very badly, they say. It was while her husband was away at sea, a year or two after they were married. She was supposed to be travelling with a Captain Scott and his wife, who know the Gregorys, but she went off alone in a boat with a young clergyman, and wrote him a passionate love letter which Mrs Gregory has seen . . .'

I did not like the sound of this, but my mind was on Louisa's own situation and I did not pay enough attention.

Louisa's daughter was born a week later. A perfectly normal delivery, Dr Turnbull said. The child healthy, Louisa well. St John wanted to call the baby Theodora and Louisa said she didn't care. He seemed besotted with the infant, his face transfigured when he held it in his arms and stared down at the swaddled form, the frowning, angry, pink little face. The room was full of flowers and gifts but Louisa was weary and indifferent.

18

I SUDDENLY FELT I COULD NOT BEAR TO STAY WITH THE CHESNEYS for Christmas. All that relentless festivity, and more farewells. I sent an excuse to Bess but did not tell Sophy, who might ask me to spend Christmas Day with them, although she was at this time much preoccupied with her brother Tom, just arrived from England. It was his first Christmas in the island, his nineteenth birthday on Boxing Day. He had come to be a clerk in Sir John's office, a cheerful, delicate-looking youth who made me think of Chatterton, the boy poet. It was hoped the climate would benefit his chest. All his strength seemed to have gone into his thick, waving chestnut hair, that russetty, dark, tortoiseshell red, such a contrast with his narrow white face.

In the end I spent Christmas Day in my lodgings with Peg Groundwater and her servant, Nellie Jack. Peg's mind was on her husband and son at sea in the southern oceans, and on past Christmasses at her little house in Stromness. Nellie said nothing of her thoughts. She was a convict woman in her fifties, morose, partially deaf, lame, not very capable. Peg wanted to send her back to the Female Factory but could not sufficiently harden her heart to do so. Nellie had been transported with a husband and son for receiving stolen goods to the value of four guineas, but both men had died. She lived in fear of the Workhouse.

My mind kept turning to London and Bergman disjointedly. I told myself that when a man proposes to a woman, of course some emotion must spring up in her. Unless the man is altogether a fool, which Bergman was far from being, some warm feeling towards him is perfectly natural, if only for his commendable taste. He must be thinking badly of me. If only I could see him and talk to him again we might part on better terms. I could explain what it would mean to me to work with Eliza in London on the bird pictures. How it might advance my prospects, lead to more work, enable me to support myself there with better success this time. Eliza believed I could. And then I thought, but what does it matter what Gus Bergman thinks? Why bother to tell him? I shall soon be gone, and in London I shall cease to think of him. It is only because I am waiting here in this dull little town that I foolishly agonise like this—and so I went round in circles.

We went, Peg, Nellie Jack and I, to early Church at St George's in Battery Point, and when we emerged the heat was already stifling. The smell of smoke was everywhere, and as the day wore on, a lavender haze thickened the air. The sun glowed through it like a sinister orange moon. There appeared to be no Orcadian words for this weather. At noon, 'the top o' the day' in Peg's parlance, we 'at wur mate'—'ate our meat'—a roast fowl neither of us had appetite for. Nellie ate alone in the kitchen because she preferred to—on account of her teeth, I think, of which she had few. Towards evening, when at last it began to grow cooler, I walked across the Battery Point and halfway down the steep lane to Sandy Bay. Rocks protruding from the hillside here made a convenient spot to sit and make pencil-and-watercolour sketches of the wild sunset flaming across the sky behind the mountain.

The sands, turning pink as the light failed, were empty save for a group of horses being exercised in the shallows. The scene was sublime, and yet I would have given it all for gloomy 'Thornfield' in a pewter-grey twilight, as it used to be when I returned from walking in the snowy woods on late winter days. A few black rooks cawing harshly above the winter skeletons of trees, snow falling past the yellow lamplight in the kitchen window, Dawlish nodding by the kitchen fire. Homesickness, like love, is not easily explained to those who have never felt it. To those who have, it will be achingly familiar.

—⁂—

I called at the Post Office two days after Christmas and found three letters. Two from Jane Eyre, written late in the northern summer, full of her plans for the garden now the house was finished. She was expecting a child in the spring. In the later one she said that since we were to leave the island shortly, she would not write again. The third was from Quigley, written on the sixth of November.

> My apologies for so long a delay in writing. I had at first little to relate and few opportunities of sending. You will be pleased to know Anna continues in health I believe bene-fitting by the warmer climates at Moreton Bay and Sydney. Unhappily I must now tell you that when we returned to Sydney the ship was seized, the owners being bankrupt, and we left cooling our heels in this expensive town.
>
> For some weeks I have hoped to have news worth writing but it is the old story, plenty of promises coming to nought. There is a great drought here in New South Wales and with it a low state of business. Two days ago I received at last an offer I have determined to accept although it will delay our return to England. When I tell you the advantages I hope you will understand.
>
> The Pelagia 423 tons is recently arrd. from London. Her owners find themselves unable to sell her cargo here. If I will take her on to Port Phillip and New Zealand, I will have a share of profits and an England run on our return. In these uncertain times I must be satisfied with this. The question is will you chuse to return to England earlier, taking passage in another vessel? I wld be glad to hear from you. A letter sent to Mrs Howe's lodging-house in York St will find us. If we do not hear from you we will come again to Hobarton

next spring. Anna sends her love and prayers. With warmest regards, your obedient servant, Edward Quigley.

PS: I enclose two hundred pounds being the monies paid by Lloyd's for your return passage, with loss of effects & etc.

The thought of this delay did not trouble me, I found. I wanted to go home, but drawing each day with Eliza was a constant pleasure I was glad to be able to continue—and I would have the chance, too, of being still in the island when her baby was born. I took Rochester's draft to the bank that week, with letters from Jane reporting Rochester in excellent health. They redeemed it at ten percent. With the insurance monies, the remainder of my own savings, and the sums I had earned from Lady Jane Franklin, I now possessed altogether the astonishing sum of five hundred and seventy-eight pounds and some shillings, the contemplation of which reassured me when I thought of the future. Eliza urged me to wait in Hobart and sail to Sydney with them at the end of June after the baby arrived. I wrote to Quigley to say I would follow this plan.

—◦◦◦—

The women and children at Government House were due to leave on New Year's Day, to sail up to New Norfolk on the *Eliza* for three weeks at the Government Cottage, but on the thirtieth of December the Chief Surveyor, Mr George Frankland, died suddenly. He was thirty-eight, a cultivated man, nephew to Lord Colville and first cousin of Sir Thomas Frankland, Baronet. He had built the lovely house 'Secheron' on the waterside at Battery Point, and entertained the young Charles Darwin there two years before. Darwin's favourite pet monkey died that week and was buried in the garden. Now it was Frankland's turn for burial—not in the garden, of course.

The planned exodus was postponed for the funeral and calls on Mrs Frankland. She, poor woman, had the unfortunate distinction of being sister to Mr William Mason; 'Mr Muster Master Mason', or 'Stone' Mason, for his hard heart. Some said it was he who invented the cruelty attributed to Governor Arthur, a flogging where each lash was delivered at the sound of a drum-tap at half-a-minute intervals, so the punishment was prolonged to an hour and a half. The Governor, it was proved, had never countenanced any such barbarity, but Mason was judged capable of anything.

John Gould's excursions were now halted for Christmas and the sojourn at New Norfolk, but Gould, who hated to be idle, grew restless during the delay caused by Frankland's death. He determined to visit other artists in Hobart to discover what they knew of lithographic printing, the method he had decided upon for his new book.

'You had better ask Mr Bock,' said Jane Franklin. 'Mr Henry Melville owns the only lithographic press and stones in the island, but he has retired to New Norfolk to finish his book, a magnum opus on the history of Freemasonry. He plans to have it illustrated when it is done, but at present he sees no one. I advised him to use Thomas Bock as his artist, and they tried the apparatus together, I believe. You'll probably find Bock at Mr Duterrau's gallery on the corner of Campbell and Patrick Streets,' she added, smiling.

Bock, a former convict, lived further up Campbell Street, she added, but his lodgings were full of children and domestic troubles. He preferred to work at Duterrau's house, which was orderly and quiet.

It was a low, six-roomed stone cottage with a central front door. A sign requested gallery visitors to take the side path to the back. Eliza, John Gould and I made our way along this through a flourishing kitchen-garden to the barn, which housed the studio and gallery. Duterrau was in his late sixties, a heavy, square-faced man with dark, greying curls; he, too, was an artist and was working slowly at a large painting on an easel, while beside him Mr Bock talked, between drinking from a mug and eating a slice of bread.

Duterrau's paintings, many of them small studies of the island's black people, were displayed side by side with French and English works he had brought out with him to sell. The picture he was engaged on was to be called 'The Conciliation'. It showed Mr George Robinson, 'the Conciliator', standing in the centre of a group of aboriginal men and women, shaking hands with their leader and vowing friendship between white races and black. Duterrau had compiled it from portraits of the natives Robinson had brought in to sit for him, but he was dissatisfied with the composition, the angle of the spears framing the central figure. He and Gould spoke about this, but my attention was caught by a small still life.

With growing excitement I saw it was surely the work of Madame Vallayer-Coster. It was almost identical to the paintings I had fallen in love with in Paris years before; the same quiet scene, imbued with a sense of mysterious meaning in just the same way. Flowers in a glass goblet, fruit on a table, a parrot. But here one glimpsed a small window behind, an enchanting fragment of distant landscape. I was seized by a great surge of desire to own it.

Miss Perigal managed Duterrau's business like the shrewd Frenchwoman she was at heart, although the Duterraus and Perigals had been Londoners for two generations, she told me. They were Huguenot families, partners in a famous clock-making business. She was Duterrau's sister-in-law, the elder sister of his wife, who had died many years before.

'Almost certainly by Madame Vallayer-Coster,' she said, 'although not signed. Mr Gregson wanted it, but it is already sold.'

My disappointment was severe; more severe, I knew, than I should feel over any mere painting. Miss Perigal said she only wished she had more such works. They would sell easily, and at present they had too little to sell. If only Mr Duterrau would continue with portrait painting as he had done when they first came here—there was a great demand for portraits in Hobart. But ever since he met Mr George Robinson and began painting the black people, he had been so affected by their plight that this subject now preoccupied him to the exclusion of all else. Which was not good for business.

—w—

Government Cottage at New Norfolk proved to be another large, shabby wooden bungalow set above the river near a picturesque rocky gorge. There were six bedrooms, guests being crowded into the usual outbuildings and huts. Pastures stretched upriver towards New Norfolk, just out of sight around the next bend in the river. Eliza was happy; the reed-beds and bush-land provided John with hunting grounds, and little Henry had grass to play in, a pony to ride and a plum tree to climb. On this visit I first saw the colony's black swans, floating among the reed-beds in their hundreds as we sailed up the Derwent. Nothing could be more elegant when they were swimming, but when sleeping, or heads-down feeding, they looked like black mops floating on the surface.

As soon as I had a morning's leisure I walked the two miles along the river path and up the steep embankment to St Matthew's Church, a clean little stone building more than a decade old. Graves on one side were dotted unevenly almost up to the wall of the Church. Two huge old eucalyptus trees lent a chequered shade to the dead and living. On this warm summer day it was welcome. Post-and-rail fences separated the graveyard from stubbled paddocks bleached by the sun. At the back, a view down the valley showed layers of hills fading into blue distance. A few minutes confirmed Bergman's account of the grave. A plain tombstone inscribed: *George Thomas Fairfax, 1767 to 1836.*

The Church was unlocked and empty. I went in and prayed for Anna and Quigley and myself, for Adèle and Jane and Rochester, and Sophy and Jane and Eleanor and Miss Williamson—and Bergman—and finding, as when I was a child, that my list was becoming embarrassingly long, I consigned all to the Lord's care and rose and looked about me. The interior was pleasant in a way quite different from my beloved London Churches, clean and spare, almost unadorned. I returned to the sunshine again and wandered, reading gravestones. Little Anne Louisa Lacey had been three when she died, her four brothers and sisters younger still. A sudden rustling beside me was accompanied by a male voice saying, 'A melancholy prospect, Mrs Adair.' Montagu and his wife had come up behind me as softly as a pair of cats.

'I find it beautiful, Mr Montagu.'

'*Et in Arcadia ego.*'

'Indeed, sir.'

'You are looking for a particular grave?'

I hesitated—but why? 'Mr George Fairfax, who may have been an associate of Mr Rowland Rochester.'

My heart beat faster, but Montagu only made a slight sound and looked vaguely away after his wife. She had gone to join their two boys, who were in the corner feeding torn-off grass to a horse with its head over the fence. We wandered that way.

'The Gospels instruct us to let the dead bury their dead,' Montagu said with his urbane smile, but I thought his eyes searched my face.

'That is not always easy.'

'No,' he agreed. 'It is common, I suppose, to be intrigued by headstones. When I was a schoolboy we were made to learn Latin epitaphs. My favourite was always Sulla's. I no longer recall the Latin, but in English it construes: "No friend ever served me and no enemy ever wronged me, whom I have not repaid in full."'

'Truly Roman, but scarcely Christian? No turning the other cheek?'

'That is for saints, Mrs Adair. We must live like Romans among the hard realities of the world. *Render unto Caesar that which is Caesar's.*'

I said nothing, and he added, 'You have a little Latin? I wonder what you make of my own family motto; *Desponendo me, non mutando me?*'

He waited.

'"Use me . . ."' I said, '"but do not . . . change me"? Or perhaps, "You may command me, but you will not change me". It is not exactly clear how it is meant. A soldier, perhaps, saying he will obey orders but will not alter his own nature? A statement—or is it a warning?'

He nodded but did not answer the question. I thought of the motto Franklin had adopted, *Nisu*: perseverance, exertion, work, struggle. We had reached Jessie Montagu and the boys. She explained that the fine weather had brought her husband down to join them. Mr Forster had already taken over the duties of Colonial Secretary in preparation for her husband's absence. They were walking to Mrs Henderson's cottage in the village, where there were always raspberries for the children at this time of year. Colonel Arthur's children, of course, had formerly come with them. Raspberries are much preferable to strawberries, are they not? The children can never get enough. Those grown at Government Cottage were not sufficient for such a large group. Her words brought another Latin tag to my mind as we separated: *Qui multum habet, plus cupit.* Those who have much desire more.

—m—

Young Henry Gould conceived a passion for fishing, and since my habit was to row slowly upriver in the dory and moor under the willows to draw, we pursued our interests together on afternoons when Eliza was resting and John Gould bird-catching. The river was narrow and placid, an invitation to pleasant idleness. One hot afternoon when we returned to the landing stage, Jane Franklin and her maid Snachall were standing watching us.

'Will you row me up to the willows, Harriet?' Jane said. 'It looks so cool there. That will be all, Snachall. Take Henry back to his mother.'

She leapt easily into the rocking craft, settled herself and said, 'You are handy at the oars, Harriet? You must not do too much, or you will coarsen your arms like a washerwoman. Where did you learn?'

'On the Thames at Henley, my lady. I lodged there several weeks one year after I had been ill.'

'Your husband did not object to your learning such a thing?'

'He was in London. My stepmother Nina was with me. She believed the exercise would do me good.'

Nina and I had intended to stay a month, but after three weeks I was better, and anxious to go back to Tom. He was in the studio with Lottie, one of our models. One of those sights you can't unsee. Her nakedness on cushions on the floor, one white knee up, one bare white breast, her head arched back with pleasure. Tom thrusting away blindly in his passion. A small consolation: he was no more faithful to Lottie than to me.

'It is astonishing what women can do,' said Jane. 'My agent at the Huon tells me he has employed a husband and wife as shingle cutters. They do everything together from the felling of the tree to the stacking of the shingles—and the woman is the neater and more hard-working of the pair, he says.'

After a pause she added, 'I have been wanting to ask you whether Sophy has spoken to you about her cousin Mary? There seems a little awkwardness between them since Mary accepted John Price. It has been hinted to me that this is jealousy on Sophy's part, but I think not. I believe Price may have proposed to Sophy first, and in refusing him, she told Mary—so now they both know Mary was his second choice. Has Sophy mentioned it to you?'

'No, nothing.'

Jane's face was leaf-shadowed by the willows as she said, 'Marriage . . . From girlhood we are taught to regard it as the object of our lives, and to many women it seems to promise freedom, but so often it only leads to more . . .'

'. . . confinements, ma'am,' I said.

'Ah, very droll, Hatty. But what is the alternative? Sophy hasn't a penny of her own. Her situation will be hard if she doesn't marry here—as her mother expects her to, of course.'

'I doubt Sophy will be easy to please.' I thought of her shudder when she spoke of men's appetites.

Jane did not hear me, or perhaps did not like the remark and decided to have one of her deaf moments. We sat, the gentle water lapping at the boat, each thinking our own thoughts, until she told me she had refused six offers before she accepted Franklin. They had been married ten years now, but had been separated more than a third of that time while he was away at sea.

19

CAPTAIN LAPLACE'S ENGLISH WAS CONSIDERABLY BETTER THAN Booth's French. The Captain, from the visiting French corvette, *L'Artemise*, was a likeable companion, surprised to find how much larger Port Arthur had grown since his last visit three years before. *L'Artemise* had been in Van Diemen's Land for two months this time, refitting and revictualling in Hobarton and making short forays up the coast to test her seaworthiness and guns. This was their last call at the peninsula, on their way out to sea and home to France.

Laplace was becoming extremely animated, his speech more rapid. Suddenly he lapsed into French entirely and Booth found it impossible to follow. It seemed the Captain needed French to express the high degree of astonishment he felt at—what? Not, Booth guessed, vegetables, although Laplace had just been called upon to admire row after row of beets and kale, peas and potatoes, carrots, Dutch turnips, tobacco plants, artichokes. They were walking—Laplace, Booth and Lempriere—between the bean rows in the Government Garden at Port Arthur. Laplace was waving a fistful of empty pea-pods. He had eaten the raw peas with relish. Scurvy had been rife this voyage; five of his men had jumped ship from the hospital in Hobarton.

Booth could catch the general tenor of his exclamations: '*éton-nant . . . sangfroid . . . insouciante . . .*' accompanied by shakings of the head and an exaggerated, humorous pursing of the lips. Not vegetables, surely?

Climbing beans, taller than the men, felt their way into the sky on curling tendrils, questioning gently in the light breeze, reaching out for each other overhead. Booth found the greenish dappled light immensely pleasing, as he did the scarlet flowers, the glimpses of hidden beans. He could hear the murmur of high voices in the distance: Lizzie collecting strawberries with the Lempriere children. On the other side of the bay he could see his own cottage and the signal mast. It was Sunday; the morning service was over. There was half an hour until luncheon. Laplace's French came faster still and Booth was entirely lost. Lempriere obliged.

'The Captain considers us astonishing. Such a penal colony! So few weapons, so few soldiers, so many more convicts than when he was last here—and only a flimsy wooden stockade to contain them! He cannot understand it. Why are prisoners allowed to act as domestic servants and boat crews? And such a ridiculously small number of solitary cells. To be sure there are leg irons, the triangle, the lash, the promise of bloody flayed flesh for those who make sins . . . er, misbehave . . . but *mon Dieu*, it is not enough!'

We French, he says, we do things differently. We comprehend prisons, punishment. We know what we are about. Protestants do not understand the nature of good and evil. We admit the English are incomparable in certain matters ('but he does not say what,' added Lempriere in a wry aside to Booth) but two things the French understand better than the English: love and prisons. No, three things: food, love and prisons. Four things only: food—which is of course to include wine—and prisons, and love, and perhaps *la mode, aussi*.

Captain Laplace laughed and began again, explaining to Lempriere—Booth could guess now—the adventure of yesterday. Well, it had been amusing. Booth could not help smiling himself. He and Laplace had been out together in the number one whaleboat, and at a certain point Booth had begun to sense an unusual mood among the six convict oarsmen. He had spoken to Laplace in bad

French, warned him to be ready in case there should be an attempt to take over the boat (Laplace had not understood a word). And then, in English, as though answering a question put to him by Laplace, he had said loudly that of course he always carried pistols and would instantly shoot without mercy to foil any attempt at escape.

But the truth was, he had forgotten to bring the guns! Laplace and Lempriere were laughing. Booth smiled broadly and explained that he believed the lash to be a punishment of *dernier* resort, indicating a failure of his system. He would rather have healthy able-bodied men who could work, than keep a hospital full of flayed invalids who were an expense first and a trouble later, seeking every chance to escape.

Laplace shrugged. 'It depends on your purpose,' he said. 'Is this settlement meant for punishment or reform? Or for the business of colonising? How do you dare train up a boat crew to such fitness?' He waved his arm in the general direction of the cove. There had been a friendly race between a crew from *L'Artemise* and Booth's number one whaleboat two days ago, and the French had lost by a wide margin. Laplace went on, 'These felons can chase a whale ten miles in a heavy sea, and you trust them not to use it against you?' He shrugged, made one of those explosive French sounds, threw up his hands.

'The purpose of this establishment is both punishment and reform,' Booth answered, sounding pompous to his own ears. 'These men must eventually form the free population of the colony, but at present they must be kept at work.' That was the necessity: building, always building. England was sending its prodigal sons in ever-increasing numbers. Booth repeated what he'd said to Arthur two years ago: keep them working and fed; be stern but fair. The Government will gain by the work, the prisoners will have no time to think of escape.

They had reached an open central area of the gardens, where there was a toolshed, water-butts, and a section of overhanging roof for shade. Here Mr Manton, the Wesleyan missionary, joined them. The conversation continued: reform or punishment, good and evil. Lempriere was talking about Rousseau, Laplace emphasising the dangers of becoming too close to one's prisoners, of knowing them too well. Manton kept clearing his throat as a prelude to interrupting—with his usual harangue on the forgiveness of sins, probably. Booth was free to pursue his own thoughts.

Although he would not admit it to Laplace, he believed his whale-boat crew was hatching a scheme of some sort. Yesterday's episode had made him certain. And whatever it was, Woolf was certainly in it. His eyes had slid away towards another prisoner, George Moss, when the guns were mentioned. Like Woolf, Moss was a London Jew, and the two men, reasonably enough, seemed to be friends. Nothing unnatural, a bond of race and experience, no doubt.

And yet Mick Walker was their accepted leader, and surely Walker would not countenance any such plan? He had too much to lose. St John Wallace appeared to be training him as a kind of model prisoner, for demonstration purposes. Maconochie would have approved. *'Monstrare, to show.'* Men, not monsters. Walker must know he was likely to gain considerably by this treatment. An early ticket of leave? A pardon? It depended on what influence Wallace could bring to bear, either with Franklin or at home. But the Arthur faction wouldn't like it.

Laplace had asked Booth about Walker after the boat race, astonished by the prisoner's extraordinary beauty, he said. Trust the French to say such a thing out loud. Laplace appeared puzzled when Booth explained Wallace's interest, and had at last shrugged, smiled, dismissing the matter with the remark that all Englishmen preferred other men to women, it was well known. Booth had smiled at the time, but it came into his mind with sudden unease that the interviews between Wallace and Walker were something like a courtship. A mutual pleasure in discovering each other's qualities—although naturally you wouldn't say so in official correspondence. Wallace had been away from the settlement for some weeks now, for Christmas and the birth of his child. It would be wise to keep an eye on how things progressed when he came back.

Booth's mind returned to the rest of the crew, all on extra rations and treated with great leniency. He must surely be mistaken about their mood. What could they possibly gain? But a sixth sense told him otherwise. Looks exchanged . . . or rather a deliberate not-looking at each other, like guilty children. A taut readiness, holding their breath to see if they were going to get away with it. Whatever 'it' was.

They treated him differently since his marriage to Lizzie. Before, they had showed a stolid acceptance, an acknowledgement of his superiority not only as Commandant but as a man. They knew him to be their equal in capacity for endurance. Now there was a new kind of assessment in their eyes, impassive, equivocal. They thought he'd gone soft. Perhaps they envied him. It was true that he spent less time tramping up and down, more time with Lizzie. Those weeks of illness had changed him. Physically he was not so strong, but more than that he had felt death's black wing brush his face, and life had begun to seem short and precious. These days he wondered more often than before what these men felt, what they thought. Which did not mean he was less diligent or allowed them to slacken, but it was probably time he changed to some other kind of work. He had written several times requesting to be transferred, applying for other positions, but it was always the same: there was nothing available at present, or if there was, others had prior claim.

Laplace was still talking about the dangers of growing to like your prisoners or be interested in them. You must keep them as you would valuable working animals: in constant awareness of your mastery. Manton spoke of conversations he'd had with Wallace about their souls, the struggle to consider each one as a spiritual being animated by a spark of the divine, and yet also a creature in bondage to evil. Laplace said it was not for a guest to criticise, but he thought the English were mad.

—⁂—

Next morning Lizzie was sick again. She was with child; they both knew it. He was delighted, she less so, he thought. He stayed with her until she crawled back to bed and slept. By the time he'd walked down to his office it was after eight o'clock. Lieutenant Williams was waiting for him. Gimpy Noles, a convict cook, had pleaded illness at muster this morning and been carried up to the hospital, where he told the doctor that an attempt was to be made to take one of the whaleboats.

Booth gave new orders. The number one boat to be hauled up on the slip whenever it was not in use, instead of tied at the jetty. The number two to be kept in the boatshed; number three on the derricks. All sails to be taken out of the boats and stored in the boatshed, a huge waste of effort but an excellent precaution. A guard must be on the shed at all times. Colour-Sergeant Killion to start at once, Sergeants Mawle, Fleming and Towson relieving on four watches. That should make them think.

Half an hour later, Booth was on his way down to the boatshed to speak to Killion, when there came the unmistakeable crack of a gunshot and then another, followed by shouting. He saw his whaleboat, black with a red streak around it, white below the waterline, flashing through the water past the jetty with a convict crew. The muster bell began to ring. It took fifteen minutes to get the number two boat out because it had just been put away, and then get a volunteer crew in and the pursuit under way. By that time the escapees had over a mile's start.

As they sped through the cleaving, glassy water, Booth sat in the stern, so furious he could not speak, his jaw clenched so tightly that later it ached for days. In hindsight it was all so clear and the nub of it was Walker. Which he hadn't wanted to believe and so he'd closed his mind to it. They couldn't have done it without bloody Walker, damn him, who'd probably had the crew ready the last few days with some vague plan they'd made after they won the race against the French. How bloody pleased they'd been about that, all the cheering, and he'd been so stupidly pleased too, thinking, well, the French will see you can have a penal establishment that isn't just a welter of blood.

Walker must have heard the new orders this morning and known that unless they acted at once their chance was gone. It would be too difficult to steal a boat if it was on the slips or in the shed, useless to try for a quick escape once the sails were kept separately. And so

Walker had decided it was now or never. He'd used the new orders as an excuse to man the boat on the pretext of taking it back to the slips from the jetty. Oh, the coolness of it! Poor Killion had accepted this and only noticed the oddity as they pulled away, eight rowers instead of six: all the number one crew, with an extra two who shouldn't have been there. Killion was probably just beginning to wonder about that when they picked up speed and went past the slips without stopping, and then a sail was hoisted and their intentions were plain.

None of it was as Booth had imagined. He'd been assuming that if they were going to try something it would be while he was in the boat with them and out some distance from the settlement. Behind the Isle of the Dead, perhaps. That's what he'd have done himself, in the hope that it would have taken longer for the sentries to see what was happening and get a pursuit going. It would have been inconvenient for them to have him in the boat, but they could easily have pitched him out into the water. Whether he drowned or reached land would hardly have signified: this was the end of them anyway. Might as well be hung for a sheep as a lamb. They'd all hang now. The stupid pitiful bloody waste of hanging a man like Walker, like Woolf, or poor young Dido Thomas. If they didn't starve or drown first.

Perfect weather for it and perfect timing. *L'Artemise* had departed on the tide last night and there was nothing coming in from Hobart today to intercept the bolters as they ran down the bay out to sea. Four of the eight men were his strongest rowers, and the number one boat handled far better than this bloody number two. For two hours he stared through the telescope at them every few minutes. The enforced inactivity chafed at his spirit. If he could have rowed half as well as any one of these men he would have taken a turn at the oars, sweated off his fury, but he would only slow them down. There was no perceptible change in the distance between the two boats until they came through the Heads and out into the open sea; then the bolters rigged a strange little extra spritsail—a scrap of canvas—and turned south.

'What the hell . . ?' he said, surprised. 'South? Why south, for God's sake?'

He'd expected they'd go north, straight for the Bass Strait islands, Sydney.

'Afeared o' the signal if they'd'a went north, sir,' said Dales. 'Afeared o'gettin' took by a boat put out from t' Neck.'

Which made sense. Although if they'd stood well offshore and struck the sails as they went past the outstation, they'd have been hard to spot. How many times had he stared from a lookout, wondering if some larger wrinkle in the fabric of the sea was a whale under the surface or merely another wave? They were heading out to sea now, away from the coast, sou'-sou'-east. Walker must know the dangers of the south and west coasts? Forty-foot waves, storms, treacherous currents and reefs.

'P'mission speak, sir. Mebbee thinkin' o' Port Davey, sir? Shipwright's place,' said Collier. 'Get unsels a brig an' main prog an' likewise.'

'If so, they won't bloody well make it. But you're right; they can't have much food or water. Do we know what they've got?'

Heads shaken. They could have no provisions in the boat, surely. The one great flaw in seizing the moment. Maybe a small scran-bag secreted in the boatshed, but that wouldn't feed eight for long.

The day wore on, the sunshine became an afternoon haze, the wind freshened and the convicts drew ahead. Around three they vanished from his telescope. They were perhaps thirty miles from the settlement, heading due south now, twenty miles off the coast. He gave the order to turn back.

Some time after midnight he was at his desk, writing again. Lizzie had come out of bed to greet him and exclaim, but he had sent her back to bed.

To the Colonial Secretary—Forster now, of course, with Montagu on the point of leaving:

Sir,

It is with no little degree of mortification and regret I have to report for the information of His Excellency the Lieutenant Governor the escape from the Settlement in a 6

Oar'd Whale Boat (commonly known as the Commandant's
Whale Boat) of the eight persons named in the margin . . .

In his haste and bone-weariness, Booth had forgotten to date the
letter. Now, reading it over, he scrawled it in: the thirteenth of February
1839. Except that, since it was twenty past two in the morning, it
was already the fourteenth. St Valentine's Day. Asleep on his feet,
he crept into the bedroom, pulling his clothes off. Lizzie was fast
asleep, her lips slightly parted. Before he fell into bed he placed on
her night table the Valentine's card and little packet containing new
hair-ribbons and a box of marzipan Laplace had brought down from
Hobart for him. Better not forget such things with a young bride,
no matter who escaped and how many would suffer mortally for it.

20

THERE WAS A 'BREAKFAST' AT GOVERNMENT HOUSE ON THE morning of the fourteenth of February 1839, but it had nothing to do with Saint Valentine's Day. It was the preliminary to yet another excursion. The weather continued glorious, as it had been all summer.

Inside Government House the atmosphere was not so cloudless. The ill-assorted house party was entering its third month, and the prevailing mood was uneasy. Too many people in close quarters, undercurrents of dissension, and the agitation of coming journeys in the air. Almost all the guests were waiting to leave the island, chafing under the strain of enforced idleness. Captain Laplace and his crew had left, bound for Port Arthur and France; John Gould was about to set out for the Wakefield Colony. The Montagus would sail in March, after which the Franklins would visit Port Phillip and the new town of Melbourne. St John Wallace was about to return to Port Arthur. Louisa was still at home after her confinement.

Eliza and I were working now on more studies of foliage, flowers, seeds and landscapes to appear as backgrounds for the birds. John Gould had also become suddenly interested in kangaroos, and while there were no true kangaroos in Van Diemen's Land, there were wallabies. 'Wobblies', as the children called them. He borrowed two, somebody's pets, and kept them in a run among the native shrubs in Government House garden, and there they grew fat while we drew them.

St John was not staying at Government House, but he was there almost daily for a series of fractious meetings about the new University College the Franklins were trying to establish. Montagu was against it. He wanted a senior school with its charter firmly in the hands of the Anglicans. Any gentleman who wished his sons to be college educated should send them to England. Those who could not afford it must do without.

These meetings were of course closed to Jane, but her husband, the Archdeacon and St John argued the Franklins' cause. The Catholics, Presbyterians, and Wesleyans all wanted a College in principle—but not in the hands of the Anglicans. The wrangling looked set to continue indefinitely. It would resume when Sir John returned in a month. Jane and Sophy would go on from Melbourne overland to New South Wales, the first women to venture on Mr Thomas Mitchell's newly surveyed road up through the Illawarra region to Sydney. Everything had been arranged and rearranged, discussed a thousand times. Now there was only the waiting to endure.

Sophy was deeply suspicious of Montagu's new affability. His fury at the Franklins over the Maconochie Affair seemed forgotten. And in spite of their differences over the college, he and Jane were now often in the centre of a group, chatting and smiling, as on that Valentine's Day morning.

'It sets my teeth on edge,' Sophy whispered, adding that you could smile and smile and be a villain.

Many outings had been contrived to relieve the situation; carriage drives and walking parties, picnics and seaweed collecting. There had been visits to the Government Gardens on the Domain, where the youngest Montagu had stayed too long in the sun and been sick among the strawberries. And the children had scratched themselves on the gooseberries and trampled the raspberry canes, to the fury of Mr Jago, the Head Gardener. After that the excursions moved further out: to the land Jane Franklin had bought in Kangaroo Valley, to the Fern Gully and the planned Native Botanical Garden.

Mr Harrison's Sea Baths and Bathing Machines in Sandy Bay had been another failure. Expensive and exhausting, wailed Sophy (Nuncle and Aunt had paid). All that undressing and dressing again while damp. She accidentally let go of her new straw bonnet and it sailed away over the water like a great . . . 'chicken', said Augusta Drewitt unhelpfully.

Sophy was in a new flirtation, with her Uncle's latest aide, Captain Ainsworth, another affable, raw-boned young giant for whom great things were planned at Home after his blooding in the colony. But he never did go back in the end. I always liked Ainsworth. Good breeding in every line of his long horsy face and every kind-hearted word of his amiable prattle. He was so tall he could be asked to straighten pictures on the wall, or reach down objects from high shelves—although fragile items tended to fall apart under his puppyish ministrations. So tall that Augusta Drewitt asked him whether he was related to Lieutenant Oliver Ainsworth, who was supposed to have been the tallest man at the battle of Waterloo, standing six feet and seven inches in his stockings. Whereupon Ainsworth looked startled and replied uneasily, 'Oh, I say! Hah, hah! Hah, hah, hah!'

'He does not appear to know who he's related to,' said Augusta disapprovingly.

'To whom he is related,' said Sophy, with an air of ownership.

Jane Franklin said *sotto voce* that what with only having arrived four weeks ago, and fallen for Sophy the moment he set foot ashore, the poor dear boy was at his wits' end. Not a long journey, perhaps, in his case.

'Was there really a Saint Valentine?' asked Augusta.

'Someone asks that every year,' said Sophy.

'If Saint Valentine had not existed we would need to invent him,' Jane Franklin said peaceably. 'Young people must have flirting and courting, otherwise how would one marry? And stationers must sell lace-paper, gilding and bad verse.'

'Hearts are a very ancient symbol, of course,' offered St John Wallace. He sat at the breakfast table on Jane Franklin's left, disturbingly handsome. Montagu, on her right, frowned. I had noticed before that Montagu appeared to dislike St John, who now continued, 'Perhaps your ladyship noticed the heart-shaped motif when you were in Egypt? It occurs frequently there. The shape is said to be derived from the seeds of the herb *silphium*, genus *Ferula*, the giant fennel. Extinct now, but so important to medicine in the ancient world that there is a specific Egyptian glyph for it.'

Jane Franklin shuddered. She had opened a valentine while he was speaking and now let it fall on the table. 'Loathsome,' she said in a low voice.

St John Wallace thought she meant him to read it. He did so and said quietly, 'A madman, my lady. Take no heed. A police matter, I should say.'

He put the letter down and Montagu reached out and took it. His face did not change as he read The Black Valentine, as it came to be known. He passed it to Forster, who read it and passed it to his wife, and thus it traversed the table, whereas it would have been better kept quiet. The gossip about it later became as painful to Jane Franklin as the valentine itself.

'Wallace is right,' said Montagu dismissively. 'A police matter.'

'What is it, Jane?' her husband called from the other end of the table.

'It is nothing, my dear,' she said cheerfully, but she looked suddenly wretched, ill and old.

It was a white rectangle with a printed border of small black flowers, probably cut from a mourning card. Lace-paper had been glued around the edges, and a ring of snakes drawn in heavy black ink in the centre, enclosing the words 'Such is Woman's Heart'. Inside the card were more snakes, a large black heart and a doggerel verse. Now that Jane Franklin had paid for the HEADS, it said, she should see fit to 'drop a tear upon the TAIL'. The end of one of the snakes had been made to stick out with, as she put it later in private, 'coarsely suggestive prominence'.

'It is about the snakes, of course,' said a small woman at my end of the table, in a low voice. She had a face like a kitten's, and wore an elaborate costume of purple silk, which gave her complexion an unhealthy look.

'I mean Lady Franklin's plan to rid the island of them once and for all.' She could not keep the contempt out of her voice. Jane Franklin was speaking to Wallace at the other end of the table. 'Well intentioned, no doubt, but scarcely wise. A waste of public money, some people say.'

'There was no public money wasted,' Sophy was scowling violently. 'My aunt paid everything from her own funds. Six hundred pounds in the first year! After which she was advised to call a halt.'

'My dear Miss Cracroft [a light laugh] I did not mean to . . .'

There was a good deal of discussion later about how the valentine came to be beside Jane Franklin's plate at the table. Sophy was sure it was Montagu's doing, but to me the whole thing was too crude for him and too carefully executed for Forster. Augusta Drewitt told me she believed it was Forster's wife. Anonymous letters are generally written by women, people say—but not always. It had exactly the secrecy and lewd schoolboy humour I associated with John Price. For all his rumoured pleasure in floggings and convict punishment, there was something vaguely womanish about him. As Chief Police Magistrate he was asked to investigate the matter, but nothing came of it.

Jane's distress was mercifully veiled when Lieutenant Stuart, like an actor entering on cue from the wings, arrived from Port Arthur with Booth's letter to Sir John. The Governor was aware of his wife's agitation, and I believe he began talking about the bolters to change the subject. News of an escape was already known from a signal late the previous afternoon, but now the details of its extraordinary boldness were evident.

'Captain Booth has married, and he is not so vigilant I suppose,' said the purple woman defiantly, her sac of poison not yet empty. 'The prisoners are all idle malingerers. When Mr Meredith came down from Great Swan Port last week he told us he saw a road-gang—so called—all the men dispersed along the shore fishing, boiling water for tea, and reclining in the shade. They need a hundred lashes apiece, I said to him, or hanging.'

'It was devilish hot that day, my dear,' said her husband.

'Language, Mr T . . .' she frowned.

Another gentleman said gruffly, 'You would be happy then, ma'am, to see the miserable conditions in which the felons are kept at Black Snake, where they are building the river crossing. I know I didn't sleep for a week after I saw it.'

Jane Franklin rose and the party began to move out to collect bonnets and coats. The sour purple woman continued her complaints to Lieutenant Stuart.

'It is not easy, ma'am,' he replied, 'to keep seven hundred men under close watch. And the leader of this escape, a man called Walker, is a particularly clever, determined rogue. It is sometimes difficult not to admire . . .'

He stopped because St John Wallace had clutched his arm.

'Walker?' he said.

'Walker, Woolf, Moss, Dixon . . . all the number one crew and two others.'

'This is my fault,' said Wallace, his face ravaged. 'Dido? The one they call Dido—Jack Thomas? Walker would not have gone without him.'

'Your fault?' said Stuart. 'The man has a bad record, Wallace.'

We were outside in the carriage drive by then and St John sank onto a seat at the edge of the gravel as though he could no longer stand.

'I encouraged Walker to think he has unusual qualities. I promised to help him. But I have not been there for two months on account of Louisa's child, and Christmas . . .'

'You weren't the only one to tell Walker he is above the ordinary. Booth has often said so.'

'We are all to blame. He will be flogged, hanged . . .' His voice was unsteady. 'Where will they go?'

Stuart shrugged. 'At present they have turned south, but it's likely they'll head north when they can. Hide among the islands in Bass Strait. Work their way up to New South Wales.'

St John bent his head and put his face in his hands.

—ᨈ—

The excursion that day was intended to be a visit to the new Tea Gardens at Crayfish Point, but we did not reach there. Just after we passed the lower end of Sandy Bay and began to wind along the narrow track around the coastal cliffs, a groom riding forward returned to say there was a rockfall ahead. The horses were unharnessed, each carriage was turned with great difficulty, and the company prepared to retreat to Lower Sandy Bay to picnic on the rocks. Jane Franklin's carriage, which had been first in the line of four, was now last, and while we stood waiting to retreat, she noticed the opening of a track among the trees. The groom told her it led up steeply to the Mount Stuart signal station.

'Ah!' she cried. 'The very thing. It will take my mind off that ghastly . . . *Solvitur ambulando*—isn't that right, Harriet? "It is solved by walking".'

Her cheerfulness returned. She had climbed Mount Wellington and every other mountain in the world she had come across; this was a mere *bagatelle*. Seeing Sophy's and Augusta's faces, she laughed and arranged for them to return with the others, and it was only Jane's maid Snachall, and a groom and I who accompanied her to the top. She leapt ahead like a hart upon the mountains, up a path so steep it resembled a crumbling earthen staircase, boulders and roots twisting every step. Snachall and I laboured behind with our holdalls and another bag each, while the groom followed with two more, these being the least we could persuade Jane to take.

Here and there on the way up, the dense bush revealed openings where shafts of sunlight descended through green glades into the fern gully below. I would have liked to sit and draw but we panted on, and when we emerged into the clearing at the top, the view was worth the climb. Our little party was greeted with surprise and welcome by the two officers at the signal station. They spread our rug at a good vantage point, put water on to boil for tea, and showed Jane our position on a chart. When they returned to their duties we ate our cold fowl and contemplated Hobart and the estuary spread below us.

'You see why I love mountains?' said Jane. 'And why they're often considered sacred? Human littleness seems insignificant in the face of such sublime . . .' A pause. 'How do you imagine the perpetrator of that vile card expected me to respond, Harriet? Did they think I would be cowed?'

She said she would like to know who had sent the card so she might ask them what they meant by it and explain that she only ever did what seemed to promise the betterment of all.

'They meant nothing, my lady. It was a hurtful, ill-judged joke.'

'I am misunderstood here. Misunderstandings occur so easily. Only a week ago, talking to Captain Laplace, I pointed to a group of convicts and said, *Voilà nos richesses*; "Here is our wealth, our riches,"—and he thought I meant it as a joke! I was never more in earnest. Convict labour is the island's most valuable resource at present—and in the end, of course, these men will form the population of the island. Does no one remember that? They are the ore out of which we must refine a society—by education and all the measures my husband's opponents deride. Perhaps the writer of the valentine thought I'd go scuttling Home with my tail between my legs?'

After a short pause she added, 'It's not as though I miss England. Do you, Harriet?'

'Yes, I do. London, particularly.'

'Ah well, London. Yes, London sometimes—for half an hour or so,' she smiled. 'But the desire for any settled home seems lacking from my composition, left out at birth. Or perhaps it's because I travelled frequently as a child with my father. Home was wherever we were. As Mr Clark, my overseer at the Huon, says of himself, "I am of a very roving disposition". He went to America but says it was not enough for him. She laughed. 'America! Not enough!'

We continued to gaze at the view while Snachall packed away.

'A good companion is the first essential for travelling,' Jane continued. 'With the right company, even disasters can be borne, as I discovered when I was in Egypt. It was three years after my husband and I were married. He was away at sea and I went to the Mediterranean to meet him. I arranged to travel for five days from Rosetta to Cairo with the British Consul to Egypt, Mr Robert Thorburn—and a married couple, a Captain and Mrs Scott. But one by one Mr Thorburn's three adult children, and then his nephew, decided to join the party—and when it came to boarding the boats ordered for the five-day voyage down the Nile, they immediately occupied the three large, clean vessels, leaving me and my maid, Lizzie Lumsden, to the single cabin in the fourth boat, which was far smaller and slower than the others. And as we discovered that night when it began to rain, there was no glass in the cabin windows. A wind came up and blew the water in until everything was drenched—which did not deter the rats, however. The boat was infested with them.

'I wrapped myself in two flannel dressing-gowns and a cloak. Lizzie Lumsden put on all her clothes—poor Lizzie, she looked like a bolster! We pushed the bedstead into the driest corner and huddled on it, wet through, rain blowing in our faces, shivering and sick from the smell of the rats. They ate a good portion of poor Lizzie's quilt,' she shuddered, laughed. 'We'd drawn it up over us, but threw it off in disgust when we saw the creatures relished the paper backings of the patchwork pieces. And Lizzie's pincushion! They fought over it until all the bran filling spilled out. Compared with the rats, the bed-lice and great black cockroaches were nothing.

'Four days and nights we endured this, scarcely sleeping or eating. Partly the thought of food made us gag, but there was no kitchen on our vessel in any case. The crew lived on dates, onions and mealy-cakes. Our kitchen and dining-room were on one of the leading vessels, and we were supposed to meet there each night when we docked at the little ports along the way. But our slow boat did not arrive until many hours after the others, by which time dinner was over and the cooking fires extinguished. And generally there was no sign of my fellow travellers—so-called. They had already disappeared ashore on the promised excursions, which I missed.

'Do you wonder that when we reached Cairo I expressed my dissatisfaction plainly and refused to continue with Thorburn and his group? Captain Scott and his wife said I must be exaggerating, and I have reason to think they later gave an ill report of me to other travellers. Indeed, a German Countess told me so. She offered to take me with her, but . . .' She hesitated. 'I had by then met a clergyman, a Swiss-German missionary very familiar with those parts. His name was Mr Rudolf Lieder.' She stopped and shook her head. 'A musician, a linguist; a scholarly man, cultivated.'

She broke off again, staring fixedly at the view. We sat silent until the signal tower behind us began creaking and clacking as the six wooden arms were hauled into new positions. When it was quiet again the lieutenant invited us to walk half a mile across the clearing to look eastwards, out to sea. The signal had been about the whaleboat absconders. He began to point into the blue distances and explain where they might be.

—m—

A few days later it was reported in the *Colonial Times* that on the day after their escape, the bolters had raided Mr Young's Fishery near Adventure Bay on Bruny Island, seizing a quantity of flour and sugar, a musket and clothing slops. They had killed a pig and taken the carcass, but offered no violence or incivility.

Days went by after that without further news; and then weeks. I thought of them on nights when I was wakeful, of trying to sleep in an open whaleboat at sea, or in the bush, hungry. Or were they already drowned, washed up among leathery black tangles of kelp in some unfrequented cove? They were strangers to me, and yet they joined Anna and Quigley and all that inward company of the absent or dead who prowl the back of the mind, unheeded for days and then vividly remembered.

Visiting Louisa and the baby, I discovered St John had been ill since Saint Valentine's Day. He had not returned to Port Arthur. He was recovering, but would see no one except James Seymour and Archdeacon Hutchins. Louisa hoped they would persuade him to give up his work here and return to England. I did not say so, but I thought St John would not leave until he knew what had become of Walker and Dido.

—⁂—

John Gould sailed on the *Potentate,* leaving Eliza more at leisure, but with a list of drawings to complete. The mood of Government House calmed after the Montagus sailed in early March. A week after Jane and Sophy left, I received an invitation from the Chesneys. They were planning a grand 'dehooney' and kangaroo hunt in April; I must go down for it and stay on afterwards. I wrote to thank them and accept, feeling it would be churlish to refuse their kindly offered hospitality a second time. I would be back in Hobarton long before the arrival of Eliza's baby in late May.

Once the family and guests were gone, the Government House servants ran up and down the stairs carrying bolsters and bedding. The drying-yard was afloat with linen billowing like sails. Empty rooms were 'turned out' and put under dust-sheets. Convicts went on with the endless whitewashing of the plank exterior, and Eliza and I worked in companionable silence punctuated by animated conversations, murmurs, fits of laughter. Towards the middle of April, John Gould returned, and he and Eliza began making preparations for their departure.

The bird skins, eggs and bones were carefully packed. Over three hundred finished drawings were laid between sheets of tissue in seven portfolios sewn into cotton cases. Dried herbs made layers above and below, and the finished bundles were swaddled in tarpaulin against damp, mice, moth, beetle and other forces of corruption. Like a twin-child with the infant to come (which would share Eliza's cabin), the package of drawings would be carried in a separate cabin with John Gould during the voyage.

21

THE MAIL COACH FOR RICHMOND WAS CROWDED WHEN IT LEFT at dawn from Kangaroo Point, the heavy dew and glittering spider-webs writing autumn's first signs across the grass. Passengers perched wherever they could find lodging on the outside of the vehicle, and inside there were six of us, yawning, squashed into jovial discomfort. Six and a damp infant, a tiny boy—who was quiet at first, but soon became shrill, eager to escape the arms of his parents, a young farming couple. He was desperate to clamber towards the interesting howls coming sporadically from a basket on the lap of the elderly woman beside me. Whenever a new howl emerged, the child would stop still and stare at us, its eyes wide as saucers.

At the approach to Mount Rumney many of us alighted and walked up the hill to save the horses, and it being by then a most beautiful day, we continued on foot down the other side, where the road curved and wound through a forest of tall eucalpyts. Sunshine dappled down into the summer-dry dusty undergrowth, two or three wooden huts became visible in parched clearings, and a bird was shouting 'be*cause*-of-it', 'be*cause*-of it', 'be*cause*-of-it' in the canopy. When we reached the bottom of the valley it was only a mile further to the baiting halt for breakfast at the Horseshoe Inn near the Cam Bridge. Here the baby ate a quantity of its parents' porridge and bacon and eggs, with bread-and-milk, sips of ale and weak tea. It was pensive by the time we resumed our seats, the little fringed eyelids drooping, and as soon as the coach moved off, it fell asleep. The child's father drew out a *Courier*, which he folded and gave to his wife. Cradling the sleeping infant across her lap and one arm, she read an article aloud in a slow, halting manner. It was about the whaleboat escapees.

'They are taken, then?' someone asked.

No, still at large. This was about a letter just come in from an isolated sawyers' and shipbuilders' camp at Port Davey on the rugged west coast. It had taken six weeks to reach Hobarton. The bolters had raided this camp and another at Macquarie Harbour. They had seized food, tobacco, guns, clothing-slops and rum, but had paid for what they took and used great courtesy, offering no threats.

'Ah! Paid, aargh!' cried the farmer, adding in broad country tones that, 'There mun be folks a-helpin' they.'

The escapees had rowed thousands of miles, read his wife laboriously, avoiding search vessels by dragging their boat ashore each night into the bush, or so it was thought. At first they had gone south and west, but now they must have doubled back, because the two most recent sightings were on the east coast. At Mr Webber's place on the Schouten Islands, they had rowed in bold as brass and professed to be in search of the runaways!

'Why, the larky divvils,' cried the farmer admiringly, slapping his knee.

A supposed 'officer', addressed by the others as 'Sir' and smartly turned out in a brown petersham coat, white duck trousers and stove-pipe hat (Walker!), had been carried out of the boat across the muddy landing-place by two of his crew. He had even questioned Mr Webber's men! But at Captain Hepburn's property further round the Schoutens, a man had recognised them and fired his musket. One of the felons—it was not known which—screamed and fell from the boat, but was hauled back in by his friends. All this was four weeks ago. Where were they now, the newspaper asked.

'Winter on the way,' said the old lady with the cat. 'They'll drown or starve or die of cold.'

An animated discussion ensued as the coach rocked along the side of the valley while I stared out the window at the shining strip of water below us, like a narrow silver lake with hills rising beyond. This inlet came to an end at last, and we turned across the bottom of the valley and rattled between bone-dry hills into the English greenery of the village. Richmond was the second largest town in the island then, with a windmill, a prison, and seven public houses along its main street. The largest was the Richmond Arms, where Polly and Liddy were waiting for me in a pony-cart with an aboriginal stable-boy called Worra at the reins, but Polly insisted on driving. She had grown tall and tomboyish. Liddy was thin and tiny still, but a new bloom of health gave her a fragile prettiness.

We trotted through the village, crossed the handsome sandstone bridge over the Coal River, and passed the tiny Catholic Church. The dusty road ran between bleached fields dotted with haystacks. A mile or so further on, 'Kenton' revealed itself gradually as an imposing square of sandstone two storeys high, half-hidden by the English trees in front, and a hamlet of barns, sheds, huts and cottages at the back. As we drove into the yard a yapping, barking, baying din began. Mr Gregson's hunting-pack—shut in the barn, said Polly.

Everything was in a state of bustle remarkable even for the hospitable Chesneys. The smell of roasting meat, ubiquitous in the colony, choked the air indoors. The kitchen thrummed with heat. Bess Chesney greeted me with affectionate distraction, shooed drowsy late-summer flies and ushered me into the drawing room, where several women sat perspiring and talking. The room seemed crowded with extra chairs. Louisa was fanning herself. The nursemaid had put baby Thea to sleep upstairs, she said. Flies tried persistently to settle on humid flesh, and buzzed at the windows. Augusta Drewitt sat with Mrs Parry, who gave me her cheek to kiss and said I was in better looks than six months ago. Julia, the wife of the Chesneys' surviving son William, was too fashionably dressed and too tightly laced for the occasion, her face beetroot with heat.

St John came in and repeated to us the story of the escapees from the *Courier*. It was still not known which one had been shot, he said, his beautiful face troubled. The *Eliza* had sailed to the Schoutens as soon as the latest news came in, but Walker may have managed to get up to the islands, the Kent Group. It would be difficult to locate them there. They could live on fish, sea birds, game, and stores left by sealers, perhaps.

At the evening meal Mr Chesney was exuberant, teasing the young ladies, tickling the babies, urging the older children to excesses of pudding and laughter. They had been overexcited all day, said Julia Chesney indulgently, ever since they'd watched the pigs killed this morning. Mr Bergman had not arrived.

At dawn next day the weather was cooler but bright. The men rode out towards the dry paddocks: Chesney and Gregson in hunting pink, the others in more motley attire. Gregson blared tantivvies on his hunting-horn, the dogs ran yelping and sniffing. When they were gone the women dawdled over breakfast with the children, or made prolonged *toilettes*, while a few of us gathered to receive Mrs Chesney's orders. Late in the morning Augusta and I were setting a children's table for luncheon outdoors in the kitchen yard when the pony-cart came back, too fast, with men on horseback behind, dust billowing round them. A pile of soft grey bodies of kangaroos filled half the bed of the cart, blotched with dark blood and clots of flies, and beside them Mr Chesney lay insensible, his head on the knees of his son William. He had suffered an apoplexy and fallen from his horse.

In the first horrified awkwardness people waited solemnly for news. Dr Coverdale was attending Chesney. No one liked to begin the meal although the men had not eaten since sunrise and the smell of savoury meat was everywhere. At last, after questioning glances, nods and murmurs, the children were fed, adults ate quickly in unnatural quiet, and the guests departed. I would have gone too, but Bess Chesney held my hand and for twenty-four hours did little but weep. After that she set about dragging her husband back from the brink of death with the Lord's help. She watched night and day at his bedside, letting me take only a few hours when she could no longer keep her eyes open. She read the New Testament aloud to him although he gave no sign of hearing, beginning with the feeding of the five thousand—something she thought would interest him—and going on to the other miracles. Withered arms restored, the woman with an issue of blood ten years, lepers, multitudes leaping up in health and thanksgiving.

'There is so much in the Bible about healing the sick,' she said in astonishment. 'Why do clergymen make so little of this and so much of sin?' she asked St John, who visited 'Kenton' every day. He replied, 'We are all in need of forgiveness.' She looked puzzled.

When there was nothing further I could do to help on these days, I went down to the river to draw. It was pleasant there, partly open, partly shaded under dun-coloured native trees or the lime-green willows. St John came that way one morning, riding Aislabie's horse to the Chesneys': every young girl's dream of a handsome stranger approaching on horseback. He dismounted and led the pretty chestnut as we walked back together. All his talk was of the escapees again, Walker and Dido in particular. He told me his opinions had changed under the influence of his acquaintance with them, and with Booth, Point Puer and Port Arthur. He now believed transportation was indefensible. He was corresponding with Maconochie, and had recently met with others leading the anti-transportation movement here. Together they were writing to England to urge their views.

—ᴍ—

After a week Chesney began to groan and stir. The weather turned cooler as winter approached. St John and Louisa returned to Hobarton and Robert McLeod called, in Richmond on yet another visit to Mrs Ross and her children. Nearly a year into her widowhood, Mrs Ross had opened the proposed school at her house, 'Carrington', about four miles distant on the other side of Richmond. She had five pupils but needed more. McLeod had persuaded William and Julia Chesney to send their eldest girls as weekly boarders; now he wanted Mrs Chesney to send Polly and also Liddy, who could help with the infants to pay her way.

'Harriet?' he said. 'I have mentioned to Susan Ross that when Mrs Chesney can spare you, you might give drawing lessons once a week while you are here. Mrs Ross cannot offer a wage at present, of course . . .'

As he rode away Mrs Chesney said, 'I always believed on the ship he had an interest in you . . . but now I wonder if it's Mrs Ross he thinks of? A widow with a little property. He has her interests much at heart, it seems. But it would need a brave man to take on thirteen stepchildren.'

—⚏—

Two weeks later, in the middle of May, Chesney opened both eyes and tried to speak, but he could make only gargling sounds and slumped back in frustration. For several days he tried, then retreated into furious silence. He no longer looked at us, but glared at the door in the wall opposite the bed as though he hoped the angel of death would come through and take him. I contemplated this wall too, on nights when I sat with him. Mrs Chesney allowed herself some rest now he was out of danger.

This room was not the Chesneys' bedchamber but a second parlour on the ground floor. It was to be a library eventually, but had neither bookcases nor books at present. The invalid had been carried here from the cart, and kept there to save running up and down stairs. The walls were distempered in palest duck-egg greenish-blue, which under the yellow lamplight took on the glow of a dawn or twilight sky in a painted landscape. 'Watchet', came to my mind, a country word used by my grandmother's maid, Sukie, for a certain colour of early morning light in spring. Now faint irregularities in the plasterwork suggested trees to me, and a cottage, and I was seized by a desire to draw on the wall. A fresco, like the ones I had seen in Italian Churches on our wedding journey. When I said this jokingly to Mrs Chesney she said, 'Why not? It might amuse Chesney.' He would take no interest in anything else. The walls would be papered in time, in any case. Or it could be painted over.

I could not use colours over such a large area, and therefore decided it must be a sepia brush-drawing with washes of tint: a pastoral prospect in the manner of last century. Why not 'Kenton' itself, as seen from the approach along the carriage drive?

Chesney's angry good eye followed my hand as the house formed in the centre. On the right I put a graceful sapling to frame the scene, life size, floor to ceiling, as though growing in the room. Fields on the left showed distant cows and sheep, and a sheen of river in Chinese white.

Mrs Chesney watched her husband watching. 'Oh look, Chesney! Harriet has caught the very shape of that hill behind us.'

Mr Chesney tried to shout. Woolna . . . walnut. I had not put in the second of the two walnut trees he'd planted beside the house twenty years ago.

I was working at it one afternoon when Mrs Chesney brought Gus Bergman in. He raised his eyebrows in mock astonishment.

'Van Diemen's Land as seen from a hill outside Rome? After Claude? Extraordinary. Everyone will be wanting one.'

It was astute; and sarcastic. Or not? This was the first time we had met since the proposal, and I was more agitated than I had expected to be. I smiled but could think of nothing to say. A short, awkward silence ensued, broken by Bess Chesney repeating the news Bergman had brought: Eliza was safely delivered of a boy, to be named Franklin Tasman Gould. Mother and child were both in excellent health. Bergman refused Mrs Chesney's offers of hospitality; she must excuse him, he was in haste.

He bowed to me and smiled and rode away, leaving me also a letter from John Gould, which I assumed would contain the same message—but when I opened it I found it concerned a change in their plans. Eliza and the child being so well, John Gould had decided to return to South Australia for another month or so, before returning here to collect his wife and sons. Only then would they go on to Sydney, at some uncertain date.

I was disappointed. I had been looking forward to travelling with the Goulds to Sydney, but when a longer, regretful note came a few days later from Eliza, I replied that it was a shame, but could not be helped. We would have longer together in Hobart, where I would soon see her and baby Franklin, and in a year or so we would be in London, working, which was the chief thing. I then wrote again to Quigley's lodging-house in Sydney, explaining the change of plans and saying I would now wait for them in Hobart.

On the day I finished the mural, letting the scene fade out across the wall, Chesney made a grumbling roar. Lifting a shaking left hand, he waved it limply at the adjoining wall.

'After Gainsborough' this time, I decided with an inward smile: a family group. Mrs Chesney in her best blue sitting on a garden seat under a tree, with Natty, Polly and Liddy on the grass leaning against her knees. Mr Chesney standing behind, arms folded, gun propped beside him, and his spaniel (dear, mad, droopy old Porter) lying at his feet, as indeed the dog lay in the sick room. Julia Chesney and her husband in the background. Chesney was soon able to say slowly and thickly to servants and visitors that 'it was a deal too flattering to him—not near handsome enough for Bess. But the house was like, very like'.

Mr Gregson, a regular visitor, said he would give me twenty guineas for two such paintings of his own house, 'Restdown', or 'Risdon', as people called it. Not on a wall, mind, but decently, on proper canvases. He was an amateur himself; his portrait of Mr Knopwood was considered a good likeness, but he wanted a professional view of his property to send Home to show his cousins how handsomely one might live here. I said that unfortunately there would be no opportunity. I was soon to leave the island.

—ᴍ—

At midwinter a Bonfire Night was held in a field by the river near the bridge. Tree trunks, dead for years from former clearing, were dragged by a team of cart-horses into a pile bigger than a cottage. The great pyre was lit before morning service on a bright cold Sunday, and by evening had burned into a red-black mountain of Hell Mouths, flaming caverns around which children played 'chasings' and shrilled and shouted in the dark.

While it was still light there was a pigeon-shoot, the prize a piece of silver plate. As it grew dark a huge orange moon rose from behind the hills, dwindling to a small, pale disc as it climbed high in the sky. The Church choir sang hymns, and later, at the supper tent, Mr Aislabie drank mulled wine in a teacup which he rested against his prominent corporation, saying with a sigh, 'Fire and lights against the darkness. What pagans we are at heart! Were you expecting to see St John and Louisa, Harriet? They are not to come after all. Now the escapees are taken, Wallace wants to stay in Hobarton for the trial, which will take place speedily, no doubt.'

The runaways had been taken ten days before at Twofold Bay, between Port Phillip and Sydney, by mere chance. The New South Wales Revenue Cutter had put in there to mend a gaff rig, and seeing a battered whaleboat containing seven men, had grown suspicious. The escapees were now being returned to Hobarton.

'Seven men? Were there not eight?' I found myself sorry to hear of their capture and hoping that one—Mick Walker perhaps—might have evaded the pursuers.

'According to the bolters' story, one quarrelled with the rest and asked to be left on Flinders Island.'

'Can St John do anything for them?'

'Gregson doesn't think so. He's of the opinion they'll hang, and I agree. *Pour encourager les autres*. Walker's crew has not been violent, but the list of their crimes is long.'

—⁂—

Each time I spoke of leaving, Bess found a reason why it must not be this week or next. At last I became anxious and insisted I could delay no longer; Anna and Quigley had said they would return in spring, and I had not yet seen Eliza and the baby. I must leave in the first week of August. On the twenty-eighth of July, George Chesney had another seizure and died later that night. Bess Chesney's sorrow this time was of a low, intense, defeated kind, her tears silent and continuous. Dr Coverdale prescribed laudanum, which let her sleep a little, but she wanted Liddy or me with her, to listen to quavering stories about George, and to add names continually to the growing list of friends and acquaintances who must be sent funeral notices, letters and mourning cards.

—⁂—

As I moved up the aisle of St Luke's in Richmond for the funeral service, I saw Gus Bergman in a pew ahead, among the large congregation. The line of his shoulders, the angled planes of his brown face, the loose dark curls—they sprang at me now like a white sail on a blue sea. I willed him to turn and give me a nod or some sign of friendliness or approval, but he was engrossed in reading the music of a hymnal. The Church was overflowing, and when the ceremony was over, a long column of walkers followed the funeral carriage and black-plumed horses as the coffin was taken down across the old wooden bridge to the graveside, which in Richmond is oddly placed on the other side of the river. Afterwards, while the family returned in carriages to 'Kenton', the rest of us began to walk back by the river path in small groups, and I looked for Bergman, but he was walking with Augusta Drewitt. They were deep in conversation and I was too proud to approach. Later at the wake, when our eyes met, I thought he was about to come across to me, but a gentleman claimed his attention and he turned away.

Bess was more herself now it came to the business of feeding people and greeting friends. When everyone had gone at last, she sank into a chair and sighed, while Liddy, kneeling at her feet, eased off the best black-buttoned boots and rubbed life back into her toes. Bess sighed again and said she believed Chesney would have enjoyed it. It was a shame he couldn't be there, it had been 'a good send-off'.

—〰—

Bess needed help with letters of condolence, and my leaving was delayed a few more days. When I reached Hobart I found a hasty, sorrowful note from Eliza. Her husband had returned early from Adelaide and was impatient to be in New South Wales. They had sailed. I missed them by less than a week. She and I had said only the most casual of goodbyes in April because we expected to meet again soon, and my grief is still raw whenever I think of it—I never saw her again.

PART THREE

22

I INTENDED TO LODGE AGAIN WITH PEG GROUNDWATER ON MY return to Hobart, but I discovered her packing, the house sold. Her husband's ship had returned with its 'greasy luck', a full load of whale oil, but he had found the great fishes less plentiful in these oceans than formerly, and wished to try Nantucket. I was pleased for Peg's sake; it meant an earlier return to Stromness for her. Nellie Jack was a pitiable sight, weeping in the kitchen corner with her apron pulled up over her face. She must go back to the Female Factory. Peg urged me to stay the three weeks until they sailed. I hoped Anna and Quigley would arrive before then.

I went immediately to see Louisa and St John, thinking he might have news about Walker or George Fairfax. But St John was highly agitated. He had not yet been allowed to see Walker, and there was, most extraordinarily, no date set for the trial. St John, furious, had now made an appointment to see Spode on both these matters. Louisa was bad tempered because the new nursemaid was unsatisfactory. Little Thea was the only happy member of the household.

A week after I settled in again, Sophy and Jane returned from Sydney. They had been five months away. Sophy showed me the small scar on her forehead caused when she was thrown from her horse outside Melbourne. She had endured most of the road to Sydney lying in the bottom of a cart, half-insensible with headache. They had stayed with Governor Sir George Gipps and his wife, but the weather was too hot, and the voyage home a nightmare. A journey which generally took ten or twelve days had taken four weeks on account of a violent storm which blew their ship far south past the mouth of the Derwent estuary, and they had trouble beating back up. Sophy was ill continuously; Aunt wrote letters and brought her journal up to date.

Jane was in high spirits, but had not yet seen the vicious newspaper articles written about her while she was away. At dinner on the first night when I saw her again, she spoke of her long talks with Sir George Gipps, who was doing tremendous good in New South Wales in spite of opposition. The town of Sydney was now fifty-one years old! A child born soon after the arrival of the First Fleet was now a grandmother, and Sydney was beginning to leave behind its brutal origins. The same could be achieved here—quicker and better because the climate was far superior to that of New South Wales: more English, more conducive to health and agriculture. The island was also more abundantly blessed with natural beauties—but it must be rechristened. 'Tasmania' was the natural choice, one word instead of a cumbersome three. People told her it would never catch on, but why not?

The Tasmania Society, established to study every aspect of the island, was now flourishing. It was time it began to produce a *Tasmanian Journal of Science*, written and published here and sent to England to extol the wonders of the place. The College difficulties must be settled, and the Museum and native botanical garden begun, and an Art Society established.

'An Art Society, Harriet!' Would I meet her the following day to discuss this?

After only an hour at Government House next day, I found myself making copies of a letter Jane had finished early in the morning, announcing a meeting to form an Art Society. It must be sent to all suitable artists in the colony, and other cultivated families.

Jane's room now more than ever resembled an 'office', but she did not appear to notice. Her desk had been moved to the side wall to make room for a table under the window, and here Miss Williamson and I sat copying—in silence mostly, occasionally looking down into the garden where the last daffodils speckled yellow along the drive. A glimpse of the estuary showed too, and I watched for approaching sails. There was no sign of Sophy. She was busy, Jane said; with the dinner book, the letter book, the engagement diary, flowers, the public and private guest lists.

Miss Williamson and I sat in a strong aroma of peppermint because she suffered with dyspepsia and sucked peppermint drops all day. She was fifty-five but seemed older, already developing the witch-featured profile of thin old women, the dowager's hump, the hooked nose curving to meet the whiskery chin. She wore plain white caps, had a persistent small cough, fussy little habits and an uncertain temper, but I was fond of her. She was well informed on many subjects, made wry little comments, and smiled sweetly when you least expected it.

On these cold spring mornings Jane, although she would have hated to know it, was the image of the female scribblers I had seen among Nan's friends in London. She did not sit at her desk, but in the green chair by the fire with her writing-slope on her lap, her small feet on the footstool in shabby red velvet slippers. She wore fingerless gloves and an old green shawl. Her hand raced across the pages, deep concentration on her face. I drew her like that in pencil, thinking her too intent to notice—but she did, and frowned. She hated to have her likeness taken. Miss Williamson asked me if she might buy the sketch and I gave it to her. She had it framed, and three years later when she went home, she gave it to Boyes, saying she would like it placed in Jane's Museum when that was finished. The drawing afterwards passed into Boyes's son's hands, and I have lately seen it ascribed to Mr Bock, who would never have drawn a sitter who was not looking directly at the viewer. He habitually used a dot of Chinese White in the eyes, too, and he would have added a flattering neckline, as I did not.

When the Art Society letters were done, Jane said to me with one of those short-sighted, intent looks, 'Your friends are not yet come, Harriet? There is a little more copying if you are willing? Miss Williamson has been kind enough to help, but she is not in the best of health. And she was employed as Eleanor's governess and must not be *put upon* now Eleanor is grown beyond her care. You have a good clerkly hand. But the most vital thing, of course,' she lowered her voice, 'is *absolute discretion.*'

My mind, steeped in foolish fiction, leapt to intrigue, although what Jane Franklin could have in that line was hard to imagine. Even so, her manner was so covert I was a little disappointed to find myself copying only the many tedious pages of the 'Feigned Issues (Distillation) Bill', as dry and unsuspicious a piece of legislation as you could imagine. It had been introduced by Sir John under pressure from England to increase revenue, and was designed to bring all distilling of spirits in the island under Government authority.

I laboured on, waiting for the secret correspondence, in the mean-time copying letters to England about seed wheat, the town water supply, shortfalls in land revenue. About a week later, a conversation with Miss Williamson at afternoon tea was enlightening. She was sitting on a window-seat, slightly apart from the rest of the family and guests, looking out at the wind-lashed garden. I carried across to her peppermint tea and a thin slice of Dundee cake which she seemed to live on.

'I have never been fond of daffodils,' she said. 'In spite of Mr Wordsworth. I find their odour unpleasant. Shakespeare is truer to life: "Lilies that fester smell far worse than weeds".' She added mildly, 'I am grateful you are to relieve me, my right arm aches, and Lady Franklin is pleased to find someone she can trust to be discreet.'

'If all the documents resemble the Distillation Bill,' I said, 'I will not be tempted to read them, let alone speak of them.'

She looked at me as though I were a dim pupil and said, 'It is not, of course, the *subject matter* which makes discretion necessary.'

She explained that if the copy clerks in St John's office or the Colonial Office noticed a word altered here and there in the Governor's wife's hand, it was nothing, but it would be unwise to let them begin to discuss how frequently Lady Franklin's handwriting converted many rambling pages into one articulate paragraph, or entirely recast—or even composed—whole documents for Whitehall. In those cases a fair copy must be made, to go to the clerks for copying.

Miss Williamson coughed, frowned, dabbed her mouth with a handkerchief, and said, 'Between ourselves, Mrs Adair, I have often found myself thinking it a shame that no one can admire Lady Franklin's letters. It seems hardly right to be obliged to hide such a light under a bushel. Or perhaps it's the parable of the talents I mean, but . . .' she shrugged, adding calmly, 'there would be outrage, of course, if it were known how much she assists.'

Sophy afterwards raised the subject while we were gathering flowers at the Gardens, as we continued to do some afternoons. She had refused to have anything to do with it. Her mother would not like it. (When Isabella was invoked, it meant Sophy was adamant, an army of two.) Beloved Aunt, from the best of motives, was Going Too Far.

'Imagine, Harriet, what the Colonial Secretary in London would *say* if he knew it was *Aunt* writing to him!' she cried. She bent and hacked at the irises, handing them backwards to me to lay in the basket.

What came into my mind was St John telling us on the *Adastra* that the Egyptian word 'almeh', which originally meant 'bluestocking', was coming to mean 'whore'. Learning in women is often regarded as only a step from depravity, he had said.

Two weeks later Sir John was forced to dismiss Gregory, the Treasurer, who refused to support the Distillation Bill. In Hobart it was known that this was because he was in business with one of the wealthy distillers, but this could not be explained to England because Gregory's interests were carefully hidden through middlemen. John Gregory had in any case been furious with Franklin ever since he was passed over for the position of acting Colonial Secretary, in favour of Forster, whom Montagu had insisted upon. The Gregorys set sail for Home vowing vengeance. Boyes told me they were as cold-hearted a couple as one could have the misfortune to encounter. Robert Murray noted in *The Colonial Times* that the Franklins quarrelled with everyone.

Still there was no sign of Quigley and Anna, no letter, and nothing from Jane Eyre, although I had written in the winter to tell her my departure was delayed.

—⚬—

At the reception for the *Lady Milford* that spring, a little aboriginal girl appeared suddenly in a red dress with short, gathered sleeves, and began to twirl and dance among the guests. Her black hair was shorn close to her head. Her eyes were dark, liquid, enormous. She began to do imitations: Jane Franklin peering shortsightedly at this, at that. Sir John, ambling along with hands behind his back, looking up at the sky, easing his short neck in its high collar. Boyes as a kangaroo, paws held up in front, chin raised, alert, hopping away. There was laughter. Those who could not see crowded in to look. A woman behind me said quietly to someone beside her, '. . . addition to the Government House menagerie.'

A vivid, affectionate child, Mathinna would come confidingly close to some unsuspecting guest, put her cheek against theirs, examine with astonishment their pale hands, face, hair, and peer into their pale eyes; prise open their lips to look into their strange pale mouths. This had to be discouraged. Mrs White did not like to have the fascinating wart on her cheek examined. Mrs Heseltine screamed and flung the child away from her French lace. Mathinna adored Eleanor's little dog—but not the cat, which she was inclined to treat with casual cruelty. At any chastisement she would fall to the floor and curl up into the picture of despair and misuse, or run gleefully away and hide for hours. She had a pet oppossum, a matter of constant complaint from the servants.

A maid was deputed to help the child wash and dress and say her prayers each morning, and the assistant housekeeper was to teach her letters, but these women were not equal to their charge. Mathinna would disappear and turn up a day or two later in the stables, or kitchen. She did not like Dr Lhotski, a new guest who appeared at about this time; a scientist, he claimed. He was fat and hugely pompous. Her imitation of him was so obscene she was whipped for it—and the antipathy was mutual. I saw him kick out at her once. But when Count Strzelecki arrived she would follow him like a shadow. A tall, gaunt, eagle-faced man, aristocratic in looks and manner, he had come to measure the heights of the principal mountains in Van Diemen's Land. While Jane was in Sydney she had persuaded him to come to the island after New South Wales. It was odd to see the mismatched pair standing together in the garden or before the fire; the pale thin Count and the small red-and-black girl.

—⁂—

In early November St John Wallace sent a note asking to see me. He and Louisa had been nearly twelve months in their cottage and he had just renewed the lease for another year. I expected to find them at war over this, but although they bickered as usual, there was an unwonted calm in the household, imposed by the new maid, a woman called Jane Fludde, a widow transported for stealing a horse while dressed as a boy.

Their last wretched servant, after many minor offences, had obtained a bottle of gin and drunk herself into hysterics. They had called a constable, but she threatened him with a broken bottle, shouting abuse. Eventually the officer coaxed her into the garden and pushed her backwards into a wheelbarrow. Being too drunk to extricate herself, she screamed like a banshee as he wheeled her away.

When Jane Fludde carried little Thea in, I thought the woman looked too small and slim to steal a horse, but when I knew her better I decided that if she wanted to steal an elephant she would manage somehow. She was Louisa's age, as homely looking as Louisa was beautiful. Her lean face might have been a young man's in its scrubbed, sharp-featured look. She had an air of authority, and treated Louisa and St John like clever children, to be humoured but reproved when necessary.

Thea, set down on the rug, crawled rapidly towards St John, and when he lifted her high and talked nonsense to her, she crowed with delight and grasped his nose. Louisa went across to them, and Jane Fludde and I stood regarding the trio. A perfect family. No. A Virgin on the Rocks with archangel: except that the infant was a girl instead of a boy, with gingery wisps escaping from the tiny frilled cap. Very Scottish-looking wisps, to my eye.

We walked into the garden and St John told me of his attempts to see Walker and his crew.

'They were captured in June and it's now November and still no date is set for the trial. It's against all precedent. When I speak to John Price—who doesn't trouble to disguise his contempt for me—he fobs me off with a threadbare story about the case taking time to prepare! Five months? Where there is no question of their guilt, and no lack of witnesses? Sir John tells me he cannot interfere with Price and Spode. Spode says it's Price's task to bring the matter to trial.'

'They will not be tried in a magistrate's court for such crimes?'

'No. They must appear before both judges, Pedder and Mr Algy Montagu, the Mad Judge. I assume it's because no civilian jury is allowed here.'

St John had been permitted to see Walker only twice. The second time the convict had a black eye, weals and bruises. He claimed the case was being delayed because the Arthur faction feared he would speak out against them at the trial. He thought they would avoid this by endlessly postponing the matter until it was no longer fresh in the public mind, when they could be quietly sentenced and hanged. (St John's voice was almost steady.) Walker had since been placed in solitary confinement and only the Prison Chaplain could see him now. In his agitation St John broke twigs off a lilac bush, snapped them into small pieces. He had protested to Spode, who said he had not authorised this, but it was in accordance with the regulations. Other visitors were 'discretionary', and Walker was considered at risk of attempting to escape again. 'Dido' Thomas was also in solitary. Dixon, Woolf, Moss and the others were together.

'I don't understand why Price involves himself?' I asked. 'He wasn't a party to whatever happened at New Norfolk. He arrived in the island three months afterwards.'

'Price and Forster are now allies in everything. Price thinks he's on the winning side with the Arthurites, and looks to his future. You will not repeat this, Harriet, I know; they have the same contempt for Franklin as for me.'

St John had now become eager to visit Copping, in the hope of learning from the former innkeepers, the Carmichaels, some detail to use against the Arthurites. He wanted me to go with him, since we might also discover more about Rowland Rochester. The best time would be at Christmas, while we were all staying at 'Kenton' with Bess Chesney. It was Bess's first Christmas without George, and Julia Chesney had decided on a reunion of the 'Adastras' to provide distraction.

'My acceptance of Bess's invitation is provisional,' I reminded him. 'If Anna and Quigley arrive we might be on our way to England by then, but if not, I'll gladly go with you.'

McLeod arrived. St John was writing articles against transportation for the *Derwent Jupiter*, McLeod's new paper. Louisa treated McLeod with an angry flirtatiousness painful to watch. He was casually friendly with her, more interested in news just arrived: our Queen had nearly perished last June, when a madman had fired two pistols into her carriage at point-blank range as she and Prince Albert drove past. By a miracle they were not hurt.

'And we have lived five months in ignorance of this!' I said. 'England might be at war with France again and we would not know!'

'Read Plato on the bucket theory of time,' advised McLeod.

'Women's minds are not formed for philosophy,' said St John. 'They are all instinct and emotion.' I kept silent, but not without an effort, reflecting that if the word 'philosophical' is taken to mean, as commonly, 'a patient, uncomplaining resignation to circumstances one cannot control', then women, perhaps more than men, had need to display the quality very frequently.

—៷៷—

At about this time I had a conversation with Jane Franklin that I recorded in my journal with a grim amusement worthy of Boyes:

Jane: I shall be sorry to lose you, Harriet. If your friends don't come soon I think I shall make a match to keep you in the island. A clergyman? A schoolteacher? Someone musical. Bergman . . . Ah, I have it! McLeod. His newspaper is begun—and heaven knows we need some benign influence in that quarter.

Me: Thank you, ma'am, but I mean to return to London to work on the bird lithographs with Eliza. Besides, Mr McLeod is interested elsewhere, I believe.

Jane: If you mean Mrs Ross, he has proposed and she has refused him. How do I know? Susan Ross's sister Charlotte Lempriere came up to town recently, and Mrs Ross of course told her. Charlotte returned to the peninsula and told Lizzie Booth, who sent a note about it to her sister Nan in Richmond. Nan spoke under a vow of secrecy to Julia Chesney, who told Mrs Parsons, who told me. *Et voilà!'*

Jane was amused but shaking her head, deploring it all.

—៷៷—

When the Groundwaters sailed I moved into another lodging house. I was boarding by the week now, expecting Anna and Quigley any day. But as time passed and there was no sign of them, I was forced to move frequently, driven out by verminous beds, a mouse plague, a room that filled with smoke whenever the kitchen fire below was alight, and fellow tenants from the too-friendly to the frighteningly sinister. Each time there was the difficulty of finding a new place, and the expense of a boy and a barrow—my possessions having multiplied somehow in spite of another hazard, a larcenous landlady. I said nothing of this to Sophy or Lady Franklin, but as generally happens in Hobart, they heard of it. I made it a joking matter, which did not deflect Jane's interest.

'You must come to us, of course,' she said at once.

I thanked her, reminded her she had even fewer bedrooms this Christmas than last. The whole rear wing was closed for repairs. The site of the new Government House had been decided, two miles upstream on the Domain.

'Why do you not buy a cottage, Harriet?' Jane said suddenly. 'I will lend you the money. It will be an excellent investment. Leave it in the hands of an agent when you go home and it will bring you a steady ten percent. You can pay me two percent when you are ready—which leaves you eight, still twice what you would get in England.'

Money interested her as another kind of practical puzzle. She had managed to invest Miss Williamson's little savings at fourteen and a half percent, Miss Williamson told me.

'Or rent a small cottage?' Jane went on. 'Even if you pay a whole quarter and leave before the end, you will hardly lose more than you do now by paying weekly and moving so frequently. It's the fourth of December today—you will hardly sail now before Christmas. Do you know Arthur Sweet, the young clerk in Sir John's office? He and Tom Cracroft are friends. His mother is a widow. She has a cottage to let in Battery Point near St George's Church.'

Jane knew such things because she was always saying to people, 'Tell me about yourself. Where do you live? What is your work? How do you manage?'

—⚏—

Ada Sweet was a Yorkshirewoman my own age, so tiny that the top of her neat cap just reached my shoulder. Her father, Old Mr Coombes, was barely taller. He and his wife owned the cottage next door to Mrs Sweet and Arthur, but Old Mrs Coombes had died, and now the widower had moved in with his daughter so the cottage could be let. By this means they would pay the mortgage until the house could be Arthur's. She would like to let to a single lady, worried about having children next door because her father worked all the ground, nearly an acre, as a kitchen garden. There was no fence between the two places. She sold some fruit and vegetables among the goods in the mixed shop at the front of her cottage.

The place to let was a crooked little house of three rooms in an odd dog-leg formation. The front door opened to a narrow hall with a room to one side, and then the hall opened into a large brick kitchen, from which a cupboard-staircase led up to a servant's attic. Another door from the kitchen opened into a bedroom, placed domino-fashion across the back. Twelve guineas the quarter. Too much, we both knew. Mrs Sweet looked at me, not unkindly, but with the look canny northerners have for daft, soft southerners, and we both knew I would agree. It was spotlessly clean, as simply furnished as a nunnery, and I was by then in love with the apple tree outside the kitchen door, and the tethered goat, and the heady new idea of independence.

—⁂—

Only one thing kept troubling me about the cottage: a small chair in the fireside corner like the one Nellie Jack had occupied at Peg's house.

I walked up to the Female Factory. It was further than I thought, and even on this sunny summer day, almost Christmas again, this place was grim, tucked under a hill on the shadowed, cold side of the Rivulet up towards the mountain. Too much like the grey school from which we had rescued Adèle. Here the smell was of strong lye, boiling linen and sour milk. There were clattering sounds of work, women's voices, the crying of babies. Nellie was in a room where prisoners of good behaviour were put to spin and weave wool into blankets. But there was no wool, said the matron. It was given by farmers, or bought if there was money, but mostly there was none. The room was freezing. Nellie sat huddled on a stool, leaning awkwardly asleep against a wall like an ancient crone. She held a tiny baby on her lap, also asleep, but both came sharply awake as we entered. Nellie had been there two months but it might have been years from the grey look of her.

When it came to signing the form to leave, her belongings were said to be one brown shawl and a walking stick. I was surprised, remembering neither, but rather an old school satchel Peg had given her, in which Nellie had kept a couple of cotton scarves, a tin brooch, hair-pins, two handkerchiefs (never used) and a set of patent false teeth (also never used) bought from a pedlar at the kitchen door. There was no satchel, said the matron. Nellie kept twitching my sleeve so we left. When we were a hundred yards from the gates, Nellie cried 'Hah!' and threw the walking stick into the ditch. After a few more steps she stopped, went back, picked it up and used it again to hobble along.

Later I saw she was not wearing her wedding ring, which I had never known her without. She said another woman had advised her on her first day there to hide it up inside herself, in her wossname, privates, like. But two women come in that night and one sat on her chest while the other searched down there and took it. One young woman kept a few coins in her hair and had it nearly all pulled out. You were better to have nothing in there. I asked her about the pretty baby. 'It won't larst,' she said. 'They don't, there.'

—⁂—

It was a wrench to leave the cottage three days before Christmas to go to 'Kenton'. I took Nellie, hoping that when I left the island Bess would employ her. I was the first 'Adastra' to arrive—and the only one, as it fell out. Rain began next morning, spoiling the raspberries and cherries, and apparently delaying Louisa, St John and James Seymour, who still did not arrive. McLeod was not expected; he was attending to his newspaper.

Christmas came and went with no sign of the missing guests and many tedious discussions of why this might be. Two days later the sun reappeared and we began pickling walnuts. Liddy, Nellie, Bess and I sat outside the kitchen door with a tub of the green fruit, and wearing old gloves to prevent our hands turning black from the juice, we pricked them soundly with a fork and tossed them into a pail of brine. A rider came into the yard and I knew it was Bergman. He was limping, and my mind flashed to Rowland Rochester.

A twisted ankle, Bergman said: it was nothing. He had returned to town for Christmas, and being now on his way back to Sorell to resume work, brought apologies from the Wallaces and Seymour. St John was ill, but he was in Seymour's care. Louisa and the baby were in excellent health.

Bergman drank Bess's famous ginger beer and made her laugh, and then asked if I would walk down to the river. I was determined to be calm in spite of a feverish tumult inside. I watched him put his old hat on again, I looked at his brown face and the rough dark curls he was pushing aside, and knew that if he asked me again to marry him, I would say yes. I wasn't sure how or when the change had come, but I was certain now. I felt happy, buoyant and breathless.

He said nothing until we turned along the bank by the reed beds and then he told me Mick Walker was dead, had died on Christmas Eve in the hospital. This was the cause of St John's illness. The *Courier* had printed the bare fact, but the circumstances were being kept quiet. Indeed, they were hard to fathom. Walker and Dixon had somehow escaped from the prison in Argyle Street two days before Christmas. They managed to bolt half a mile down the road to Wapping, a rookery of shanties between the theatre, wharf and slaughterhouse. Walker had then managed to get a message to St John, who went down there . . .

'. . . which must have taken some courage,' Bergman added. 'The place is so dangerous even the constables leave it alone. Walker told Wallace that he and Dixon had been deliberately allowed to get away so they could be "shot while attempting to escape".'

While Walker was speaking the slum was raided. Gaolers and constables burst in and Walker and Dixon were shot. They were taken to the hospital, where Walker died late on Christmas Eve. St John had insisted on staying with him, and when Walker died he began raving and trying to prevent the body from being taken away for burial in an unmarked grave.

'Dixon is still alive but Seymour doubts he can survive,' Bergman said.

Through Seymour, Wallace had sent for Bergman and asked him to take me to find the Carmichaels at Copping.

'But why? What is the use now? Can nothing be done about John Price, about this corruption?' I was too angry for tears, choked by a helpless sense of injustice.

'That's just it. Wallace believes the Arthurites must be called to account. And the Carmichaels may know something which will help the case,' said Bergman.

He told me he had three days of work at Sorell to finish, and after that, if I was willing, we would go. His manner was friendly, but cool and businesslike. He added that there had been no shipping arrivals over Christmas, no sign of Anna and Quigley. He gave me the address of Quigley's agents in Sydney and advised me to write for news.

With the walnuts soaking we began on the jam. Through all the pitting cherries, weighing precious sugar, sorting jam crocks and jars, my mind would persist in returning to Bergman's coolness, Walker's death, Anna's and Quigley's delay. We made twenty-eight pounds of cherry conserve on the morning James Seymour arrived. Dixon was dead. St John, as before, needed not so much a doctor as a theologian. Archdeacon Hutchins was with him.

23

I REACHED SORELL BY COACH FROM THE CHESNEYS' WITHOUT incident, and met Bergman, who was waiting with the pony-trap. Sorell to Forcett is some seven or eight miles, which passed easily enough, though not without a degree of discomfort from the plank seat that made me glad the ride was no longer. The day was warm, warmer than any day in the previous January, as we both said. I asked whether he had seen St John or Louisa, but he had been working at East Bay Neck for a week and had no news. Other topics failed us too: we could not seem to fall into our old comfortable manner together, and after a few attempts I began to think he did not want to talk, and we travelled in silence.

At Forcett I lodged the night with the Misses Driscoll, whose main livelihood was poultry, two acres alive with turkeys, chicken, geese, ducks, and flocks of tiny quail, which seemed to flee from under every bush. Their servant, Yankey Tom, a black man, took the cart, and I was shown into a small white room, while Bergman rode away to his camp nearby. In the morning we set off again. Once more the day rose quickly to heat, and our stilted conversation met with no better success than the day before.

Just before noon we jolted up to a farm gate on which hung two recently skinned hides, still bloody, black with flies. A hut was visible in a clearing beyond, among tall gum trees. Smoke rose from the chimney. Once through the gate the building revealed itself as two huts set at right angles with a gap between. A rank stench filled the air. A rough-coated dog dutifully drew attention to us in deep unthreatening barks. Outside the larger hut, where a wooden bench and table stood against a sunny wall, a young woman plucking a fowl looked up from dowsing it in a bucket of water. She paused and stared as we approached, did not smile. Bergman lifted his hat and asked if this was the Carmichaels' property.

'Dinah!' she shouted.

A little girl in a cotton pinafore and bare feet came out of the hut, clasping a rag doll. She stared at us and wheeled back inside, appearing again almost immediately, clinging behind the skirts of a woman about my own age, carrying another small child on one hip. Bergman gave our names and said we would like to speak with her—or her husband—on a private matter. The women wiped their hands on their aprons, their expressions guarded. He said I was a friend of Mr George Fairfax and would like to know something more of how he had died at New Norfolk. Perhaps she had seen how it happened?

'Dinah,' said the older woman, pointing at herself. 'Sal,' pointing at the young woman. 'My husband's sister.'

They turned into the hut and we followed with the small package of gifts Bess Chesney had provided: a length of calico, tea, jars of jam, walnuts and several recent newspapers. The women kept their eyes away from it. The interior of the cabin was airlessly hot. Flies droned in circles. It was one long wooden room with two alcoves, each curtained off by a blanket pegged to a rope across it. The far end wall was stone, most of it being a wide fireplace where a pot steamed on a hook above a fire. I was offered a chair and Dinah apologised for the smell; they were boiling tallow for candles on a fire out the back.

When we were settled, Bergman repeated that we did not want to cause trouble, but would like to hear anything they could tell us. George Fairfax had died the night of the Bridge Meeting?

Dinah said slowly, 'Aye, a terrible hot day it was—like today.'

Led carefully by Bergman, she admitted eight or ten gov'ment gen'lemen were in New Norfolk that night for the meeting—not lodged at The Eagle, but at the Bush Inn above the river. And so when the Fairfaxes came off the coach at midday—the two Mr Fairfaxes and Mrs Fairfax and the daughter—there warn't no beds left at the Bush, so they was sent across to The Eagle.

'The two Mr Fairfaxes?' asked Bergman, after the slightest hesitation.

Yes, the two gen'lemen (patiently, as though Bergman were a little backward).

'Did they say where they had come from?'

Yes, but then, no. The older gentleman, Mr George Fairfax, he wrote in the book Harris's Landing, but that was wrong. Harris's was on the other side of the river where the bridge was to be built—and he didn't live there any more than she did. He'd come on the coach hadn't he? No one lived there. Mr Magistrate Harcourt grazed his horses on it.

'The younger man was Mr Rowland Fairfax?' I asked.

She looked doubtful. She could not rightly say, now. It being such a hot day, Mrs Fairfax and her daughter had stayed in the back parlour reading while the two men went out walking and came back, and later they went out again to the meeting at the Bush Inn. The daughter was about thirteen. She and Sal spoke a few words when Sal took in some barley water. She, Dinah, was not taking much notice because Mr Henry Arthur came in about that time, to visit his brother Mr Charles Arthur, and that put her on edge. You had to keep an eye on Mr Henry.

Mr Charles Arthur was generally magistrate up north at Muddy Plains, but he was at New Norfolk because he'd changed places with Mr Thomas Mason, the one they called 'Mister Muster Master Mason'. Mr Mason had been in trouble a few months previous, for insulting another gentleman. There was talk he must lose his place, but Governor Arthur let him change for six months with Mr Charles Arthur instead.

Mr Henry said he would join his brother, who had already left for the meeting, but he stayed and stayed and in the end did not go—all on account of Mr George Stephens, the brother of Mr Alfred Stephens, Lawyer Stephens, who was there too. Mr Henry and Mr George called for brandy and water and persuaded Mr Montesquieu and Mr Ross to play at cards. Which she didn't like on account of when Mr Henry Arthur was gaming and drinking there was no saying what he might do. He had once rid a horse up the stairs into the Launceston Hotel and got the poor beast stuck so it had to be shot. And another time he tried to climb the spiked front railings of a respectable house and got himself stuck hanging by the breeches, shouting and threatening any who tried to help. And Mr Ross just as wild sometimes—and her husband Seth was away, gone to the meeting too.

Dinah noticed Sal staring at her and fell silent.

At any rate—Dinah spoke quickly now as though to get finished—after the meeting the two Mr Fairfaxes were walking back and the older one had a fit as they came in and died.

'A fit?'

'Yes, an apperlectic fit, the doctor said.'

'Was it your local doctor?' I asked. 'A good man?'

'Our Doctor Maynard was good,' she nodded at me. 'But it weren't him. They fetched Dr Brand from the meeting, a gov'ment gen'leman.'

After a pause she added: it being that hot, the poor man was buried quick and she was sorry for our loss but there it was. Sal brushed something from her skirt and began to breathe again. The two women exchanged a look. Bergman and I too exchanged a look of suddenly renewed complicity and interest. The Arthurites had brought in an Arthurite doctor, not the local man.

There were voices outside, sounds of horses and men, and the women rose and began to set out bowls on the table with platters and spoons. Sal peered through the one tiny window, in which a dry hill was framed. The little girl stared at me but looked away shyly when I smiled at her.

The hut erupted suddenly with the entrance of three men; large active limbs, the smell of hot working bodies, horses, leather and smoke. They took off their hats, acknowledged us with brief nods. Two sat at the table, where one produced a knife and begun cutting wedges from a large round damper Sal had put down beside the grey-brown slab of cold meat. The second man hacked slices from this. The third, evidently Dinah's husband, came and shook hands with Bergman, nodded at me, and indicated that Bergman should sit at the table. The little girl clung beside her father until he hoisted her onto his lap with a 'whhoa-hup, lass' and fed her morsels from the point of a knife.

Dinah handed me the two-year-old. He sat on my knee, staring into my face, fingers in his mouth, nose running a greenish slime, shocked into silence by this betrayal. His mother wiped his nose with a rough pinch of a rag, swung the iron arm to bring the pot off the fire and dealt stew into the bowls Sal handed to and fro. The heat in the room grew even more stifling. The men ate, grunting a few phrases, cutting more meat and a second damper. Another man, lizardy and old, came slowly in. Bent and gnomish, he might have been a hundred. He sat, was served, sucked his stew noisily. Every time I looked towards the table he caught my eye, winked, and grinned gummily. I looked away. When the meal was ended, he limped slowly past me, chucked the toddler under the chin, and quick as a snake reached out a hand to pinch my upper arm between finger and thumb. I winced at the fierce nip.

'No fa'aat on she,' he cackled.

Dinah whisked at him with a cloth.

'Git out, yer'ould divvil,' she called after him.

The men left, taking Bergman with them. Dinah took the toddler and fed him damper crusts dipped in stew. Sal brought another baby from one of the curtained alcoves, unbuttoned her bodice and attached the infant to a nipple. Its little fists opened and closed. The small girl stood on tiptoe at the edge of the table, her eyes just above the level of it, humming softly and making hills out of the crumbs on its surface.

'What is your name?' I asked her gently.

'Jane,' she whispered.

They invited me to help myself to the stew, which was greasy but good. There was tea to follow, black and sugary. Sal put the baby back to sleep and went outside, calling little Jane to follow her.

Taking my chance, repeating that I did not mean to cause trouble, I drew the books from my bag and asked Dinah if she could tell me about them. She flushed and said she had not stolen them, she had found them at the inn, left behind. She went to the door and looked out, shut it and came back.

'I knew this'd come,' she said. 'I said to Seth, this is a bad day's work. It's bin on my mind these two years. Why do you want to know?'

'We are looking for a man called Mr Rowland Rochester. We thought he and George Fairfax might be the same man. Do you know the name Rochester?'

She shook her head and said, 'Seth heard Mick Walker is dead? Constable Walker. Killed? That's a right wicked thing, if it is so. He and Seth come out on the transport together, the *Medina*—a good man.'

'I'm very sorry. It is true.'

She looked at me steadily, her eyes welling with tears, and spoke with great bitterness. 'Poor Mick Walker. 'e never did harm to nobody. Dead all on account of Mr Henry Arthur, may he rot. It might of bin Seth.'

She seemed to come to a decision and began speaking so fast it was not easy to follow.

The real reason why Henry Arthur had come to New Norfolk was not to see his brother, nor for the meeting, but on account of a girl, a convict-assigned servant working at the inn. Nan. Poor silly girl. She believed he would marry her. Mr Henry made Nan sit beside him to bring luck in his playing, but it done him not a speck of good. He lost, and being drunk grew quarrelsome and said he did not like the way George Stephen looked at Nan. 'What are you looking at?' he said, and fired a pistol through the window—that was nothing new—but Nan got up and ran out the back. George Stephen told Henry he was a fool and should consider what his uncle the Governor would do if he heard of Henry's goings-on.

Mr Henry quietened a bit but soon began again, saying George Stephen and Hugh Ross were cheating. She did not see who began the fight but they knocked over the table and bottles and glasses and cards. The gun was on the table and fell to the floor. Someone picked it up and fired twice just as Nan came back in, followed by Mr Charles Arthur and Mick Walker, returned from the meeting. Nan was suddenly on the floor lying there all bloody and Mr Henry on his knees beside her white as starch, blubbing like a schoolboy, pulling at her and moaning, 'Come on, Nan, get up,' and Mr Ross trembling so he couldn't hardly stand.

Then Mr George Stephen picked Nan up in his arms and carried her into the back parlour just as Mrs Fairfax came downstairs to see what the noise was. At the same time the two Fairfax men came in from the meeting, and that was when the older Mr Fairfax, seeing the body and blood, took his fit. Mr Charles sent George Stephen to fetch the doctor and Mr Alfred Stephen from the Bush Inn. They told her, Dinah, and Mrs Fairfax too, that Nan had only fainted. But Dinah saw the way Nan's head hung backward, her eyes and mouth open, and the blood. The poor girl was past help. Mrs Fairfax said nothing but rushed away upstairs to her daughter.

When Seth came back, he and Mick Walker carried the dead man up to his room. Alfred Stephen was in a terrible state, red-faced and sweating and mopping hisself with a great handkercher. Then younger Mr Fairfax said he and his family must leave at once. It seemed strange that they would go without waiting for a funeral. There was something strange about it all. He wanted to take his wife and the child away then and there, although it was just past midnight! Mick Walker persuaded them to wait a while, and later he took them down in a skiff to the Black Snake to catch the morning coach. Fairfax also gave Mick money for the burial of the older man, and for a headstone.

When the Fairfaxes were gone she had found the books left behind. She had thought they might do to teach Jane her letters, but she did not know how to begin and when Harry Bentley the pedlar came, she had given them to him in exchange for—she indicated the shelf by the fire. A chipped china plate with a border of painted flowers, propped standing up with a stone. The only object of beauty in the place. I suddenly wished I'd brought some more interesting gift than the jam and walnuts in the package.

And straight after, Dinah was continuing, Mick Walker was taken for housebreaking, which she did not believe—and Mr Henry came and told Seth to say nothing of what had happened or it might be blamed on Seth, and he didn't want another sentence, did he? If they kept quiet, something might be done for them. Later they were offered this place. Seth had been wanting to breed horses and this run was on a good creek, but lonely, not like the inn.

Strangely lonely, I thought, to a woman used to the coming and going of an inn. And at night, the small clearing would be full of wild shadows, and the tall whispering crowding gum trees and the thick dark undergrowth alive with the scrabbling of unknown creatures. And if they took Seth away . . .

I promised Dinah I would do everything in my power to make sure no harm came to her from the story she had told me. I had brought nothing with me except what I took everywhere: the small sketchbook, now about a quarter used, a tiny watercolour box and a couple of brushes and pencils. I gave them to Dinah.

'For Jane,' I said.

—m—

The last barred gate was shut behind us by mid-afternoon, and as we rattled away down the track the humid afternoon was building to a storm, the air no fresher than in the hut. I was weighing up what to say, but need not have troubled. Seth had told Bergman the same story, with an added detail: Mick Walker had arranged for Nan to be buried in the same grave with Fairfax. The sexton was an old man, a heavy drinker. When he drowned in the river a month later, nobody was surprised.

'Two Fairfaxes!' I exclaimed. 'Where did they go afterwards? Wouldn't the Carmichaels have had to account for losing a servant?'

'They probably reported her "absent from her place of work".' Bergman, too, was clearly exhilarated by what we had heard. 'Female convicts disappear from the records more easily than men. If they're assigned outside the main townships they may not come under the eye of the authorities for years.'

'You can't blame the Carmichaels for keeping quiet,' I said, 'but why would the Fairfaxes agree to say nothing? Why did they want to leave so quickly? Do you suppose the younger man *was* Rowland Rochester?'

'We don't even know who George Fairfax is—or was. The younger man could simply be his son. But Rowland Rochester is almost beside the point now. This is the kind of thing people have been trying to prove against the Arthurites for years. No wonder Alfred Stephen and the rest were determined to prevent Arthur finding out. He'd have had no compunction about letting the law deal with all of them, even his chief officers. At any rate, St John Wallace now has the evidence he wants.'

'But you can't tell him?' My voice was too harsh. 'If he is half mad, as you say, he will use it and the Carmichaels will suffer.'

'Of course I must tell him,' he said, taking a sideways glance at me from his driving, his face suddenly serious. 'This is exactly what he is looking for. Arthurites colluding to hide a death they have caused? Walker falsely accused? Imagine the outcry!'

'But what about Dinah and the children?' I was too hot, breathless. 'How would they survive if Seth was sent back to prison like Walker?'

'They will be safer if everything is out in the open.'

'How can you say so? The Arthurites will take revenge on the Carmichaels and escape punishment themselves. Montagu and Forster are not directly involved. They will plead ignorance, twist the story . . .'

Bergman spoke impatiently. 'They are accessories to murder! Or manslaughter at least.'

'But Dinah, trying to survive in that hut . . .'

He looked at me sideways again. 'You dislike the bush yourself, and therefore assume everyone feels the same. Sal and Dinah may be freer than you.'

I kept my voice as calm as I could manage. 'What do you mean?'

'They are working for themselves, on their own property. In England they must have worked for someone else all their lives. But England is always best with you.'

I had been hot already, now I was burning. I felt perspiration soaking my hair under my bonnet, trickling down the back of my neck and between my shoulder blades. I knew I was red-faced, damp and ugly with heat.

'Are you suggesting I should lie to Wallace?' he asked.

'You could tell him about George Fairfax's death, about the other Fairfax. Not mention the girl.'

'But the death of the girl is the crucial point!' I could feel his growing exasperation.

'It's only hearsay! Unless the grave is exhumed to find the two bodies—and the Arthurites would never let that happen. The Fairfaxes must be found and induced to speak out, and then the Carmichaels will not need to. And we will know once and for all whether Fairfax is Rowland . . .'

'If the Fairfaxes haven't spoken before, why would they now?' he said. 'The Arthurites bought the Carmichaels' silence with threats and gifts—they probably used the same means on the Fairfaxes . . . You speak of doing harm, but what about the harm you will do to Rowland Rochester and his family if he has a bigamous second wife and a child?'

'Rowland counts for more than Dinah and the children?'

'No! But Dinah, Sal and the children have more connection with the real evils the Arthurites have done in this colony. Grabbing land for wealthy absentee landlords in England, nepotism, a greedy disregard for every interest but their own. Wallace is right; they must be stopped or they'll continue. Will you wait for others to fall victim?'

We jogged along in steaming irritable silence until he said, 'You say, "find the Fairfaxes"—but by now they could be anywhere. Sydney,

England, New Zealand, the Indies. In any case, Rowland Rochester is *not the point*. Can you not see beyond the personal? There are larger issues at stake.'

Everything was over. I was lectured like a child.

'Perhaps,' I said bitterly, 'it's because when men begin to talk about the larger view, it often seems to involve some loss or injury for women and children.'

What I now furiously, incoherently felt, was that I was powerless to save Dinah and her family, and so were he and St John. We could do nothing—only stumble along behind the Arthurites on the dark path their greed and secrecy had carved. They would destroy whomever they pleased, by accident or choice, to save themselves.

While I struggled to find words for this, he said in a hard voice, 'Well, the whole matter has very little to do with me . . .' he grimaced, made a dismissive gesture as he brushed a fly away from his face. 'Against my better judgement, I'll say nothing at present to St John about the girl's death. But when he is more recovered . . .'

'I shall leave the island soon,' I said. 'When I'm gone you can do as you like.'

We were only a silent, angry, suffering mile now from Forcett, an immeasurable gulf between us. Thunder rumbled behind the hills, roiling masses of purple-grey cloud spread across the sky, but the rain would not fall. We clattered back into the poultry yard and Yankey Tom helped me down. Bergman raised his hat, gave his attention to helping unhitch the cart, and rode away without a backward look. I spent the hot night tossing on the little cot, mulling over the painful mess of it all. The storm broke in the early hours of the morning. It brought rain and coolness and I wearily slept.

I did not see him next morning. It being a market day in Sorell, I travelled back with Yankey Tom and one of the Miss Driscolls, in a cart full of poultry dead and alive, and a strong, sickly odour of blood and feathers.

—⚏—

After my return to 'Kenton' I remained full of disgust and fury—with myself, Bergman, the island, and the whole Rowland matter. I vowed to wait no longer for Anna and Quigley; I would book my passage home as soon as I reached Hobart again; shake the dust of this quarrelsome, brutal little colony off my feet. But Mr Gregson, visiting 'Kenton', urged me again to paint views of his house, and I allowed myself to be persuaded. I went to 'Risdon' in late February, directly from the Chesneys by the back road over Grasstree Hill, sending a note of my whereabouts to the Post Office in Hobart.

The Gregsons' household was like the Chesneys' in being large and sociable, but elegant beyond compare, its setting an earthly paradise at the edge of the Derwent. Verdant gardens and orchards spread along the river and native bushland clothed the hill behind. Mrs Gregson and her two grown-up, unmarried daughters welcomed me kindly. Another daughter was married and expecting a child; their son had just sailed for England to study the law. Feeling empty on this account, the Gregsons had filled the house with six or seven guests.

Everything here was serenely well ordered and the scents of late summer filled the calm, light rooms. The company was cultivated and elegant but without formality. I was free to wander all day, drawing and painting. When I finished Mr Gregson's commission, he and his wife encouraged me to stay on to add to the portfolio of works I could sell in England. In the atmosphere of kindness there, I began to think I'd be a fool to hurry into leaving on account of a fit of bad temper with the island and Bergman.

The trial of Walker's six fellow-absconders was set for the first week of March, and Gregson went up to town to attend. He was due home on the Thursday, but a note came from him to say the trial was delayed, and it was not until late on the Friday evening after the family had dined that he came in, with Booth, who looked tired, but was full of good humour, as always.

'No, my dear, we have not eaten,' Gregson answered his wife, 'we are indeed famished. We waited in town for the evening edition of the *Courier*—and might as well have saved ourselves the trouble—since they are no wiser than we, it appears. Will you sit again with us, my dear, while we eat? Harriet, will you take a glass of wine while we tell our news?'

'The hearing, as you know, was set down for Tuesday before both judges, Pedder and Montagu, but it was adjourned until the following day on account of the "absence of a material witness". That was Booth here, of course, delayed in coming up to town.'

'The *Isabella* came down,' said Booth, 'but she struck an obstacle in the water just before Wedge Bay . . .'

'On Wednesday the trial was adjourned again until Thursday,' continued Gregson, 'by which time,' he turned to me, 'your friend St John Wallace was in a pitiable state of agitation. The man is a mass of sensibility.'

'It was unfortunate,' added Booth. 'When we came to the court-house on Thursday morning we discovered four men had been hanged an hour earlier and a great crowd was there to see it. I thought Wallace would collapse, but he didn't say a word.'

'. . . though to look at his face,' Gregson said, 'you'd have thought he'd seen the Gorgon's head. And when the trial at last began, we expected days of evidence and debate—both their Honours being garrulous gentlemen. But what did we get? Nothing! All over and done in great haste. The charge was read, "absconding from Port Arthur"—no mention of other crimes—and a guilty plea recorded. And then the sentence! "To be severally transported for life." There was great astonishment in the court, as you may imagine, both at the sentence and the manner of it. It was commonly believed they'd hang.'

'Transportation means hard labour on a chain gang, as you know,' said Booth, 'or return to Port Arthur. Wallace is determined to negotiate for Port Arthur so they will come under my care again.'

'Who will decide?'

'John Price, or Spode, or both in consultation. If it's Price it's hopeless, I'd say.'

One of the newspapers had recently claimed Price had been seen in disguise in one of the lowest pothouses in town, trying to entrap an unwary sinner.

'I've seen many an odd business here,' continued Gregson, 'but this is one of the oddest—and we haven't yet come to the most curious thing. Look there in the newspaper. Do you see the names of the men? John Jones, Nicholas Head Lewis, George Moss, James Wolf and James County. No mention of Jack Thomas, the one they call Dido. He did not appear. Where is he? Wallace hopes it means they've accepted his plea that Dido should be charged separately because he is somewhat simple-minded—but nothing was said. Now there will be another wait I suppose, to see what happens next. Oh, bye the bye, I called at the Post Office, Harriet, and have letters for you.'

The first was from Sophy.

16th February, 1840

I am told you have spent the Christmas season making likenesses of half the citizens of Richmond. Perhaps you will have better leisure now at 'Restdown' or Risdon as people call it. Landscapes are less trying than People to paint I sh'd think but Vanity being Universal you will no doubt be soon in reckquisition for portraits again.

The new clergyman has arrived his name is Mr John Philip Gell. He is twenty-three, looks seventeen, and has all the composure of a bishop three times his age. He gives speaches in Greek and Latin which we hasten to Admire although I for one do not understand a syllable. He also speaks French and German, and Dr Arnold of Rugby (who has sent him out at the request of Nuncle and Aunt) says he is very brilliant but Harriet he does so remind me of a Sheep. Not the Timid kind of sheep, the Stubborn kind. (See how I trust you. But the truth is I would not care if he knew.)

He is thin and pale. Hair and face sallow-yellow, both worn long to the shoulders. He cultivates a ginger frizz of side-whiskers which he appears to imagine adds gravitas to his youthful phyzignignionomy. Whiskers are worn everywhere in England now, he informes us, the fashion being set by Prince Albert, Queen Victoria's affiancé (German! And her first cousin! Aunt does not approve.)

Gell is to be principal of the New College. Aunt has set her Heart on it as you know, but Nay-Sayers are Legion. Forster repeats the objections Montagu made before he left, parrotting as he was taught, and arguing for an upper-form school in Hobarton, whereas Aunt believes some land at the New Norfolk Cottage should be given up to build the College. It would make it all the more prestigious and keep the boys from idling in town during their studies. Dear Aunt at once reads into Mr Gell all her own Cleverness and Good Nature. She calls him the Son she would like to have had, and praises his Profound and Original mind and pure and Noble Feelings. As for Eleanor she is madly in love with him and makes no secret of it. Nearly sixteen, and less discretion than a twelve-year-old. I would have been whipped at her age for such folly.

Nuncle is beset by cares of State but looks forward to the coming of the Magnetic Expedition with his old friends Captain James Ross and Captain Francis Crozier. The Lady Hamilton brings news that their ships the Erebus and the Terror left England last September. They will reach VDL this winter after spending the summer months in the southern ice. You will understand from all this, Harriet, how I long for a Friend with whom I may laugh at Mr Gell and bite my thumb at the Arthur Faction. I hope you will soon return to us here at the Palace(!). Let me know as soon as you arrive.

Your most affectionate friend,
Sophy Cracroft

The other letter was a reply from Padgett & Marshall, The Universal Shipping Company, 23 George Street, Sydney, in answer to my questions about Quigley's ship:

> . . . regret to inform that the brig Firefly burthen 343 tons was damaged in the harbour at Port Nicholson, New Zealand. There being presently no further news, we cannot . . .

Had they changed to another ship? Been delayed there for repairs? Where were they now?

—⁂—

When Nellie Jack and I at last returned to the cottage at the beginning of April, there was a parcel waiting for me. A manservant had brought it to the door weeks ago, Ada Sweet said. She had not sent it on because she thought I would return before this. It was the painting by Madame Vallayer-Coster that I'd seen at Duterrau's studio, and a letter from Gus Bergman dated in February, a week after our meeting with the Carmichaels.

> Dear Harriet,
>
> You must please allow me to give you this. A parting gift, an apology. I should not have spoken as I did in our last conversation. In my defense I will say only that I have been on the receiving end of one of Henry Arthur's drunken attacks, and Seth Carmichael's story revived old fury. But enough of that. You will be reluctant to accept this I know, but it was clearly meant to belong to you. I bought it more than a year ago, intending to give it to you then, but the opportunity I hoped for did not arise.
>
> You will observe that the bird here is free, not caged as in the paintings of Madame Vallayer-Coster you described to me. It may fly whenever it chooses. Gould explained to me that this is Platycercus caledonicus, or the green rosella, first described by the German naturalist Johann Friedrich Gmelin

in 1788. It is migratory, a rare thing in parrots, apparently. Herr Gmelin wrongly believed the specimen he owned had come from New Caledonia, hence the misnomer. Gould kindly told me a great deal more, as you may imagine—far more than I can readily remember—my interest being rather pictorial and personal than zoological.

James Calder and I set off again tomorrow for the Marlborough region and the Frenchman's Cap, with a dozen 'bad laddies' as Calder calls them, to get a start before autumn on clearing the track the Franklins will use next spring when they visit this sublime part of the island. Not that our felons are truly 'bad', we find them trustworthy and eager for the work. On my return I go to Lady Franklin's settlement at the Huon, and after that to the east coast for a month at least, thus you and I are unlikely to meet again even if your leaving is further delayed.

Mr Boyd has replaced Frankland as Chief Surveyor (I wish it had been Calder), and we have new instructions which increase our load of surveying, just when the number of surveyors is being reduced! But the world is mad, as you and I have always known. Art and music are the only sanity. God bless you, Harriet, and keep you in health and pleasant paths for the future.

Gustave Bergman.

I shed tears then, at the same time laughing with pleasure at such a perfect, clever gift. He must have known that every time I looked at it I would think of him—which made me hope that he was not so entirely indifferent to me as he had seemed at our last meeting. But the parcel had lain here so many weeks! It would seem I had not troubled to reply! I had removed my bonnet and gloves, but now I put them on again hastily, and wiping my eyes and calling to Nellie that I was going for a walk, I set off to Bergman's cottage. I would knock and ask for him, or at least explain to his servant Durrell that

I had only just returned. But the place had a closed, empty look. A woman sweeping the path next door said Mr Bergman was away. He had taken Durrell with him. She was to air and dust the place each week. They would return in late autumn.

I returned to the cottage, shrugged off my outdoor wear, sat down, and throwing caution to the winds, wrote Gus a letter. I poured into it the burden of what I had thought and felt since his proposal. I said that if it were possible he still felt the same, my answer must be different now.

Before I could change my mind I sealed it and took it round again to Bergman's cottage. After knocking on two doors I found the woman who was to air the house and gave her a coin to put the letter in a place where Mr Bergman might find it the moment he returned.

—⁂—

On my first visit to the Franklins again, Sophy took me by the arm as we went in to tea, and with a look of eye-rolling significance drew me across the room to meet Mr Gell—who was indeed, as she had said in her letter, a pale, underdone-looking youth of imperturbable composure. I said I hoped his voyage out had been tolerable, and received in return a brief sermon on Duty—but not brief *enough*, as I said to Sophy later. She listened to him with the satisfaction of a ringmaster showing off a performing seal. Jane Franklin came over and teased Gell for his erudition. He, clearly knowing himself a favourite with her, replied with easy confidence. Eleanor hung beside them, cow-eyed and prickly with jealousy.

24

'SO FORSTER HAS GOT HIS HARPOON INTO ME,' BOOTH THOUGHT, 'and now he will never let it out.'

Forster sat opposite him at the table in the small meeting room at Government House—no informal breakfast session now—explaining there was to be yet another enquiry into escapes from Port Arthur.

'. . . deplorable affair of Walker and the whale boat last year. It should not have been possible in my opinion . . . was never properly explained. And another escape this summer. We must account to London.'

Sir John sat at the head of the table saying little. Forster was doing all the talking. Josiah Spode, Chief Superintendent of Convicts, sat next to John Price, who looked . . . pleased with himself, Booth thought. Smug. On Price's other side sat a man who had no right to be there, a former convict, Stringer Wynn. While he was at Port Arthur he'd been known as Tickler Wynn, or 'Stinger' or 'the Butcher', because of his former role as flagellator at Sarah Island. He was Constable Wynn now, some sort of bullyboy handmaiden of Price's. Outside the window a breeze shook white blossom from a bright, tossing tree. The sky was forget-me-not blue. Booth would have liked to be striding along a beach, singing. A junior clerk wrote rapidly in shorthand.

Forster continued. 'We must determine why escapes have become more frequent.'

'With respect, sir,' said Booth. He spoke rapidly because he knew Forster would soon stop him. 'I have addressed that question in several reports. There is no mystery about it, as I have tried to explain. We are receiving new prisoners at an impossible rate, which has created severe difficulties in accommodation and provisioning. Newcomers must be put to building work or cultivation in ever-enlarging gangs with too few experienced overseers.

'At the same time, as a result of the first two enquiries, I am required to punish even the smallest misdemeanours.' His sittings as magistrate took up far too much time now. 'Prisoners under such strict rule become all the more eager to escape. The mood is infectious, and greatly increased by the agitation of continual newcomers. I have also been ordered to reduce those little rewards and incentives—extra rations and so forth—which to my mind are essential to keeping a well-ordered . . .'

Forster raised his hand in a brusque gesture, giving Booth a hostile look—or perhaps it was just his ruined face or the pain of his gout. He had been ill again.

'Am I to understand, Captain, that in your view, attempts to escape can best be reduced by ceasing to punish offenders? You argue that we are to provide them with inducements to remain in prison?'

John Price snorted.

'Sir . . .' said Booth.

'Write down your opinions, Captain. The new enquiry will consider them,' Forster said, his bulging eyes magnified by the lorgnette.

'Sir . . .' Booth began again, but Forster glared, did not stop.

'With sufficient vigilance, escape is impossible. That is my opinion, as I have made abundantly clear. But this is not the time for discussion. The enquiry . . .'

Booth turned to Sir John.

'Your Excellency, again I must protest. Mr Forster has raised the matter of the Walker escape. It is the talk of the town that the penalties meted out to Walker's men were hardly such as to deter others. Their trials were long-delayed and Walker's death has been a matter of public comment. All this, and yet I am instructed to allot twenty-five lashes for the merest . . .'

Booth clasped his hands over his papers, did not want them to shake in case it looked like fear or weakness rather than the fury it was. Forster's face was purple. He slammed his fist down on the table.

'Mr Forster?' said Sir John uncomfortably. 'Do you wish to . . . ?'

'We are not met to hear your opinions, Booth!' shouted Forster. 'You will be silent or quit the room, sir. We are here to advise you of the new enquiry and to remind you of your obligations—as it appears you need reminding. And . . .' he paused briefly, 'to acquaint you with the news that under orders received from London, the assignment of male prisoners ceases from today. Henceforth, all male prisoners will be confined in Probation Stations. You have submitted sites for these, Captain, and have known it was in prospect. The stations must now be built with all speed.

'Transportation to New South Wales will cease before the end of the year, and Van Diemen's Land will receive an increased number of felons. You are required to provide immediately a detailed scheme for the disposition and employment of prisoners of various classes.

'We must have, I insist on—all speed, without delay.'

'Delay!' Booth fumed to Lizzie back at the peninsula the following night. 'They ask the impossible. We are building as fast as we can go— have been for years—and now we are to go faster! And to compound everything, England sends no instructions as to how the new system is to be managed! Merely, "Cease assignment. Begin probation." And Forster, well aware of the difficulties, simply repeats the order to me. When I pressed for details he could not avoid admitting—or rather it was Sir John who said—that there are no details. The Colonial Office in London protects itself by specifying as little as possible. If they wish to criticise later or change their minds, they will say it was not ordered to be done in that way!'

He paced. Lizzie spooned yellow mush into little Amelia, nestled on her lap and in the crook of her arm. Amy's round brown eyes followed him. She did not look at the approaching spoon, but at him, and yet as the spoon came near, her mouth opened in a little circle, closed on it, mumbled and pursed gently.

'What does Sir John say?'

'He is in difficulties too. Before Montagu went to England it was agreed that he should try to persuade London to retain the assignment system, but if they would not, he should at least argue that the new Probation Stations must be widely spread around the island. We were all in accord—the outskirts of the small inland townships would be best: Bothwell, Ouse, Kempton, Jericho . . .

'Prisoners could maintain local roads, bridges, public buildings. They'd have access to existing Churches and chaplains, and at least some small contact with civilians. But all that is gone overboard. Boyes says that when Montagu reached England he found the tide of opinion against him and changed sides without a murmur. "At Mr Montagu's recommendation", we now hear, all Probation Stations are to be on the peninsula, away from settled areas. Disastrous in every way!

'No provision for chaplains. The Archdeacon, Wallace, Lillie, the Wesleyans—they're all furious. They say it's a sign that ideas of Christian reform have vanished. From now on it will be punishment only. The irony of it! The Molesworth Committee ends by bringing about a harsher system than the one they decried—and poor Maconochie becomes known as the instigator of a method he never intended. But the crowning insult is that Sir John hears none of this directly from Montagu. Everything is sent to Forster, who doles out scraps to the Governor.'

Tonight Lizzie was sympathetic. Sometimes she was bored and impatient when he spoke of such things. He knew she wondered if he was partly at fault. He should somehow be able to manage it all better. She wanted him to put in a request to leave the peninsula; he was more than willing now. And it was not only these new irritations; sometimes lately, when he looked at little Melly, his work struck him as strange; a life spent imprisoning other men. Even a few years ago he had believed he was on the side of the angels, working for the general good, but he no longer had that confidence. Perhaps it was the stupidities required of him as a magistrate, or a greater recognition of his own failings, but he no longer felt easy with judging others. It had to be done, of course; but he did not want to be the one to do it. Walker's death and the escape had contributed to his dissatisfaction, too.

Why, Lizzie asked again, couldn't Booth be transferred to the Richmond gaol? Her sister and brother-in-law were settled outside Richmond. Booth explained again that the places there were filled. And he knew it suited Forster to keep him here. Getting the work done, a useful scapegoat for whatever objections turned up later from Home.

Some nights now he was visited by a dream in which he lay flat on his back on hard ground, tied down, pegged out and anchored with guy-ropes, like an illustration from *Gulliver's Travels*, which he had loved as a boy. Only it was not the tiny people of Lilliput who swarmed disgustingly over him, but heavy-bellied, rat-like creatures, dragging a dark slime, weighing on his chest until he could not breathe. In these dreams he struggled to rise, to accomplish something desperately urgent, though he could never remember what it was, only that some horror would ensue if it were not done. But he could never get free, and woke in a fever, sweating and gasping.

Lizzie made him see the doctor, but he believed the dream came from those nights when he was lost in the bush. His greatest fear then had not been of dying, but of native tigers or devil-cats getting past the dogs to tear at his legs, fingers—even his face—while he was still alive.

He applied for the vacant position of Chief Postmaster—and was told, as always, that 'others had prior claim'.

25

DIDO WAS BEING RELEASED INTO ST JOHN'S CARE, WE LEARNED that autumn. The other members of Walker's crew were sentenced to terms on Norfolk Island, but since Maconochie had recently been appointed Commandant there, St John was sanguine about their fate. There was no sign of Anna and Quigley, and no news. I worked relentlessly all winter, accepting every commission I was offered, laid aside more money, grew even fonder of the cottage, and lived with only Nellie Jack's arthritic complaints to trouble me—apart from the moments when I allowed myself to think of Bergman, and to wonder whether my letter had reached him. On some days I thought of that heartfelt outpouring with hot shame and regret. At other times I thought, like Pontius Pilate, 'What I have written, I have written.'

One commission came from Mrs Parry, for portraits of her grandchildren.

'Have you met Mr Gell?' she asked me. 'The latest ornament to the Franklin circle?' She sighed and laughed. 'Pompous young puppy. I'd give three of him to have old Bobby Knopwood back. And what is the matter with St John Wallace? He used to be amusing, but he talks of nothing now but the Arthurites. He seems determined to provoke a quarrel with them. John Price ignores it; Forster cannot be bothered to notice because he is ill and negligent—but when Montagu returns the fur will fly.'

—⁂—

The winter straggled on and I forced myself to believe that Bergman was still on the east coast. Bess Chesney moved to town. Susan Ross had transferred her school from 'Carrington' in Richmond to 'Paraclete', a pretty, Italianate house on Knocklofty hill at the northern boundary of Hobart Town. James Ross had built 'Paraclete' years earlier on his first land grant, but after his death Susan could not afford to keep both properties, and 'Carrington' was put up for sale. 'Paraclete' was smaller but close to town, which she hoped might attract more pupils. Polly's cousins, William and Julia's children, were to move with the school as full boarders, and Polly wanted to do the same, urging that Liddy must also go with her. Bess Chesney deplored the idea, but could refuse them nothing.

For a month Bess suffered the dullness of the girls' absence on Saturdays and Sundays at Richmond, and then she made up her mind to move to town as well, to 'see a little society before she was quite past everything'. Polly and Liddy and the cousins could then stay with her weekly, as before. William and Julia could have 'Kenton', and come to her when they wanted a taste of city life. She bought a large cottage in Argyle Street near the Scotch Church, and it was there, in August, that we heard the sound of cannons in the harbour.

'Seven guns,' cried Mrs Chesney. 'An English ship.'

Her manservant, John Crabbe, who was on a stepladder putting up curtains, said, 'And here is the answer from the Battery, ma'am. Seven again. The Magnetical Expedition, I shouldn't wonder.'

'Lord, John. What do you know of magneticals?'

It was the *Terror* that day, under the command of Captain Francis Crozier. The *Erebus*, with Captain James Ross, arrived two days later. Both ships were 'bombs' or bombardiers, built to carry fixed mortars for firing at shore targets from the sea: harbour entrances, gun emplacements. The mortars, weighing three tons each and many times more powerful than cannons, had such violent recoil on firing that they must burst apart the hull of any ordinary ship. Thus 'bombs' had triple reinforced hulls, which made them perfect for use in the polar regions, where they could withstand the great force of the shifting ice-fields.

Jane Franklin called them 'the Captains'; to everyone else they were 'Ross-and-Crozier'. Never the other way around, although Crozier was several years older than Ross: forty-five that year. Ross was the taller, and ridiculously thin. Spindly, leonine, heroic-eccentric. The handsomest man in the Navy, some said. His red-grey hair sprang mane-like from his brow in great sculptured waves. His gestures were large, his talk cheerfully ferocious. He was leader of the expedition as a whole. Crozier was shorter but still tall: Irish, plump, dark, round-faced, milder. The crown of his head was bald, with a frizz of tiny black curls at ear-level. He was not quieter than Ross exactly, he loved to dance and had a fine baritone singing voice, but Ross was the virtuoso talker, declamatory, eager. Crozier, who seemed always to be watching his friend with admiring amusement, fell in love with Sophy almost immediately—too late, alas. She was smitten with James Ross from the moment she saw him, she said.

'Such perversity,' murmured Mary, smiling, watching Sophy watch Ross. It was September 1840, three weeks after the arrival of the ships and early spring again, late afternoon. We were on the Domain above the Government Gardens at the site where they were building the Observatory, one of the main reasons for the visit of the Magnetic Expedition. On this voyage Ross and Crozier were expected to determine the exact position of the South Pole, but also to set up an observatory which would join Van Diemen's Land to a chain of such establishments around the globe. After a week's work the former bush was now a raw wasteland echoing to the sound of axes, saws and hammering, strewn with peg-markers and string-lines, piles of bricks and timber. Men ran across planks laid on the mud, pushing barrows laden with bricks, digging trenches, carrying timber. Two hundred convicts and a large proportion of two ships' crews swarmed like ants from a disturbed nest, with the same obscure, urgent purpose. Ross, ten yards on our left, leaning close to Sophy, pointed into the sky and described with one arm an arc to the ground. I had thought Bergman might be here, but he was not.

'Ross has a fiancée in England, as Sophy knows perfectly well,' she continued. 'Her name is Anne. She has been waiting eighteen months and it will probably be another two years before she sees him. Is it merely accidental that Sophy always chooses gentlemen already promised elsewhere?'

Mary Boyes reminded me of Nina, my stepmother: a long face with mild, drooping brown eyes full of amusement, nut-brown hair always escaping at the back. We had met frequently at Government House, becoming close that winter, when Boyes asked me to paint her portrait.

'I can't imagine Sophy ever leaving "Aunt" and "Nuncle", can you?' she continued. 'Is it possible to be in love with a whole family? Perhaps she is deterred from marriage, as anyone might be, by the experience of her poor cousin Mary . . . But look, there's Henry Kay, such a charming sight in his uniform. You can see why Jane Franklin was worried when she found he was with the Expedition.'

Jane had thought Eleanor might fall in love with Lieutenant Kay, the very model of a dashing young officer. He was the son of Eleanor's aunt on her mother's side, Mrs Kay, and therefore Eleanor Franklin's first cousin. Jane disapproved of marriages between first cousins.

'How could she guess Eleanor would be blind to Kay's charm, all her horizon being filled with Gell,' added Mary, '. . . who begins to respond, I think?'

'Eleanor is an unlikely choice for him.' I watched Ross point again at the sky. The men planning to watch the stars, the women interested in a different kind of magnetic attraction.

'No one could call her bookish,' Mary conceded, 'but I imagine he's one of those men who prefer their wives to leave the learning to them. Eleanor is clever in her own way—and profoundly devout, which may be more important to him. He'd have to be a fool not to consider it. He has no fortune, while she will inherit her mother's money when she comes of age. And some of her father's too, eventually, I suppose. Not a vast fortune, but highly respectable. Oh, Hatty, hark at me, I sound just like my mother.'

'She's very young,' I said.

Mary smiled, 'Not so young as I was at sixteen. Were you not in love at that age? Poor Crozier. He kneels at Sophy's feet and she falls over him to get to Ross. George calls them the Three Blind Mice. He drew a wicked sketch. Ross as the leading mouse—a lion-mouse,' Mary began to laugh, 'wearing a Captain's hat and looking blindfolded through a telescope at the South Pole. Sophy behind him, blindfolded too, her hand stretched forward onto his shoulder, with Crozier behind her in the same way, all three stumbling along in a line.'

Mary wiped tears of laughter from her face. 'So comical, but George tore it up. He knows he'll get himself into trouble one of these days.' She shivered suddenly. 'It's cold. Let's go back and have tea. You can see how my garden comes along.'

The Boyes had lived in town until two years earlier, at Fitzroy Place, just up the hill from Government House, near the barracks. But new cottages had begun pressing close around them, so they had moved out this mile or so to New Town, as other senior officials were doing. Hobart was changing, growing, Mary said—except the Mountain, which had no doubt been brooding over the sea here in the same way when the Romans invaded England.

26

BOOTH, STANDING A HUNDRED YARDS BEHIND THE BEACH AT Slopen Main, experienced a surge of joy in defiance of the vexations crowding his mind. The water of the estuary was blue, the sky bluer still. His spirits had always been lifted by these first intimations of spring, the brilliant light, the mild, lively little breeze. It was late October, more than a month until summer, and yet as sublimely fair a day as a man could wish. His eyes fell to the beautiful drainage trench at his feet: five feet wide, four deep, half a mile long and heading for the beach, and he grew hot with irritation again. It must now be abandoned. Looking up, he saw Bergman, who had been away on the east coast for a month, striding towards him looking warm and dusty, flapping his wide-brimmed hat against the early flies.

'A handsome ditch,' Bergman said as he came up, smiling. 'Is it deep enough? What happens at the beach end, some sort of lock-gate?'

Booth made an irritable sound. 'Word has come to leave it. There's to be no station here, only on the island.' He nodded towards the glittering sea and tiny Slopen Island, little more than a large rock offshore.

Bergman grimaced. They had both recommended Slopen Main as a site for one of the first Probation Stations on account of its abundant fresh water, a good track in from the coal mines, and a small constable's station already in place. This consisted of a cottage, barn and stable built a decade earlier when Lawyer Gellibrand had owned the land. When Governor Arthur resumed the peninsula for prisons, Gellibrand had accepted an alternative grant, but he had already begun draining the marshy ground and cleared twelve acres behind the beach near the lagoon, a perfect site. But on an inspection visit, the Governor revealed a stubborn, inconvenient attraction to Slopen Island, and announced the first station would be there.

In vain Booth and Bergman had pointed out that the island had no water and was too small for subsistence agriculture—not to mention the problem of transporting building materials across by boat. In spite of this, building on the island had begun.

Bergman had then been called away, but Booth had persisted, suggesting to Franklin that it would be easier to build on the island if they at least extended the station at Slopen Main to include a Barracks and storehouse. The Governor had seemed to concede, but now, a month later, with the trench well under way and a preliminary survey completed, the written order had come: there would be no Probation Station at Slopen Main, only on the island. The station at the coal mines would be enlarged, and another established at Saltwater River, a few miles south.

Booth explained all this to Bergman as they turned back towards the mines, passing a labouring gang hauling timber. As soon as they were out of earshot, Bergman said, 'Stuart says you've resigned? It can't be true?'

Booth nodded. 'Forster was here last week. Said he was shocked to find the Barracks not yet built on the island. Men living in tents and "primitive" bark huts, standing idle.' He grimaced and flung one arm out in exasperation. 'Not yet built! What does he expect?'

Bergman grunted in sympathy. 'But you didn't resign over Forster's idiot remarks?'

'No. I kept my temper, told him we'd made excellent progress considering we're working with men straight off a transport, mostly unskilled. Two experienced overseers when we need five. Men idle because there are not enough hammers, nails, picks, shovels. No forge. Everything dependent on the weather for getting boats to and fro.'

Booth added grimly, 'I wanted to make him understand that this is just the beginning—because he doesn't, or doesn't choose to. It's not just this site—it's the whole mad enterprise! Forster should be jumping up and down, writing home a barrage of complaints—but he won't risk offending Whitehall. Simply tells me to get on with it.'

'What did he say?'

'Told me he wouldn't accept excuses for my incompetence. Said he'd write an adverse report of me to London—and if I continued to add insolence to my other failings, he'd dismiss me. Stared goggle-eyed at me through that blasted eye-glass and walked away. Probably intends to let Montagu deal with the problem when he comes back. If he comes back. Two days later I received notice to appear at another tribunal—to answer why I've given extra rations to the labouring men. Twelve hours a day working their guts out to build at the speed we need! And my judges were to be—you won't believe this—the Medical Officer here and the Supervisor at the Mines. Men under my command!'

Bergman grimaced again.

'I wrote back,' Booth continued, 'not to Forster, to the Governor—saying that conditions here are nearly impossible. If I cannot even issue extra rations without an Enquiry in which men under my command are appointed to judge my orders, my position is untenable. Regretfully therefore . . . and etcetera . . .'

'But you don't really want to leave . . . ?'

'Not without another position to go to. But you should have heard Forster, Gus. Threatening me, and enjoying it. When the truth is he needs me here—to get the Stations built and serve as his scapegoat. It wouldn't be easy to replace me just now.'

At least he hoped not. If his resignation were accepted, he must rejoin his Regiment—in India now—and Booth was appalled to find how profoundly the thought dismayed him. They turned away towards the lagoon again and entered a grove of she-oaks. Bergman said

328

suddenly, 'Why not come up to town for a few days? Have a private word with the Governor? Forster's caused him trouble too. They've let things slide while Montagu's been away. And now the Magnetic Expedition is here, Sir John is even less inclined to stick to his desk. But Montagu is coming back in March. Four months—which will put the wind up a few people, Forster among them.'

Birds were massed ahead of them on the water, squabbling and calling. It was good advice, Booth knew, but money was tight again, and if the worst came to the worst they'd need every penny. A trip to town would do Lizzie good, though. Poor girl, she needed a change. She'd had a miscarriage in the winter, and had been despondent since, missing her mother. There'd be the expense of staying in Hobart for three or four nights, but after that Lizzie could go to her sister at Richmond, and he could stay a few days in barracks . . .

'Use my cottage if you like,' Bergman said. 'It's small . . . but if Lizzie doesn't mind . . . If I have to go away Durrell will look after you. He sleeps in the kitchen at the back. And if I am there, I'll use the loft over the stable.'

They spoke of possible arrangements and Booth asked, 'Any news of Rochester?'

Bergman hesitated. 'Nothing since I went with Harriet Adair to see the Carmichaels—and we . . . fell out over how to proceed.'

'You and she . . . Lizzie and I thought . . .'

'So did I—but I was wrong, apparently. I sent a note of apology but I've heard nothing since. St John Wallace tells me she has booked a passage for England, leaving in December.'

A raw nerve, evidently. Booth did not like to probe beyond asking, 'What will you do?'

Bergman sounded weary. 'Wash my hands of the whole business.'

Later that day Booth applied for leave, but he did not tell Lizzie until three days later when, with a swiftness that surprised him, the request was approved. She flung her arms around his neck, 'Oh, you are a dear man, so you are.'

329

They went up in the first week of November, Booth's request for a meeting with the Governor having been granted with, again, unusual alacrity.

'Sounds to me as though they're looking for a way out,' said Bergman, who was in residence at his cottage that week.

It was so. The Governor made a muted apology; Forster did not appear. Franklin had been shocked, he said, by Booth's taking the matter so personally. No slur was intended against the Commandant's exemplary record. It was Forster's duty to see regulations obeyed—a little over-zealous in this case, perhaps. Forster not well. Everybody under strain. All these confounded changes. Everybody's interests best served if Booth would withdraw his resignation and bring Mrs Booth to dine at Government House this evening. Meet Ross and Crozier. And the Observatory tomorrow? Heard about the Observatory? Magnetic Expedition?

Booth had not known how tightly he was braced for disaster. His shoulders relaxed and the albatross weight slipped off his heart again. Dinner that night with the Franklins was informal and easy, and he'd won another battle, if not the war. He could have returned to the peninsula with equanimity, if it had not been for an incident the following night.

In the afternoon they went to the Observatory with the Franklins, but Lizzie was disappointed by it. She murmured to Booth that she had been to Greenwich seven years ago when she was twelve, and sure she knew this one could not be like that! But, honest to goodness, will you look at it! Three little cabins with a flagpole! Why, he had more books and pretty brass instruments himself at home! He was still laughing when Sophy Cracroft came up to suggest a walk in the Government Gardens nearby. She took Lizzie by the arm and went ahead while Booth followed with Lady Franklin, who said, 'This Magnetic visit has quite restored my husband. You notice it, Captain? He's back to his old self, merry as a cricket.'

Booth bowed and smiled. It struck him as an odd remark. Jane was so clever; she had been telling him about the Troughton telescope and 'the black drop effect'—and yet this comment seemed to miss the point entirely. Sir John's high spirits since the arrival of Ross and Crozier were surely an indication of how unhappy he had been before? And the cause was plain as a pikestaff, as Lizzie would say; the role of Governor did not suit him.

But Jane did not see him in all-male company, of course. After dinner last night when the ladies withdrew, the talk had turned to Desolation Island, one of Ross and Crozier's ports of call on the way here: the strange cloud formations, the giant Kerguelen cabbages. Franklin's plump face had lit up like that of a ragamuffin gazing in a sweetshop window. Booth had almost laughed. But he recognised the look that followed, too; that of a man planning escape. Franklin was desperate to return to his beloved shipboard life.

And yet here was Lady Franklin beaming on his arm not twenty-four hours later, and explaining that when her husband's first term of six years as Governor was over, they would accept another the same length, as Governor Arthur had done.

'Staying on will not mean cutting ourselves off from northern friends,' she said, 'or scientific pursuits. The Captains' arrival proves that. And Henry Kay is here, and young Joseph Hooker, though we see little of him. He is not fond of society. He is ship's surgeon on this voyage but his real passion is the same as that of his father, Mr William Hooker—Head of Kew Gardens, you know. Both are botanists to the marrow. You see, Captain, Van Diemen's Land is now truly part of a world-wide community of scientific men.'

Horatio Tennyson had arrived too, she continued. Had Booth met Horry? He was the young brother of Alfred, the poet. The Tennysons were related to the Franklins by marriage, since Alfred had married one of the Sellwood girls, poor Emily. Horry had so far proved to be as dreadfully reckless, idle, and eccentric as the rest of the Tennysons, but he might improve. Allowances must be made for his upbringing. When he was young he had seen the ghost of a severed head walking along the shrubbery path. In that benighted rectory anything was possible. Jane gave a faint shudder before rushing on.

'And Sir John Barrow's son Peter is to become catechist at Port Arthur, as you know—and the Goulds intend to return. Even Dr Arnold of Rugby—this will astonish you—has written that he would love to take charge of the new College himself, when all factions are satisfied and it can begin at last.'

And think of Dr Lhotski—well, not Lhotski perhaps—like Horry Tennyson, he was of dubious value. Think of Captain Laplace and all the charming French naval men whose ships seemed to abound in these latitudes! Think of the dear Count, Strzelecki, whose company Sir John so greatly enjoyed. They had wrangled like brothers over the Wollaston boiling point method of determining the heights of mountains . . .think of all the other wonderful men here—why, her husband might wish to continue in Tasmania even *after* twelve years as Governor! A scientific retirement here would be the very thing! This was the place for discoveries. The northern hemisphere was all known and stale. The only thing left *there* was the exploration of the Northwest Passage, and Sir John was far too old for that now.

'You had better not let him hear you say it, my lady.' Booth uneasily took a jocular line, but Jane Franklin repeated firmly, 'Fifty-five next April. Far too old for an Arctic winter. The Admiralty would not allow it.'

Again Booth was silent. Last night the question of a new voyage in search of the Northwest Passage had also arisen among the gentlemen, and it was clear that Franklin had discussed it before with Ross and Crozier. Who among the old Arctic Lions at the Admiralty could be counted on to back the venture? Who would oppose? Why should Sir John not take the *Erebus* and *Terror* when the Magnetic Expedition was over? The bombs had performed superbly so far, and their strengths and weaknesses would be even better known by the time they returned to Hobart next autumn after another summer in the southern ice. Their return to London in two years would coincide roughly with the end of the Governor's first term here . . .

'My brother James is also on his way, ma'am,' Booth said. Changing the subject. 'My eldest brother, and his wife and children. He has been

332

Captain of the *Trinculo* for a decade, but is now to have three years "on the beach" and will spend much of it here.'

As they walked on it came to Booth that he should sell his commission, leave the Army. It would bring in a useful amount. Pay off his debts again, hold a little in reserve against James's arrival—bound to need money then.

He was in excellent spirits that night when he and Lizzie joined a party going to the Theatre Royal. The moving spirit was Augusta Drewitt. Her sister and brother-in-law were in town, and they had persuaded Bergman to escort her. The Franklins were not involved, they did not approve of plays, except Shakespeare perhaps. This was a satire on the Magnetic Expedition. Lizzie would have preferred to see Mr Loon's Menagerie Troupe, but said philosophically that the play might be ludicrous and amusing at any rate.

Ludicrous indeed, thought Booth, laughing in spite of himself. Mr Jarvis was playing the part of Franklin as a grotesque, a Sir John Falstaff, a tub of lard so genuinely reeling drunk he forgot his lines. Wags from the pit threw peanuts and jeered, 'Make 'im walk the plank'. The snow and icebergs were well done, however, and Mrs Jarvis as 'Fame' came down on a gilded swing and crowned Ross and Crozier with laurel wreaths. She gave her husband an angry slap, which set the house roaring, and the Misses Adelaide, Emily and Kitty Jarvis, 'spirits of the North', ended the play with an energetic dance. To keep warm probably, said Bergman.

It was the first time Booth had been in the new theatre, which really was the pretty little gem everyone called it, but as the crowd began to leave at the end, the great defect of its design became clear. An elegant curved staircase descended from the dress circle and boxes into the foyer—but unfortunately the pit also opened into the back of this area. The pit doors were supposed to remain closed until the upstairs audience had gone, but the penny and peanuts crowd were in no mood to wait. They came thrusting out to mix loudly with their two- and five-shilling superiors, turning the foyer into a struggling mass surging towards the outer doors.

Lizzie held tightly to Booth's arm. She was fearless by nature, but small, easily shoved by the crowd. Augusta clung to Bergman. Her sister and brother-in-law were still on the staircase behind. In the midst of it Booth felt someone staring at him. Among the backs of heads four yards in front, a pale face was turned to look back at him. A woman, not young, her expression filled with alarm. She turned quickly away. A two-shilling patron, or even a five, judging by her head and bearing. Booth decided he did not know her and turned away, before recognition came like the flare of a match: Catherine Tyndale, Rowland Rochester's woman. Older, of course. Her hair done differently. He scanned the heads near her for Rowland but there was no one resembling him.

He could not abandon Lizzie and push forward—and in any case, he could hardly seize the woman, demand explanations. While he hesitated, her part of the crowd reached the street, and he saw she was with a tall young man and a dark young woman. They moved briskly towards a line of carriages waiting further along where it was darker. Bergman was pushed closer to Booth at that moment, and he was able to point and say, 'Rowland Rochester's wife'. The words were half lost in the hubbub, but Bergman looked in that direction.

At this point, the crowd, which had been inching forward, seemed to lose momentum and stop. Looking about him in frustration, Booth saw Mr Tulip Wright, the former District Constable, nonchalant among the jostling mob. The front edges of his black coat were pulled wide apart to reveal his barrel chest; his thumbs were hooked into the armholes of a very splendid purple satin waistcoat. His high collar cradled two or three chins and a verdant swathe of emerald cravat.

'Evening, gents,' he said, and nodding outwards, 'An 'oss gorn down in the road.' Booth reflected that men like Tulip Wright always do know what is going on, in spite of having no visible source of information.

'I thought you were gone to Port Phillip?'

'The wife's expecting. Come back to 'er mother for the 'appy event.' He jerked his head back towards the stage. 'Bit of a larf, eh?'

'Do you know who that carriage belongs to?' Booth asked, pointing.

Tulip considered, thrusting his underlip forward to show his poor opinion of it. 'H'eddicated guess—an 'ired lug from The Ship—being as the jarvey's Billy Ryan. Want me ter suss 'oo's 'ad it ternite?'

Bergman, listening too, shook his head. 'We were interested in the horse.'

Tulip eyed them doubtfully but said no more.

It was midnight before they reached the cottage, and in a few words they agreed Bergman should speak to Billy Ryan. There was no time to say more: Lizzie called Booth away, and next morning, at first light, the couple left to take ferry and coach to Richmond.

—∞—

Booth did not return to Hobart until the Monday evening three days later. He and Bergman met at the cottage in the early evening and adjourned to a chop-house near the new wharf.

'The carriage was hired by an elderly widow,' said Bergman. 'A Mrs Ritchie in Fitzroy Place. She had visitors; it was they who went to the play. Their name was Fairfax.'

'Ah . . .'

Bergman nodded. 'I wasn't sure whether to leave it to you or follow it up. But I didn't know when you'd be back, and decided not to wait. I walked up there and asked if I could speak to Mr or Mrs Fairfax.' He smiled. 'A voice from inside called, "Who is it, Dora?" and out came Mrs Ritchie. Straight as a die, no-nonsense. I said a friend and I thought we'd seen Mrs Fairfax at the play. We had been acquainted with the Fairfaxes in the West Indies, and would like to meet them again.

'She said they'd gone, and she would certainly not pass their address to any stranger who came knocking—but she'd make the same offer to me as to the other gentleman who'd called earlier. If I would write down my name and address, and a sentence to show my *bona fides*, she would forward it to the Fairfaxes when she next had occasion to write.

'I did so, and asked whether the other gentleman who had called was dressed in elaborate style. She looked at me for a moment and then said she supposed there was no harm in telling me, as I seemed to know anyway; it was the Constable, Mr Tulip Wright. He claimed to have found a pair of gloves at the theatre belonging to Mrs Fairfax. After that I went to the coach depot and learned the Fairfaxes had travelled to Launceston on Saturday morning. Then I went hunting for Tulip and asked him what he meant by it.'

'He's one of Forster's cronies.'

'They've fallen out. Forster owes him money. And Tulip says he doesn't like the company Forster keeps nowadays. Told me he's not against "a bit o' violence in the right place", but there's some kinds of violence is "downright narsty". Butcher Wynn's kind, and John Price's.'

'You believe him?'

'I don't think he'd have been so indignant about Forster if it wasn't true. He says Forster owes big gambling debts and has chosen to forget the small ones. When I asked Tulip why he'd gone to Mrs Ritchie's, he said he was just curious. But it occurred to me that Tulip could be employed to go to Launceston and look for Fairfax—if St John Wallace agrees, of course.'

He hesitated. 'There's something else I should explain to you.'

He recounted to Booth what the Carmichaels had said.

'And you haven't told St John?'

'No.'

'He'll have to be told now. We can't leave him in ignorance that Catherine Tyndale is here—which suggests that Rowland is too.'

They walked up to Davey Street, were admitted by Mrs Fludde, and found Louisa at the piano and McLeod standing by the fire. St John was down at the Church, they said. He had eaten dinner with them and then gone to a Church meeting.

Booth and Bergman walked down the hill again as it began to grow dark. Neither made any comment on the strangely domestic scene they had witnessed. They found St John with Dido, locking up the vestry. He opened it again, Dido relit a lamp, and in its golden light St John's splendid profile outlined itself against the black cassocks ranged on hooks along the wall. They sat on three straight chairs among the musty smell of garments. Dido stood at St John's side, avoiding Booth's gaze, shifting between his good foot and the thick, built-up sole of his club foot. The convict's face was young, unformed, a piece of dough not fully modelled into the detail of a face.

Wallace listened while they explained, let a silence fall before he said, 'There is no need for Mr Tulip Wright's assistance. I know where Fairfax is.'

Booth frowned. Bergman said, 'You know? How long have you known? Why did you not say so? I thought you wanted the Arthurites brought to justice? Have you told Mrs Adair?'

Wallace shook his head, smiling.

'It has been a hard lesson for me,' he said, irritatingly calm, 'but salutary. After Walker died I was greatly troubled in mind, as you know. But I at last began to understand that I had been wrong about him. He was a dark angel, tempting me. He led me into the belief that I could do good through my own righteousness.' His face took on a sombre expression. 'Pride, the sin of Lucifer, the greatest sin. Now the Lord has given me this man, one of his lowliest servants, to help me continue my work.'

He laid his hand gently on Dido's shoulder. '"Judgement is mine, saith the Lord." Those who caused Walker's death must be left to Him. Their punishment will be more fitting than anything I, or any court of law, could devise. Even now I can see it beginning. Henry Arthur lying on the brink of death at his brother's house, a ruin of drink and debauchery. Forster ill and floundering in a debtor's mire of his own making; Montagu returning to this island against his will, because for all his cunning he has not achieved the preferment he craves.

'Even Governor Arthur.' He nodded at Booth. 'You've told me how, when it came to leaving, Arthur wept—but why did he leave if he did not wish to? He had land, money. He could have stayed as a gentleman farmer, a member of the Councils, contributing to the island from which he'd taken so much. He went back because he was a prisoner of England's ideas of advancement and his own greed; hungry always for higher rank, greater wealth.'

'But the crimes of his followers are not matters of private morality,' said Bergman, visibly angry now. 'They have concealed a violent death . . .'

'I know what they have done. I met Fairfax, he told me.'

'Fairfax *told* you? Then why have you not . . . ? If you let their offences pass, you make a mockery of the justice this island is supposed to serve. Many of the wretches imprisoned here are less guilty than the men who sit in judgement on them.'

St John smiled, shrugged. 'You speak as though wickedness in high places were new, Bergman. *Quis custodiet ipsos custodes* is a very old question: "Who shall judge the judges?" My business is with God's law, not the human variety. In six months I shall return to England to argue against transportation—when the Huon chapel is finished and the new College is properly begun.'

'Dido must stay—for the term of his natural life,' said Booth.

The convict ducked his head convulsively, made a gulping noise.

'He will come with me,' said Wallace, his jaw tightening. 'Who will prevent it? You, Captain? The Colonial Office has wiped his name from the records. He is dead to them. It is time Louisa went home, too. Her character is weak, she needs guidance.'

'And Rowland?' asked Bergman. 'Where is he? Of course you'll write to the Rochesters in England about him, and explain it all to Mrs Adair?'

'My conversation with him was under the seal of the confessional. Circumstances make it necessary for him to preserve his secret at present. And Mrs Adair is about to sail home.'

—⁓—

On the last day of his leave, Booth joined the Government House party that sailed up to New Norfolk for the Governor's laying of the foundation stone of the new College, dedicated to Christ. Coins were laid underneath the stone, with copies of an oration by Gell in his several languages. Ten days later, when Lizzie came home bearing a *Colonial Times,* Booth read that the newly laid foundation stone had been jemmied up by 'a person or persons unknown'. Everything under it was gone. And the *Erebus* and *Terror* had sailed, to spend summer exploring the southern ice. They would return in autumn, April or May.

27

AT THE END OF WINTER, IN LATE AUGUST, I HAD TOLD LOUISA I would leave for England. The Mountain had been covered in snow down to the foothills the day I said it, a great white bastion against a blue sky, the bright air as chilly as I believed Bergman now felt towards me. No reply had come to my note. I had not seen him for months. I knew from Louisa that he had been in town for a day or two now and again, which probably meant that he was avoiding me.

I was sitting on the hearthrug in Louisa's parlour, in front of the fire, building a tower of blocks with Thea.

Louisa said, off-handedly, 'Augusta Drewitt seems to have overcome her dislike of marrying here. She speaks constantly of Bergman these days. She is three-and-twenty, and begins to despair, I suppose.'

My back was half-turned to her; she was sitting in a chair looking through a magazine I had brought her, but the fire would have excused my burning face in any case.

'Gus and Gusta,' I said mockingly. Then I added that I was tired of waiting for Anna and Quigley, and would return to England soon.

'You think of your time here as waiting?' Louisa said, interested. 'Why not think of it as staying on until you are tired of it? I am coming round to that view myself.'

I shook my head, and when I left her I hurried down to the wharf, feeling compounded of fire and ice, frozen on the outside as the cold wind scoured my face, burning within. I discovered the *Lady Dorothea* would sail at the beginning of December and booked a passage. I would be in England by spring, and I was glad of it, I told myself. But the heart is a contrary organ, with a mind of its own, and I discovered mine had put out tendrils and attached them to certain aspects of Hobarton during these three years. No sooner was the deposit paid than I began to think of the friends I would miss, and of saying farewell to my snug little cottage, and how I would never see again certain favourite views through odd gateways and now-familiar trees to the Derwent.

'You are thirty-seven,' said Mary Boyes crossly, 'making an excellent living doing what you love—and since Hobartians appear to have an insatiable propensity for having their portraits taken, why on earth are you leaving?'

And there was Nellie Jack. Fifty-nine, a tireless grumbler with a contrary streak, but we managed comfortably together, suited each other. She pottered with old Mr Coombes in the garden, helped out in Ada's shop, fussed over an old stray cat. Bess Chesney had three servants, already one too many. She would take Nellie in, but Nellie would be a fifth wheel, a known charity case—and the cat must be left behind. When I told her I was leaving, her face dropped into a look of weary hopelessness very terrible to me. She nodded curtly and set her mouth to stop it wobbling. All the blows in her life had taught her this: mute resignation to the fates which had so often used her so ill. I had to turn away to hide my own eyes, filling with tears.

I had heard no more about the *Firefly*, a fact Sir John Franklin assured me must mean that it had not been sunk or mortally damaged. 'Ships are expensive items, Hatty,' he said, 'news of them is always shared. Word of a wreck goes about like wildfire.' And so I allowed myself to imagine Anna and Quigley, sailing in foreign seas, always expecting to return here, but their coming always deferred by chance or necessity. And every time I looked at the still life painting I thought of Gus, with irritation, anger, hope, tenderness, sorrow—depending on the day and hour.

In November, a month before I was due to leave, I thought he might be at New Norfolk for Sir John's laying of the foundation stone for the College, but instead I saw Booth.

'I had hoped to see you here,' he said.

He recounted the story of seeing Catherine Tyndale at the theatre, but my attention was distracted by his mention of Bergman. He had been in Hobart and not called on me. He had gone to the play with Augusta Drewitt. I was surprised and irritated to learn St John had not trusted me enough to tell me he had discovered Rowland, and curious about the latter's whereabouts. It soon struck me, however, that this only added to my freedom. The Rochester business was now wholly St John's affair, out of my hands.

'Gus is now gone to the Huon for a fortnight,' added Booth casually. 'From there he'll join James Calder in the western wilderness for the summer. They'll take a party of convicts to clear the track again for the Governor's expedition in January.'

Over the next days I schooled myself to accept that I had seen Gus for the last time, but towards the end of November I received notice that the Lady Dorothea was delayed in Cape Town, and would not now sail from Hobart until February. At the same time, the Franklins decided to postpone their west coast expedition, and it came to me that Gus and Calder might return to Hobart for Christmas.

The reason given for the Franklins' postponement was the Governor's volume of work—which was true, Sophy told me, but it had more to do with the growing attachment between Eleanor and John Gell. Gell was taking leave over Christmas to visit his brother, who was secretary to Colonel Gawler, Governor of the new Wakefield Colony in South Australia, and Jane decided she and Eleanor would go also. The young couple's feelings would be usefully tested under the strains of travel, and it was important to forge links between all Governors in the Antipodes. Besides, Jane was curious to see Adelaide. Sophy was happy to stay in Hobart. Sydney had been too hot last year and Adelaide would be hotter, and the town was so new there could be nothing worth seeing. She would have Tom and Nuncle to herself for a month, 'and as your sailing is so fortunately delayed, Harriet,' she added, 'we can spend your last days here together.'

Sophy was eager for company in those weeks before Christmas. Nuncle was busy and Tom had the *grippe,* which became prolonged and worrying, and as soon as Jane, Eleanor and Gell left, the rains came. We read aloud to Tom, walked when the weather allowed, and when he was convalescing set up skittles in the ballroom and competed until the cavernous, shabby room echoed with his barking laugh, his wheezy cough. And so we came to Christmas, and then 1841. *Annus horribilis* for the Franklins, a decisive year for me. At one time I used to believe that if only Jane Franklin had stayed at home that December, the dramatic events which followed might have been avoided, but now I understand that everything was moving relentlessly to one conclusion by then.

—⁂—

Christmas luncheon at Government House was subdued. The Governor appeared not in spirits, or at least, not in those of a metaphysical kind. He was imbibing a good deal of the other sort, both before and during the meal. More than he would have been allowed if Jane had been there. He sat silent while the young people talked, emitting now and then a huge walrus sigh.

I never felt I understood the Governor as I did Jane Franklin. He could be talkative and companionable, or nearly mute. And the mystery of the silent person is that you cannot be sure whether deep waters, or nothing at all, run below the surface. I'd felt this with Anna, too. On that Christmas Day, however, I could guess some of the demons haunting the Governor's silence.

The Magnetic Expedition had gone and he longed to be with it. Instead he must wrestle with a mountain of neglected paperwork. Montagu was expected back in two months, with a keen eye for the Governor's failings and heaven knows what impossible new edicts from London. Jane, Eleanor and Gell were away, and the newspapers had launched another savage rebuke against his wife. *Only a woman possessed by a mania for travel could choose to desert her husband at the Yuletide with no other purpose than a whim of novelty.* Jane professed to despise such attacks, but she would grow tremulous and pale and have the headache.

And he was under attack too, most recently by William Gates, a political prisoner, a lively anti-British rebel recently deported to Van Diemen's Land from Upper Canada by Colonel Arthur, who was now Governor there. Gates was writing tirades about the unfinished projects in the island. The Wellington Bridge, the New Norfolk Bridge, the new Government House, the east coast road, the water supply in Hobart—which was in a dire state, and summer now here again with nothing done. A cartoon circulating just then showed the Governor as a bloated grotesque, a pig-governor at trough, with a table napkin the size of a bed sheet tucked under his chins. He was gorging himself on a roasted ox, swilling it down with tankards of rum. Sir John had managed to laugh at the lampoon. An uncomfortable laugh.

If Archdeacon Hutchins had been there, the Governor would have talked to him, but Hutchins had quarrelled with the Franklins over the proposed College. The Governor wanted no discrimination between the sects of Christianity when taking in students or employing masters; Hutchins believed Anglicans should have preference. He also demanded that Sir John refuse an enquiry into the conduct of Reverend Ewing, Head of the Orphan School. No ordained minister should be so shockingly suspected. But I knew from Sophy that the Visiting Surgeon at the School had written a letter of complaint about Ewing's licence with girls in his care; an Enquiry could not be avoided.

Now Sir John's eye fell on the young people: Sophy and Tom, Henry Kay and Arthur Sweet, and again I could imagine some of his thoughts. These children were a comfort, but also another profound source of worry. Tom, allowed down to dinner for the first time in a month, was making his sister laugh, but emitting terrible coughs, and Dr Bedford had spoken bleakly about the lad's chest. Tom was consumptive. Would Isabella want her son at home? The Franklins had debated the question. Sir John had never had much to do with his older sister, but he thought not. Isabella had made it clear that Sophy must not be returned to her. Sophy must marry. But Sophy had turned down two or three suitors already. Poor Ainsworth had made her an offer last week and was now miserable. Why would Sophy not have him? They had all grown fond of Ainsworth. A sound, cheerful fellow of good family . . . The poor silly girl hadn't a penny to her name; what did she think to live on for the rest of her life?

Sir John's glance fell on Mary, sitting opposite him, demure as a lamb, expecting another child. He shuddered visibly, took another drink. (Sweet little Mary, poor orphaned Mary—and who knows what horrors . . .) I knew both he and Jane deeply regretted they had not known enough to stop that marriage. Franklin did not look at John Price but lifted his eyes to the windows, the grey scene outside. It was raining, ropes of water twisting down the glass. Trees lashing and leaning just like the January of their arrival four years ago. He had been four years stranded ashore! And the rain had leaked into another bedroom yesterday. This place was a bottomless pit for expense. But the young never troubled about such things. Ah, to be young again, a pretty young Midshipman.

'In those days my hair was chestnut, of course,' he said happily, 'long and waving like Eleanor's . . .'

He had told these stories many times; how he had looked so girlish he was made to act the heroine in skits got up on the ships at New Year.

Henry Kay and Tom now instantly begged to be allowed a small private fancy-dress party on New Year's Eve, and Sophy, who would have faced the devil to give Tom what he wanted, said it was not, after all, like *acting in plays*. 'Dressing up at New Year is a great naval tradition, is it not, Uncle?'

'Indeed, my dear. Ross and Crozier will be engaged in just the same way this week on their icy shelf.'

He cleared his throat to disguise the regretful tone.

—◊—

On New Year's Eve, Sophy was Britannia, draped in a white sheet girdled with gold, and wearing a little gold helmet. She would have preferred to be Justice, she explained to Boyes and Mary, but having to dance blindfold would have been too awkward.

'And then you must have limped as well,' said Boyes at once, '"Since Justice is not only blind but lame amongst us", as Otway says.'

Boyes looked as he always did: black frock coat, grey waistcoat. At first I thought he intended some joke about impersonating himself, 'The Colonial Auditor' or 'the anonymous author', which would be like his humour. But then I saw a small black book lettered DIARY, protruding from a pocket, and some kind of plant or weed hanging from the other pocket, and I guessed he was meant to be John Evelyn, the diarist and gardener.

Mary laughed and nodded, and said, 'And I am a portion of his shrubbery!' She was in a green dress with paper flowers pinned all across it and a bird's nest attached at her waist. Boyes said, 'You do better than I, Hatty. Coming in we passed a man personating a Spanish muleteer—or so I thought, but on addressing him in that language I discovered it to be young Arthur Sweet from Sir John's office, who speaks only English—and that imperfectly, like all the young. He claims to be Richard the Third.'

Sophy had given me a blue-sprigged dress from the box, front-laced and with side panniers.

John Price was in black. Black doublet and hose, tight-buttoned jerkin, hat with a red feather in it. The devil himself. He looked pleased with the effect this was having on the rest of the company. His wife, soon to produce her second infant, had stayed at home. Tom was the Artful Dodger. Nuncle, under Sophy's direction, made a Captain Cook somewhat larger than the original. Henry Kay wore Fool's motley, with a long tail of frayed rope and a lion's head from some old performance. He was a Bunyip, he said, the curious creature someone had recently lectured about at the Mechanics Institute.

346

Bergman was not in fancy dress. He appeared at the door when the dancing had already begun and stood as though he were looking for someone. He saw me, came across and, taking my hand, said, smiling widely, 'You *are* here! I can't believe it. Boyes told me only today. I thought you had sailed.'

'I sent you a note . . .'

'I have only just received it.'

'I thought you had decided not to answer it.'

'It has been following me about, missing me.'

'You have been away a long time.'

'I'm a fool. I should have come to see you.'

We smiled at each other and could not stop. Henry Kay asked if we would play. He had been unable to hire musicians at such short notice. I kept losing my place, glancing at Bergman and flushing because I felt his eyes on me. He laughed and stopped and said, 'Hatty, Hatty, why have we wasted a year?'

Nothing had changed since the gloomy Christmas luncheon a week before—and everything had. Later, at supper in the verandah room, Sir John offered a toast to absent friends: Jane, Eleanor and Gell in the heat of Adelaide; Ross and Crozier in the snowy wastes. A servant refilled his glass.

'At this time of year it will be light all night on the ice,' Franklin said. 'On festive evenings the Eskimo women would come for the *kooniging*, kissing and welcoming the *kabloona* from the far lands with great affection . . .' He cleared his throat and said hastily that Eskimo words had fascinated him from the beginning. *Kikerktak* for King William Island, *eshemutta* for the ships' captains. The senior Captain was *Toolooark*. Crozier they called *Aglooka*, but he did not know why.

Somebody said the colours of the play-acting on the ships must be strangely vivid against that silent white expanse, and Sir John said, 'Ah, white. People say white, but . . . You are an artist, Mrs Adair; you know how many shades of white there are, and how it may carry a host of other tints. *Emerald* in the depths of the bergs, with every blue you can conceive of . . . And the aurora in winter—immense green veils twisting across the skies.

'And silent, no, that is wrong too. Always creaking and cracking as the ice moves and the barky shifts. Then the rush of avalanches thundering down the great bergs into the sea, and the bark or yip of seals and walruses—howling of the dogs—a strange musical whistling of the winds . . .'

Deeply immersed, he came to a stop, found himself at the table and took a handful of cherries.

Just before midnight the party made its way back to the drawing room. Bergman and I loitered behind. We stood looking out at the river and recalling the night Booth was lost, when we had walked through the streets arm in arm. He took my hand, his own warm and alive with all its mysterious vitality, familiar and strange. Flows of desire coursed through me, making me weak, making me laugh. The clock struck midnight and the clamour of bells began. He kissed me, a light New Year's kiss; but then we were in each other's arms and would have stayed there, murmuring, unable to let go of each other, but we knew that if we did not soon rejoin the others, someone would come to find us.

I felt we were shining like a pair of Roman Candles, but no one seemed to notice. The party dispersed in good wishes and farewells and we walked outside and hurried through the streets hand-in-hand, exchanging New Year greetings with a few passers-by. We stopped to kiss again in the shadows of a great tree, and ran on, laughing. At my cottage we shed our clothes, and that night was as ardent and joyful as if we had been sixteen, as tender and easy as though we were long married. We lay rib-to-rib afterwards, skin to warm skin, and the joy I felt then was the beginning of our marriage, although the ceremony itself must wait.

Gus was committed to leaving in four days to go to the west coast again with James Calder. They would be away two months, clearing new growth from the Frenchman's track, setting food caches and making preparations for the Franklins' delayed expedition, now to begin in early February after Jane and Eleanor returned from Adelaide. Jane and Sir John would ride up to meet Gus, Calder, and the convict party at Marlborough above New Norfolk.

We agreed to say nothing of our affairs until Bergman returned, but in the days before his departure he came to me late every night and left before dawn each morning, cautious of my reputation until our announcement was made.

—◊◊◊—

Gus had been gone a week when I came home one afternoon through Minto Lane, opened the back gate, and saw Mrs Tench, the sailor-woman from the *Adastra*. She was standing in the garden under the apple tree. Only the red-and-white stripes of her skirt made her visible in the mottled shade. She wore a man's shirt with an embroidered dark green waistcoat. Her long grey pigtail hung down her back from under a chip hat, which was tied over the crown and under her chin with a faded blue scarf. Old Mr Coombes was hoeing in the vegetable patch. He raised his hat to me, indicating Mrs Tench with a slight motion of his head. She was feeding a windfall to the tethered goat, smoking a clay pipe, letting the smoke trickle from the corner of her mouth. She saw me and nodded, unhurried. A pounding began in my chest.

'Anna?' I said. 'The Captain?'

She took the pipe from her mouth and nodded again. 'Mrs R is at the Hope and Anchor.'

'And Captain Quigley?'

She looked at me, said nothing. We went into the kitchen and sat at the table. The Captain was dead, had died in Valparaíso. From the deep pocket of her skirt she brought an oilskin packet. A letter headed 'Auckland 10th March 1840': ten months ago.

Dear Harriet,

When I accepted this voyage it was in expectation of an easy run from Sydney with good profit, but now we are arrived it proves no such thing either by error or I am deceived. The cargo never intended for this Bay of Islands but promised to a new colony further south. After much argument with the agent here I see little choice but to carry it onward to this place they call Wanganewi.

There was a space and then:

More dispute. I have succeeded in making favourable terms being an additional fee and percentage on delivery which I

The writing broke off and the remaining two small pages were filled with jottings: latitude and longitude, sums of money, disconnected sentences. One of these recorded their arrival in Nelson on the sixteenth of April 1840.

Much violent sentiment here against the New Zealand Company and Wakefields. Many claim to have been robbed or misled. Rumours that the Government of New South Wales will look into all lands sold by the Company and reclaim what was wrongfully obtained from the Mowri people. Some will lose what they bought in good faith.

Mrs Tench said a group of angry settlers had boarded the vessel and refused to leave. They demanded Quigley take them to Valparaíso to join an earlier party of disgruntled emigrants. If Quigley did not agree they would take the ship by force, but if he would sail them to Valparaíso he would be paid when they arrived, and the ship would be his again. The Captain was rageful, but at last agreed.

Four days after they reached Valparaíso, it being the fever season, the Captain fell to the ground while walking to the harbour-master's and was carried back to the ship. But Mrs Tench believed he knew he was ailing long before. A week earlier he had given her these papers and some money—all gone now—saying if anything should happen to him, she must take Mrs R back to Van Diemen's Land to

Mrs Adair, 'who will make certain you do not lose by it'. She looked me squarely in the eye.

After Quigley's death the first mate had taken command of the ship. He would not sail west against the winds, and so it had been the long way back—eastwards round by Cape Town once more. At last they came through Bass Strait to Port Phillip, where she and Anna disembarked. Her brother and sister-in-law stayed with the barky and went on to Sydney. She had brought Anna across to Launceston and then south on the coach to Hobarton.

'How is Mrs Rochester? How did she take Quigley's death?' I asked.

A shrug, a long look, a puff at the pipe.

When I arrived at the Hope and Anchor, Anna was sitting in the same room we had occupied three years ago. At first glance she seemed little changed. Her face was a trifle heavier, round, brown and as strong featured as ever. But she had gained flesh in the body, too, and was now nearly as large as she had been in the attic. She looked at me so blankly I thought for a moment she did not recognise me, and then, 'Harriet,' she decided placidly. She smiled and put out her hand, but could not rise unassisted from the chair to greet me.

She gave no sign of it having been three years since we met, and showed no desire to speak of her travels. When I asked about them, she considered for a time and then said slowly she had liked Moreton Bay. Quigley had bought her a blue silk there and Mrs Tench let it out. But Quigley was dead and Mrs Tench looked after her now. She liked Sydney, too. Other places she had not liked. Neither then nor later did she ask about Rowland, or show any curiosity as to how I had passed the time in her absence.

Mrs Tench lifted the hem of Anna's gown and showed me her ankles, much swollen. Anna regarded them with mild interest, as though they belonged to someone else. I sent a message to the hospital and James Seymour came next day to examine her, by which time we had removed her to the cottage. Each time he asked her a question she looked to Mrs Tench to supply the answer. At last he and I returned to the parlour while Mrs Tench dressed Anna.

'She may have had a small seizure. More than one, perhaps. Her mind is slower than it was? The heart is irregular and there are signs of a dropsy, but I cannot tell how quickly the fluid is gathering.'

'But she is not ill? She could make the voyage home to England?'

He hesitated. 'If I observed her for another month I could answer you—judge whether her condition is changing and to what degree. How old is she?'

'Thirty-eight. My own age.'

'Medically speaking, she could be twice that. Are you anxious to leave?'

'No! Quite the opposite!' Reddening, I explained the situation, asking him to say nothing of it elsewhere.

'Ah, at last! He is a lucky man—and you will be happy, I'm sure.'

He told me he had decided to return to England. He loved the island, but felt torn between the two places. I sympathised, wondering silently whether he would attend Anna on the voyage home if she was fit to travel—with Mrs Tench perhaps? Or must I take her to England and then return to Gus? I could not bear the thought. I would not consider it until he returned, by which time Seymour might have better news of Anna's health.

Her old guitar was among her few remaining belongings, but she never played it now. She seemed content to sit and do nothing but watch the comings and goings of the household: Mrs Tench, who washed and dressed and cared for her as if she were a child; or me, or Nellie Jack, or even Aristo, the coloured parrot, which sat on a perch beside Anna, eating apple or carrot. Ada Sweet came in and out, and there was Mrs Tench's dog, Dasher, a grey-brown lurcher; a poacher's dog, silent and absolutely attentive to her command.

It was clear from the beginning that Mrs Tench intended to stay, for which I felt only relief. She said she had slept under kitchen tables before, aye, and atop o' them too, but we moved about until Anna had the large back bedroom, which opened from the kitchen and had

French windows onto the garden. I had the front parlour, unused before, and Mrs Tench was supposed to share the attic with Nellie, but generally slept on a palliasse in the kitchen.

An old wooden bench turned up in the garden one day, placed against the cottage wall under a pear tree, and Anna and Mrs T, as she liked to be called, often sat side by side dozing on it as the summer went on. I thought Anna spoke less and less, but Mrs T reported conversations. Anna said she had a fancy for a beefsteak for her dinner, or a nice piece of fish, or a tin of ginger biscuits, or new gloves and stockings. These requests were always perfectly reasonable, and it soon seemed practical to give Mrs T not only a weekly wage but also a modest allowance to supplement the meals and housekeeping Ada Sweet provided.

My only uneasiness was connected with the daily gin, porter and wine for nurse and patient. Anna was accustomed to her 'little drops', Mrs Tench said. 'Could not sleep proper without'—as well I knew. And after all, she kept a check on the amount Anna consumed, and nothing untoward occurred. Most evenings Mrs T went down to The Black Swan, or The Case is Altered, letting herself in long after I'd put Anna to bed and gone to my room, but if I wanted to go out she would stay with Anna.

—⁂—

Jane, Eleanor and Gell returned early in February, Jane full of the energy travel always seemed to give her, eager for the west coast journey. But three days after they arrived, the *Favourite* put in to Hobart, bound for New Zealand under the command of another of Sir John's old friends, Captain Hobson. He dined *en famille*, and spoke of the infant colonies in New Zealand and their mutual friend Captain Owen Stanley of the *Britomart*, who was now Senior Officer at the Akaroa Station. The following day Jane called me in and told me she had accepted Captain Hobson's offer of a passage to New Zealand; would I go as her companion? I explained Anna's situation, saying nothing of Gus. When the *Favourite* sailed a few days later,

Jane and Miss Williamson were aboard and the west coast expedition was postponed once more. The news was sent to Gus and James Calder, and they packed up camp again and were in Hobart by the first week of March.

My lease of the cottage was due for renewal on Lady Day, the twenty-seventh of March, but early in the month Ada came to tell me she could not renew: she must sell. Like so many small businesses, her shop was doing poorly. She would have closed it, but in these hard times there were widows who relied on being able to buy a penn'orth of tea or tobacco from her, a cup of flour or an egg. She was paying mortgages on both cottages and falling behind. The newspapers had lists of foreclosures and insolvencies. Her father wanted to sell this cottage to clear the debt on her own.

They could raise the rent, I said, or I would lend them money—but they had a horror of borrowing and believed the bad times would not end soon. It was former conversations with Jane Franklin that made me think of buying the cottage myself. Anna could then stay where she was comfortable and Old Mr Coombes could continue to garden both plots. Gus approved. We would live in his house after we married, but it was hardly big enough for us and Durrell and Billy Knox, Gus's new apprentice—and the land it stood on was tiny. Ada's cottage had half an acre, which meant that in the future we might add rooms and live there.

We were married on the fifth of April. I went to Government House beforehand, somewhat apprehensively, to tell Sophy the news. Her moral scruples were puritanical. Gus had once had a convict mistress; he might be Jewish; I was a widow: any one of these circumstances might bring her strong disapproval. And besides, she had once made reference to our remaining bosom friends when we returned to England—perhaps even living together—and although I had laughed away the comment and she had never repeated it, I suspected it might linger in her mind.

It was the first time I had been to the 'Palace' uninvited; I had always taken care not to presume on the friendship. The footman would have sent me straight upstairs but I said I would wait in the morning room. When Sophy came in I said I hoped for her good wishes. She took the invitation, turned her back on me and walked away to the window. After a moment she let the note fall unopened to the ground and turned back, and from the look on her face I knew there would be a scene. By the time she spoke, I was expecting almost anything except what she did say.

'Why does Mr Therry come so often to see you?'

'He comes to see Anna, who has returned unwell, as you know. She asked to see a priest. She was educated in a convent. Father Therry is a good, spiritual sort of man.'

Too late I remembered she did not care for the word 'spiritual'. The look on her face now was familiar; righteous indignation girded for battle.

'A "spiritual sort of man"?' Her voice was contemptuous. 'Then why is he such an enemy to my uncle? He publicly accuses Nuncle of holding back a thousand pounds intended for the building of the Roman Church—when it is Mr Therry's own fault that the money cannot be used. He does not supply the documents London requires.'

'But Mr Therry has written to the newspapers saying Sir John is not to blame.'

She ignored this. 'And that vile newspaperman, Mr Gilbert Robinson. He is Bergman's friend too. I wonder at *you* though, Harriet, at this betrayal from *you*. You have had ample opportunity—through the charity of my aunt—of seeing how the vicious population of this place seizes any opportunity to slander our family. But one should not expect gratitude, I suppose.'

I knew her words were childish, meant to hurt because she was hurt, but this was painful and unjust, and I grew agitated. Sophy and Jane had been good to me, but I had given faithful service too, and borne much. Before I could speak, not trusting myself to choose from the flood of words welling up in me, she cried urgently, 'Why are you doing this, Harriet? Because you are afraid of being poor? But this is not worth it. You will have to bear his touch, his hands . . .' She made a strangled sound.

'I love him.'

Again she ignored me. 'Disloyalty is your besetting sin. A second marriage is also a kind of disloyalty, is it not? Which is why there must always be some disgust attached to the idea of a widow marrying again. Aunt will be disappointed in you.' Her young face was filled with cold dislike, but I could see she was not yet finished, only waiting to begin again.

I hesitated, but if I stayed I would say something unforgivable. I turned and walked out. She called something after me but I did not stop.

—⁓—

St John Wallace married us at St George's Church. It was to have been a small ceremony, but Mrs Parry brought her daughter Marion and the four great-grandchildren whose portraits I had painted, and Booth, Lizzie and Amelia came to town with the Lempriere family. I wore silver-grey silk and Louisa sewed white silk roses for my hair, and I remembered Jane and Rochester's marriage on the *Adastra*.

Boyes gave me away. Booth was best man. Old Mr Coombes made me a posy of late roses and sweet peas that smelled like heaven. He stayed with Anna at the cottage while we were at the Church; the service would have been too exhausting for her. We collected them in the carriage afterwards and went to Bess Chesney's; she had insisted on giving us a wedding breakfast. Anna was quiet, smiling—pleased with the outing, but weak, having difficulty in moving. She kept forgetting what the occasion was all about.

Rising to propose the loyal toast, Boyes told us the *Duncan* was just in, carrying London newspapers from last December. They announced the birth of the Princess Royal, Her Majesty's first child. We drank the health of mother and infant, reported to be doing well; but there would be no Brevet or Promotion on this occasion, the baby not being a Prince of Wales.

Bess Chesney shed tears when we left and Nellie wept too, although she and Anna were coming home in the carriage with us. We had decided to postpone our wedding journey until spring, when we would go down to Gus's little hut on the river at the Huon for a week or two. In the meantime there was all the pleasure in the world in waking every morning in each other's arms.

—∞—

Gus's cottage, being small and fastidiously well kept by Durrell, needed no attention from me. I was working on portraits for two or three families, but also spent several hours each day and some evenings at Minto Lane helping Mrs T and Nellie, since Anna could not be left alone. She was cheerful and in no pain, but daily weaker.

'Coco!' she said one day, looking at splendid Aristo, Mrs T's bird. 'Maman's parrot was Coco. Coquette. Cocky, cock, prick. "Qui est là? Je m'appelle Coco." Poor Coco died when Coulibri burned—on the railing—screeching—when they set fire to the house. Coulibri means "Hummingbird" you know, Harriet. A tall house—white—bigger than an ajoupa—green jalousies—the verandah all broken. Vines growing through the ceiling of Maman's chamber and balcony.'

She paused so long I thought this unusual flow had come to an end, but then she began again.

'In the boiling-house no sugar, only cane-trash and rats and the duppy—the ghost, a spirit from obeah. When the fire came Maman took Pierre, my little brother—but he died as they ran. Christophine holds to me—we run with Sass Thomas and Despa, his mother. The rest all gone.' Another long pause. 'Mr Mason—did he burn?' She frowned. 'Ah, he always burned . . .' followed by a burst of salacious French.

'He was like the Old One himself, Beelzebub. Mr Samedi. Cruel for white flesh, black flesh. Hands under the chin, under the skirt, thick wet lips. Come here, little Anna, little daughter. Annette, Marionette. Come here, girl. Christophine said, "I will kill him." But she is afraid for her soul. If she kill him she will burn in hell.'

Her eyes had closed, I thought she was asleep, but after a minute she murmured, 'Coco, coquette, cocky, cock, Antoinette, marionette . . .'.

———

I had written to Mrs Fairfax many times with no reply, most recently to tell her of our marriage. Before this could possibly have reached England, I received a puzzling letter from her. She was leaving Brighton-on-Sea. Jane and Rochester had invited her to return to 'Ferndean' and she preferred the country. She looked forward to seeing me when I returned, and hoped she could count on my discretion now as in the past. She begged I would say nothing to Mr Rochester or Jane of what had occurred. She had only ever done what she believed to be for the best. What Rowland had asked her to do.

28

BOOTH, SITTING IN CHURCH AT PORT ARTHUR ON THE FIRST Sunday in May, grew drowsy. The sermon murmured on. Lizzie, close against his side in her new green merino, was emitting the soporific warmth of a small roosting hen. His own clothes too, were new and warm, bought while they were in Hobart for Bergman's wedding three weeks before. Civvies now. Coat, waistcoat, linen, cravat, bought from the sale of his commission. After twenty-five years in uniform he felt odd in them, like an actor playing a gentleman.

Strange words from the pulpit brought his mind back to the sermon: *Mene mene tekel upharsin.* He had loved those words as a child for their very strangeness. 'Thou hast been weighed in the balances and found wanting, and therefore shall thy kingdom be taken from thee'. If he had been so inclined he might find that ominous. Tomorrow he was to appear in Hobart before another committee, for reasons he had not yet been told.

The weighing of good and bad deeds after death had been vivid to him as a child. He'd pictured a small pair of scales like his father's, with a brass pan hanging at each side on fine gold chains. Good deeds would be in one pan like a heap of diamonds; bad deeds blackly fused together like a lump of coal on the other. The balance would waver—drop remorselessly to left or right. These days he preferred

Bergman's idea: the Creator of the universe must be a joyful Mind, an inventor who loved His creation and would understand an honest mistake. But then again, it would not be God doing the weighing-up at tomorrow's committee but Mr John Montagu, a less forgiving article altogether.

The Colonial Secretary had returned two months ago and had been alarmingly quiet since. Still, whatever it was this time, Booth felt he had nothing to fear. What he had accomplished in the last six months would speak for itself. The Ralph's Bay Railway and Saltwater River Probation Station finished; three more stations under way; a new barracks at Port Arthur; a dormitory at Point Puer; foundations for the flour mill; a huge crop of wheat and vegetables. They'd worked like demons, he, his officers and the men. Murderers, forgers, thieves, incorrigibles; he was proud of them all.

As he and Lizzie walked back down the hill after Church, they saw the *Vansittart* sail in to pick him up, and later, under an autumn sky as cloudless blue as a Dutchman's trousers, he leaned against its rail, feeling the joyful energy of the cutter flying before the breeze, and thought again about Montagu—whose mood was far from joyful, apparently. He'd returned empty-handed. No Lieutenant Governorship, not even a position closer to England. And Jessie Montagu had discovered a week after they returned that she was expecting another child, which could hardly be welcome news.

The *True Colonist* wrote (and how it would infuriate Montagu, their printing it!) that his two years away had cost all the four thousand pounds raised from the sale of the contents of 'Stowell'. He'd paid nothing off the loan from Arthur, they added, except monthly interest, which was in arrears. He must still have four thousand from the sale of the house itself, but this must be used to buy and equip a new residence, at effectively half the value of what he'd owned before. In the meantime the Montagus were living with the Forsters at 'Wyvenhoe', which would not improve the Colonial Secretary's temper. And it would not be just the meals! 'Stowell' was only a stone's throw from

'Wyvenhoe', and every time he stepped outside, Montagu would glimpse his old home, lost to him now, bought by the Mad Judge.

If Jane Franklin had been in the island when the Montagus returned, Booth thought, she would surely have invited them into Government House again and flattered the Colonial Secretary into a better humour, but she was still in New Zealand, where she had sprained her ankle badly in a fall. The Governor and Miss Cracroft, if they had thought of asking the Montagus to stay, must have decided against it. Poor Jane. Her accident sounded painful but typical. She had wandered out of her quarters one night to admire the moon or the view, or something, and forgetting the lodge was on a raised platform about three feet high, had walked straight off the edge.

Another unpleasant surprise for Montagu would have been Ross and Crozier's intimacy with the Franklins, not to mention the shipload of Franklin's relatives and friends come to increase the Government House 'coterie', as the *True Colonist* called it. Ross had friends in high places in England. And there had been defections from the Arthurites, too. The Turnbulls, father and son, had been Arthurites but were now at least equally Franklinites. Boyes and Dr Bedford, the Mad Judge and James Calder, if not wholly converted, were certainly Janeites.

Booth waited twenty minutes outside the Governor's office and was being ushered in by Henslowe, Sir John's new secretary, when George Boyes's tall, thin figure emerged from another door and came past him.

'Booth,' he nodded a greeting, lifting his eyebrows, adding quietly as he passed, 'Giving away the cabbage crop again? Transgressing with other vegetables?'

He continued on his way with the sardonic smile he cultivated, but ten minutes later it was clear to Booth that this was no laughing matter.

There was no sign of Forster, only Franklin and Henslowe, Montagu and a senior man, Asquith, from the Attorney General's Department, and his clerk. It was Montagu who read aloud the item for investigation: the sale of a vessel built at Port Arthur, ordered by Mr Charles Swanston of the Derwent Bank and Derwent Steamship

Company, finished and delivered to him last year. There appeared to be grave objections to the transaction, which might be construed as a deliberate attempt to defraud Her Majesty's Government.

The ship had been sold to Swanston's company for three hundred and fifty-two pounds, ten shillings and tenpence, a price calculated using the convict rate for labour. If it had been calculated using the commercial rate, the cost would have been two thousand five hundred pounds. The question was, had the low price been by error—or design? Mr Swanston had immediately fitted engines and sold it to a friend for seven thousand pounds. Had there been an arrangement by which Captain Booth was paid the difference?

'I strongly object, Your Excellency.' Booth was on his feet.

'Nevertheless,' said Montagu calmly. 'We must ask, Captain, why you used the convict labour rate in calculating the sale price?'

'Mr Forster instructed me to do so.'

'You have a record of this?'

'No. Mr Forster spoke of it while we were conversing, and I subsequently wrote a letter to him confirming that I would make the calculation on that basis, as he had advised. My letter should be in the files.' But it would not be, of course. 'I most vehemently deny receiving any advantage from the sale.'

But somebody had. Booth's heart jumped erratically for a queasy minute, during which he wondered whether he was about to have a fit, then it resumed a heavy fast throb. Forster? Who else? Forster had given Swanston the cheap sale in exchange for cancellation of some debt, and he, Booth, had been played for the gullible fool he was. Montagu had no doubt returned from England knowing nothing of it, had found it among the records, and seeing how fishy it would appear to Whitehall, decided to kill two birds with one stone. Stab Booth in the vitals and save his ugly brother-in-law's neck. No use threatening to resign this time: it would only seem like guilt.

'You have recently bought land at York Plains, Captain?'

Montagu, having laid his red herring at their feet, was purring quietly behind the desk. 'And yet until a few months ago your financial state was—straitened, shall I say? You owed a debt to your agent which you have also recently paid?'

'I sold my commission. That alone is the source of my expenditure. Sir. The sale of the ship to Swanston took place last year.'

'Hmm. You might have delayed spending, of course, to defer suspicion.'

'A bad business,' muttered Franklin. 'Henslowe, will you note . . .'

Captain Booth—they were still calling him that—*you are required to submit a full account of your version of the sale in an affidavit sworn before a magistrate. It will be forwarded to Lord Stanley in England with other papers in the case.*

—⁂—

Booth walked across the wharves and up into the Battery, blind with more fury than he had ever felt in his life. Forster had turned to him casually after they'd talked about the sale. 'You'll use the convict rate of labour in calculating the price, of course.' And he hadn't given it an instant's thought: assumed Swanston had ordered the ship from Port Arthur for that very reason—because it was cheaper than a commercial boat-builder. He walked swiftly down the hill to Sandy Bay where he would be unlikely to see anyone he knew, and strode along the shore for nearly an hour before he turned back. Talk to Bergman, he decided, coming back through Battery Point.

Mr and Mrs Bergman were not at home, Durrell said. They had gone to visit Mr Duterrau, the painter, who was to give a lecture tonight at the Mechanics Institute. They would dine with him and go to the lecture afterwards. Durrell produced a hand-bill advertising Duterrau's paper on 'The School of Athens as it Assimilates with the Mechanics Institution'. He and Billy Knox would go too, after a bite. Had the Captain eaten? Booth, finding himself suddenly ravenous at the aroma of stew, and recalling that he had not eaten for hours, shared their meal and grog. There was distraction in talking to Durrell and carrot-haired, blushing Billy Knox, a former Point Puer boy Booth had recommended for the apprenticeship with Bergman.

363

The boy was taller than Booth now, narrow as a plank, and as stiff and speechless until Durrell drew him into talk about the Huon settlement. They walked together to the hall afterwards, separating at the door when Booth, seeing no sign of Bergman and Harriet, joined St John Wallace and Louisa, from whom he learned that Duterrau was ill. The Reverend Ewing had stepped in at short notice to speak on 'The Migrating Caterpillar', and would stay the night afterwards with the Wallaces. He didn't want to ride three miles back to the Orphan School very late, only to return early next morning for the enquiry into his handling of the school, due to begin the following day.

When the lecture was over Booth could not have said a word about caterpillars. He was not the only one: there had been loud snoring. The audience began to leave, and Booth would have gone quickly too, but St John and Louisa, forced to wait for Ewing, began speaking to him. In the end they were the last to leave, except for a clerk waiting to lock up and extinguish the lamps lighting the few stone steps outside the door.

Booth stepped aside to let Louisa and St John go first down to the road. Ewing was behind him. As he stepped down onto the street Booth saw two men approaching: John Price and Stringer Wynn. As they came past, Wynn veered out of his path to collide with St John, shoving with such brutal intent that St John staggered and fell against the building. Wynn grasped St John's arm in a tight grip and cried loudly, 'Oh dear, sorry, sir. What 'ave I done? 'Ere, let me get you steady.'

'Let me go. What on earth do you think you're doing?' said St John.

Wynn took no notice. He turned to Ewing, and leering into his face, said, 'Well, if it ain't *Mister* Ewing as well. *Mister* Wallace and *Mister* Ewing. Two *men of God*. Black and white like the soul of a sinner or a pair o' magpies. Heckle and Peckle both. Ewing takes the little girls and you 'as the boys? Is that how it goes, eh, Wallace?' Booth was speechless with astonishment: he saw Lizzie's shocked face and put out a hand to steady her as she backed towards the railing by the steps.

St John spoke to John Price, 'Will you tolerate this?'

'Sorry, Wallace, wasn't listening,' said Price. He fixed his monocle in his eye and added, 'What say, Stringer?'

'Quotin' the Bible, sir. Sayin' as 'ow you can't touch pitch an' not be defiled. Ain't that so, gen'lemen?'

Ewing was bent over, gasping strangely. Booth moved towards Wynn, who stepped easily back, grinning, and took up a pugilist's stance with his fists up. He danced away from Booth, lithe, young, in peak condition, saying, 'Keep aht of it, Cap'n. Ain't you in enough trouble? Or so I hear.'

Laughing still, he danced towards St John and away again, working his fists, taunting, and then came close, suddenly thrusting his right fist to within an inch of Wallace's chin. Louisa screamed. Wynn stepped back and held up his hands.

'Never touched 'im, ma'am. Jus' my liddle joke, see? No 'arm done, sir? Leastways, not this time. Not but what there might come a night when it'll be a different story. A bit o' sport between us one dark night, eh, gen'lemen?'

'Will you stand there and do nothing, Price?' said Booth. Three years ago he would have leapt at this man. He was furious now to recognise in himself neither the will nor the capacity.

Price pulled at a chain across his waistcoat until a watch emerged, consulted it and said languidly, 'Must be off. Come along, Wynn.'

St John seemed about to rush at them as they walked away. Booth restrained him.

'Go to your wife,' he said. Louisa had sunk onto the steps.

Booth went in search of a cab, and when they reached the cottage, Mrs Fludde took Louisa to bed. Ewing gulped down two brandies, chattering with shock and outrage, and then staggered off to sleep. When they were alone, Booth said to St John, 'You will report this, of course.'

'Report it to whom? The Chief Police Magistrate—Forster? His assistant—John Price?' St John gave a distorted smile. 'They would call it a misunderstanding. Their word against ours.'

Wynn had threatened before to horsewhip him in public, he added. And he had received two anonymous letters, destroyed now, because their filthy contents did not bear showing. At any rate, he and Louisa would sail for home in a month, early July. He believed these brutes would not dare anything more in the meantime.

—⁂—

I heard Booth's story when he came to see Gus early the following morning, before he returned to the peninsula. I went immediately to see whether there was anything I could do for Louisa, expecting to find her prostrated. It was almost winter, but sunny. She was sitting in a basket chair outside the French windows under a leafless tree, knitting, which I had never seen her do before, wrestling the needles and worsted in the awkward manner of beginners. She held her head slightly to one side in concentration, her thick golden hair carefully looped back, her blue eyes untroubled when she stopped and looked up at me. Little Thea, nearly three, copper curls tied with blue ribbons in two bunches, played on a rug with the cat. She put her face up to me for a kiss and hug. Jane Fludde went out to fetch tea.

'Of course they dislike St John,' said Louisa calmly, reaching the end of a row and holding the work up to gaze at it with satisfaction. 'What does he expect? He has let them know he has something against them. Something they would rather conceal. He has hinted it to McLeod, who tells me. St John tells me nothing. McLeod says John Price hates Dido Thomas. He hates all convicts, thinks they get away with too much.'

Fludde came in with the tea things and Louisa added, 'Perhaps Edward Rochester was right to be afraid of coming here. This is not England, however much it tries to be. You begin to wonder why we thought some things so important.'

'What things?'

'Oh, manners, rules. McLeod says society in this colony is in some ways stricter than the Court of London. It has to be, he says, because people are afraid we are so far from England all the rules will break down.' She rested her knitting in her lap. 'I wonder if you know how fortunate you are, Harriet?' she added. 'To be certain from a child what your gift is, what you want to do. It has taken me so long to find out what I want to do. I don't want to go back, now.'

'Good heavens, Louisa. What has changed you? What do you want to do?'

'The *Adastra* changed me, and you, and Mrs Tench, and Jane Fludde, and McLeod . . .'

She gave me a smile full of meaning. St John and Dido came in then, and I had no opportunity to ask the question again.

—m—

The Magnetic Expedition returned that week. They had found their great ice land, which prevented them approaching within a hundred and fifty miles of the pole. Nevertheless, they had been able to plot the pole's position accurately, and could prove errors in the American charts, which showed mountains and prairies in places where the *Erebus* and *Terror* had sailed across open water. The most spectacular sight had been two mountains on the snowy continent, one a volcano erupting smoke and flame. They had named them Mount Erebus and Mount Terror.

Planning now began for the great *Erebus* and *Terror* ball, perhaps the most famous celebration ever held in Hobart. Souvenir programmes of the great occasion, printed on blue silk, are treasured to this day by some families in the colony. The sight of them still has the power to make me agitated and melancholy.

The rift with Sophy meant that I did not see her during this time, but I heard the progress of the arrangements from Gus and Calder, who were again assisting with observations at the Rossbank Observatory—and also from Old Mr Coombes and Ada, who reported Arthur Sweet's gleanings from the Governor's office. The date was set for the first of June, to allow a month for preparations. Jane Franklin was still in New Zealand, but it was hoped she would be home by then. At any rate, the ball could not wait. The Expedition must soon leave to go to Sydney and New Zealand, and south into the ice again for the spring melt. The ball would be held on the decks of the two ships, as grand and glittering an affair as they could make it, Ross and Crozier declared. It would express their inadequate thanks to the Franklins and all friends in the colony, for the months of entertainment and assistance the Expedition had received.

Everything needful would be done by the ships' crews, they insisted. The Government House ladies must resign themselves to being honoured guests, untroubled by preparations, merely arriving on the night to gasp and wonder at what the jack tars had wrought. But Sophy and Eleanor, bursting with anticipatory fervour, could not be denied activity. Sailors and servants wore a track up through the garden between the ships and Government House. On the up-journey went bunting, flags and pennants for the ladies' inspection, laundering and repair. Back down to the ships went cutlery, crockery, chairs, tables, cushions, rugs, mirrors, hairbrushes, pins, lavender water and *sal volatile*—even the portrait of Queen Victoria which Peter Barrow had given to Jane Franklin. This was to be prominently displayed, framed by small lamps and tasteful greenery arranged by Sophy. There were paper garlands to make, and ribbon favours, and an archway of greenery (by Sophy) to adorn the gangway to the ships. The newspapers warned the hopeful that there could be only two hundred guests; the ships could take no more.

Sophy was advising Ross and Crozier on the invitations and I could imagine her difficulties. The official party numbered forty at least, leaving only a hundred and sixty for other guests. It was a matter of choosing whom to leave out. Someone would be affronted. The Franklins had made enemies before by handing out invitations and then rescinding them; or by inviting only one half of a couple.

Bergman and I received no invitation; we had not expected one. The day before the ball, however, there came a handwritten note from Ross, delivered by a sailor, apologising for 'the unaccountable confusion' by which our invitation had not been sent. If we could forgive this deplorable mistake, he and Crozier must still hope to enjoy the pleasure of our company. Gus had taken a heavy share of shifts at the Observatory, and I guessed someone had suddenly noticed the omission and drawn it to Ross's attention. Gus wanted to send an excuse. He did not like crushes, and I could not accompany him; Anna was sinking lower every day. But I argued that it would be ungracious not to go after Ross's kind letter.

'It will be your last occasion with the 'Obs Men' before they sail,' I said. 'And otherwise what will you do? Only sit alone by the fire while I'm at the Minto Lane cottage with Anna. Besides, I want to know everything!'

He gave an amused husbandly groan, but agreed to go.

Until a few days before this, Anna had still been able to sit in a chair for an hour or two each day. To eat soup and toast by the fire, or look out the window, or receive visitors—Bess Chesney, Liddy and Polly, Father Therry. But the effort had grown more and more laborious, and on the morning before the ball, she was too weak to leave her bed. I walked over to the hospital to leave a note asking James Seymour to come, and on the way I saw for the first time the full extent of preparations for the grand occasion.

The eastern side of the grounds of Government House had been fenced off for a month; now a new road was revealed: creating a semi-circular drive to allow carriages to pass across the front of Government House to reach the *Erebus* and *Terror*, which were lashed together side by side at the wharf. The vehicles could then continue on past the Customs House and back up to Davey Street without turning. The *Terror* was on the sea side, the *Erebus* nearest to the wharf, and joined to it by a bridge of small boats with planking laid across them to form a path. As I walked by—one of many curious onlookers—this wooden footbridge was being tented over with canvas to form an entrance arcade the length of a large room and perhaps a yard and a half wide.

That night, oil lamps were hung at intervals along the interior of this arcade, and Ross and Crozier stood at the entrance under Sophy's green arch, greeting the guests as they came from the carriages. The deck of the *Erebus*, sheltered under a spread of sails, was for dancing, its cabins taken over as dressing rooms for the ladies. Supper tables were set on the *Terror*. The night was fiercely cold but dry, no doubt in answer to fervent prayers rising heavenwards from the latitude of 40 degrees south, like smoke from a great chimney. It was three years almost to the day since Booth had been lost.

The military band of the 51st Regiment supplied spirited music, the *True Colonist* noted next day, and after a couple of hours of dancing, the guests repaired to supper. 'To Mr Walond, the Mess-master of the Barracks, praise was due for the elegant arrangement and decoration of the long tables, and to Mr Gardiner, the confectioner of Macquarie St, loud accolades for the sumptuous provision of viands,' declared the *Courier*. Large quantities of champagne were consumed, one reporter noted, but so lavishly was it provided, he added wistfully, that there was likely to have been a good deal left over afterwards. Captain Ross proposed the Loyal Toast and the health of the Lieutenant Governor. Lieutenant Henry Kay proposed Lady Franklin, best of friends, regrettably absent but warmly in their thoughts, and then he toasted the fair Ladies of Hobart Town. Mr Knight spoke to 'the Navy', which Captain Crozier answered.

Gus spent most of the evening talking with James Calder, joined at various times by Booth, Boyes, Henry Kay and others. He was not called upon to dance, far more men than women being present, but he did have half a turn with Louisa. She had been dancing with McLeod, he said, talking intently until she left him abruptly and moved away. Seeing Bergman, she said, 'Will you be kind enough, Mr Bergman?'

She was trembling, Gus said, in suppressed rage and near tears, he thought, but when McLeod came up and reclaimed her, she made no objection and danced away with him again. McLeod also took her in to supper, where they continued to talk; urgently, quietly, and not altogether amicably, by the look of it. St John was in a corner with Archdeacon Hutchins and Seymour. He took old Mrs Parry in to supper.

Louisa and St John had come with Archdeacon Hutchins and his wife Rachel in their carriage, and it was planned that these four would also leave early together, before the other guests finished their supper and the dancing resumed. But when Wallace went to fetch Louisa, she was clearly unwilling to go. For a moment it seemed she would resist, then she followed him reluctantly.

McLeod stood looking after her for a moment, and then he, too, followed. St John led the way off the *Terror* onto the *Erebus*, where a servant stood waiting with the wraps, and when these were resumed, the party entered the covered way leading to the shore. McLeod caught up with Louisa and began to speak urgently with her again. Rachel Hutchins went first onto the board-way, steadied by the Archdeacon. The tide was on the turn and the planking rose and fell underfoot with a queasy half-roll. Louisa and McLeod went in next, followed by St John.

The chief witnesses at the inquest were Mr Tulip Wright and Mr Walter Nesbit, universally known as the 'Bell-Man'. He was not the town-crier, but the owner of Hobarton's only business for setting up servants' bells in the houses of the well-to-do. He had repaired and extended the old contraption at Government House the previous year, but when money grew tight that summer his trade suffered, and he worked occasionally as a coachman for his friend Mr Broughton. He was yarning with the Archdeacon's coachman when the Archdeacon and Rachel emerged from the covered way.

The Archdeacon helped his wife into the carriage and stood back to wait for Louisa to enter, but she, McLeod and St John were still some way behind. As Louisa stepped off the planking and onto the wharf, she pulled her arm away from McLeod, turned, and struck him across the face. He caught hold of her, St John stepped up to them and McLeod let go of Louisa and said something 'in a belligerent manner' to St John, Mr Nesbit reported. At that moment a young man appeared from behind the carriages, apparently coming to the aid of St John, while another man also ran in to join the melee. Mr Nesbit thought he recognised this last one as Stringer Wynn, but he could not be certain because a fight had begun and one of the hanging lamps had been knocked into the river.

Nesbit and Tulip Wright could not agree on how long it was—not long—before there was a scream, and a figure toppled and fell into the water between the wharf and the first lighter. A second figure dived in after the first. The military band had started up again to signal dancing would resume, and people were leaving the supper tables, scraping their chairs and chattering in a general movement from the *Terror* back onto the *Erebus*. Mr Nesbit did not believe these events on the wharf would have been audible or visible from the ships.

Tulip Wright restrained Mr St John Wallace, who appeared ready to leap into the water. Wallace was bloody about the head and face from a blow. After a time he ceased to struggle and fell silent. It was his wife who had fallen in, and Dido Thomas who dived after her. The whole incident lasted five or ten minutes from beginning to end. In Wright's opinion no one could have lasted long in that icy water. He believed the two drowned had become lodged under the small boats forming the causeway to the *Erebus* and *Terror*. The verdict was death by misadventure. The bodies were never found.

—⁊⁊—

It was the Archdeacon who prevented what might have been a scandal. He spoke to Tulip Wright, Nesbit, and Billy Gawler, his coachman, promising their silence would be not only honourable, but well rewarded. He then thought quickly, and chose to go straight to Ross and lay the problem before him, rather than the Governor. He told Ross there had been an 'accident', probably fatal, involving St John Wallace, his lady wife, and a convict. It had better be kept quiet—to protect reputations and ensure no pall was cast over an otherwise brilliant evening.

Ross's response was swift. He went immediately to the scene, where he, too, spoke to Tulip, Gawler, and Nesbit. The only others who knew what had happened were St John, still limp in Tulip's grasp, and McLeod, who had disappeared, two other coachmen who had only seen a fight, and two members of the *Erebus* crew on guard at the entrance to the covered way. Ross assured the Archdeacon that he would answer for them. They would say nothing. It was the one evening of the year, fortunately, when the newspapermen, who would otherwise be a danger, were out of the way safely eating—and of course drinking—at the ball.

The Archdeacon looked at Ross and said thoughtfully, 'It would certainly not do to let it be widely known that the name St John shouted and called across the water was "Dido", not "Louisa".'

—⁓—

Early next morning, the Wednesday, the Archdeacon looked in at St John Wallace, who had been brought to the Archdeacon's house and given a strong sleeping draught. Hutchins then went, by an arrangement made the night before, to meet Ross at Government House, where they would jointly tell Sir John of the drownings.

Franklin was astonished and bemused. He seemed to imagine at first that it was St John and Louisa who had died. It took some time to get things straight, but when he did understand, he, too, was adamant that no one must know of it. A short paragraph about Louisa Wallace's 'sudden regrettable demise' would be given to the *Colonial Times*, the *Courier*, and the *Advertiser* on Friday, their publication day. The Governor invited the Archdeacon to return the following evening to dine, when Ross and Crozier would be there too.

The dinner proved immensely convivial, in spite of the tragic circumstances surrounding it. Towards the end the Governor remembered to ask, 'Where is Stringer Wynn? What does he say for himself?'

Stringer Wynn could not be found, the Archdeacon said. A few days later he was discovered dead in the cellar of The Shades, a disreputable tavern.

On the morning after Franklin's dinner party, the Friday morning, the Archdeacon rose at half-past six, pulled back the curtains and said to Rachel, who was still in bed, 'I think we shall have a fine day, dear.' He went through the door to his dressing room and a few moments later she heard the servant's bell ring three times in short, agitated pulls. This was unusual. He rarely wanted a servant at this time. Thinking some article he needed was not in place, she rose, wrapped a shawl about her and entered the dressing room just as the servant arrived, but by then the Archdeacon was insensible on the floor and a few minutes later he expired.

Rachel returned to Wales and lived with her father in straitened circumstances until he died. By that time they had moved from the parish where his living had been, and my letters went unanswered.

—⁜—

I knew nothing of all this until three days after the ball. From the Tuesday night of the ball until the Friday of the Archdeacon's death, I was watching by Anna's bedside at the cottage in Minto Lane. James Seymour had said any hour might be her last, and Mrs T, Nellie and I stayed with her by turns. After a few hours I would walk home to spend time with Gus, or sleep, then return to her bedside. Even Gus did not know of Louisa's death until the Friday afternoon, when he saw it in the *Colonial Times*. He went immediately to the Wallaces' cottage, and discovered from Mrs Fludde that St John was ill in Dr Bedford's new private hospital, and was not allowed visitors. As before, his illness was more mental than bodily, although there was a head wound. He had asked to see the Archdeacon, and so they had been forced to tell him that the Archdeacon was dead. This news had worsened St John's condition. Gus decided against telling me then.

On that night, the Friday of the Archdeacon's death, Father Therry came to administer the last rites to Anna at about nine o'clock. She died shortly before midnight without waking. As I walked home with Gus I thought of her life. She was dead at thirty-eight, my own age. Beauty, wealth, rank; she had possessed them all in some degree, but what good had they brought her? She had never known a home of her own, or children, or the satisfactions of learning, or pleasant work. Had she known other joys I could not imagine? Had she been happy with Quigley? Unanswerable questions.

When we reached home and sat for a moment to warm ourselves by the fire, Gus gently told me that I must prepare myself for more bad news. There had been another death—Louisa's.

Anna's death had been long expected; Louisa's was not. A wave of anguished sorrow overwhelmed me as he spoke, and I could hardly comprehend or believe what he was saying.

'Is there no chance she can have survived?' I cried, trembling and sick with a helpless sense that this could not be real, not true. It seemed impossible, desperately unjust. I wanted it to be St John who had died.

When I could speak without breaking down, I told Gus everything Louisa had told me about her marriage, and about McLeod, which I had not felt it right to do while she was alive.

'Could that be the cause of the quarrel? Because Louisa told McLeod at the ball that Thea is his daughter?'

'If so, he seems to have denied it,' Gus said. 'But then he followed them, and said something to St John? About Dido, or the marriage, or Thea . . . which began the fight?'

'So St John may know the truth now. Oh, what will that mean for Thea? And what about Stringer Wynn? Where is he?'

'He's vanished.' Gus shook his head uncertainly. 'He's been spoiling for a fight with St John.' He paused. 'Louisa probably didn't know it, but if she did tell McLeod, it was a bad time to do so. He's been paying court to a Mrs Henderson. She's Scottish, a few years older than McLeod. Arrived three months ago from New South Wales and bought a substantial property at Magra. She was not at the ball.'

We slept at last, fitfully, and the following morning Gus would have stayed with me, but when I said I would walk over to the Wallaces' cottage, he let me go. I found James Seymour there with Jane Fludde and Thea. St John wanted Fludde to continue caring for the child, but Seymour thought it would be well if I came to visit Thea when I could. No one had seen McLeod. The office of the *Derwent Jupiter* was closed.

Fludde was composed, brisk and calm as always, but her eyes were red-rimmed. She was cautious with me at first, but gradually, as we bathed, dressed and fed Thea together, or played with her before the fire on those melancholy winter days, she softened.

After a month she told me she had two children herself, two boys of twelve and fourteen left in Liverpool with her sister. She also had a girl, five, in the Orphan School at New Town, a bad place. Louisa had promised to help her write a letter to her sister—but it had never been done, somehow. It could be sent to the corner shop. The shopkeeper had a son living foreign and was always fetching letters from the post office. He would read it to her sister. I wrote a letter at Fludde's dictation and posted it, gaining her strong approbation. My reward was to take Thea home with me for a night, while Fludde accomplished an overdue 'proper turn-out' she had been itching for.

Thea was nearly three. Always a contented baby, she was now a lively, strong-willed infant whose character looked set to match her carrotty hair. She liked Gus, patting his brown face and smiling at him, making him chuckle. Nellie Jack allowed her to stroke the old cat, carefully, and Ada and even Mrs Tench came in to dandle and smile and fuss. My heart was wrenched with pleasure and pain together as I watched her pretty ways and remembered my own children—and Louisa, and Anna.

Anna's funeral was small. She had wanted a Roman mass, which meant that few of our friends attended. She is buried in the graveyard near the old Customs House just above the harbour. The headstone carries her name, dates, and the word *Resurgam*; 'I shall rise again'.

After the funeral Mrs T came to me and said she would go. Find her sister, perhaps. I asked if she would not stay at least until the winter was over. Longer if she liked. After some demur, she did. I offered her money but she said to keep it until she was ready. In late spring she asked for it and I gave her a hundred pounds. She counted it, nodded, tucked it into her bodice and walked away with Dasher and her old pipe, and her clothes in a bundle tied at the end of a stout stick, leaving Aristo with us.

Nellie Jack moved in with Ada Sweet and her father. Old Mr Coombes had asked her to marry him but she would not. She was fond of him she told me, 'But her teeth did not allow of it.' At any rate, whatever arrangement existed between the three seemed peculiarly amicable. The Minto Lane cottage was thus empty, and Gus and I began to make plans to enlarge it so we might live there.

29

JANE FRANKLIN RETURNED FROM NEW ZEALAND IN JULY, FOUR weeks after the ball, and the newspapers at once resumed their vicious criticism of her 'unfeminine passion for travelling, which amounts to a mania'. Sir John was ridiculed for allowing her to evade her wifely duties and go rambling about the world.

'It is all Montagu, of course,' said Mrs Parry, calling on me to gossip. 'And Robert Murray.'

'But why? What have the Franklins ever done but forgive Montagu his trespasses?'

'The Arthurites blame them for everything. The ending of assigned convict labour, the low state of business—the unseasonal rain. And forgiveness, humph!' She threw up her thin old hands, heavy with rings. 'Forgiveness from those one hates is like salt rubbed into a wound. Montagu loathes the Franklins and blames Jane for his failure to achieve any preferment in England.'

'But she wrote references and letters of introduction for him!'

She shrugged. 'No doubt he suspects she acted as he would have done himself—write in laudatory fashion, and then write again privately to convey a worse opinion. To the pure all things are pure; to the suspicious everyone is corrupt.'

'Isn't Montagu looking for a new house? Are his thoughts not sufficiently occupied between that and Government affairs?'

'He cannot find a house, or not one he can afford. He wants the grandeur of "Stowell" at half the price. Which only increases his dissatisfaction until he goes about like the Devil, seeking whom he might devour.'

By this time my quarrel with Sophy had lasted two months and seemed beyond repair. She sent no note or card when Anna and Louisa died, and contrived not to see us at the Archdeacon's funeral. I was sorry, but also rather guiltily relieved. Sophy's friendship was demanding, often forcing me to leave work I was enjoying to answer her pleas for company or help. In any case, the happiness of my life with Gus left no time for regrets.

I was therefore astonished one afternoon about a week after Jane's return, when Durrell hurried in to say the Governor's carriage was at the door with the Governor's ladies, asking if they might come in. It was a day when I had Thea, and I went out with her in my arms to greet them. Jane, Sophy, Eleanor and Miss Williamson had come to invite us to a final private dinner the Franklins would give for Ross and Crozier before the Magnetic Expedition sailed in a few days.

'Oh, you little love,' cried Eleanor, taking Thea into her arms. And with this distraction, and their interest in our tiny cottage, and the desperate attempts of Durrell to produce a creditable tea, Sophy and I were able to exchange a few words again. Jane, who was still hobbling from the injury to her ankle in New Zealand, drew me aside in Durrell's vegetable garden and wished me happy in my marriage, adding in a lower tone, 'I was shocked beyond expression to hear of Louisa Wallace's death. A dreadful business. And the Archdeacon's so quickly following! I am sorry too, about your friend Mrs Rochester— but Louisa!' She shook her head.

I was wondering whether Sophy had decided to say nothing of our quarrel, or whether Jane had wanted to be a peacemaker—or had chosen to ignore what she preferred not to know.

On the night of the final dinner with 'the Captains', Jane's limp was still evident, but she was in excellent spirits. At one end of the reception room a table held a display of beautiful Maori gifts—and one object out of keeping with these. It was a double-bed patchwork quilt pieced by convict women on the *Rajah*, newly arrived. Miss Kezia Hayter, the matron on the voyage, had persuaded the women to make the quilt as a gift to Mrs Elizabeth Fry, the famous Quaker prison visitor in London, their benefactress, and Miss Hayter's friend. The fabrics came from the sewing pouches that Mrs Fry's London Ladies Committee supplied to every convict woman transported. Miss Hayter had asked Jane to have the gift sent home to England, and also to help establish a Ladies Committee in Hobart, to visit female convicts.

'I have a bad conscience about Mrs Fry,' Jane admitted with a rueful smile. 'Four years ago, before we left London, I promised to send her a report on the Situation of Female Convicts in the island, and . . .' she groaned, 'it is still not done.'

But once the Ladies Committee was begun, the report would be easy. She was counting on me for the Committee—but it must wait another month; Sir John was to tour the Richmond region in early August, and she would go with him. It was a perfect opportunity to call on Captain Booth's brother James, who had now arrived in the island and established himself and his family in a handsome stone house on the road into Richmond, about half a mile from the town. James Booth's years as a naval Captain meant the visit was essential, even without their friendship for 'our' Booth.

—⁓—

In the end the first meeting of the Ladies Committee did not take place until early September. It was 'by invitation', but Jane must have invited quite a number, I thought, because she was plainly mortified by the few who arrived on the designated evening. Apart from Jane herself, there was Miss Williamson, Miss Kezia Hayter, myself, and four women I did not know. No Sophy.

I had assumed Miss Hayter would be a Quaker like Mrs Fry, but she was not, although she was devoutly religious. She was small, dark, pretty, and at twenty-four, much younger than I had expected. She blushed when Jane gave her good wishes on her engagement to Captain Charles Ferguson, Master of the *Rajah*. At that first meeting we accomplished only the formal request that the Governor be Patron of our Society and his wife Patroness, and the business of our name. After three hours of a discussion at once convoluted, pedantic, heated and inane, we voted to call ourselves 'The Society in Aid of the Measures of Government for the Religious and General Instruction of the Female Convicts of Van Diemen's Land', a title which owed more to irritable exhaustion than consensus.

At the second meeting a fortnight later, the membership had dwindled to four. We sat in a row like schoolgirls for an hour while Jane read aloud a draft of her report to Mrs Fry, plainly anticipating a chorus of approval at the end. Instead there was dismayed silence. Her harsh criticism of the convict women was particularly severe against those who returned to the Female Factory to bear illegitimate children. They must be separated from their babies immediately after the birth, in Jane's view.

The more we politely demurred, the more adamant she became. Maternal attachment, she argued—always supposing these women capable of feeling any such sentiment—must be sacrificed for the welfare of the child, whose future would best be ensured by removing it from the pernicious influence of the parent. We protested that this would make these children virtually orphans at birth. Jane nodded approvingly; the Orphan Asylum would raise and educate them properly. The meeting ended with dissatisfaction on all sides.

As I was trying to leave quickly, Jane called to me. 'Harriet! Could you spare a moment?'

I had never felt less in sympathy with her than I did just then, but she was a friend, and tonight she looked . . . 'forlorn' was the word that came to mind. Dejected and lonely.

'Your friends at Richmond, Harriet,' she said when we were seated again. 'What are they saying about this Coverdale Affair, as the newspapers call it? Do the locals really blame Sir John, or are Robert Murray and his cronies making a mountain out of a molehill again? Don't be afraid to tell me the truth. I need to know.'

Another awkward matter. I knew from Mrs Chesney that many at Richmond, formerly strong supporters of the Franklins, were angry about what they considered to be Sir John's unjust treatment of their popular young doctor, John Coverdale. Coverdale had been the subject of a complaint, and there had been an enquiry, with a verdict that the doctor should be merely reprimanded. But the Governor had dismissed him, and the decision was deeply resented.

Before I could answer, Jane added, 'In reality it is neither mountain nor molehill, but a sign that Montagu is scheming again, plotting against us.'

'What makes you think Montagu is behind it?' I asked.

She looked at me directly, and said, 'You know my husband, Harriet—his dislike of paperwork. Montagu put the order for Coverdale's dismissal in front of Sir John and recommended him to sign—and John did so, without knowing the full circumstances.'

With his mind on matters more congenial to him, I thought. His new lighthouses, and his ideas for a naval base here, the Observatory . . .

'And why shouldn't he sign?' Jane continued, 'If his Colonial Secretary tells him to?'

'But why would Montagu want Coverdale dismissed?'

'Oh, Montagu doesn't care about Coverdale. His aim is to disgrace us. To make my husband look a fool. I begin to believe he plans to bring about our dismissal—because he loathes us, or in the hope of claiming the Governorship himself. He kept quiet while Ross and Crozier were here, but now they're gone, these attacks begin again.'

'But there's been a petition from Richmond?' I said, 'And Coverdale is reinstated?'

'Sir John has ordered his reinstatement; Montagu refuses to comply. He accuses me of drawing up the petition, of inciting the Richmond people to protest—in order to give my husband an excuse for reversing a bad decision!'

'Mrs Parry says Mr Aislabie has written to the *Colonial Times* admitting that it was he who got up the petition . . .'

'Yes—but Robert Murray won't publish it. I doubt any of the papers will. The Derwent Bank—Montagu is of course a Director with Swanston—holds the mortgages on all the newspapers in the island except Gilbert Robertson's. . . .'

I said what I could in the way of comfort, thinking all the time how frustrating it must be for her. If she were Governor, she would out-manoeuvre Montagu, but instead she could only watch and be loyally silent as her husband blundered on. When I reported the conversation to Gus, he thought Jane had good reason to be worried, and at the next meeting of the Ladies Committee, there was more evidence of this.

I arrived late and most reluctantly for this third meeting, on the tenth of October—to find Jane alone in the room, pale, furious, melancholy.

'Montagu has won,' she said. 'He and his cronies, Murray and the Macdowells. Swanston. I have been made to look an utter fool. Miss Hayter has withdrawn from the Committee and refuses to have any further dealings with female convicts. All on account of a vicious, contemptible attack in the press.'

The newspapers had been flung on the table; two articles declaring it immoral for respectable women, especially unmarried ones, to associate with convict females. The other three women on the Committee had immediately resigned too. There was also an article in a London newspaper charging her with 'petticoat government' and interfering in matters of her husband's office. The piece had been written by Murray and sent by him to London months ago.

'To be vilified by the local press is one thing,' Jane said, her voice unsteady. 'I am accustomed to it—as much as one can ever be. But to be pilloried in London! The lies and distortions these colonial papers stoop to are not known there. Some will choose to believe their calumny.'

She looked ill and I felt sorry for her. Her hair had begun to fall out again, as it had before when she was suffering with nerves. Marie had been able to dress it so that it hardly showed, but Marie had left to be married. She and her lieutenant were settling at the Huon on ten acres, which, Gus told me, Jane had given them on generous terms. The new maid, Stewart, was less skilful with hair, better with a needle.

—⁂—

There was a lull of two weeks then, although the newspaper attacks on Jane did not stop. I was at the 'Palace' in early November working on a portrait of Tom, which Jane intended for his mother Isabella, when Sophy rushed in, furious. An hour before, she and Aunt had been at work in the anteroom when Nuncle came in, greatly agitated. Montagu had been with him for *three hours* complaining of Jane. He claimed she had made slanderous 'insinuations' about the Arthurites and Montagu—to Forster!

'As though Aunt would speak to Forster about Montagu!' Sophy cried. 'Or about anything of importance! But Montagu is so plausible—and my uncle so little accustomed to dealing with barefaced liars—he does not know what to believe. He asked Aunt, "Have you said anything which could be so misconstrued?" and then to me, "And you, Miss? Have you been interfering? You had better tell me if you are in any doubt."'

Sophy paced about until Tom calmed her again.

'And Aunt replied, "How can you ask us, John? What kind of fool must I be, to criticise Montagu to Forster? This is ridiculous. He wants to drive a wedge between us. How I wish you had called me in to answer him directly."'

Jane then wrote to Montagu without telling Sir John, denying all his accusations and strongly objecting to his method of tackling her husband behind her back. Montagu replied, not to Jane, but to Sir John. He had been monstrously insulted, called a liar. He would never again enter Government House while Lady Franklin was in residence, nor would he allow his wife to do so. He began a policy of working to the letter of his duty, making everything as awkward as possible for the Governor.

He had previously been used to dealing with about half the paperwork himself, trivial matters which only wasted the Governor's time. Now he did nothing: every scrap of paper, every change of time for a meeting, every most minor issue, was laid before Sir John. While feigning reticence, Montagu also made sure his rift with the Franklins was widely known. The Arthurite *Van Diemen's Chronicle* redoubled its viciousness; the Arthurite MacDowells called a public meeting to discuss the Governor's inadequacies; hecklers disturbed Franklin's public speeches and jeered the Vice-Regal carriage.

—⁂—

This year's Regatta was postponed until February in the hope of better weather later in the summer. Rain had deluged the last two Decembers.

'Thank Heavens! One less thing,' cried Jane Franklin. 'All I want now is peace and obscurity.'

But the Horticultural Society Prizegiving was in late November. She had promised to judge the Best Potato Bed, the Best Small Garden, the Best Vegetable Plot, the Finest Compost. For a whole long hot day she must go about in the carriage admiring rhubarb, mangelwurzels, leeks, geraniums, mixed herbaceous borders; remembering names, accepting jam, posies, giant marrows. A retinue was essential: Sophy and Eleanor, Miss Williamson and myself.

We were running late that morning. Sophy had lost a shoe. We waited in the carriage. It was found; we were away. A hundred yards outside the gates there was a disturbance. A small woman with a child in her arms, shouting at the open carriage, trying to stop it, calling and waving as it left her behind.

'Oh stop, please stop!' I cried. It was Jane Fludde, with Thea. I was out before the carriage halted, ignoring the cries of Jane and Sophy, waving the driver on, turning to run back. As the horses pulled away again, I thought I heard Sophy say, 'Well, honestly . . . !'

Fludde's face like stone. Trying to find me. St John. Thea must go into the Orphan School. Today. She, Fludde, had tried to argue. He was adamant. Whereupon she had run from the house with Thea. 'But why, why?' Because she was a child of sin.

He opened the door himself. An angel of death. Thin, hollow-eyed, saintly.

'Ah, Harriet. I have been expecting you.' Calmly.

He led me into his study. Fludde and Thea went to the parlour.

'Why?' I asked.

'Because she is no child of mine, but McLeod's bastard.' Righteousness disguising a perfect revenge. Did he know it, or not? He gave a smile before adding, 'I thought you and my wife were such friends, Harriet. I made sure she would have told you.'

He could not say their names. A perfect day outside, excellent for viewing marrows and posies. I opened my mouth to say, *but Louisa did tell me*, and begin the long argument, but before I could start, he cried in triumph, 'So she *was* ashamed, or she would have told you. She never showed any sign of remorse to me, no flicker of guilt. Corrupted to the core. It will be no use to argue with me, Harriet. I have thought and prayed and made up my mind. I shall go to India again, where I shall soon die. No English constitution survives long in that climate. In this reduced state I shall not last. The child shall become Mr Ewing's ward.'

He smiled at me, his face beautiful, kindly. 'I thought at first of taking her with me to India to die beside me, but this is the better solution. She is a child of this colony. Her fate shall follow its fortunes.'

My mind was filled with a violent hot wind, burning but not consumed, beyond fear, fury, beyond pain, searching.

'How do you know,' I said, 'that Thea is McLeod's child?' Merely enquiring. As calm as he.

He smiled. 'Louisa told me so herself. She told McLeod at the ball.'

'What did McLeod say? Did he confirm it?'

The smile faded. 'No. But why should he?'

'Louisa was angry with you these last months. She would have said anything to hurt you.'

He looked at me, acknowledging the truth of it.

'Louisa never showed any sign of guilt or remorse to you,' I said slowly, musing, as it were, 'nor to me. She did not tell me McLeod was the father—and yet she did talk about other intimate matters. Your marriage, for instance . . .' I paused, watching St John's face. Blank, but a slight flicker. I added, 'McLeod does not acknowledge the child—and this sudden claim came out when Louisa was very bitter against you. Are you very certain Thea is not your child?'

'Yes,' he said, adding, 'The child has ginger hair. She resembles McLeod.'

I made a movement as though I would rise and leave, saying, 'Am I wrong in thinking—Louisa said—your sister Mary has auburn hair?'

He did not reply, stared into an imaginary distance.

'If Thea was your own child,' I said, 'would you wish her to go to the Orphanage? Is Ewing the best guardian you can imagine? Gus and I would . . .'

For a terrible moment I thought I had overplayed my hand. Cursed myself, cursed St John, willed him to fall dead at my feet.

'Bergman? You?' He was astonished.

'I cannot bear children of my own, St John.' I did rise now, forced myself to move towards the door. Nina would have been proud of me. Casually, I continued, 'And Fludde, of course, Fludde could come to us as nursemaid still.'

I knew he had a soft spot for Fludde. He approved of her reticence, her stoicism. But nevertheless, it seemed he was going to let me leave. He sat silent, unmoving. My mind searched for delay. I looked at him, noticing the first grey hairs in his side-whiskers; they only made him look wiser, more distinguished. Behind his head were chintz curtains Louisa had chosen, beneath his feet the India carpet she had bought in Kolcutta, badly worn at one corner, which we had decided to put under the desk. Smiling, my mind in a red rage, I decided that if he said nothing further I would simply go to Fludde on my way out, seize

Thea and take her. Gus would disapprove but he would understand and help me. The veins in my neck throbbed. I felt ill. I reached the door of the study, turned and said mildly, 'You will let us know, St John, before you sail?'

'Wait, Harriet. You really believe she would have . . . That she tried to deceive me . . . That Thea is truly . . .'

And it was done. By a mild smile and a great lie, I secured Thea and Fludde to myself and Gus. There was much more to endure, of course: two weeks of ghastly fear that St John might renege on the promise I exacted then—but in the end it was done. Gus, after his first astonishment, took no persuading. 'How the devil did you manage Wallace?' was all he said at first. When I explained he shook his head at me, smiled, and said he must speak privately to McLeod—who would only say he was about to marry Mrs Henderson, whom he had been courting. She was childless and preferred to remain so.

Gus also stipulated that St John must allow us to adopt Thea legally, which, to my distress, delayed matters further until the documents could be drawn up. I was in an agony of apprehension until the ink was dried on the last line and St John Wallace on his way to England, where he would farewell his sisters before leaving for India. But long before then, it was as though he were already far from this colony in his mind, gone forward to the fatal task he had set himself. He signed the papers almost absentmindedly, kissed Thea and bade her be a good girl, telling her they would meet again in a better place.

—⚭—

During those harrowing weeks of waiting until Thea was finally ours, my mind was wholly occupied with her, with St John, Fludde, the progress of the legal papers, and my gratitude to Gus, who calmly brought it all to fruition. I had no feelings left to spare for anything beyond. And yet when I look back, the 'Barrow Letter' remains for me the perhaps the strangest episode of those months—all the more because it carried echoes of Louisa's life.

Henslowe, Sir John's secretary, who told us about it, believed Montagu was behind this too, but I cannot be sure. The Colonial Secretary's malignant influence seemed everywhere at that time, and some crimes of which he was innocent may have been added to his score.

It came in late November, a glowing sunny morning: not quite summer. There were patches of high wispy cloud and the promise of a warm day. Henslowe took the private mail into the small breakfast room and put it beside the Governor, who looked up from his plate and set down his knife. He pushed aside the top items and pulled out the fattest. Jane was not yet downstairs.

'Ah, from John Barrow. A good start to the day,' Sir John said to Sophy, who was sitting beside him.

The packet was unusually bulky, Henslowe said. Sir John leaned it against the silver cruet set in front of him while he finished his meal. And then, Henslowe continued, Miss Cracroft put down her teacup and picked up the letter—which was odd, startling. She would not, as a rule, touch Sir John's correspondence—and the next thing she had risen from her chair and was walking rapidly to the door, taking the letter with her.

Sir John had meanwhile turned away towards Mrs Wilson, who had just brought a fresh pot of coffee to the table. When he turned back, the letter was gone.

'Henslowe . . . ?'

'I believe Miss Cracroft took it upstairs, sir,' said Henslowe, only just recovering from the shock of seeing it happen.

Sir John hesitated, looking displeased, put down his cup, rose and went out. Mrs Wilson looked at Henslowe but he would not meet her gaze. She picked up the cold coffee-pot—it was a good thing it was empty, Henslowe said—left the room and had begun to cross the hall when she froze and dropped the pot, because a bloodcurdling noise had come from upstairs, a terrible roar like that of an animal in pain.

It came again, a great bellow this time, which must be Sir John because there was no one else it could be, although Henslowe had never heard anything like it before. He ran out of the dining-room and started up the stairs but stopped abruptly near the top when both he and Mrs Wilson distinctly heard Sir John shout, 'How dare you, madam! How dare you! You have ruined me with my oldest friend. And as for you, miss . . . Go away from me! Get out of my sight. I cannot bear to look at you. Go to your room. I shall speak to you later.'

They had burned the letter. There it lay, a heap of ashes on the hearth. Jane and Sophy stood beside it, heaving with emotion. Sophy ran from the room. Jane's explanation, given to Sir John first, and then Henslowe, and afterwards written to her sister and repeated to Mary and George Boyes, is patent nonsense. She said she had ordered Sophy to throw the letter in the fire because she wanted to save her husband from a rupture with his old friend Sir John Barrow. She claimed Barrow had written things painfully critical of Sir John, based on ill-informed reports sent to him by his son Peter, catechist at Point Puer. Peter Barrow blamed the Franklins for the fact that he had not been chosen to go to Norfolk Island as aide to Maconochie, whose opinions on convict matters Peter now wholly endorsed.

Sophy and Jane were immediately sent to New Norfolk for 'a rest'—but it was banishment, and they knew it. They had been there a week when Jane suffered an 'attack', and first Dr Turnbull and then Seymour went up to see her. Her writing arm was limp, almost useless, and she complained of feeling weak and ill. She spoke of sailing home to England without her husband—something hardly believable. Only with the coming of Christmas, a month later, was some measure of family unity restored. Jane and Sophy were allowed to return to Hobart for the celebrations, which were even more subdued than the year before.

What was really in the Barrow Letter? Was this another attempt by Montagu to drive a wedge between the Franklins? Did he get hold of something damaging to Jane, while he was still in England, and give it, or send it, to Sir John Barrow? They had been warned it was coming: that is the only thing Sophy has ever said to me about it. I cannot help thinking it was a copy, or even the original, of Jane's passionate farewell letter to Rudolf Lieder in Egypt. It is not impossible. There were people in Van Diemen's Land who were friends of the woman who later became Lieder's wife. I can think of nothing else Jane would have so desperately wanted to conceal from her husband.

Whatever it was, Jane's powers of language eventually repaired the damage, although scars remained. Weeks later she wrote to Barrow, and he was persuaded to resume his friendship with Sir John. The longest shadow fell on Sophy. Her uncle never fully trusted her again. He wanted to send her home at once, but Jane managed to dissuade him.

—⁂—

In mid-December, while all this was happening, there came a letter carrying another blow. A grief-stricken note from John Gould told us Eliza had died in August, of a fever following the delivery of her sixth child. This was so terrible to me that even now I cannot write of it without burning tears. With her death I lost the last vestige of any desire to return to England.

—⁂—

All through this time, the newspapers continued their attacks on Jane, the most vicious and ill-founded being in the *Van Diemen's Chronicle*, set up only six months before by Thomas Macdowell, former editor of the *Hobart Town Courier*, and his brother Edward, formerly Solicitor General, both close friends of Montagu and Swanston. When the paper began, Montagu had asked Sir John for permission to issue news bulletins from his office to the *Chronicle* alone, thus making it an unofficial 'gazette'. The Governor agreed, and the *Chronicle* proclaimed in its pages that it 'afforded its readers the only authentic official information in reference to Government matters'. Now, however, when Franklin called Montagu in to ask him to have the attacks on Jane stopped, Montagu denied any connection with it.

'But of course you are connected with it! Do you not recall asking me for a subsidy in June or July? And for permission to pass bulletins from your office? Are not the Macdowells your particular friends?' said the Governor, astonished.

Montagu shook his head. 'Much as it pains me to refer to it,' he said, 'you must know, sir, that your memory—or lack of it—is the great joke of the colony. My own memory, by contrast, is known for its accuracy. If it comes to a challenge, which of us will be believed?'

The Governor gaped at Montagu for a moment, Henslowe said, as though he could not believe his ears, and then replied, 'And you consider that the manner in which you have just addressed me—confounded impudence—is not a challenge in itself? You are disgracefully mistaken, sir. You had better apologise at once. I shall then consider whether to issue an official reprimand.'

Montagu stood silent, gave an almost imperceptible shrug.

'Good Lord!' said Franklin, 'Have you gone mad? You are relieved of your duties, sir. Dismissed for insolence. With immediate effect.'

Montagu grew pale, turned and left the room. He only began to grow nervous, Henslowe said, when the Governor appointed Boyes to act as Colonial Secretary until England should make a new appointment, and refused Montagu's request for another interview. He began to understand Sir John might stick to the decision this time.

'The Governor holds all the cards,' Boyes said, 'if only he can play them—which, unfortunately, I doubt.'

Montagu wrote an apology, but the Governor refused to rescind the dismissal. It was now the week before Christmas and Jane had returned to Government House from New Norfolk. Montagu sent a note begging her for an interview. She was not well and refused, but at last agreed. Montagu was in a terrible state, weeping and trembling. She felt for him in spite of all he had done. If Whitehall backed Sir John's decision, he was ruined. Dismissal for insolence from a post of Colonial Secretary was too great a fall ever to be reversed.

Montagu must have said a great deal more to Jane than she ever repeated, but after a time they were both weeping, she admitted. She told him his letter of apology was so formal it sounded insincere. They rewrote it together. Sir John, not knowing Jane had largely composed this second letter, was so affected by it that he almost relented, but decided he must not give way. This was the turning point. Montagu was convinced that the Franklins had planned this last humiliation: Jane making him recast the letter while secretly knowing it would be useless. His fury redoubled and he arranged to leave immediately for England, repeating to anyone who would listen: 'I'll sweat him, see if I don't. I'll persecute John Franklin as long as he lives.'

The Franklins now prepared to endure an anxious wait: eight months, at least, to hear whether Montagu's dismissal was accepted by the Colonial Secretary in London, Lord Stanley. Jane suffered a relapse. She could not help thinking fearfully of several earlier dismissals—the former Treasurer, Mr Gregory, was one—so reluctantly and with such grating unpleasantness approved by Lord Stanley. If the decision should fall the wrong way, it would be Sir John and not Montagu who suffered.

—m—

The Great Census was supposed to be taken on the first day of 1842, but Arthur Sweet, who was in charge of completing the form for the 'Palace', celebrated the New Year with Tom Cracroft and several bottles of claret, port and other spirituous liquors. The result was that he did not fill in the form until the fourth of January, by which time everyone had a different opinion of how many had been in the house on the last night of the old year. In the end he wrote 'forty-one', which was about right. Twenty-five servants and sixteen family and friends, and the whole place falling around them.

30

You said to write when I could not sleep my dearest, and so here I am, all obedience, thinking of you in your tent and wondering whether you are awake too, and thinking of me among your many cares. I count the days until you return, and trust the rain lashing my window has already passed over you, leaving clear skies for the remainder of your expedition.

THIS IS THE BEGINNING OF A LETTER I WROTE TO GUS ON THE fifth of April, the first anniversary of our marriage, when I was not the only one worrying about the rain. After so many postponements, the Franklins had set out for the west at last, dangerously late in the season. Autumn was not the time to begin an expedition through a region of 'impervious forests, rugged mountains, tremendous gullies, impetuous rivers and torrents and swamps and morasses', as Calder had warned them.

Gus and Calder had spent most of January on the Frenchman's track with the convict party, making ready in case the Franklins should decide to proceed with the long-planned journey, which the Montagu affair and Jane's illness had again thrown in doubt. Indeed, when they returned to Hobart in early February, Sir John told them it must be abandoned for the third summer in a row. Jane was not

393

strong and he was behind in his work, having spent the last three weeks writing a tortuous account of the Coverdale Affair to Lord Stanley in London.

Franklin was determined to lay bare now the saga of the Arthurites' power in the colony. The dismissal of Montagu was not the work of a moment. Years of treachery must be recounted, every accusation supported by copies of the minutes of endless meetings, copies of letters and sworn statements of witnesses.

Boyes shook his head and predicted this document would do Franklin more harm than all his enemies put together, but he could not dissuade the Governor from sending it. Jane relied on being able to edit it, but at the crucial time she was too ill. Inevitably, therefore, it was four times longer than it should have been, full of longwinded outrage, blustering pompous digressions.

Nobody in the colony, not even Boyes, read the document until it was published two years later in London, by which time Jane had cut it ruthlessly. The original was sent that February on the same ship that carried Montagu to England to make his case in person. When it arrived in London the wordy mass was scanned with increasing impatience, while Montagu, called in to speak to it, had only to deny each point with the dignified brevity he immediately guessed Lord Stanley would prefer. In Montagu's plausible presence the accusations were made to look like the ramblings of an old naval buffoon.

Montagu may also have taken the opportunity to point out how curiously this document differed from earlier crisp letters sent to London over Sir John's signature. Lord Stanley would not have missed the point. Either Sir John's powers had waned alarmingly, or there had been other minds at work, and Sir John's not the most cogent of them, whether his former helper had been Montagu, or disgracefully, Lady Franklin. Montagu certainly implied that he could have said a great deal more about the Franklins if he had not chosen gentlemanly reticence. But news of this treachery only came to us much later.

In the meantime Jane suddenly revived, as she was wont to do at the mention of travel, and became eager for the expedition to

'Transylvania', the old name for the wild western region of the island. An absence from town would restore them, she argued. Their low spirits were the result of three months in a man-made wilderness, with petty human malice tearing at their vitals, forests of dark intention, thickets of misunderstanding. Like any hurt animal they must drag themselves into the real wilderness to lick their wounds. Healing would come in the sublime purity of Nature. This journey might bring hardships too, but of a nobler kind. After these terrible weeks of confinement—she in her sickroom, her husband at his desk—there would be joy in the mere physical activities of riding, walking.

The orders were reversed, and Gus and Calder went up again to restore provisions and shelters as speedily as possible. Before they left, Sir John laid the foundation stone for Jane's glyptotek Museum at Ancanthe, her native botanical garden in Kangaroo Valley. This was her response to England's refusal to fund an object so unnecessary to a convict colony; she would build it herself.

In the end it was the twenty-ninth of March before the Franklins' expedition started on horseback from New Norfolk. Autumn was in the air, bright mornings fiercely cold and heavy with dew, nights suddenly freezing. The party included three more than originally planned. Sir John had intended to bring only his aide, Mr Bagot, but now Boyle, his orderly, was there too. There was Jane and her maid Stewart, Calder and Gus, and two late additions: Dr Milligan, and Mr David Burns, a newspaperman recently arrived in the island. And a dozen convicts.

Rain began on the second day as they made their way to the base camp at Lake St Clair, which they reached on the second of April. The next day they left the horses and began to walk, although Jane had her sedan chair, and on some afternoons used this. Calder had planned for the group to stay together, but when they reached the Lake he confessed to Gus, watching the rain, that he thought the party could not now hope to reach Macquarie Harbour. The narrow river gorges quickly became impassable when torrents came flooding down from the peaks. They would be forced back at some point. He asked Gus to return to New Norfolk to collect another half-dozen convicts and bring more supplies up to this camp in case of a rapid retreat.

They had allowed eight days to walk the sixty-six miles through the bush from Lake St Clair to the Gordon River, and a week to sail home on the *Breeze*, which would be waiting for them in Macquarie Harbour. The Captain had instructions not to stay at the rendezvous after the eighteenth of April. If they were not there by then, he should assume they had turned back. We expected them in Hobart on the twenty-second or twenty-fourth of April. Jane had spoken confidently of being on the *Breeze* by the sixteenth, Sir John's fifty-sixth birthday. And here was another reason, I believe, why Jane was determined to continue with the expedition. If they had been in Hobart on the Governor's birthday some kind of celebration would have been inescapable. In their present mood they could not bear the idea. The pity of friends would be as hard to stomach as the crowing of enemies.

There was no sign of the party on the twenty-second or twenty-fourth—nor a week later. And no news of them from the Lake St Clair camp. The *Colonial Times* and the *Courier* spoke of the 'doomed expedition', which they reminded readers they had always condemned. Boyes, now acting Colonial Secretary and therefore officially in charge of the colony in Sir John's absence, remained sanguine until the first of May, when he received a note from Gus, still waiting at Lake St Clair. The rivers were in spate, and he believed the party must be trapped between two flooded canyons.

There was an enclosure in this for me, and I learned for the first time that Gus was not with the main party, and rejoiced selfishly and too soon. By the twentieth of May, when they were a month overdue, the papers could talk only of the 'lost' expedition. The weather was bitter. Sophy and Eleanor were not speaking to each other because Eleanor had said they must be dead, and Sophy had said it sounded as though she wished them to be, and Eleanor had said Sophy was wicked and horrid, and Sophy had said where was Eleanor's religion now? Gus and his convicts set out from Lake St Clair to search, taking as many stores as they could carry.

On the twenty-fourth of May, over a month late, the *Eliza* came blithely up the Derwent carrying the Franklins safe and sound. By the skin of their teeth they had reached the *Breeze* before it departed, but the ship had then been imprisoned for nearly three weeks in Macquarie Harbour, unable to get out of the vast bay into the open sea through 'Hell's Gates', the dangerous narrow opening. Once through, they had met the *Eliza* and transferred into her.

Invited to dinner to hear of the adventure, I could not help laughing at Jane's account of their adventures: Stewart's reckless bravery, the plum pudding Jane had kept secret until her husband's birthday and carved into slivers, a slice for everyone, convicts as well. By this time they had been living on three ounces of salt pork a day each. Mr Burns, the journalist, read *Master Humphrey's Clock* during the days of waiting in the bush, his tears at the fate of Dickens's Little Nell joining with the ever-falling rain. But at every mention of snow, sleet, freezing conditions, swollen rivers, I fought down a rising terror, and when I returned home that night, I went into Thea's nursery and sat by her little sleeping form and prayed and wept. There had been no news of Gus and the convict search party since they left Lake St Clair.

A week later came the fourth anniversary of Booth's being lost and found, and he and Lizzie came to town for a dinner at Government House. I was invited again but could not bear to go, my mind now half-paralysed, able to think only of Gus. Booth and Lizzie called on me next day. Thea, three-and-a-half now, was eight or nine months older than little Amy Booth, but the two infants were much intrigued with each other. While the two little girls carefully examined each other and Thea's playthings, Booth told me Jane had dissolved into tears while speaking of Gus's party. She had said she would gladly bear the expense of every possible further extension of the search. Booth reminded me that he had survived, alone and without food. Gus, with plenty of supplies, would easily do so. He and his men were no doubt holed up snugly somewhere, waiting out the weather. I was comforted—until they were gone.

Booth had also received good news. The steamship affair was settled: he was exonerated. And he was to be Supervisor of the Orphan School at New Town. The Reverend Ewing had been stood down after the Board of Enquiry found his behaviour indecent in more than one case. While I rejoiced for Booth and Lizzie, dragging words together to respond to their pleasure, smiling over the two lovely infants, it was difficult for me to attend properly to anything but my growing fears for Gus. It was only later that I began to think of the ironies of Booth becoming head of the orphanage. Did he ever think of his own children by Caralin? Wonder whether they were in an orphanage somewhere in the West Indies?

I had already learned during these weeks that fear permeates one's whole mind and body like an illness. In the first week or two when Gus was missing I was merely restless, so that only certain kinds of physical activity brought relief. Fludde and I pushed Thea in the baby carriage all the way down to Sandy Bay beach on several days when it was not too wet or cold. The sight of her little figure made plump by outdoor mufflers and bonnets could always make me smile—and yet I was reluctant to leave the house in case news came while I was away. Poor Durrell seemed to feel the same. He pruned the huge mulberry tree, sawing for days and stacking the wood, while Fludde and Thea and I gathered the twigs and leaves and built a damp winter bonfire. Whenever Durrell caught my eye he would say in a long nodding flow, 'All is well, yus, yus, and all shall be well, yus, and all manner of things shall be well, yus.'

Long after Fludde had taken Thea in, rosy with cold and running about, I stood in the dusk feeding and raking the smouldering heap, half praying, watching the smoke rise into the windless air until I was driven inside by more rain.

Mary Boyes, Bess Chesney, Jane Franklin all asked me to stay with them. I was grateful, but could not bear any company but Durrell and Fludde and Thea—and Nellie Jack, who insisted on coming to stay with us. Each day of the following two weeks was more wretched than the last. All my effort went into not allowing myself to think two recurring thoughts: that Gus's party had lost the track and was wandering into the depths of the treacherous horizontal scrub, and that this was a terrible punishment for my lie to St John Wallace.

On the twenty-first of June, snow covered the mountain down to the foothills. I had eaten little for three weeks. The *Derwent Jupiter* that day carried another article about the lost party and the surveying of the track. Mr Bergman had been married only a year, they wrote, to a widow, Mrs Harriet Adair, companion to the late Mrs Rowland Rochester, both passengers on the ill-fated *Adastra*. I sat thinking over the last four years, growing colder and colder, unable to force myself to get up and attend the dying fire. It seemed useless to do anything but sit there until I died.

I was saved by Nellie, who came out of bed in curl papers and nightgown, scolding me as if I were a child, re-lighting the fire, asking what Mr Bergman would say when he came home to find me 'a skellington'; how I must be brave for little Thea's sake. The tears rolled down her face and when I began to cry with her I could not stop.

On the morning of the twenty-fourth of June, Gregson arrived. He burst into tears when he saw my face and I nearly collapsed because I thought the news was bad, but he shouted, 'No, Harriet, they are found! Bear up. All is well!' Gus and four of the convicts had walked out to Lake St Clair and had been carried to New Norfolk. Gregson had sent his schooner up to bring Gus and the convicts back, the *Vansittart* and the *Eliza* being still away on the west coast searching. Now he would take me to 'Risdon', where they were recovering. Two other convicts, too weak to walk out, had been left on Sarah Island. They were rescued by sea several days later.

—◊◊◊—

When I saw Gus I wept even more. His dear face so sunken and thin! Our belief that they had plenty of provisions was mistaken. Their packs had been washed away as they crossed a river in torrent.

It was a week before we could tear ourselves away from the Gregsons' kindness, and when we returned to the cottage, to the joyous welcome of Durrell and Nellie, Thea and Fludde, we found a pile of notes and letters directed to us through the newspapers. Kind messages from neighbours and friends, people whose properties Gus had surveyed, and from people we did not know at all. Durrell had kept them in a basket and we sat before the fire together, opening them, exclaiming and exchanging pages or reading them aloud, while Thea scribbled with a crayon on any paper she could grab.

Dear Mrs Bergman,

Please accept my sincere good wishes on the safe return of your husband. We have not met, but I have read in the Derwent Jupiter that you came to this island as companion to the late Mrs Rowland Rochester? If this is true—one cannot always believe the newspapers—we have a mutual connection in Mrs Alice Fairfax, a cousin to my husband. We understand that for some time you have been enquiring about Rowland Rochester on behalf of his family. I would be grateful to speak with you, and believe you might also wish it. I will come to you, or abide by whatever arrangement you suggest, but would be grateful if we could speak privately.

Yours faithfully,

Catherine Fairfax.

—w—

She was not late, but I had been waiting half an hour at the window by the time she came walking along. She looked at the cottage and then at the other side of the road. This small place was not what she had expected. It was early July, cold but bright. Gus and I had decided that Catherine Fairfax might be more inclined to speak if it was only she and I together. Gus had business in the town in any case. He would return in the middle of the day to see how we progressed.

The removal of bonnet, gloves, cape allowed us time to consider each other. She was dressed with care and taste in a grey costume elegantly piped with black along the seams. I was in grey too. I saw it cross her mind that we were alike. A similar age and height, her hair darker than mine. Both our faces a little too thin and worried. She carried herself more gracefully than I, perhaps accustomed to regular horse-riding, I thought.

'You were Anna Mason's friend,' she said when we were seated by the fire. 'I am sorry for her passing. Her life was difficult, I know.'

'You were Catherine Tyndale?' I asked. 'Your husband is Rowland Fairfax? Is he still alive? Does he know you are here?'

She nodded, half-smiling. 'He would have come with me, but he is in poor health, not equal to the journey these days.' She hesitated and then added, 'You have spoken to Booth, of course. And therefore you know, probably, or have guessed, that Rowland and I have lived as man and wife for seventeen years, although it was impossible for us to be truly married. Our lives have been shadowed by this secret. No one else knows it. Not our daughter, nor my parents . . . only Alice Fairfax, who has written faithfully over the years.'

'You have corresponded with Alice Fairfax?' I asked in astonishment. 'She has always known where Rowland was? Why did she not say so?'

She smiled, shook her head. 'Poor Alice. They say women can't keep secrets but Alice has kept this one. It has been the guilty pleasure of her existence—and as I said, the bane of mine. Alice's husband died two years after their marriage, as she must have told you, leaving her with nothing. She loved her cousin Lucy—they were brought up as sisters—but she never could abide Lucy's husband, old Mr Rochester. I believe she kept the secret to spite him at first.'

'But why did she not tell Edward Rochester after his father died?'

'She was afraid by then. She had enjoyed the secret at first when it seemed she was helping Rowland, but like all secrets it took on a life of its own—grew and twisted, and she began to understand that she did not know the whole story. Alice told you, I think, that Rowland went to Spanish Town to arrange the marriage for his brother—but she did not know Rowland had fallen in love with Anna, nor that they had married before his father could prevent the match.'

'But why should he prevent it?' I asked. 'Surely he did not care which of his sons married Anna? It was only the dowry that mattered to him?'

'Not quite. What Alice did not tell you was that Old Rochester suddenly claimed to have suspected for years that Rowland was not his own child, but the son of George Fairfax, Lucy's cousin. Just after Rowland left for Spanish Town, the family solicitor, the present Mr John Gray's father, grew ill, and according to Rowland's father, revealed on his deathbed that this was true . . . but whether it is we are not certain. Rowland once asked George, who denied it, but I used to think there were resemblances—and in later years, the two grew close.

'At any rate, Old Mr Rochester arrived in Spanish Town saying Rowland was not his son. But he wanted it kept secret. He wanted Rowland to return to England and marry Lady Mary Faringdon as arranged. If he did so, old Rochester would continue to acknowledge him and give him an annuity. If not, Rowland would be cut off without a shilling. In either case, he would not inherit 'Thornfield'. Put 'Thornfield' into the hands of George Fairfax's child? Never.

'When Rowland told his father he had already married Anna, the old man was furious at first, but then suddenly declared it did not matter. It was just an "Irish marriage"—a Catholic service with no legal force in England. Anna could still marry Edward. Rowland could still marry Lady Mary.

'Rowland, finding it useless to talk to his father, tried to leave the island with Anna, to sail to Demerara, where he had a small property in his own name, which he could sell. He knew he would have no other money once he quarrelled with his father. But Anna's father and brother came aboard their ship before it could sail, seized Anna and took her back to the convent. After fruitless attempts to see her, Rowland went to Demerara himself, planning to sell the property to provide himself with funds. He thought he would be back in Spanish Town before his brother Edward arrived.

'But the Slave Revolt had begun and Demerara was in confusion. Rowland sold his estate cheaply to a neighbour who had always coveted it—that was the money in his jacket when Booth found him, but the Masons had followed him and challenged him to a duel. Before it could take place, Rowland was set upon, shot, and left for dead. He would have died, he says, except for the arrival of a group of slaves who rescued him.'

Our small parlour seemed close and dim that day, filled to bursting with the strangeness of our conversation. The sky outside showed blue and fair. Fludde had taken Thea for a walk to the shore. Catherine and I were both agitated, and I suggested we too should walk, talking as we went. We girded ourselves against the cold, and Catherine resumed her story, as though she wanted it to be over.

'Most of this I only learned later, of course. When Rowland moved into the hills as our neighbour, my servants used to tell me about the sick Englishman. I went to see if there was anything I could do, and as Rowland recovered we talked. He was in love with Anna, determined to find her and take her to England.'

She looked at me directly. 'I was twenty and had been married three years. I was lonely in the hills—but that was better than when my husband did arrive—with half a dozen Barracks friends and their island women; drinking, playing cards and quarrelling into the night. My husband was hardly more than a boy, mild enough when he was not in drink, but the rum made him wild. Rowland saw my situation, and when I begged him to let me come when he took Anna to England, he was too kind to refuse. We left Saint Vincent and went straight to the convent in Spanish Town, but the nuns told us Anna had been married to his brother and the couple had left the island.'

'And that was when you collected the baby—Anna's daughter?' I said.

She stopped, her face turned red and white, and I thought she would faint. 'How did you know? You have not told anyone?'

'It has only this minute come to me. Booth mentioned that your only child was a boy, and when you mentioned your daughter . . .'

We had reached the top of the steep lane leading down to the shore at Sandy Bay. Halfway down was the rocky outcrop where I had more than once sat painting. We rested there now and she stared ahead.

'I would have told you. That's why I came. My daughter is married now and expecting a child, and I want to know whether her mother was really . . . whether there is any prospect that . . . But first I must explain. My son was sickly from birth. He died while we were in Spanish Town. The nuns saw my grief—if it had not been for that, I do not think they would have given us the baby. When Rowland first demanded to know what had happened to Anna's child, they said it had died, but a few days later they sent a servant to bring us back and gave us Maria. She was seven months old—so beautiful, so healthy. Our safety lay in the fact that Mason did not want Edward Rochester to know Anna had had a child, and so he had concealed it carefully. Nobody knew.'

She paused, wiped her eyes and said. 'Once we had Maria, everything changed between us, Rowland and I. It felt as though we were her parents. I would have done anything to keep her, and was already half in love with him because he had been so good to me. Rowland believed he had lost Anna to his brother, and being so much together, both in distress, we . . .' She paused and then continued, 'By the time we reached England we were united. I took Maria to my parents. God forgive me, I told them my husband and son had died—that Maria was the orphan child of a woman I had known. They believed anything possible in the colonies. Lies, piling on lies, I was terrified at myself, at where it would all lead. Rowland, meanwhile, went to 'Thornfield' to see whether his father could be brought to reconsider, but the old man said he had only one son now. Edward. He ordered Rowland out, threatened to have him shot or arrested on charges of trespass if he ever returned.'

'So you decided to emigrate,' I said. 'To join George Fairfax, who might be Rowland's father.'

'No!' She had spirit enough to be amused now. 'It was my parents who emigrated. It was one of the reasons why I was so eager to return to England to see them before they left. They had written to tell me they would join my brother, a Lieutenant in the Fortieth Regiment here. He had fallen in love, and sold out of the Army to marry and settle. When Rowland came back to me, we talked endlessly about what we might do—and suddenly it seemed perfectly sensible to go with them; a perfect opportunity to start again in a place where no one would know us, far away from England and the Indies.' She was recovering herself, and smiled again now. 'Well—it seemed far away then—but can you imagine what we felt eight years later when we heard the Twenty-first was to come to Van Diemen's Land? I knew my husband was dead by then, but it meant Booth would come—and all my husband's former friends in the Regiment . . .'

'So you have been all this time in the island?'

'My brother settled in the north, near Port Dalrymple, and first my parents, and then Rowland and I, joined him. Rowland had spoken with Alice Fairfax while he was at 'Thornfield'—he was always a favourite of hers—and told her the whole story. Being sentimental and romantic, as you know, she immediately wished to help. She sent him to see her cousin George, near Liverpool. He was a widower, childless, and after a year, he too, came out to the island. Someone on the ship persuaded him to buy land at New Norfolk, which he did rather hastily when he arrived—but afterwards he too came north.'

It was now nearly midday. We turned back towards the cottage for luncheon. I was eager to hear Catherine's account of what had happened at New Norfolk, but she began to tell me about Maria, now eighteen and married to the son of a prominent family in the north. Her first confinement was approaching.

'When I saw the paragraph in the newspaper, I thought of coming immediately to see you, unannounced, but Rowland persuaded me to write.'

She seemed to have difficulty in framing what she now wanted to say, but after some hesitation began again.

'Rowland says he saw no madness in Anna when they married—but she was very unlike young English women—on account of her strange upbringing. She had seen few other white children, was brought up by black servants. Her mother seems to have been alternately doting and distant. And then Anna had years in the convent. She knew things an English girl would be ashamed to know, but was ignorant of many common matters—which might make some people judge her mad.' Catherine hesitated again. 'But I have heard of women whose madness only begins after they have borne a child . . .'

I told her I believed Anna's madness had been brought about by the unhappiness of her life, adding what little I knew. She looked grateful, but only half-comforted. We walked on in silence, but as we passed St George's Church she stopped and asked me if I would go in with her and swear on the Bible to keep her secrets. She apologised. She trusted me, but this was a matter of life and death to her.

It was cold and still and silent in there that winter's day, after the sun and buffeting wind outside. There was the lectern, the great golden eagle guarding the Book, and I looked at each small brass feather and at the fierce eyes watching and not-watching me. Should Edward Rochester be told about his brother, and his niece? I thought of who would be made happy and who unhappy by the telling. I thought of the rules men had made for us women to live by, and how sometimes we must ignore these and live by our own rules. I thought of Jane Eyre and Jane Franklin struggling free of the nets cast around them, and I thought of Thea—and I told Catherine I would promise to say nothing about Maria, but Gus might feel it necessary to tell Edward his brother was here. And I put my hand on the Book and swore.

—⚹—

By the time we reached the cottage Gus was home, and as we sat at luncheon, we came at last to the matter of New Norfolk.

'George Fairfax bought the land,' Catherine said, 'and put it into the hands of a man down here called Lascalles, a magistrate but also a rogue. In the beginning we used to come to Hobarton once a year, but when the school became established we did not have the leisure, and as I said, Rowland's health is not good.'

'School?'

'My brother always wished to begin a school. A farm-school, to provide pupils with a sound basic education, but also some agricultural training. He and my father bought a property with a large house, 'Rutherlea', and began with four boys. This year we have twenty-one, from seven years old to seventeen. My mother and I are matrons, with maidservants, of course. Rowland, who has always been scholarly, teaches Latin, history, grammar. But you see how awkward it was when we stumbled on the trouble at New Norfolk. The shooting of that poor girl . . . any gossip might have revealed the secret that we were not truly married. It would have ruined the school—not only our own livelihood, but my brother's and father's.'

They had come south that February because George saw a notice of the Bridge Meeting in the *Courier,* and wondered why he had received no word of it from Lascalles. He decided to come down and see Lascalles and attend the meeting, in case it should affect his property. Catherine, Rowland, and Maria joined him for a summer excursion. Catherine's account of the episode at New Norfolk scarcely differed from what Dinah had told us. At the meeting Cousin George discovered his land had been resumed to the Government almost a year before, and sold to a friend of the Arthur faction. He was beside himself with anger. Perhaps that was what had caused his fatal attack, or perhaps it was seeing the dead girl.

All Catherine's fears had been for her daughter and the school, and when Rowland began to understand the import of what they had seen, he decided they must leave as quickly as possible. He arranged it all with Mr Alfred Stephen and the local constable, Mr Mick Walker, who promised to see to George's burial the following day. It seemed disrespectful to go, but George was dead, and if they stayed they risked everything.

Constable Walker took them downriver in a skiff and landed them at Black Snake Inn, where they could meet Cox's coach going north. Mr Stephen assured them the matter would be kept entirely quiet, in everyone's interests. At the Black Snake there was difficulty over the coach seats, and then just as they were boarding the diligence at last, they saw Booth! She was so ill with worry she had had pains in her chest all the way home. When they reached 'Rutherlea' again, she had never been so glad to see any place in her life.

St John Wallace had found them by accident. He had read a pamphlet against transportation written by her father, and called at the school while he was in the north. Her father introduced several of the schoolmasters, naming among them Mr Rowland Fairfax.

Rowland died two years after Catherine told me this story. Catherine and I corresponded until she died twelve months ago. Her daughter Maria had only the one child, a boy, a great comfort to his mother and grandmother, but he disappointed his father's family by having no interest in farming. He converted to the Church of Rome in his twenties, and by the age of thirty-four was a Catholic priest in Melbourne, where many lady parishioners apparently sighed over his dark good looks, which were believed to be of Italian origin. They were devastated when he died of a fever on a visit to Rome. They are all three dead now, he, Catherine and Maria, and I have kept Catherine's secret, as I promised, until it can harm no one.

—◊—

Lord Stanley to Sir John Franklin,

Your proceedings in this case of Mr Montagu do not appear to me to have been well judged, and your suspension of him from office is not, in my opinion, sufficiently vindicated. I find no reason to impute to Mr Montagu any unworthy or dishonest acts. He is entitled to be entirely acquitted of blame. It is gratifying to me to have it in my power to offer to him the vacant office of Colonial Secretary at the Cape of Good Hope, which he has cheerfully accepted. I have undiminished confidence in his disposition and ability.

This letter began to be distributed on street corners in Hobart that autumn. The Franklins refused to believe it was genuine, since they had heard nothing further from England, but a month later they received the original. Lord Stanley had given a copy to Montagu, and only later posted it to Sir John. The printed version had come from a copy that Montagu, in his triumph, sent straight to Forster.

Franklin was stoical, Jane incredulous. How could this happen? How dare Lord Stanley treat her husband in such a fashion, lay him open to such public humiliation? She asked the question (more than once) of Mr Bicheno, who now arrived to take the position of Colonial Secretary. He could supply no answer. He was large and benign, similar to Sir John in appearance. They made, as Jane said, 'a droll-looking pair, so alike in age and size and bonhomie'. Had they always been working together, she added, their time in the island would have had a happier outcome. This new contentment did not quite make up for the humiliations of the 'Black Book', a volume Bicheno had unwittingly brought with him, sent from Montagu to Swanston, a compilation of documents supposed to prove the Franklins' depravity, beginning with Montagu's claim that Lady Franklin was 'a scheming dangerous woman, with an altogether malign influence on her imbecile husband'. It was handed about among the Arthurites and a copy 'for the better information of the public' was available for perusal at the Derwent Bank.

Now the Franklins waited to discover whether Sir John would be replaced. They had expected this to be mentioned in Lord Stanley's letter, but there was no news until, in *The London Times* dated the 24th February 1843 and received in Hobart in July, Jane saw a notice that Sir John Eardley Wilmot had been appointed Governor of Van Diemen's Land.

Two weeks after she saw it, Sir Eardley Wilmot arrived. By error he landed on an unfrequented part of the coast—and still Sir John had received no letter of official notification that he was to be recalled. At last the *Gilmore* came in with it, a duplicate; the original arrived on the *Eamont* a day later. Forced to make a hurried, undignified, inconvenient exit from the 'Palace', the Franklins went to stay with Ainsworth, and later moved to the cottage at New Norfolk. Jane was ill with suppressed anger, Sir John almost bemused, it seemed, by the sudden turn of events. In the meantime, the *Rajah* returned, Miss Kezia Hayter and Captain Ferguson were married, and the vessel sailed again with the newlyweds and the Franklin party aboard. At Port Phillip the Franklins transferred to the *Flying Fish*, bound for England.

—⁓—

Thea called us Ma and Pa, even though she knew—we made no secret of it—that Louisa was her real mother. We said nothing about McLeod. I still don't think that was wrong. We finished rebuilding the cottage I'd bought from old Mr Coombes, adding several more rooms, and moved there. Fludde reclaimed her daughter Betty from the Orphanage, and she was brought up with Thea. A quiet child with light-brown hair and her mother's swift, interrogating, self-sufficient look, Betty, more than Thea, always wanted to draw when I drew, and read avidly from the moment she learned to. Thea would throw herself sprawling in a chair and read for a whole afternoon with an intent expression, but what she loved most was animals and an active life of walking and riding.

Every summer we spent two months living on Gus's land beside the Huon River, in a little cabin that always reminded me of Dinah Carmichael's: a great fireplace made of stones, curtained-off bed-places and a long table with chairs. The children of the family living nearest us there were three boys, who grew up almost as brothers with Thea and Betty. We rowed on the lucent tea-coloured water among the reeds and moorhens, walked on the quiet tracks between the great gums, read away wet days before the fire. Here I learned to love the landscape I had once feared, and to see in it not always beauty, but glimpses of the sublime.

31

IN 1851, SEVEN YEARS AFTER THE FRANKLINS LEFT VAN DIEMEN'S
Land, Gus, Thea, and I travelled to England for a year. Tasmania had
sent three hundred and ninety-four items to the Great Exhibition
in London, which Gus was eager to visit, and we thought Thea old
enough now to enjoy the travel and benefit by a stay in the great
city. She was thirteen that year. I was also curious to see London
again myself, although my old hungry yearning for it had long gone.
We arrived in mid-September, by which time the price of entry to
the Exhibition had dropped to a shilling and it was full of families.
Someone had written to *The Times* suggesting that a portion of the
entrance money should go towards the search for Sir John Franklin
and the *Erebus* and *Terror*, vanished six years before into the vast white
secrecy of the Arctic.

Faced with the splendour of the Crystal Palace, the huge glass
arcades, the magnificent tree growing in the main hall—the grandeur
of it all—I felt, as I said to Gus, very colonial. I admired it, and yet
could not help feeling I preferred the simplicity we were accustomed
to. Gus laughed and looked at me affectionately.

'The difference between grand and grandiose is in the eye of the
beholder, perhaps,' he said. 'We're country mice these days.'

Once inside, the Exhibition was almost beyond imagining.

'Oh, look, Ma! Pa, look!' Thea was still the bright, forthright child she had always been, only fitfully aware of being now a young lady. She pored over the machinery and tools with Gus; the working looms, printing presses, daguerreotype machines, and her favourite, the vast steam hammer which could gently crack an egg. At last I urged them on to the Russian vases twice the height of a man, the life-sized elephant statue, the plethora of clothes and textiles, the vast array of musical instruments. We bought a Tempest Prognosticator worked by leeches, and illustrated cards to send home. Like the Queen and Prince Albert, we visited three times that autumn, wandering through the crowded rooms until we were so weary we could marvel no more.

For Thea, London itself was also a great exhibition; every street an astonishment of finery and filth; trains and thronging people. For me it was much the same, but not exactly the place I'd carried in my imagination for twelve years. I felt a similar jolt of strangeness when we called on Jane Franklin. She and Sophy had been living in her father's house in Bedford Place, but had recently moved to rooms in Spring Gardens, not far from the Admiralty.

When we were first shown in to see her she seemed for a moment a stranger: a small, thin old lady wearing the kind of lace cap Jane had always disliked. But the room was familiar: Persian carpets, flowers, books, curios, the writing slope put aside on a chair. And as soon as she smiled and spoke, her personality was vivid and irresistible as ever, the sense of a quick, eager intelligence that Robert Murray and others had so deeply resented in the Governor's wife. She kissed me, took Gus's hand and pressed it, turned to Thea with a smile, 'This is Thea. What glorious hair! You are as beautiful as your mother.' She smiled. 'Both your mothers.'

Thea's hair was a glory, a joyous thing; strangers often smiled with pleasure at the shining fall of copper-coloured waves down her back. Her face lacked Louisa's madonna perfection, but I loved it all the better for the more generous mouth, the clear, considering grey eyes with no trace of Louisa's fierce blue discontent.

'What do you think of London?' Jane asked her.

'I like the zoo, my lady,' said Thea. She hesitated. 'But I do not think I should like to live here always.'

Jane smiled and said, 'You prefer your island? I'm inclined to agree with you. Hobart is very lovely.'

'I like the Huon even better,' said Thea.

'Oh, the Huon!' Jane turned to Gus. 'I suppose I should not recognise it now?'

As Gus, Thea and Jane began to talk about the Huon, Sophy drew me aside. She was now 'quite stout', as she had warned in a recent letter. Black bombazine stretched tightly across her ample bosom (always apt to heave), her troubled heart. I had come to the conclusion many years before that she did not like being young. She found it too agitating, too beset with troubling decisions: all those messy, perilous possibilities of love, marriage, children. Now she had apparently decided at the age of thirty-eight to embrace elderliness as a safe port beyond the storms of youth. She wanted to thank me, as she had already done in letters, for my attentions to her poor dearest brother Tom. He had died two years earlier in Hobart—the weak chest again. During his last illness he had lived with Mary and John Pride, who had moved to New Town.

'And now her *fifth* child by That Man!' hissed Sophy. 'Poor Mary, she always seemed so stoical, so determined not to let us see she regretted her marriage. And so we were quite unprepared for that ghastly outburst just before we left. It upset us all—as though we had not enough troubles at the time.'

In the last two weeks before the Franklins' departure from Hobart, Mary had fallen into a strange madness of grief. She trailed behind Jane and Sophy, weeping as they supervised the packing. We tried to reassure her. Tom Cracroft and Henry Kay were staying on, and she had many good friends in the town; but Mary could not be consoled—and the talk of leaving Tom sent Sophy into floods of tears.

'Our nerves were in shreds by the time we boarded the ship,' Sophy added. 'And we were desperately anxious all the way home. Not just on Mary's account. We were braced to endure more newspaper scandal over the Montagu quarrel—and we knew my uncle would never have a suitable post while Lord Stanley was in office.'

But when they arrived in London they discovered to their chagrin that nobody cared a fig about Montagu's wickedness or Lord Stanley's ill-treatment of Franklin. England was in crisis, the Government tottering over the repeal of the Corn Laws. A squabble in a distant colony was like the cry of a spoilt infant. Lord Stanley had refused to re-open the case or even grant Franklin an interview.

'It was unjust, disgraceful.'

Only the old 'Arctics' were sympathetic. Sir John Barrow had already begun preparations for a new expedition to decide, finally, the question of the Northwest Passage. He wanted his dashing young protégé, James Fitzjames, to lead it, but Fitzjames had annoyed the Admiralty and the Royal Society, and they wanted Ross and Crozier— and Ross had married his Anne at last, and promised not to leave England for two years. In May 1845, eleven months after the family returned to London, the *Erebus* and *Terror* set off with Franklin as Captain of the *Erebus* and leader of the best-equipped expedition in the history of Arctic exploration. Fitzjames was his second, Crozier was commander of the *Terror*.

All this we learned from letters at the time, and during '48 and '49 we waited for news of their triumphant return, but none came. There was still none a year later when the decade ended. Sophy's letters had begun to rage against the Admiralty, reluctant to send search vessels. Jane was raising money for a private search, churning out letters of appeal for help. The American shipping magnate Mr Henry Grinnell had subscribed $5,000, and then raised it to $10,000. After Jane's next letter he made it $15,000, and when he read the note she sent to thank him, he raised the sum to $30,000. A letter she wrote to the President of the United States was said by the MP Sir Robert Inglis to be 'the most admirable letter ever addressed by man or woman, to man or woman'.

Now, a year later, there were more difficulties, Sophy confided. 'Aunt's family have turned against her. That is why we are here in

Spring Gardens—why we had to leave her father's house. He insists she must give up spending money on the search for Uncle. He wants her to leave all in the hands of the Admiralty—who do nothing! Her sister Mary Simpkinson—and Mary's husband, and her son Frank—all support old Mr Griffin, of course.'

Eleanor Franklin, too, wished to abandon the search. She had married Gell ('the wedding day fixed without Aunt Jane's knowledge,' Sophy had written to us, her letters fizzing and crackling with fury) and by 1850 the Gells believed Sir John was dead.

'All this is sad and shocking,' Sophy's familiar handwriting had come tearing across the page. 'The Gells know Aunt has only a life income and no capital. She is living in a straitened manner, which grieves me and would astonish you, Harriet, and all our distant friends. My uncle had only the *interest* of his *first* wife's fortune, whereas my aunt gave him all hers, capital and income. If it were not for her generosity, her own fortune, or rather the remnant of it, would not now pass to the Gells.

'The Gells are opposed to sending another ship and to every plan devised by my aunt,' she wrote. 'Gell asks Jane to sign a contract that she will repay all she is spending on the search, back to the time of Sir John's death, if he is discovered to be dead. . . Gell is requesting plate, linen and pictures belonging to Sir John . . .'

The lamb-faced clergyman Jane had called 'her son' was showing the wolf beneath the skin—unless it was all done at Ella's insistence, as Sophy believed. As we talked that day in London I began to understand Jane's situation.

'While Uncle is presumed still alive, Aunt, as his agent, can spend the interest of his monies and her own on the search,' Sophy said, 'but if he is declared dead, she will lose control of his estate—and much of her own, which was given into Nuncle's control when she married. It will almost certainly become part of the residue left to Eleanor—though nobody knows exactly how the will is written.'

I asked how the search stood at present.

'There is a ship preparing in Aberdeen . . . Which reminds me . . .' She turned to Jane, and said almost sternly, 'If you are quite determined, Aunt, on going to Aberdeen, I suppose I had better go to the station and enquire about trains and tickets. For myself, I cannot believe that acting on messages ostensibly from the dead is an entirely Christian . . .'

She rang sharply for her bonnet and wraps and began fussing with purses and gloves, while Jane said, 'Leave it until later, Sophy, and then take a hansom.'

'Good heavens, no—the expense! No, of course I shall walk. My leg is almost painless today.'

'Will you allow us to escort you, Miss Cracroft?' asked Gus. 'Thea and I? We'll take you in a cab and bring you back in no time. We're immensely fond of jaunting about London—and we love railway stations—and have only a limited time to indulge ourselves.'

Sophy protested but at last capitulated, and when Jane and I were left together Jane told me this was all on account of a letter from a clairvoyant, which Sophy disapproved of. They had received such letters before, of course—too many—but this one was not in the usual mould.

'The writer is a Captain Coppin,' Jane said, 'a bluff old sea-dog, salt of the earth and briny, and what's more he's kept the matter quiet for nearly a year, which does not look to me like a thirst for notoriety. I can imagine him smoking a ruminative pipe over it night after night until at last his wife has persuaded him to write to me—about his daughters: Annie, who is ten and very much alive, and poor little 'Weasy' (for Louisa), who would have been five except that she has been dead these twelve months.'

Six weeks after her funeral, Weasy had appeared to Annie, heralded by a ball of bluish light, Jane continued. The Captain's three other children also saw their dead sister, and later the ghost-child fell into the habit of sitting at the table with them at mealtimes. The Captain, unable to see the little girl, felt at something of a loss. Casting about for conversation, he asked suddenly: was Sir John Franklin still alive?

Where was the lost expedition? Then Annie cried out in astonishment because to her the room seemed to fill with snow and ice. She saw large round childish handwriting appear on the wall, saying *Erebus and Terror, Sir John Franklin, Lancaster Sound, Prince Regent Inlet, Point Victory, Victoria Channel*, and she drew a chart at Weasy's direction—which the Captain judged remarkably accurate, though Annie had never seen such a chart before. In consequence of all this, the Captain ventured to take the liberty of suggesting that Lady Franklin's search vessels might be looking in the wrong place, since all their attention seemed fixed on the Wellington Channel.

Jane had thus determined to go to Aberdeen at once, where the little *Prince Albert*, ninety tons, was preparing to leave. She did go the following day (Sophy stayed in London). Captain Forsyth of the *Prince Albert* listened respectfully, but did not alter his course, and again, nothing was found.

But I am leaping too far ahead; we knew this only later. As we left at the end of that London visit, Jane handed me a book.

'Alfred's poetry,' she said smiling. 'Remarkable, but more your taste than mine, Harriet.'

She always preferred factual works: memoirs, travellers' tales, books about natural sciences. Poetry she considered rather rich emotional fare, allowable in small helpings, like pudding, although some of it—Wordsworth, say—could pass as philosophy or religion at a pinch. Novels she thought mostly dramatic nonsense.

When Gus and I looked at the book that night in our hotel room after Thea was in bed, we found it was Jane's own copy of Tennyson's *In Memoriam A.H.H.* Alfred was 'Family', of course, and now the Laureate. The long elegiac poem had been published the previous year, 1850, just about the time when Jane must have been facing the possibility that her husband might be dead, even if she would not admit it. A faint asterisk in pencil marked one of the verses:

The Man we loved was there on deck,
But thrice as large as man he bent

To greet us. Up the side I went,
And fell in silence on his neck.

But in the poem this was a dream, and Jane had written beside it: *So Alfred has them too, these dreams of the beloved dead.*

A week later, when we called on John Gould in Broad Street, he said, 'Lady Franklin is still refusing to admit they are dead, I suppose? Of course they are dead. Franklin should never have been allowed to go on the expedition, let alone lead it! A man of nine-and-fifty, grossly overweight, with a perpetual cough? He was only given the place because people were sorry for him over that business with Montagu.'

'The Arctic Circle is large,' said Gus mildly. 'There are many places where they might have taken refuge. It is only six years; they had enough provisions for that length of time.'

Gould shrugged and said, 'Well, I have given Jane Franklin ten pounds towards her search—though I judge it useless.'

He added with candid pleasure that he was able to give such a large amount, in spite of having children to educate, because he found himself suddenly beginning to be wealthy—and curiously enough, this was all because he had *not* been invited to display his work at the Great Exhibition! He was Europe's most famous bird collector—and yet the Committee had passed him over! So he had set up his own display in Regent's Park: a Hummingbird House.

'Have you seen it?'

We had. Gould had displayed the exquisite little birds with all his skill, poised as though they were arrested in mid-flight, hovering among flowers in their iridescent colours, their tiny impossible perfection. London had become hummingbird mad, and thousands were being slaughtered in the wild to satisfy the craze. A consequence he had not intended.

'But the real joke is that I am the *only* person made rich by the Exhibition,' he chuckled.

Those who had been invited to show in Prince Albert's Exhibition were not paid, but the Hummingbird House was making him wealthy.

He could have given Jane Franklin twenty pounds, but would not throw money away.

—⚊—

We spent Christmas that year with Jane and Rochester at 'Ferndean'. The house was beautiful and they were flourishing. Jane's memoirs had been published by then, and in certain circles she was becoming celebrated, but she was more concerned with the dame schools she had set up in Hay and Milton. She and Adèle, who was now her secretary-companion, visited the classes. Thomas, the same age as Thea, was at Eton, but just then at home for the holiday. He was rather lordly with Thea until he discovered she could shoot an arrow at a target in the barn a little better than he. He softened further when she made much of his dog, Raffy, and his pony, Tarquin; and his rabbits, his pet sheep. Rochester was a magistrate now, and owner of a prize flock of Romney Marsh, a breed he could defend at length against their rival, the Dishley Leicester. We learned a great deal about sheep during that visit. We had told them in letters of Anna's death, and Rowland's, but the subject was not mentioned.

It was the trains in England that most captivated Gus on that first visit. He never tired of train travel, nor of discovering the new surveying methods developed from cutting rail-lines across England.

When we returned to Hobarton towards the end of '52, we learned to our great sorrow that Booth had died while we were away; of heart disease, in his fifty-first year. His death was not entirely unexpected: his chest had been weak since he was lost. He knew his heart was precarious, but it never affected his cheerfulness; it only made him try desperately to economise so Lizzie would be well provided for after he was gone. But both he and Lizzie were sociable and liked to live in style, and Lizzie insisted they keep a carriage, in spite of Booth's grumbles that it wasn't necessary. Lizzie had a temper, though, and Booth hated quarrels. They were the first family in the colony to have a croquet lawn made, some years before it became madly fashionable, because Lizzie had played the game at a great house in

Dublin when she was young. And although Booth again protested at the expense (they were still only renting the mansion from Spode, never managed to buy it), there were many joyful summer days when we all (the Boyses too) played there with the children. They were a great family for games and excursions. But the result was that when Booth died, Lizzie, after fifteen years as a much-indulged wife, was almost penniless at the age of thirty-two. Amy was a year younger than Thea, Charlotte was six. Gus helped Lizzie write to the Colonial Office to secure a small pension, and she and the girls returned to England. She never married again but became Matron at several schools in Berkshire, Bath, and then at Denbigh in Wales near Ruthin, where her mother was living, also widowed by then.

John Price was one of those who showed a malevolent interest in the fate of the *Erebus* and *Terror*, but by the time we eventually heard more of the Expedition, he was dead, murdered by a group of convicts at Williamstown, near Melbourne. Seven men were hanged for it. Which, as Sophy later wrote, seemed a pity.

It was not until 1859, two years after Price's death, that we heard a cairn had been found with a message in it from the Expedition. Weasy's cairn, Jane called it in her letter to me, because it was found exactly where Captain Coppin's spirit-child had indicated—at Point Victory in Victoria Channel, Prince Regent's Inlet. Even then, the two messages found in the cannister were short and unsatisfactory. Sir John had died two years into the voyage, in 1847, and after another winter beset in ice, Fitzjames wrote a brief addition: the survivors were abandoning the ships to walk to safety via the Great Fish River. This was not enough. The search must go on.

In 1870 we went to London a second time. Thea had by then been married ten years to a young orchardist, Robert Kerr, a son of our neighbours at the Huon. They had three children: Alice, Louisa and William, to whom Thea was an admirable mother, loving but brisk, active and good-humoured. (And I found being a grandmother—which I had never expected to be—so much easier than being a mother. The same pleasures, so much less anxiety.) Robert now wanted to visit his cousins in Dundee. We would go with them as far as London to help with the children on the ship, after which Gus had arranged a two-month tour of railway workshops around England. He was charged with buying a railway engine for Tasmania's first private passenger line. I would stay with Jane and Sophy in London for the summer.

We arrived in London and waved Thea, Robert, and the children off to Scotland, only to discover Jane had changed her plans. She and Sophy must go to San Francisco and then Alaska. I must go with them.

Gus groaned when I told him. 'Jane! I'd forgotten how high-handed she . . . You don't want to do that, Hattie? More travel . . . But you can't stay alone in London all summer. I'll have to give up the tour. If we go to Leeds I can try to . . .'

He had been planning this for two years and was desperate to do it. For a moment I considered going to Jane and Rochester, but as I said to Gus, Sitka had a certain curious appeal. I had never heard of it until Jane and Sophy described it, but then it sounded to me very like Hobart. Both towns are on islands, little more than large villages wedged between mountains and sea at opposite ends of the earth. Hobart turns its back on the great Transylvanian wilderness with an air of whistling in the dark, of defiant liveliness; Sitka has the great north behind it. Hobart huddles at the water's edge gazing out towards the far distance where Europe lies, invisible but ever-present. Even at this date it still had a frontier rawness overlaid by a hopeful, sometimes desperate, gentility.

But no, said Jane. She did not believe Sitka would be like Hobart. For thousands of years it had belonged to the Tlingit Indians, who were overrun in 1799 by the Russians. The Russians held on to it until 1867, when they sold it to the Americans—and for the last three years it had been an American Army base. Part Indian, part Russian, part American; an intriguing mixture.

I will not dwell on the tedious journey, but by the fifteenth of May 1870 Jane, Sophy and I were in Sitka's harbour waiting aboard the *Newburn*, the ship that had carried us up from San Francisco, until somewhere could be found for us to stay. Sitka being small and having few visitors, it had no hotel, we now discovered. Nowhere to lodge us, and Jane's maid Marie, and a manservant, Lawrence.

Sophy, who seemed to have grown more devout, spent the days of waiting reading her old Bible and book of sermons, both of which I remembered from Van Diemen's Land: full of fraying silk page-markers, pieces of crumbling palm from long-ago Palm Sundays, and ancient brown pressed pansies. Jane's reading matter came from 'the Box', a small metal trunk holding books, charts and letters connected with the many search parties she had urged out over the years. Her eyes were very poor now, she used a strong lens for short periods. Generally Sophy or I read aloud to her—but it was hardly necessary; the Arctic was written on her heart, she said.

After three days a house was found, to rent furnished from a merchant going south for the summer. When we stepped ashore at last, it was cold in spite of the bright sun, a wind sharp as glass parting our furs and watering our eyes, whipping and rattling a flagpole nearby. We walked the few hundred yards up from the wharf to the two-storey log-house, which had a front door onto Sitka's main street. This led into a short hall, where a staircase mounted to the living quarters: sitting-room and bedroom, kitchen and dining-room. Jane would sleep in the bedroom, Sophy in the dining room, and I in the kitchen, which would not be used for cooking. Our meals would be sent in from the bakery down the street. Marie the maid was allotted a kind of cupboard in the upstairs entry, Lawrence had a corner in the hall below.

Sophy grimaced at the furnishings, neatly simple in the American style, none of the upholstered cosiness of London. Walls and ceilings were lined with boards painted an ochre colour, and the heating came from a small black stove on four legs, like some agreeable domestic pet. Through one window you could see the water and two tiny islands, each with its neat family of pointed firs. The window on the other side showed a row of sharp little mountains behind the town.

We had just finished luncheon on our third afternoon when Lawrence came in to say that General Davis, the Army Commander of Sitka, had come visiting. He proved to be a tall, spare, courteous man who deferred to Aunt with such grace he won Sophy over immediately.

'The Better Sort of American,' she said afterwards.

The General apologised for not calling sooner. He had been away on his last inspection. Alaska was henceforth to be governed from the Territory of Oregon, and General Davis and his family had been transferred to Portland. His wife and household had gone ahead, and he was here for a final week with only his manservant, otherwise he would have had the pleasure of inviting us to be his guests during our stay. A shame, we agreed afterwards, we would have liked to stay in Baranof Castle, a huge ornate wooden house named after an early Russian governor, more recently used by the Army Commander here.

'But if there is any other way in which I can assist, ma'am . . .'

Jane asked him to lend his authority to the collection or report of anything that might be connected with the loss of the *Erebus* and *Terror*. Relics of any kind, however small; stories, however wild. She would offer a reward of two thousand pounds for 'significant information' and wanted it known she would purchase 'suitable objects'.

General Davis nodded, hesitated, and said gently, 'I am ashamed to say I do not recall exactly how many years it has been now, my lady? Twenty-five?'

'Twenty,' said Jane and Sophy together. They knew their lines.

'We count it twenty,' Sophy explained, 'because although the expedition left England in May of 1845, they carried enough provisions for five years—seven at a pinch—and therefore we did not begin to consider them *truly* lost until *after* 1850 . . .'

'My husband hoped to make a speedy journey, of course,' (Jane now) 'to be home within two years. But he warned us a hard season might detain him far longer.'

General Davis replied politely that he would do what he could; that the Arctic is vast, but Sitka is the old capital, called New Archangel by the Russians, and any news or trade-able object found by whalers or fur-trappers might eventually make its way here. The Inuit, or Esquimaux, or 'Huskimay' people, he said, do not set great store by paper and were unlikely to save anything of that kind, but they keep practical objects, knives and so on. The Indians, by contrast, take excellent care of paper or books, handing them down to their children.

'Have there been other finds?' he asked.

'Many small ones over the years, but all of them more puzzling than explanatory,' said Jane. A great quantity of monogrammed silverware belonging to the ships' officers, for instance. Franklin's men seem to have lugged all their spoons and forks into a whaleboat, which they intended to drag a thousand miles over the ice—and yet they'd left behind a large supply of chocolate, when provisions would be vital? Why was this?

Sophy fetched a small package wrapped in linen and showed General Davis the spoons carrying Sir John's crest. General Davis said quietly that it was an honour to have seen them. Sophy repeated several times later that he made 'a most *favourable* impression'.

I began a letter to Gus.

> Jane was right, dearest, Sitka is not like Hobart, but I believe you would love it, and find myself continually wishing you were here to see the skill of these buildings all made of logs or planks, even the huge ones like St Michael's Church, also called the Russian Cathedral. It has an elegant onion dome of wooden shingles painted yellow, and sits almost in the centre of the town on a slight rise, with the Indian village on one side and the American Army compound on the other.

Over the next two weeks I added to this letter: a visit from the Army wives, and one from an eccentric Army Captain calling himself 'Prince Thoreau'; a visit to the Indian village. In the third week I tried to write but could not. As the sun moved towards the solstice, a strange malaise gripped all three of us. To my imagination it seemed to emanate from Jane, who was quiet and feverish with a burning desire to find some trace of the expedition. Nothing had come in. Marie and Lawrence ran away together the same week; perhaps they felt it too.

We were scarcely sleeping; day and night seemed one. There is no midnight sun in Sitka, but in the middle of summer it is never entirely dark. About an hour before midnight the sun dips below the horizon for a short time, leaving the world lit with a golden crepuscular glow, an effulgent twilight which seems to make the mind at once languid and preternaturally active. We closed the curtains at first and tried to sleep, but restlessness often drove us outdoors, where the yellow sky seemed an extension of the earth, another path waiting to be taken.

Sophy, after complaining for a week, took a heavy dose of chloral one night and fell deeply asleep. Jane and I shared a bottle of sweet yellow wine one of the Army wives had brought us. Later I dozed and then woke, lay thinking about Gus and Thea, becoming gradually aware of shuffling noises in Jane's room. It was not quite two in the morning. I heard the click of Jane's door and soft footsteps. A creak of the stair as someone descended. Clicks of the downstairs lock, a thud as the front door closed. Silence. Jane never went out alone, would never do so at night.

It took me two minutes to pull on slippers and a short jacket over my nightdress. When I emerged from the front door I could see Jane plainly, a lone figure in a white nightgown and shawl hobbling away along the empty road towards the Indian village, in the warm magical night. I ran to her, but when I came close I saw she was sleepwalking and hesitated to touch her. Her eyes were open, but glazed, fixed. I called softly, 'Jane, Jane', but she did not stop. We reached a little bridge crossing a stream where the water came rushing down from the mountains. Snow-melt, icy even now in summer. Then she wavered and veered off the road, and I thought she must stray into the water, and so caught hold of her arm. Nearby were some boulders with broad flat tops where we had rested when we walked to the Indian village, and I led her to these and sat her down, my arm through hers. She began to speak to me—in a delirium I thought at first.

'Reports of a blue-eyed woman among the Apache—snatched from settlers when she was a child thirty years ago. And Mrs Eliza Fraser in Australia found with an aboriginal tribe three years after she was thought lost in a shipwreck. And the convict William Buckley!' Jane laughed. 'What a sight for the Port Phillip survey party! Six feet seven inches tall and clad only in skins—walking out of the bush when he had been believed dead for thirty-two years! And after all,' her voice was firm, 'there have been rumours over the years of a white man living among the Inuits.'

Then I understood her forlorn hope. That somewhere out there in those thousands of miles of shimmering white there was a survivor from Franklin's expedition, England still glimmering fitfully in the depths of his ice-altered mind. Jane gripped my arm as though she would make me see it, and I thought, Oh Lord, if only it were true!

A man brought in to us in bulky furs, his nose and the lower half of his face covered by a mask of caribou skin chewed to air-penetrable softness by an Inuit woman (there would have to be an Inuit woman to have kept him alive). Suddenly he might say English words, 'God Save the Queen'. Or his own name, or the name of his leader, 'Franklin'. If only it could be Fitzjames, who still haunted Jane even more than all the others! Because he was young and brilliant, and if he had perished, lost such a future, probably while obeying orders he did not agree with.

'We have discovered nothing here,' Jane whispered. 'It is my fault.'

She felt that if only she tried hard enough, she should be able to will the objects to reveal themselves. They must be there. Two hundred metal canisters for messages, a thousand volumes of reading matter on each ship, costumes for amateur theatricals, boots, shoes, medals . . . Sometimes, she said, she tried to send her mind out like a bird speeding across thousands of miles of ice, scanning for a dark speck: a man, a ship. At other times she tried to make herself an emptiness into which the ice and wind might flow, bringing . . . what? A voice? A vision? She worried that her fears and furies made a silent chaos around her so that nothing could get through.

She had forgiven everyone now, except herself. Of course she had known her husband was too old for the voyage. He had only been given the expedition because of the humiliations in Tasmania. She had not tried to dissuade him because she agreed with what Parry had said to Lord Haddington: 'If you don't let Franklin go the man will die of disappointment.' But it had led to the deaths of not only her husband, but a hundred and twenty-eight men besides. All those mothers, wives and families, all that long waiting. Jane groaned. This was a burden weighing heavier on her every day for twenty years. If giving up her own life could have brought them back, she would have done it in an instant.

'You could not have dissuaded him,' I argued. 'He would have gone no matter what—and so would every man of his crew.'

'Not enough kindness, not enough love,' she muttered, shaking her head, not heeding me. She knew she loved her husband more now than when they were together; not the old man as he would be with his elderly smells, his fumbling and deafness; it was the idea of him she loved, noble, heroic.

Eleanor, too, her stepchild, she had not loved enough.

'You know Ella is dead?' Jane looked at me, her face troubled. 'We were so shocked. Gell took her with their little boys to Wales on holiday, but there had been scarlet fever in the village. Her children sickened with it; she nursed them through, but died herself.'

At the funeral Gell had held out an olive branch; how could she refuse? Now Ella's little boys came to Jane's London garden to help sweep up the autumn leaves and make a bonfire, and she paid them in 'wages and rations': bright new-minted pennies and ginger cake.

Mathinna. She had not loved Mathinna; she had been dreadfully sorry for the child. How could she leave that bright little girl to die among the ghastliness of the stricken tribe at Flinders Island? But she, Jane, had not spent enough time with Mathinna. Perhaps if she had ignored the doctors' advice and brought her back to England with them? But the Orphan School with Booth as supervisor had promised well. Why had Mathinna been taken out of the school? Three aboriginal children Jane had tried to help, and only one had lived happily, the boy who became a constable at Muddy Plains. The other boy had run away, and Mathinna had died tragically, drowned in a puddle while the worse for drink, the newspapers said.

Sophy. Perhaps, in Sophy's case, she had done a little spark of good. She had loved Sophy like a daughter, and yet—never to be spoken, of course, hardly to be thought—perhaps it had been Sophy in the end who caused the failure of the expedition?

'Crozier proposed to her again two days before the *Erebus* and *Terror* sailed, and she refused him again—with great severity, he told me. He was in a pitiable state.'

'But . . .' I hesitated. 'Sophy could not marry him if she did not love him?'

'No,' said Jane, 'but she had kept him hoping for five years. Why not let him hope for another two, during the long hard voyage? Instead she told him she felt nothing for him, would never marry him.'

And thus when the expedition left, Crozier was in a state of melancholia, and taking too much rum as consolation. 'That was plain from a letter Ross showed me, the very last one Crozier sent from the Whale Fish Island just before they entered the ice.'

After her husband died, she added, Crozier must have assumed command, with Fitzjames as his second. But Fitzjames had no practical experience of the Arctic, his field was magnetics, and Crozier was probably in no fit state to lead; devastated by Sophy, missing Ross.

'Then blame Ross for marrying Anne,' I said, 'or the Admiralty—or chance, fate, destiny . . .'

But Jane was following her own thoughts. 'Men believe women have no power, and yet great matters may turn on a woman's emotions.'

I hesitated for a moment, and then told her how I had lied to St John Wallace to prevent Thea going into the Orphan School. Jane's face showed her shock. She shook her head, but then after a minute she hugged me and said she could not find it in her heart to blame me. 'He died in India, I suppose? St John?'

'No,' I said unable to resist a laugh. 'He went to the hill station at Darjeeling, where the Army wives go for the hot weather—and thrives there, according to Jane Rochester.'

We sat in contented silence as the sun began to rise like a vision of glory, angels and archangels and all the company of heaven soaring up to the great vault above us from a burst of golden rays across the horizon. The waters of the sound became a shimmering molten mass, the sight grew in splendour every moment. Wisps of lavender clouds flamed deepest crimson, and the world was remade in an ecstasy of light and colour.

'This,' said Jane, tears running down her face, 'this is what they saw. What they were drawn back to see again and again.'

Later, a wagonette came towards us along the road, and I begged a ride for us back to the lodgings.

'Passing strange,' I said to Gus when we were together again in London—and after I had been saturated with blissful news of railways, tunnels, steam engines, routes and scenery, 'that it might have been Sophy's character that caused the loss of the expedition.'

Gus was dressing for dinner. He raised his eyebrows at me and repeated the objections I had made. When I told him Jane's answer he said smiling, 'Only very young men, or very ignorant ones, underestimate the power of women. Was anything found in Sitka, in the end?'

'No, nothing.'

—◊—

In 1876 Gus and I went to England for the third time—the last, it must be—for a ceremony at Westminster Abbey installing a memorial to Franklin. We arrived in July, two weeks before the nominated date, only to find Jane had died a few days before. She was eighty-three. Sophy was sixty-two—fat, inconsolable, and again facing a return to live with her mother. No hope of rescue this time.

The day of Jane's funeral was cold and grey although it was the middle of summer. England so green: that old surprise again. She was buried at Kensal Green Cemetery beside her sister Mary. As we drove to our hotel afterwards the heavens opened and rain came down like floods of tears for every one of our scattered dead.

The unveiling ceremony in Westminster Abbey two weeks later seemed an anti-climax. The Abbey was magnificently itself, stone lifted to heights beyond possibility, the sublime enfolding the human in intricate embrace. We were too few in a corner, a cold little gathering. Sir George Back was the only one who looked warm—large, ruddy, gleaming with prosperity. Beside him was old Mrs Osmar, widow of the purser of the *Erebus*. She was fragile and fine as ancient lace, needing her daughter's assistance for every move. Mrs Blanky, widow of the ice-master, was equally ancient but much different. Her vivid brown eyes glared from a shrunken little brown face; her scrawny determination strong as tarred twine. Sophy stood next to her, almost a caricature spinster. Shabby, umbrella'd, deaf, the last surviving authority on the wishes of Nuncle and Aunt, shouting 'Hush!' in ringing tones.

Sir George Back performed the unveiling. Another irony, I said to Gus. George Back was one of the few people in the world Sir John detested, because of Back's selfishness on two very early Arctic journeys. We had often heard the story in the old collapsing Palace a million miles away.

And then it was time. The veil was drawn back and there was the bust of Sir John in Carrara marble.

'A fine heroic portrait,' murmured Sir George to the surrounding air, 'but not a perfect likeness.' He read aloud, sonorously, Tennyson's lines:

Not here! The White North has thy bones; and Thou
Heroic sailor-soul
Art passing on Thine happier voyage now,
Towards no Earthly Pole.

Afterwards Gus and I went to Regent's Park and sat in the Zoological Gardens and talked about Eliza Gould; a fond old couple, holding hands. The prisoners behind these bars were neatly labelled. Shrill children fed the monkeys who swung about looking, as the Queen had said when she visited the monkey house, 'dreadfully, horribly human'. Perhaps it's true, I thought, perhaps we are no longer angels or devils, as we once believed we were, but merely animals, as Mr Darwin insists.

'I shall be glad to be getting home,' I said.

We called on Sophy once more before we sailed. She was copying out her aunt's correspondence which she had been retrieving for years, and changing words, as I have said before, leaving out lines, destroying some letters altogether.

Seeing the expression on our faces, Sophy grew defensive: 'I lived with Aunt for forty-five years—*forty-five years*—and nobody, no, not even my uncle, understood her as I did. I think I might be allowed to know, Harriet, what my aunt meant. What she would have wished.'

She was beginning to breathe gaspily, always a sign that her feelings were hurt and yet she knew she might be in the wrong. As we took our leave she went back to her editing, protecting dearest Aunt and Nuncle from posterity, deciding what should be kept, and what should vanish as though it had never been.

Acknowledgements

ANY NOVEL WRITTEN OVER NEARLY FORTY YEARS, AS THIS ONE has been, must acquire debts of gratitude to a host of people. Foremost comes my family—*sine qua non*—my husband Brian, Kate and David, and Elizabeth; Richard and Jane; Sheila, John, and Lyn, all of whom have given me unflagging support. I'm particularly grateful to Kate and to Elizabeth McMahon, who read the manuscript innumerable times and made many acute suggestions. And to Bruce Cornelius, with whom it all began.

Dear friends were early readers: Ruth Blair, Jenny and Paul Boam, Trauti and David Reynolds, Mary and Saxby Pridmore. Their encouragement kept me going; their companionship and hospitality have enriched my life as well as my work. Margaret Scott, Sarah Day and Cassandra Pybus were supporters from the outset; Caroline Lurie kindly read an unfinished draft; Maureen Matthews always told me I could do it. Amanda Lohrey has been the most generous and perceptive mentor a writer could have in the later stages.

My heartfelt thanks to Hannah Fink, who introduced me to my agent, Gaby Naher, who then showed the manuscript to publisher Jane Palfreyman at Allen & Unwin. I am immensely grateful to Gaby and Jane for their confidence in *Wild Island*, and would like to thank the Allen & Unwin team, especially senior editor Sarah Baker, for their friendly expertise.

From the beginning I had wonderful help with historical research. Gillian Winter and Margaret Glover gave me a wide array of useful archive references. Margaret Glover's 'Women and Children at Port Arthur' was an early pleasure (together with many other articles published in the papers and proceedings of THRA, the Tasmanian Historical Research Association), and the beautiful *First Views of Lake St Clair*, by Gillian Winter and Tony Brown, has been a recent one. I am very grateful to Ronnie Bramich and his family for access to his fascinating thesis on the development of old Government House in Hobart. Cynthia and David Hooker gave me *The Fate of Franklin* by Roderic Owen just when I needed it. Kerry Dunbabin and John Evans shared their wide knowledge of the peninsula and east coast areas. The modern Lempriere family took the trouble to bring me copies of their forebears' family tree. Alison Alexander's *Obliged to Submit* (later *Governors' Ladies*) fed my interest in the period; her prize-winning monograph, *The Ambitions of Jane Franklin*, was published by Allen & Unwin just as *Wild Island* was finished.

Many other writers have enlarged my knowledge, but a few books have been particularly important: *The Journal of Charles O'Hara Booth* edited by Dora Heard; Volume 1 of L. Robson's *A History of Tasmania*; Kathleen Fitzpatrick's *Sir John Franklin in Tasmania, 1837–1843*; also Ian Brand's *Escape from Port Arthur*; Ken McGoogan's *Lady Franklin's Revenge*; Penny Russell's *This Errant Lady: Jane Franklin's Overland Journey to Port Phillip and Sydney, 1839*, and Joyce Eyre's master's thesis on 'The Franklin-Montagu Dispute' (for knowledge of which I'm indebted to Ruth Blair and Ralph Spaulding). I borrowed Mrs Chesney's shopping list from *Kettle on the Hob: A Family in Van Diemen's Land, 1828–1885* by Frances Cotton.

The staffs of the Tasmaniana Library, the Allport Library and Museum of Fine Arts, and the Library of The Royal Society of Tasmania were always patient and helpful.

I am very grateful to Arts Tasmania for a Small Grant; to *Southerly* for publishing two extracts from early drafts of the novel; and to the Australian Society of Authors for a 'Mini-Mentorship' towards manuscript development.

Profuse gratitude, always, to Charlotte Bronte for *Jane Eyre* and to Jean Rhys for *Wide Sargasso Sea*. Errors and omissions are, regrettably, all my own work.